# CURSE
# BREAKER

Book 2 in the Weapon of Mass Seduction series

## JACKIE EGAN

Dev editor: Lopt & Cropt Editing Services
Line editor: Lopt & Cropt Editing Services
Cover design : Cleo Moran / Devoted Pages Designs
Interior Formatting: Cleo Moran / Devoted Pages Designs

*For the women who were betrayed by those who were supposed to protect you, the women who have been ignored, dismissed, taken advantage of, used like property and discarded like they were nothing… this is for you.*

*CB is for everyone that's had to overcome their darkest nights, rebuild their life from the bottom up, and had to claw their way back to who they were.*

*May we all find our inner Bellatrix warrior, and may the universe let us watch those who betrayed us receive their karma.*

*For all my badass woman:*

*I see you.*

*I hear you.*

*I'm with you.*

# PLAYLIST

James Newton Howard- The Hanging Tree
Smash into Pieces- Real One
Florence + the machine- Cosmic Love
Rival and Cadmium- Just Breathe
From Fall to Spring- The Cursed One
Tyrone Briggs- The Cost
Florence + the machine- Seven Devils
Paramore- Decode
Catch your Breath- Savages
Fight the fade- (Not) Enough
Florence + the machine- Jenny of Oldstone
Ruelle- Game of Survival
Teddy Swims- Lose Control

# PRONUNCIATIONS

Hidi- Hee-dee
Tenuma- Teh-new-muh
Koen- Ko-in
Sperantia- Spur-an-tee-uh
Quirina- cure-een-uh
Mellani- Mel-on-ee
Fira- Fear-uh
Lothar- low-thar

# TRIGGER WARNING

Dear valued reader, this book contains topics that could be difficult for some readers. If you're sensitive to certain topics, please be aware that, while not described on page, this book deals with S.A.

Please read with caution.

# SOUL SNATCHER (REFRESHER:

The kingdom of Tenuma is home to Princess Bellatrix, a woman who has been cursed by a mysterious enchantress at the request of her mother, the queen, in order to protect her from any man whose intentions aren't pure. Her curse? A soul-snatching pussy that turns any man who sleeps with her for the wrong reasons into a soulless daemon.

Bellatrix's parents currently rule the kingdom with an iron fist, leaving its people struggling and scrambling to survive. Koen Archer, a local handyman, is summoned by the queen to complete a labor request at the castle. Desperate to provide for his mother and little sister, he accepts, despite his hatred for Bellatrix, and his mother's apprehension.

What should have been a simple job ends up changing the trajectory of his life, when he realizes there's more to Bellatrix than meets the eye. He finds himself being drawn to her time and time again, eager to find out more about the princess who has it all, yet seems so sad.

Both Bellatrix and Koen have separately been given magical protection bracelets that tingle whenever they're near each other. But what does it mean?

Bellatrix is desperate to prove herself worthy of wearing the crown as queen one day, but begins to realize that her parents' demands are too much for her to bear. After meeting Koen Archer, she decides that while she wants to be queen to make a positive impact, she wants more out of life. She wants a man who will love and cherish her. A man that sees her as more than the Soul Snatcher.

A chance encounter in the forest has both Bellatrix and Koen running for their lives from a mythical creature long thought dead: a dragon. Their night in hiding changes everything for them, as they're brought closer in a way neither of them expected. With a dragon on the loose terrorizing Tenuma, the townspeople are terrified, wondering how many more there might be. And the bigger question is, why are they back now?

As Koen and Bellatrix struggle to find the meaning of their bracelets and their attraction to one another, the queen's disapproval of their relationship becomes more apparent, causing friction between the two families.

After Bellatrix is attacked in her bedroom by a man claiming to be the son of the king of Sperantia, Koen finds himself in new territory as he avenges the princess.

Not long after, Tenuma receives a deadly attack from Sperantia. Their soldiers arrive on dragonback, terrorizing the entire kingdom, leaving it almost completely in rubble. While the people of Tenuma seek safety behind the castle walls, Bellatrix is eager to help and rushes to the rooftop for a better vantage point. When she doesn't return, an anxious Koen decides to go after her, only to find that she's been captured by the king of Sperantia—who happens to be none other than Koen's estranged father.

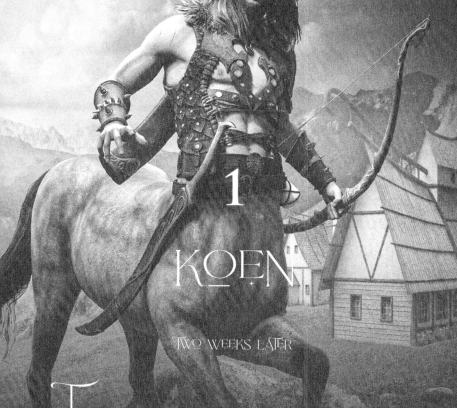

# 1

## KOEN

There are some things that stroking your dick just can't fix.

That's what I tell myself when I'm in the shower, chasing that once-blissful high to the image of her beautiful face as I fist my cock. The act would indicate that I'm sexually frustrated, though it's not the case at all. Grief has its own demands for release. I wasn't able to save her, and now I can't even bring myself to orgasm. It's not her body I miss, but her heart. Her face. Her soul. The desperate need to override the unabating rage inside, only leaves me feeling emptier and more pathetic.

They say when you lose someone close to you, you can almost feel the world stand still for a moment. As if the universe has stopped breathing, a moment of silence for the loss of one of its souls.

I have yet to feel that heaviness, so I have to believe Bellatrix is still here, still alive. My girl is resilient. She will survive this until I can get to her.

Princess Bellatrix was abducted by my father, who's somehow the new ruler of Sperantia. Knowledge that my family and I weren't privy to until recently. The same blood that flows through his greedy veins is the same that travels through mine, and I can't help but feel responsible for what's happened to our land. As if all of Tenuma is watching me, silently blaming me, not only for the attack, but for the abduction of our princess as well.

I hear my mother coming up behind me, and I brace myself for an uncomfortable conversation.

"Where are you going?" she asks with caution, knowing my temper has a short fuse these days.

"To the castle," I say in a clipped tone.

My mother sighs with disappointment and exhaustion with my attitude. I've never given my mother much trouble, seeing as I've always felt this innate need to take care of her and my little sister, Mellani. "Again?"

"If I can just get in—" I start, but she cuts me off.

"What? What happens if you get inside?" she asks, her frustration growing.

I finish tying up my boots, stand, and head for the door. "It's been weeks. I need to know why she isn't back yet. The king and queen have done *nothing* to bring her home."

My mother grabs my arm firmly and spins me around, forcing me to look at her. "Koen, please. This has to stop. The queen announced that she's in talks with Sperantia. Let her take care of things. This isn't your fight."

I scoff. "I won't stop until she's home."

Her eyes plead with me. "They've turned you away every single day. You're putting yourself in danger, son. I'm trying to protect you."

A laugh devoid of any humor bursts from my chest. "Protect me? Mother, I'm a grown man. I don't need protection. I need transparency. I've spent my life doing everything I can for you and Mel. Had I known you have been lying and hiding things from me—"

"What? What would you have done differently? Would you have left us? Let us starve? Let us fend for ourselves?" She already knows the answer. I'm not my father, and I never would have done to them what he did to the three of us under any circumstance, but I'm still choosing to take my anger out on her.

My mother desperately tried to talk me out of accepting a job at the castle for extra money all those months ago. All this time I assumed her hatred for the royal family was due to their poor policies and high taxes—only to find out that my mother is on a first-name basis with the queen. There's more she's hiding from me, and until she's honest with me, every request, every conversation will be met with resistance.

"I'm not getting into this right now, Mother. When you want to be tell me everything, then we can talk. Until then, I'm not interested," I say coldly, and walk out the door, closing it behind me and exhaling another long breath. I don't get very far down the pathway before I hear the door opening behind me. Expecting my mother, I turn around hesitantly to find Mel chasing after me.

"Koen!" she yelps.

I set my things down on the ground and turn towards her. I feel for her the most. Mel has seen everything and yet understands it all the least. Coming face-to-face with a father she barely knows and watching him abduct a woman she's gotten close to can't make much sense to her young mind.

"Hey, sweet girl," I say gently, bending down to embrace her.

"You didn't say bye to me." Mel has her best pouty face on but underneath it, I can tell how sad she is that Mother and I are fighting, that I've been distant. That I'm leaving her again.

I caress her cheek with my thumb, giving her a sad smile. "I'm sorry, Mel. I'm just in a hurry, but you know I'll always come back for you."

She shakes her head sniffling. "Not always."

I know she's referring to the few times I didn't make it home when I was with Bellatrix. The memories hit like a dagger in the chest, making it hard to breathe. Tucking her brown curls behind her ear, I reply, "Mel, I will always come back for you. Even if it's late. I love you. You don't have to worry about that."

Her big brown eyes are watery as she stares up at me. "Promise?"

"With my life, Mel."

I kiss the top of her head, and she scurries back inside out of the cold. I turn and begin the trek to the castle where I can wallow in my misery, away from my mother's pleading eyes and my sister's confusion.

I shift into my centaur form once I get to the woods. I thought it would feel strange to shift so openly this way, but if anything, it feels…freeing. Though shifting is common in Tenuma, aside from a few nearby neighbors who have the ability, I don't personally know many people with the gift. The power I feel in my legs and back, and the ease with which I can now travel great distances without exhausting myself, makes the journey to and from the castle a breeze.

It's been two weeks since the princess was taken by my father, and aside from the queen making a few announcements that she's in talks with him, we don't actually know anything. There have been no updates, and frankly that's unacceptable to me.

Some days it feels like I'm the only one concerned that she's been taken. I don't see any commotion at the castle, and aside from the extra guards around the perimeter, it's like nothing happened at all.

As I approach the castle gates back in my human form, I can already see the men out front exchanging words and rolling their eyes in my direction. They're sick of seeing me every day. Sick of turning me away with no information. But I'm not one to easily give up.

"Good day, gentlemen. I'm here to see the queen," I say like I have every day since the abduction.

The two men standing directly in front of the gate entrance give me a blank stare. "Go home," one of the men replies.

"I'm not leaving until I see the queen. Princess Bellatrix has been missing for two weeks. What are you doing to get her back?"

One of the men shifts the large sword in his hands, capturing my full attention. "We are doing what we're told. Now do what you're told, and go back home before you find yourself in trouble."

I stare back at the man, not yet ready to give in. I thought that if I kept showing up, eventually the queen would hear me out. Why wouldn't she? My only goal is getting Bellatrix back, and surely that's her number one priority right now too. But there has been zero movement on Tenuma's end to get her back.

"Please, let me inside. I'm not here to cause more problems. All I want is to help. I will do anything. Just let me talk to her," I plead.

"The queen is not interested in speaking with you, as we've told you multiple times. She is taking care of the situation with her daughter, and doesn't need a *commoner's* assistance. You don't belong here. Now leave, or we'll make you leave," one of the men threatens, while a group of men approach from behind with their weapons drawn.

I throw my hands up in the air in surrender and slowly back away. Before I leave, I make one last attempt to reach the queen, hoping she's somewhere nearby watching and listening as I shout towards the castle. "I'm never going to give up. I won't stop until she's home! You've done nothing for weeks, and she could be dead! Tenuma will never forget if you let her die in Sperantia! Do you hear me?"

The men close in on me, and it's officially my time to go. I quickly retreat from the castle, and head for the one place that's been my solitude. The only place I've ever truly felt at home and at peace.

The forest.

My large hooves trample through the snow between the trees, as I make my way towards one of my hideout caves. Once inside, I slip back into my human form, and pull on a pair of trousers and a long-sleeve top. The backpack in the corner holds my current vice and new favorite pastime.

I pop the top off the amber bottle and lift it to my lips. I draw a greedy pull of the strong whiskey, letting it make its way down, burning off the remnants of anger from my visit at the castle.

With Nik's bar destroyed, I've taken every bottle we've had at home and turned this safety hideout into my own private bar. It's lonely and sort of pathetic, but it's all I have.

The last few weeks have been an agonizing combination of being told to fuck off and drinking in the woods by myself. The tension at home has been steadily growing, and I know that if I can't stomp out the roaring rage inside me, things will erupt in an ugly way.

It's not just that Bellatrix was taken, and it's not only that it was at my father's hand.

It's the secrets that have been kept from me. The way that my mother knew of my gift, but neglected to tell me. I've made peace with my gift—hell, I even like my gift. But why couldn't my mother be honest with me? What was the point of lying when instead she could have been preparing me for the first time I shifted?

I know I'm being unfair, and I know that my actions as of late have made life harder for her. But every time I try to stifle the frustration around my mother, all I see is the betrayal, the secrets, the lies. If I have to turn into a monster in order for people to finally be honest with me, then so be it.

This has changed me forever, and I don't know if I'll like who I am at the end of it all.

# 2

# BELLATRIX

I twist my arms in an attempt to find a more comfortable position for the rope on my wrists. The frayed edges dig into my skin, making me wince. It definitely doesn't have the same effect as it did when I was in my own bedroom getting tied up and played with. I think I can safely say this won't be a part of my sexual lifestyle going forward.

Presuming I make it out of here alive, that is.

My heart beats, which means I'm still alive, even though I feel anything but. Spending my days stuck to a bed isn't living. It's huge, comfortable and plush, but I may as well be chained to a pole on a damp concrete floor. It's still a prison to me.

If Tenuma is a winter wonderland, the realm of Sperantia is a hellscape. The window next to the bed reveals the same scenery

I've been staring at for…I don't know how long. I've lost count of the days. They all bleed together into one infernal scene of reddish, gray skies, skeletal trees in the distance, and relentless gusts of wind that blow around thick dust and dirt, making it feel like I'm inside of a dusty snow globe.

The only thing that gets me through the long days is the sound of Koen in my head calling after me. The anger and desperation in his voice is enough for me to know that he won't leave me here to die.

I don't expect my mother and father to be doing much to find me. Given their resources and power, they could have gotten me out of here by now if they wanted to. For whatever reason, they've left me here, but I know Koen is somewhere fighting for me.

I keep waiting for my bracelet to tingle, to tell me he's near, that he's about to bring me home, but so far I haven't felt a thing. As the days go on, it's getting more and more difficult to keep believing I'll ever leave this room.

*"Why am I here?" I beg, holding back a sob. I refuse to cry in front of these people. I refuse to show them any sort of weakness. The blindfold slides off one eye, and I can see ugliness all around me. A land devoid of life.*

*A male's voice responds, "You'll find out soon enough, Princess."*

*"Where have you taken me?" I ask a different question, hoping to land on one he'll answer.*

*"Sperantia. The land that will soon rule them all," he responds smugly.*

*I shift uncomfortably with my hands bound and my eyes still mostly covered. We're waiting outside a large gray building, for what I don't know.*

*"Please, let me go. My family will give you whatever you want." Surely this man is after money, or some sort of power I can barter with.*

*A sinister laugh escapes him. "Oh, Princess, I already have what*

*I want."*

*The combination of his laugh and ominous words sends a chill over my flesh, and my body stiffens even further.*

*Frightened, I am unable to think of a way to respond when another man approaches.*

*"Where have you been? You should have been out here waiting for our arrival, not the other way around," the man holding me scolds whoever has just joined us.*

*"Apologies, Your Majesty. We have been preparing for her arrival," the new voice gives a shaky response. It's evident he's terrified of the man restraining me, His Majesty the king of Sperantia.*

*No, no, no. Instead of sending his men to find me, he personally abducted me. Kings never do their own dirty work. Whatever he has planned won't be good for me or for Tenuma.*

The opening and slamming of a door pulls me back to the present.

My gaze snaps to the door to find a sweaty guard staring at me with a dark gaze that moves up and down my body. The oversized sleeping gown I'm in isn't revealing, but I might as well be sprawled across this bed naked by the way this man is salivating from the doorway.

"Princess, would you like some help with your shower today?" The man makes no effort to hide his intentions.

My heart begins to race, and I try to keep my face neutral. Showing fear would only make this worse. Though, before I have a chance to respond, a now-familiar woman appears from behind the man.

She enters carrying a tray. As one of the castle's handmaidens, it seems to be her job to tend to me. She feeds me, brings me water, and takes me to the bathroom a few times a day before tying me up again. Though not friendly, she's not cruel either. More importantly, I've never had to wonder if she might violate me.

I've asked her many questions when she's come in, but she never answers. The only time she speaks is when she's giving commands. No matter how much talking I do, she gives nothing back. I slip her small details about myself, hoping to find a connection, but she's not interested.

"Thank you for getting the door for me. These trays sure can get heavy," the woman tells the guard as she sets the tray down on the bedside table.

I watch as she shoots him a look I can't read. The silent exchange only heightens my anxiety until the man, caught off guard, simply nods and exits the room shutting the door behind him. The woman and I are left alone, and I instantly feel my breathing return to normal.

She offers me water, and I lean forward to take it, remembering my mistake in not accepting anything the first few days, which made me too weak to voluntarily keep up the defiance. As much as I wanted to prove to myself and these strangers that I didn't need anything from them, I quickly realized my need for survival surpassed anything I was trying to prove.

The water is cold and soothing down my throat. Though I've been kept indoors, dust pervades the air, creating a thick filmy layer inside of my mouth that's evolved into an abrasive cough.

She takes the glass away when I pull back, and offers me some toast. Afterwards, a few bites of fruit and meat. Once I've had my fill, I lean back against the bed and take another good look at the woman in front of me.

She has tanned skin that looks smooth and healthy. Her dark hair is pinned back tightly in a bun at the top of her head, and her brown almond eyes reveal nothing except for maybe a hint of sadness. She has high, sharp cheekbones and thin lips that point down at the corners. She's a few inches shorter than me, and her slouchy posture makes her look even smaller. Her figure is petite but full, not that different from Quirina.

"Thank you for the food. It's delicious, though I'd be lying if I said I didn't miss the food from home," I say, trying to keep things light.

No response.

This is usually how our visits go, so I continue. "We have this incredible dessert in my kingdom. A vanilla-strawberry swirl cake. It's the perfect amount of sweetness, and you can't imagine how soft it is."

She's doing her best to avoid eye contact, but I know she's listening.

"Why am I here?" I ask, hoping today's the day I'll get answers.

She doesn't reply. She gathers the dishes on the tray and moves them over to the small table by the door. The room is too dry, too warm. There's no fireplace like there is in my own room in Tenuma, though in this overheated wasteland, I'm grateful for that. The bed is flanked with two side tables that are bare but for a small light globe on each one that automatically turn on each night. The bathroom is oversized and luxurious. There's a shower and a giant tub that would otherwise be wonderful for soaking and relaxing. The room is grand but monochrome in shades of dull beige and gray.

She sets the tray down and comes back to untie my straps from the bed to take me on one of our routine bathroom trips. As we walk, I try again. "Please, why am I here? You must know something."

More silence.

I rest my hand on her forearm. "Please. What's going to happen to me here?"

Her eyes quickly move to the door, and then back to me. She shakes her head, telling me that she can't say.

She wants to, though.

I don't say anything. This is the most I've gotten out of her since I've been here, and I don't want to scare her off. After a few moments she finally speaks.

"I can't say. I-I can't be sure." Her voice, barely a whisper, rattles with nerves.

My eyes immediately well up with tears at the fact that she's finally speaking to me. I'm so grateful I could hug her. I've been the one doing all of the talking the last few weeks. The only conversations I've had have been with the sleazy guards who make sexual comments and eye-fuck me from the door.

I match the quietness of her voice. "I'm just scared. I know you can't help me, but if I know what I'm going into, I can at least mentally prepare myself."

She releases a heavy breath, and I can tell she's holding back. "I…"

I nod, urging her to keep going.

"I really don't know anything. Lord Lothar doesn't tell me anything. I'm only a handmaiden, told to look after you until you were needed."

I haven't heard from Lothar since the day he brought me here, but it only adds to the anxiety I have, wondering which day will be the one that he comes to find me.

"What's your name?"

Her voice is still low and controlled. "Hidi."

"Hidi," I repeat quietly. "Thank you." I retreat into the bathroom, shutting the door behind me.

Opening the door a little while later, having finished using the restroom and scrubbing the dirt off my body in a cold shower, Hidi leads me back to the bed where I'll be tied up once again. Her hands are always gentle with me, so I know whatever issue this kingdom has with me, it does not extend to this woman.

As she's securing my hands to the frame, I glance up at her

face, noticing her brown eyes have flecks of gold in them. She's beautiful. It would be easy to hate her, but she's no monster. She's a woman with no status, no power, simply trying to do her job.

Once she's finished, she steps back and looks at me for a moment, hesitating before she leaves the room. I wait for whatever she might say or do. But I'm left feeling even more confused when she turns and walks out without uttering another word.

I don't know when I fell asleep, but sometime later a thunderous noise startles me awake. The same noise that wakes me most days. A booming, painful cry, louder than anything I've heard before I came to Sperantia.

*Dragons.*

Up until recently, I believed dragons were an extinct species that were more legend than real. I never expected to witness them in my lifetime.

Whatever they're enduring is bad—if I had to guess, it's torture. It's difficult to listen to, and it goes on for hours at a time. Though the anguish comes from mythical creatures, the sound of pain is a universal language. It's hard to imagine what they're experiencing to release such an agonizing cry. I fear I might suffer the same fate. Both imprisoned for the benefit of the king.

I know what it's like not to be in control of your own body. To have others dictate what you'll endure, no matter the cost. I don't know how Sperantia and King Lothar came into possession of these animals, but I'm certain that they're not here by choice.

The minutes tick by as I try drowning out the sounds of their cries, by humming, talking to myself, covering my ears with pillows, but none of it overpowers the shrieks and cries that come from outside the walls. My heart aches with every cry. Hearing these creatures endure such pain is a torture all on its own.

# 3

# KOEN

It's torturous.

The pounding at my temples tells me I had too much whiskey last night. With a groan I turn on my side, hoping to reach for a glass of water nearby, only for my arm to land on Mellani.

"Argh," she grumbles in her sleep as my large arm lands on her small frame.

I cringe and lift my arm back off of her, hoping not to fully wake her.

When did I get home?

The sky outside the window looks dark, so it must still be early.

Stretching my aching limbs, I stand and quietly make my way to the washroom as my full bladder threatens to burst. I lean over the toilet with my hand pressed into the wall above, my throbbing head hangs heavily. I swear my piss is pure whiskey.

As I internally argue with myself that these hangovers aren't worth it, I try to imagine myself falling asleep without the numbing comfort and realize it's probably not going to happen.

I try to quietly make my way back to my makeshift bed on the floor but lose my balance and bump into one of the walls between my mother's room and the main living space. Immediately I freeze, holding my breath, waiting to hear if my clumsiness woke my mother or sister. A few long moments pass, and just when I think I'm in the clear, my mother's door slowly creaks open behind me.

"Koen? Is that you, son?" She rubs at her sleepy eyes, trying to assess the situation.

Spinning around slowly, I attempt to seem sober. "Sorry, I was using the washroom."

Her eyes narrow, as she inspects the strange way I'm holding onto the wall for support, the way my bloodshot eyes can barely stay open, and the obvious stench of whiskey wafting off my skin. I don't know why I bother trying to lie; I'm not hiding a damn thing. Even if I was good at deception, she's my mother, and I know she sees right through it.

She saw Bellatrix coming long before I did, apparently.

Just one of the many secrets that were kept from me.

I begin to feel that familiar bubble of anger rising in my gut.

Then again, it could be all the whiskey I consumed threatening to evict itself from my body.

My mother motions for me to come into her room. I reluctantly follow, knowing this will likely be another lecture, but not wanting to wake Mellani, I decide it's probably best to cooperate. She sits on the edge of the bed and takes my hand to guide me down to the mattress.

"Do you want to talk to me yet, or do you want to continue down this path of self-destruction?" she asks softly.

"Depends. Do you want to tell the truth for once, or do you want to continue to avoid it?"

I know I'm being harsh, but I want her to finally be honest with me. Apparently if I don't fight for it, the truth won't be given.

She sighs heavily, trying to conceal her frustration. It's clear that the long line of patience she's gifted me is nearing its end.

"Ko, baby, listen to me." She uses her thumb and forefinger to guide my chin so I'm looking directly at her. "I would never do anything to harm you or your sister. You two are the most important parts of my life, the *only* important parts of my life. I'm not perfect, but I'm doing the best I can. I'm sorry you felt that it was a betrayal."

I jerk my face away from her hand, and stare at the floor. What she's saying is true, I know it is. But all the anger swirling inside of me needs a scapegoat. I can't make a one-man rescue mission to save the princess, and I can't punish the person who took her. He's my father. Regardless of the hurt he's caused, I don't know that I'm ready to kill him. I've already killed a half-brother I didn't even know existed. It's all changed me, and I'm grappling with the foreign emotions that have surfaced along with it.

"It's not just you. Everyone is keeping secrets from me, and I'm walking around like the town moron who didn't know his father was the evil ruler of another kingdom. Nobody wants to hear about their life from an outside source." Everything that's come out in the last few weeks has made me feel stupid, humiliated, lost, and angry.

The room is quiet for a moment as my mother takes in what I've said, likely searching for a response that won't make me shut down like every other time.

My gaze, still downward, travels to the bracelet I haven't taken off. I was told it was for protection. Protection from the princess. But that was always within my control. I never needed a bracelet for that. It's yet another unanswered question that my mother kept from me.

"Why the bracelet? What does the damn tingling mean? It

only tingles when I'm around the princess, and now, nothing." I pause, feeling that familiar lump in my throat. "Is she dead?"

She exhales. "I don't know," she says, sounding disappointed that she can't give me a better answer.

My head jerks up at her. "You don't know?"

"I don't know if she's alive or not, baby. That's not what the bracelet is for."

My head slumps back down. As much as I want answers to everything that's come to light, that's the one question I really needed an answer for. Not knowing is plaguing me.

"What is the bracelet for? The truth."

"While it was intended for protection, yes, there's a little more to it," She pauses, and I can feel the air in the room shift. "I know you're smart enough not to get twisted up with someone who's bad for you, so it was intended to be extra precaution. I don't *really* know her, so I wanted to make sure you wouldn't be pressured into a situation you didn't voluntarily get into. The bracelet would act as a deterrent from her. It was supposed to act as a sort of force field, and push you two apart whenever you were near."

My eyebrows furrow in confusion, because that sure as fuck didn't happen. "Okay, well, I don't think it worked."

"Right, and the only reason it would tingle is if…" she trails off.

"If what, Mother?" I snap, feeling my patience thinning by the second.

"If you two were True Mates."

Her words make the room spin, and I know it's no longer from the whiskey.

"She's my True Mate," I say slowly, needing to feel how each syllable feels coming off my tongue.

"Yes." The finality with which she says the words knocks the wind out of me.

My True Mate.

How can I be Bellatrix's True Mate? Compared to her, I'm nothing. Nobody.

I'm trying to understand exactly what this means for me, for us. I'm familiar with the concept of True Mates, the ones we are predestined to be with. The perfect counterpart created for us. Though we have the freedom to be with anyone of our choosing, a True Mate is the soul the Gods designed for us to be with. But they are rare and difficult to find, and most people aren't capable of being alone, so they opt for companionship over searching for their match.

The stories passed down from each generation all tell the same tale of how each of us has one True Mate. Only one. The Gods carefully curated one other person to perfectly fit into our lives, and once we found them, nothing could break the connection. Before I knew Bellatrix, I never gave the possibility of a True Mate a second thought. But how can I deny the intense connection we have?

"What does this mean?" I ask, my eyes pleading for more.

"It means that yes, there's a lot of answers you're still due, but all this anger you're feeling is not because of that, it's because you're without your mate. Once a person has found their mate, being without them can be more painful than a fatal flesh wound."

"Fuck!" I don't even know where to place the current anger I'm feeling because it's all rolled into one giant orb of tension that rocks around in my chest every damn day, each clash reminding me of the pain of it all. "Did you know all along that she was my mate?"

My mother shakes her head, and as much as I want to label her a liar, I know she's not. "No. Not at first. As time went on, I had a pretty good idea. Then you told me about your bracelet sensation, and it became clear."

"Why would my mate be somebody that I could never have?

Is this some sick joke?" I whisper shout.

What I told Bellatrix was the truth—I'd have her anyway I can. She's more than sex, more than what her body can ever offer me. But it's hard to understand why my True Mate would be somebody that has this curse upon her. Someone I could never truly be with or build a family with.

"I don't have an answer for that. I wish I did. Nobody knows why or how a person gets mated with another," she tells me gently. "Life doesn't always come with answers."

My frustration comes to a boil. "Why would someone put this curse on her? I could kill the person that did this to her!" I realize I'm getting loud, but as the new information starts to settle, I feel everything boil over. "We need to find this monster and make them reverse it."

I swear I see my mother flinch during my ranting.

"Koen, I wish it was that easy. But please, don't talk like this." Her voice is still low, devoid of any anger or frustration. If anything, I hear sadness. Guilt, maybe.

"Why? It might be. Has anyone ever tried to reverse it?"

"It can't happen," she insists, her lips turning downward.

"Mother, if we—" I try to continue arguing, but she raises her palm to me, cutting me off.

"I know you're feeling a lot of anger and it feels very justified, but it's not the way. Anger is never the answer. What's done is done, and all you can do is move forward," she tells me firmly.

I scoff, not having the words to respond to such absurdity.

She wants me to just come to terms with the fact that I've been lied to and betrayed by almost everybody in my life. That my mate was taken from me before we had the chance to realize what we were to each other. The intense agony and suffering I've felt since she was taken makes all the more sense now. A part of my soul went right along with her.

"I can't move forward. Not with the princess, not with…*him*." The father I refuse to call by name.

My mother nods slightly and pats my leg with one hand. "You should get some sleep."

Eager to end another shitty conversation, I stand to leave, but when I grab the doorknob my mother's voice stops me.

"Please start taking care of yourself," she says, causing me to turn around and face her. "You reek of alcohol, and she needs you," She juts her chin toward the living room where Mellani is asleep.

"I know she does, and unlike that pathetic excuse for a father, I'll always be there for her." My voice takes on an edge at having to think about our father.

"Then I would think you'd be able to recall all the drinking and anger he brought home." She pauses when she sees my face fall. "Don't you think Mel deserves better than having both men in her life do this to her?"

My stomach twists as her words sink in. Hearing my mother compare me to that man knocks me off the moral high ground I've been settled on. I've worked my whole adult life trying not to be anything like him. In the blink of an eye, I slipped and fell right into the role he left vacant all those years ago.

Shame washes over me, and I can't look my mother in the eyes. I quickly turn back around and quietly close the door behind me. I climb back onto the cot next to Mellani, feeling lower than I thought I could. Knowing I've allowed my grief to take over and let my sister down pains me in a horrifying new way.

Something tells me that those words have been bouncing around in my mother's head for a while, and I hate that I forced her to say them aloud. I hate even more that what she said is true. I've been so busy being angry at everyone else's behavior and actions that I've been blind to my own.

While I don't think I can eliminate the anger that afflicts

me, continuing this way isn't an option. If I'm being honest with myself, I don't care much what happens to me, but I can't let my actions hurt my mother or Mellani any longer. It's time to make things right.

# 4

# BELLATRIX

This feels so good, so right.

Big, firm hands slowly drift their way up my legs, along my stomach and breasts, and land softly against the base of my neck. I can feel his body heat, the comforting weight of him when he shifts his body directly over me, positioning himself between my legs. His knee pushes them wider apart, and he settles himself into me like a puzzle piece clicking into place. I welcome his advances, and while this song and dance usually feels forced, this feels right. He belongs here.

"I need you," I whisper into his ear, as he plants kisses on my neck.

His kisses and gentle bites feel euphoric, and even though I'll wear his marks after this I can't bring myself to make him stop. I relish it. My stomach warms, my heart races, and I can feel my pussy starting to *get wet, pulsing with desire.*

*He pulls back, and I finally face him. Koen. He looks so handsome and intense. I feel like he's staring into my soul.*

*"Kiss me, please." I need more. I need his lips on mine.*

*He smiles a devilish grin, and presses his lips to mine firmly, kissing me hungrily. Our lips conjoin perfectly, and our tongues dance together as if they're old friends who've memorized each other's moves.*

*He tastes like home.*

*His hand slides between my legs and his fingers slip into my wetness. He groans, his noises only adding to my own pleasure. I push my hips up to meet him, forcing his fingers to sink deeper inside of me.*

*"Does that feel good, Princess?" he asks in a low, husky voice.*

*His voice alone could get me off. The look in his eyes threatens to send me over the edge. His desire is not just a need for my body, it's a need for me. To be as close to me as possible. I can feel the way he needs my heart, my soul.*

*I nod my head in approval, and barely force out a breathy "Yes" when he abruptly pulls his fingers out, leaving me empty. But I know it won't be for long. We both know what he's about to do. It could be deadly, and yet neither one of us is able to resist any longer…*

My eyes open, and the dream fades into oblivion. Reality hits me hard when I remember that I'm still being held prisoner in Sperantia. Koen was never here, and I'll likely never see him again.

My soul aches for him in a way I never knew possible. It's like missing a limb, not yet accustomed to the loss, still feeling those phantom pains.

Devastation and loneliness make another mark on my heart, like it's tallying up the tragedies of my life. I attempt to wipe the tears falling down my cheeks with my shoulder, since my hands are bound. An uncomfortable position, but one I've strangely gotten used to. Once you get settled in, even hell becomes manageable.

"Good morning, Princess." A woman's voice startles me.

Hidi.

I turn my face in an attempt to hide the fact that I've been crying. But it's pointless. Hidi sits next to me, setting a tray of tea and food on the small table next to the bed. My gaze follows the tray, noticing a small change to the usual array of meats and toast.

My eyes immediately well up at the sight. Next to the typical offerings is a tantalizing piece of vanilla-strawberry swirl cake.

I never expected her to retain the information I gave her the other day, nor did I expect to see a piece on my tray this morning. It's more than cake, it's a peace offering.

A simple token of joy, in an otherwise doomed situation. It's enough to remind me that there's still good in people, and there's still hope. A kindness like this could never come from someone cruel. Swallowing the lump in my throat, I clear my throat, turning away from the tray.

"Would you like a minute, Princess?" she asks gently. As small a gesture that it is, it reminds me that I'm not just a prisoner. I'm still allowed some say. For a moment it makes me forget my situation, and reminds me of the kindness Quirina always showed me. Compassion like that cannot be faked. People will always show you who they are if you look close enough, and this small act of kindness tells me that she's not one of *them*. She doesn't belong here. She's a good person, and she just might be my way out.

I shake my head. "No, thank you. Just a bad dream."

"I'm sorry to hear that," she says and stands to untie my hands from the bed.

As she's working on the ties, I can't help but wonder why they're needed. "Why do you continue to tie my hands?"

"What?" I'm not sure if she just didn't hear me, or is confused by my question.

"Why do you keep tying me back up? I don't have weapons, I wouldn't survive a jump out the window, and the door is locked from the outside. Why am I kept tied to the bed?"

"Princess, I just do as I'm told. I know nothing." She tries to lie, fairly convincingly if it weren't for the way her hands shake.

I've never given her any reason to fear me, so I know she's not afraid. At least not of me. She's hiding something.

I'm desperate for an ally, so I let it slide.

"Nobody but you has come to me since I've been here. How long has it been? A few weeks? Please, can't you grant me this small freedom? I'm no threat to you." I'm begging for scraps, and as pathetic as it feels, I no longer have the capacity to care.

"I can't," she says, shaking her head. It's wavering, and I catch a hint of remorse.

My hands fall loose as she finishes with the ropes, and I take both of hers in mine gently before she takes me to the washroom. Aside from her guiding me to the washroom, this is the first physical contact I've had. An unexpected wave of emotion washes over me.

"Please." I gaze into her eyes. I know there's a decent person inside of her. I might be a prisoner in her land, but she calls me by my formal title. She's showing me respect, even when she doesn't have to.

Her face is splotchy, and her eyes begin to glisten. She stares down at our intertwined hands, appearing equally affected by the touch as I am.

She starts to speak but is interrupted by a deafening cry from outside the castle somewhere. I drop her hands, the noise causing us both to startle, and then freeze in place while the echo fades out. Dragon cries. The sound blasts through the room once more. My soul aches knowing these creatures are in such pain.

Once the crying and screeching stops, my sadness turns to

anger, and I find myself shouting at the one and only person I've interacted with in weeks. "Why is he doing this?"

Hidi stumbles backwards a few steps. Her eyes well up with tears and her hand covers her mouth to prevent the sobs racking her shoulders from escaping.

The dragon cries fade out again, and I lift my head to face her. "I'm sorry I shouted at you," I say, and decide to try something different today. "I don't know what you know about me, but I'm cursed. Back home, years ago, my mother had a curse put on me so I couldn't be taken advantage of by unworthy men." I chuckle at the irony.

Hidi's feet scuffle against the cold tile floor as she makes her way back over to me and sits next to me. Opening up to her might be a mistake. She might be planted here to see what I do or say, but at this point what do I have left to lose?

"I spend my nights with different suitors, sleeping with man after man to find my king. One man worthy of surviving the night with me. Only the man who isn't using me for my title or riches will survive a night in my bed. But there's only one man I want to share it with, and I can never risk that with him."

"What's his name?" Hidi asks timidly.

A slow reminiscent smile spreads across my face. "Koen. He's the only man that saw me for more than I had to offer. The only one that ever stood up for me, protected me."

Hidi stares at me for a few moments, studying the heartache in the lines of my face. Tears fill my eyes, overflowing down my cheeks, but I don't wipe them away. I let her see the pain, and the longing. I let her see that I was a person with a life before I came here.

"They're weapons," she starts, but when she sees my confused expression, she continues, "The dragons." Her eyes shift to the window then back at me.

I nod in understanding. "The dragons attacked us, destroyed

my kingdom."

"Lothar's army tortures them into submission. They're inherently docile animals, believe it or not. They can be dangerous, but it's not their instinct to harm others."

Her knowledge of the dragons stuns me. I've only heard about dragons from stories passed down, but she talks of them as if they're a house pet she's been around her entire life. The way she defends them seems personal.

I take a deep breath. "Did this kingdom have dragons before the king obtained them? How do you know all of this?"

I watch as memories flicker behind her eyes, and a genuine smile lights up her face. "It was many years ago when they first arrived here. I can't recall how old I was, maybe just before I became a woman."

I figure we're about the same age, so it would be around the same time that the curse was put upon me.

"I never thought I'd actually see one. One day, I was playing in front of my house with my brother, and in the distance, we spotted this small creature." She stops to laugh. "Well, I guess it wasn't small, but small compared to what they are now."

"Are you saying you and your brother found a dragon? The very first one?" I ask, my head spinning at the revelation.

She nods. "It should have been terrifying. In retrospect, we were foolish to have wandered up to a creature that was believed to have been dead for thousands of years. But it's strange, we weren't scared at all. Somehow we knew that she wasn't going to hurt us. We approached her, and held out our hands the same way we would with any other small animal. She sniffed us loudly with her long snout, and then licked us. We couldn't believe it. She was so gentle and immediately friendly and trusting. My mom just about had a stroke when she saw us that close to a wild animal." She chuckles to herself again.

"What happened between then and now? How are there

so many? Is the dragon from your story here?" I'm shooting off questions because there are too many crowding my mind.

Hidi nods, and her entire face turns mournful. "She's here."

*She.* The word sounds so intimate coming from her, so deeply personal. I'm scared to let her continue. Her expression tells me this story doesn't have a happy ending.

An audible swallow fills the room and she wraps her arms around herself. "Mirielle is what we called her. Once my mother got over the shock of seeing a dragon in front of her and her children, we lured it back to our yard, and hid it in the back fenced area. I wasn't sure at the time why, but I know now what my mother knew then. If anyone saw her, she would be in danger, and so would we."

I fully turn my body towards her, giving her my full attention. "If you don't want to continue—if it's too painful, I mean—you don't need to go on."

She waves a hand in front of her. "No, I want to. It's been so long since I've met somebody who didn't know the story. It'll be good to talk about it. It feels good to talk about her." She takes a calming breath. "We were somehow able to keep her existence a secret for a few years. She got large quite fast so we couldn't keep her in our yard, but we found a vacant cave deep within the trees, where we knew nobody would wander. It was close enough to our home, and over time we created a routine with her. In the mornings, my mother and my brother and I would walk the distance to the cave, and she'd be waiting for us out of sight at the back of the cave. We'd call for her, and she'd come bouncing out like a rabbit, excited to see us. We'd bring her any food we could, although we suspected that based on her growth and size, she was hunting and finding her own food just fine. The food we brought Miri was more like snacks. A way for us all to bond."

The love she has for that dragon is easy to see. Her emotions flare from joy to sorrow and back again.

"She was so beautiful. I know they're huge animals, and to most people they look terrifying, but I knew her as a baby. All I see is that sweet curious face I knew when she was small. She has the most beautiful eyes, one a golden brown, and the other a brilliant green. I told my mother I wanted eyes like Miri's. I still do. I was so envious of her. Her great big wings that could take her high above the trees, her gorgeous eyes, even her tough white flesh. To me, it seemed like this incredible armor that I thought nothing could penetrate." She pauses. "I was wrong. I don't envy her anymore."

"What happened? Why is she here?"

"I'll give you one guess."

"Lothar."

She nods.

"How did he get possession of her?" I know that my questions will cause her to dig up a painful memory, but something in me is striving for answers, as if tied to my own fate.

A rogue tear tries to slide down her face, but she aggressively wipes it away. "Word got out about her, because, well, you can't keep an animal of that size secret forever. Especially when the monarchy wants to harness her for power. One day she was just gone. I was on my way to bring her treats one morning, and instead of being greeted by Miri, there were armed guards in front of the cave. They saw me approaching and I tried to run back, but I was brought here and…" She trails off, and I can tell it's too painful for her to finish.

I gently touch her hand, attempting to comfort her, even though I have no actual relief to offer. I give her a sad smile and nod, letting her know she can continue when she's ready.

"They…" She starts, but her voice breaks as the emotion becomes too much. She clears her throat, and tries again. "Sorry. I was the only one Miri would let close, so they needed me to be a trainer of sorts."

My eyebrows furrow in disbelief. "They wanted you to train her to *kill*?"

She shakes her head. "They wanted me to train her to be obedient."

A shiver goes down my spine, and I can't help but think that's exactly why I'm here. My entire life, I wanted to be free from the hold my own family had on me, and now I'm just a slave for a different king. I thought obedience was the only way to win my parents over and see me as a good daughter and a strong queen, but they never did. Now I know that all this time, being obedient to evil only allows room for more evil doings to occur. It was never about obedience, it was about control.

If there's anything I've learned from my parents, it's that rulers will always seek control over the strongest individuals to prevent their own downfall, and preserve their power.

Looking into Hidi's eyes, I see heartbreak, but I also see strength. I don't know why this woman was placed as my caretaker, but right now it feels like fate. Because when I look at her, I see a plan beginning to form.

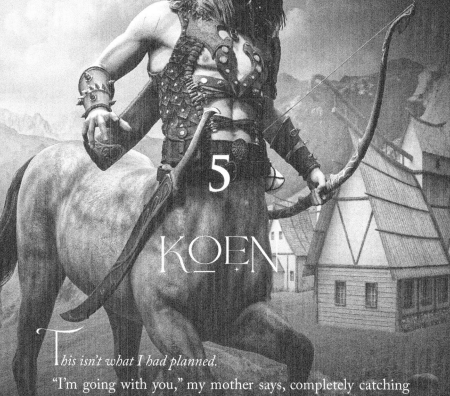

# 5

## KOEN

*This isn't what I had planned.*

"I'm going with you," my mother says, completely catching me off guard.

"I don't think that's a great idea, Mother."

She sighs heavily. "Something about this doesn't feel right."

I cross my arms in front of my chest. "Do you ever plan on telling me how she knows you, or why she seemed so perturbed to see you the day of the attack?"

Suddenly my mother has nothing to say. How convenient.

"Look, I love you, but I don't want you to come. After weeks of begging to speak with the queen, they're finally allowing me to see her. I don't know why, but I need to find out."

A summons slipped under our door a few days ago requested my attendance for a meeting at the castle. I'm not sure what the king and queen will say, and frankly it might not be safe for me to go alone, but I'm desperate for any news of Bellatrix, so I can't resist.

"Are you going in your animal form?" she asks. It's the first time she's ever addressed my shapeshifting gift.

I shrug. "Possibly. I've mostly gotten used to shifting, and it gets me to the castle faster."

She reaches out and gently places her hand on my forearm. "I should have told you. Prepared you for the possibility of shifting. I didn't know how to start the conversation. If I could go back, I'd do things differently, but I can't. Just know that the gods have blessed you with an incredible gift, and not everyone gets that privilege."

Shifters, enchantresses, divination, and nature-based magic have been known around Tenuma, so my ability to shift doesn't make me an outcast by any means. If anything, it makes me feel closer to my mother. The magic in my veins comes from her. I want to let go of my anger and resentment to share this with her, but I'm not there yet.

"Please, I think I should go with you. Just in case," she insists.

"Mother, please. I don't need you there, and Mellani shouldn't be there either. She's been through enough, and that family isn't to be trusted. She's seen enough. I'm not traumatizing her a second time." I watch as her face softens.

Mellani doesn't have many people in her life she can trust. She became very close with Bellatrix in a short time, and Mel had to watch her own father abduct her friend. Stirring up difficult memories for her doesn't seem right.

"Please be careful with the queen. She's not like Bellatrix. She won't hesitate to kill you." Her lips tremble.

I've been acting like an ass for weeks with my drinking and outbursts, but my mother's love for me hasn't dropped an ounce. If I was able to focus on anything other than the bubbling anger in my chest, I would take that love and let it fill me up like the whiskey I've been drowning myself in. But right now, I'm only capable of one emotion: anger.

Anticipation dances through my veins when I'm granted entrance through the front gates at the castle. After weeks of showing up and being turned away, I'm finally going to get some answers. I plod up the long walkway to the castle. My boots leave deep imprints in the thin layer of snow still blanketing most of the ground, creating a soft crunching noise as the snow gives way underneath.

I pause before I reach the doors, glancing upward. To the windows where I first caught sight of Bellatrix. The moment that I truly saw her for the first time, as someone other than the cold-hearted princess she was pretending to be. The same windows that I saw her masturbate beneath, the moment I realized the attraction was mutual.

My anger slips for just a moment, and I can feel a smile tug at my lips. The memories wash over me like I'm basking in the sun on a warm day, without a care in the world.

I'm jolted back to reality at the sound of my name.

"Koen," the queen calls.

I want to scream at her for what she's done, but I force myself to nod. A moment passes and once she realizes there will be no pleasantries here, she waves an arm in, inviting me in.

I've never seen her this way. The soft tone, the demure expression. She almost seems scared, or sad. Surely it's only my imagination. There's no way a mother could do the awful things she's done to her daughter if she were capable of actual human emotions.

I follow the queen inside, and she gestures to a sitting room on the right. As we make our way over, my gaze travels to the long dining table to the left where Bellatrix ate, to the stairs where she descended in her extravagant gowns. Every emotion is stirring in my chest, and I have to force a cough to keep it all tucked away. Holding my emotions at bay keeps my centaur form safely in place, now a daily struggle for me. Heightened emotions make it more difficult, and this woman brings out all the ugliness in me.

Once we're alone inside the room, I glance around expecting to see guards or the king waiting.

But it's only us.

Too much silence has passed, and standing before her makes my skin crawl, so I want to get this over with as quickly as I can. "Do you have news of Bellatrix?"

She swallows whatever emotion she's concealing and offers me a seat. I shake my head and instead lean against a doorway crossing my arms. "Suit yourself," she tells me, taking a seat on a plush maroon couch big enough for four.

My eyes track her every move, and I intentionally keep my distance from her. My mother's warning was well-founded.

"Well, I've been outside the castle wall for weeks trying to get in here to talk, so let's hear it. What's this about?"

"The war. Bellatrix. About how we're getting her back."

She's still talking about her in the present tense. The more days that passed, the more I concluded that I might never see Bellatrix again. Like the waking of a sleeping limb, the pins and needles of hope are reviving the life inside of me. I manage to hold my composure. "And how are we going to get her back?"

"I was hoping you could help me with that."

My frustration boils over. I push off the wall and point a finger at her. "You're her mother! You and that husband of yours have every tool you could need to find her and bring her home! It's been weeks! What have you been doing?"

My shouting has drawn the attention of the guards, and I hear heavy boots rushing towards us. I glance behind me to see three armed men looking as angry as I feel. They halt suddenly, and I turn back to see the queen holding up a hand and shaking her head, keeping them at bay. They hesitantly back away, leaving us to our conversation.

The queen takes a calming breath, and as she looks at me I see her eyes well up. "I've been planning my husband's funeral."

The information hits me like a ton of bricks.

"I need you to keep this between us. With our borders already sensitive to invasion, I can't have word getting out that our ruler is no longer living."

She's not wrong. The kingdom values the king over a queen, which is why her mother was so adamant about Bellatrix finding a man to rule with, so if anyone knew the king was dead, we'd be in serious trouble.

I rub the back of my neck in frustration and confusion. "Why tell me? You don't even like me."

She chuckles, but it's devoid of any humor. "My daughter likes you. I think she might love you, actually."

My head spins every time this woman opens her mouth.

"You don't seem to like her very much," I say bluntly.

I want her to challenge me, scream at me, tell me I'm wrong. I want her to show me any sort of emotion that tells me that somewhere inside she cares for her only child.

That's the thing about expectations, though—more often than not, we break our own hearts hoping people will meet them.

"There's so much you wouldn't understand, Koen," she says, as if it's the only explanation that's needed.

I shake my head. "No. Enough of the bullshit. You need to give me more than that."

She sighs like I've annoyed and exhausted her. "It's easy to hate a person when you don't know their intentions."

A loud hostile laugh erupts from my chest. "Intentions? Are you serious? Intent is meaningless when your actions are evil. You are nothing more than a villain. And the funny thing about villains is they never see themselves as the bad guy." If my gift was shooting fire from my eyes, this whole room would be ablaze now. "Every villain has a reason for their actions. But slapping an excuse on your evil deeds doesn't make them any less evil."

I glare at her, and I can see my words penetrate like a dagger, a wound that's captured her attention. I want her to feel every ounce of pain that she's caused her daughter. I want her to feel something, anything.

"What would you know about any of this? Everything I've done has been to protect her. You wouldn't understand. You're just a poor man from the village," she sneers.

My hands begin to tremble with anger and something more. "Oh yeah? I'm just a powerless man, huh?"

I explode into my animal form. Towering over her, I look down at her tiny human form and we both know how easily it would be to end her with the stomp of my hoof. "Can you do this? Because it looks to me that I've got more power than even our *mighty* queen."

Her eyes widen, but she stays still. Afraid to move.

Having made my point, I shove my emotions back under, snap back into my human form, and quickly dress. I turn to walk away, unable to listen to anymore of her excuses, but the words she speaks next stop me in my tracks.

"Have you asked your mother how we know each other, Koen?"

I hate the way she says my name, like scolding a toddler. I turn around and give her a quizzical glare.

"Have you?" she taunts.

I step back into the room directly in front of her this time, a few feet back. "Feel free to enlighten me."

A slimy grin spreads across her face. She's a cat with a mouse, choosing to toy with it before the inevitable meal. She rises from the couch as if planning to walk away with the bait she's dangling over my head.

I hold up an arm to stop her from walking out.

"Tell me," I demand, my voice low but firm.

With both hands she smooths down the fabric of her black suede dress as if she's bored of this conversation and has better things to do. When she glances up at me, her face reveals the same sentiment.

"Who do you think put that curse on Bellatrix all those years ago?"

The implication lands like a bomb. The room is spinning, and I fall backwards on the chair as the blast hits me. Gripping the chair arms for support, I glance up at the queen again. "You're lying."

She pulls her lips in together, I assume to disguise a smirk.

"Just because you destroyed your own family, it gives you no right to try and destroy mine," I growl at her.

"It makes no difference to me whether you believe me or not. That's a problem for you and your mother. What I'm concerned with is how I'm going to get my daughter back. I was hoping we could put our differences aside and come together. For Bellatrix. Do you want to bring her home or not?"

I run my hands through my thick hair, frustration seeping out of my pores. "What am I supposed to do? You have an entire army."

She takes a step towards me. "Because of what you are. You helped fight off the dragons and Lothar's army by yourself."

I cringe at her use of my father's name. One he didn't always go by. The new identity he assumed when he left our family and fled Tenuma also included a new name. According to newly revealed information, he managed, with a group of power-hungry criminals, to overthrow Sperantia's weak kingdom and put himself into power. Would things be different had we known Sperantia's new king was my father? Subconsciously, I feel responsible. As if I could have stopped him.

"Plus, he's your father, and you know him. You have inside information the rest of us don't. That gives you the upper hand. We will use anything at this point to get her back."

I scoff. "He left my family a long time ago. He was a stranger to us then, and he's a stranger now."

"So is that a no, then?"

She's baiting me, and I know it. Yet, I find myself unable to turn away, not with Bellatrix's life on the line. This is what I wanted after all. I wanted action towards bringing her home.

Leave it to the person that put us in the middle of a mess to place the responsibility of cleaning it up solely onto somebody else.

"Of course I'll help get her back. I'd do anything for her," I spit back. While a part of me feels like it's an overshare, another part knows it's something she's already aware of. I couldn't hide my feelings for Bellatrix if I tried. And I did try.

She folds her hands in front of her. "I was hoping you'd say that."

I'm not sure why I'm agreeing to this, and I sure as hell don't know if I should be trusting a word she says, but Gods help me, I can't say no to anything that might bring the princess home.

Despite my instincts aggressively waving a red flag at me, screaming for me to turn and walk out of here right now, I stand. "Let's hear this plan of yours."

# 6

# BELLATRIX

"What's your plan?" Hidi surprises me as she enters the room while I was preoccupied trying to undo the ropes on my wrists.

"I, uh, what?" I stumble and fail to land on any actual words.

"What's your plan here? Even if you made your way out of those binds, where are you going to go?" she asks in a way that seems more curious than accusatory.

"There's no plan. I wasn't doing anything. Just adjusting. These are very uncomfortable." I'm not altogether lying.

After Hidi confided in me last week about the dragon that was taken from her, our dynamic changed. We went from captive and caretaker to two women who were both wronged by the same terrible man. Having somebody open up and show you what matters most to them blurs the lines of a situation like this. She has pulled back the last few days, not speaking much and keeping her visits shorter than usual.

But each day she brings me a piece of strawberry swirled cake.

Her detached behavior shouldn't bother me, but it does. I want to ask her about it, but I understand. She's between a rock and a hard place, trying to do what she needs to do to survive. I don't know why she's still here or what she has to lose, but I'm sure helping me in any way wouldn't be beneficial to her.

She approaches me to undo the ropes. Once free, she gently caresses my wounds. "Your wrists look redder today. Are they bothering you much?"

I'm taken aback by the moment of comfort and closeness. "I'm okay."

The corners of her mouth turn down, evidently seeing through my lie. "I can bring you a salve for that tomorrow."

She releases my wrists and holds up an arm gesturing towards the bathroom. Like a flower trying to bloom in winter, our friendship is fighting against the situation we're in. She's resisting it, but I can see that she cares.

"Thank you. And thank you for the cake." I slide off the bed and make my way across the room. She doesn't follow me the way she usually does.

Closing the door behind me, I turn the bath water as hot as it will go and sink beneath it. Aside from the usual layer of dust and dirt floating around Sperantia, I don't accumulate much filth sitting in a bed all day, but it's nice to retain some of the basic human needs to make me feel like I'm still a person.

Sinking until only my head sticks out, hot water covering me like a protective cloak, I allow myself to cry. My eyes might be red when I come out, but I won't give anybody the satisfaction of watching or hearing me cry. Even Hidi.

Typically, I can be in and out of the bathroom pretty quickly, but today I'm taking longer than necessary. I felt like I was getting closer to Hidi, breaking down her barriers, and now her walls are higher than ever. If the situation were different, I think we'd be friends. She reminds me of Quirina in so many ways. She's loyal, kind, comforting, and compassionate in a way that makes me sometimes forget that I'm not in the company of a friend.

After I've dried myself off and dressed in one of the simple cloth dresses they've left for me—which are always too big—I open the door and realize I'm alone.

I stand in the doorway unsure why I've been left alone and unbound. It feels like a trick, and I'm too spooked to move.

Has she finally given into my wishes and gifted me this small freedom?

Will she return to tie me back up?

I thought being left untied would make this more bearable, but it's oddly unsettling. Hidi has shot down every request not to tie me up, either by flat-out telling me no or not responding to the question all together.

Why now?

"Princess," a voice calls softly.

I don't know where the voice comes from. My head whips around the room, looking for the source. I'm too scared to respond.

"Princess. Don't panic. It's Hidi," she says quietly. Her voice is close, as if right next to me. But I can't see her.

Full-body goosebumps break out on my flesh and the hair on the back of my neck stands up.

Maybe this is a dream.

"H-Hidi? Where are you?" I hold onto the bathroom door frame for support.

She answers by materializing right before me with the wave of a hand. As if she's wiping over a cold, foggy window to give me visibility to what's beyond it.

I stumble backwards, shocked by what I'm seeing.

"You have the power of invisibility."

"And intangibility," she adds.

Even though I have a "power" of sorts, it's shocking when others reveal their own, especially when theirs are more of a gift and a lot less of a curse. Not only can Hidi appear and disappear at will, but she can also move through solid objects, like walls.

"Why are you showing me this?" I ask with as much confusion as intrigue.

"It could be the way," she whispers cryptically. I quickly catch on to her attempt at keeping our conversation from reaching the guard at the door.

"Are you saying what I think you're saying?" I don't want to get my hopes up, but her statement floats like a lifeboat in the middle of the ocean. A misread sliver of hope would be soul-crushing if I'm wrong. Physical wounds, I think I could handle, as the pain lessens over time. But the emotional pain demanding to be carried 24/7 is unbearable. Currently I'm grasping for a tether that I'm scared is just a mirage.

Her lips turn upwards, and her head starts to nod when the door to the room swings open.

Hidi spins around like a kid who was just caught going through her parents' belongings. My muscles tense and my chin begins to tremble as we both gaze over to the intruder.

"Your Majesty," Hidi announces formally, bending rigidly at the waist, bowing to her king.

Deep lines stretch across Lothar's weathered face like dark valleys full of secrets. The long wavy dark hair that hangs loose underneath his crown matches the thick beard on his face. If his narrowed eyes didn't emit pure hatred, one might find him handsome. He's tall with broad shoulders. A physique that tells me he's a man who has taken care of his body the majority of his life. Though all the care in the kingdom couldn't erase the way his poisonous heart left its mark on his face.

Lothar ignores her, and his eyes land directly on me. "Ah, there's my princess."

His voice is deep and hoarse, almost like it hurts to speak. His words make me shudder, which I try to hide by holding onto the door frame.

The king must catch it because his thin lips form a sly grin, and the tongue that slides over his bottom lip feels like it is slithering all over my body. Inside I'm screaming, but I stand still. Like a deer in the woods, afraid to make a move, hoping the mountain lion won't see me. But he doesn't need provocation to attack, he hunts for sport.

"Handmaiden, excuse yourself. The princess and I have much to discuss."

She nods her head. "Of course, Your Majesty," she responds dutifully, and exits the room.

Though she's powerless to protect me, I immediately feel vulnerable. She won't be witness to whatever happens next, and the desire to jump out the window and hope I sprout dragon wings intensifies. So does the desire to tell him to go fuck himself.

Lothar slowly makes his way further into the room, closing the distance between us. His scent brings me back to that long, uncomfortable journey on dragon-back, when sweat, dirt, and smoke permeated my senses for hours.

"I've been eager to see you, my beautiful princess." His words slide through the room as if carried by oil, and I have the urge to leap out of their reach. I don't know what he wants with me, and I'm terrified to find out.

My mouth doesn't open to respond. My expression doesn't change, but the bead of sweat dripping down the side of my face gives me away.

"You should know better than anyone that when a king speaks to you, you respond."

"W-why are you doing this? What do you want?" My voice comes out shakier than I was hoping. I'm unable to control my quivering lips. I cross my arms over my chest, as if both consoling and protecting myself.

So much for feigning strength.

"I thought it was fairly obvious, my dear." He chuckles. When I still look lost, he continues. "Your gift. That wonderful gift you've been given."

*No.*

His face turns from entertained to angry quicker than the time it takes for an arrow to shoot through its target. "What do you mean, no?" I'm confused by his question and then realize I've been shaking my head. "Nobody tells me no, princess."

I force my head to stop shaking, which is harder than I expected.

"You are the perfect woman to rule with. That gift of yours is just what I need to enhance my power over this and all other lands," he says with a cunning look in his eyes.

"Curse," I spit back.

"Excuse me?"

"It's a curse, *not* a gift."

"Ah, yes, well, that all depends on the way you look at it."

My eyes instinctively narrow at him. "There's only one way to look at it. You're a fool. You can't survive it, any more than the rest of the men that tried. I'm of no use to you. Let me go."

He laughs smugly. "Oh Princess, I would never put my own hands on you, let alone lie with you."

"I will never help you gain more power. You'll have to kill me," I shout.

The asshole actually laughs. "My son is right. You're something else."

His son—the man Koen killed for assaulting me.

I'm the reason his son is dead. No wonder I'm here.

Suddenly my skin turns cold, and I feel like I might be sick. He wants revenge.

"You and Koen have gotten pretty close, no?"

"What does he have to do with any of this?" I attempt to keep my face neutral, praying to the Gods that Lothar doesn't know it was Koen who ended his son's life.

"Your mother really left you in the dark, didn't she?"

With a puffed-out chest, he takes a step towards me. He lifts one finger and slowly traces it down my face. "How do you think I was able to find you, sweet princess? Koen is my son, and he led me right to you."

The ground feels unsteady beneath my feet. I blink rapidly, trying to focus on the face in front of me. It somehow looks completely different than it did a moment ago.

The long dark hair, thick beard, and gray eyes are a perfect match for Koen's. They have a similar height and build, and I feel stupid for not having seen it before. There's no doubt that this man is Koen's father.

"Koen would never betray me. He said you left his family years ago." Something isn't adding up, but I don't know what.

Lothar takes another deliberate step towards me, and I retreat backwards into the bathroom, ready to slam the door in his face.

"How do you think I knew where and how to find you, my dear?" he taunts, leaving me feeling dizzy.

No, Koen wouldn't have betrayed me.

Though everyone else has me, so what's one more person? My heart clenches. Not Koen.

"No. He killed the son you sent to kill me. Why would he kill his own brother?"

I see his jaw grind. "Both of my sons are very much alive, and they helped me get exactly what I wanted."

I retreat fully into the bathroom and slam the door behind me, crumbling to the ground.

Koen is the only man I've ever trusted. Is it possible he did this to me?

How could he be the sweet attentive brother to Mellani *and* the monster his father claims he is?

It feels like the world just flipped upside down, and everything I thought I knew is no longer real. There's nobody looking for me, and I'm truly alone. The man I thought cared for me and had my back has been plotting against me with his evil father. I can't help but feel like my heart was just torn into with sheers, leaving it a shredded mess in my chest.

"Settle in, Princess. You're not going anywhere. I'll be back to discuss my plans for you," Lothar shouts from the other side of the door. A few moments later I hear the bedroom door open and close.

I don't know how long I sit on the floor sobbing into my hands. I no longer care who hears me. I've finally accepted that I won't be leaving this horrid place. Not that it would matter, because there's nothing left waiting for me in Tenuma anymore.

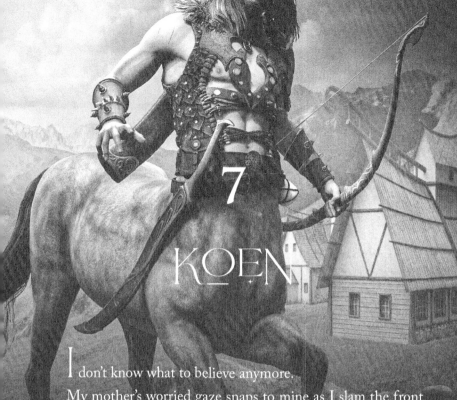

# 7

# KOEN

I don't know what to believe anymore.

My mother's worried gaze snaps to mine as I slam the front door to our cottage. After my conversation with the queen, I ran home for answers from the one woman who has them.

"Koen, baby, is everything okay? What happened?" she asks, rising from her chair and approaching me as I stand in the entrance of our home.

"Is it true?"

Her eyebrows cinch together, and I see her swallow. "Is what true?"

Mellani lays on her stomach on the ground where she was working on a picture, but now watches us intently. I shouldn't have this conversation like this, but I can't wait any longer. "Don't do that, Mother. It's time for answers. Was it you who put the curse on Bellatrix?"

Her lips form a thin line, and she pulls them inward and nods her head.

"I'm so sorry. Please, let's sit down and talk." She pauses and walks over to Mel. "Sweetheart, will you go color in my room so I can talk to your brother for a few minutes, please?"

"Okay, Mommy. Can I color on the bed?" she asks innocently.

"Of course you can, but please be careful," she tells her, helping Mel collect her colors from the ground.

Once Mellani is in my mother's room with the door closed, my mother sits on the couch, and pats the cushion for me to sit next to her. I reluctantly take the seat next to her, but face forward. I'm not ready to look her in the eyes. Not ready to accept what she's done.

"So, you talked to the queen then," she begins.

I nod.

"It's not what you think, Koen. I never wanted to curse that sweet girl."

"But you did," I say through clenched teeth.

"I wasn't exactly given a choice, my son."

I turn my gaze to hers, finally looking at her. There's guilt, shame, and sorrow in her eyes. I wish I hadn't looked.

"What do you mean? How is this even possible? You've known Bellatrix and the queen all along?"

She nods. "I'm sorry. I should have told you."

"Why didn't you?"

She sighs. "Never in my wildest dreams did I think that you would end up anywhere near Bellatrix."

"But I did. And you saw that we were becoming close. You had so many opportunities to tell me, and you didn't."

"I know, baby, and I'm so sorry for that. I should have. My actions, everything I've ever done, were in the spirit of protecting you and Mel."

"What do you mean, you didn't have a choice? How did this

happen?"

"The queen approached me years ago and told me her plan for the curse for her daughter. I tried to object, but once she threatened your life, I didn't have a choice. I was to cast the spell, and should I resist or reveal to you or anyone else what I had done, she would have you killed."

I take a deep breath, letting the information sink in. This entire time I've hated the person who cast this spell on Bellatrix, and it turns out it was my own mother.

"Is that why you didn't want me to take the job at the castle?" I ask.

"Yes. I wasn't as worried about you falling into the princess's trap, but I know firsthand how dangerous that entire family is. I never wanted you anywhere near them."

"This is so fucked up. All this time, it was you."

"I'm very sorry I lied to you. But it saved your life, and as much as I hate what Bellatrix is going through, I don't regret my decision. I did what I had to do for my family. For you. You know I would never harm that poor girl willingly. You can be mad at me and blame me all you want, but her mother is the one who did this to her. I was merely a conduit to complete the curse."

My mother and Mellani are the most important people in my life, so if my back was up against the wall like my mother's was, would I make the same choice? Even though it's easy to look at from the outside and know that what happened to Bellatrix was wrong, I also know that I'd do anything to protect my family.

"Can't you reverse it, take the curse away?" I ask.

She shakes her head. "I wish it were that simple, baby."

Defeat sits heavy in my chest. I lay my head in my hands, unable to bear the weight. "Why can't you?"

"You know I don't have my power anymore. I haven't had most of my powers for some time now. Since I cast that spell on

Bellatrix."

My head jerks up at her confession. "Why then?"

"All magic has a cost, and this one had a big price tag. We're punished when we use magic for evil."

Her confession both softens me towards my mother and hardens my anger toward the queen. The way the queen tried to bait me with that revelation made it seem as if my mother was the culprit for the entire situation. She conveniently left out a few key pieces of information.

"If there was a way to stop it, I would. I'd never let that sweet girl continue to suffer. There's only one way to end the curse."

My heart begins to beat wildly in my chest at the possibility of ending this curse once and for all.

"How?"

"The curse will be lifted with her mother's death."

"Was that your idea?" I ask.

She nods, not quite proudly, but not ashamed either. "If I had no choice but to ruin that little girl's life, I wasn't going to let that woman escape unscathed. It was her doing, and if she wanted it, I told her there would be a price for her to pay as well."

My mother is a badass.

All of the anger I felt for my mother shrivels up and falls away. Understanding does wonders for anger and assumptions. Some of the missing pieces have begun to snap into place, and I'm starting to make sense of what's been happening.

"Does Bellatrix know that you were the one who cursed her?" I ask, wondering if maybe the princess knew all along and reeling me in was her version of payback.

Immediate relief floods my body when my mother shakes her head.

"No. The night I cursed her, I was in disguise. While the

queen knew who I was, I was never revealed to Bellatrix. I never wanted to be associated with what I had done. She doesn't know who I am, nor does she have any previous knowledge of who you are," she explains as if reading my mind.

"I wish you had trusted me enough to handle the truth."

"Like you trusted me with the truth of your feelings for her?" she counters.

"That's not the same," I respond stubbornly, crossing my arms.

"No, but you knew it would worry me. You kept that information to yourself to protect me, same as I did. I never wanted to hurt you, and once I learned of your feelings for one another, I panicked. With the attack and your father taking her on top of all of that, it's been a lot to wrap my head around."

I nod. I've been stuck in my own world of misery, that I forget that others have been trudging through their own turmoil. "Did you know he changed his name?"

She shakes her head. "To find out that he's the king of Sperantia with a new name hasn't been easy to digest either. I hate thinking that I used to share a home with that man. He's a stranger."

I reach out and grab her hand. "I'm sorry. For everything. I'm going to get Bellatrix back, and we will all be okay."

"Did the queen have any information on Bellatrix?"

I fill her in on how the queen appointed me the head of the search. In exchange for my help, I demanded that my family be taken care of in the way of payment, so we don't have to worry about food. It's one less thing to think about, and I can focus on the mission to find Bellatrix.

"That sounds dangerous," my mother concludes.

"Probably. But I can't sit here and continue to do nothing."

"Why does she want *you* involved?"

A peculiar question considering the revelation of her own

involvement with the queen. "Because of my father. Apparently I have insight she claims not to have herself."

"What will that mean for you? I don't want you risking your life any more than you already have."

"If we want her back, I don't have a choice. I have to get her back."

My mother takes a cleansing breath, and her rigid posture slackens.

"What's a mission?" Mel chimes in from the hallway as she emerges from my mother's room.

"It's like an adventure, sweet girl." A partial truth. Mel has dealt with enough, and I refuse to give her another thing to worry about.

"Oooh, can I go?" she asks excitedly.

I chuckle. "Not this time, Mel."

She gives an exaggerated frown. "Okay."

Mel goes back to the room, and I rise and walk to the kitchen to prepare a snack for the three of us. My mother follows, pulling out a few plates as I begin cutting up some fruit.

I place a few wedges of apple on each plate, handing them to my mother. "I'm going to visit Nik and see if he would be willing to join the rescue. We'll need all the men we can get, and it would be nice to have somebody I trust alongside."

"I'm sure you won't have any trouble convincing him to go with you."

I wish I could feel the confidence my mother has. She's right, he is a good man. But my selfishness and misplaced anger in these past few weeks might have ruined any possibility of having him by my side. Unfortunately my mother hasn't been the only one that's seen the wrath of my anger. I haven't been the best version of myself, nor have I been a good friend to him, so I don't know how willing he will be to join me on what could very well be a suicide mission.

Hell, for all I know, the queen is sending me into a trap so she can find a better man for Bellatrix should she ever return home.

Nik and I have been friends for a long time, so I hope that the foundation of our friendship is strong enough to withstand the last few weeks of hell I've put everyone through.

# 8

# BELLATRIX

Get me out of this hell.

"Yes?" A knock on the door reminds me that I'm still holed up in the bathroom. Maybe if I close my eyes with enough force, I'll disappear into thin air like Hidi did.

"Princess, are you okay in there?" Hidi's voice is comforting compared to the voice I thought I would hear.

I press the palms of my hand deep into my eyes until I see stars. Rocking back and forth on the floor with my knees pulled up to my chest, I curse myself. I feel so stupid.

Lothar's voice bounces around in my head.

*"Settle in, Princess. You're not going anywhere. I'll be back to discuss my plans for you."*

A shiver runs through my body as I recall his words from a few hours ago. I think it was a few hours ago, but I've been lying here for so long, it could be a whole new day.

Soft knocking at the door pulls me back to the present as Hidi tries to lure me out of the washroom. "I need you to eat something. Can you come out please?"

When I don't answer, she continues, "Princess, you do know that I can come in there, right? Did you forget what I showed you?"

I swing the door open to face her. She stares back smugly, clearly proud to have gotten me off the washroom floor.

"So, are you going to tell me *why* you showed me?" I ask, slowly making my way around her, heading for the window. I don't want to go back to the bed that's been my prison for much too long.

Instead of answering my question, she points out something I missed in the midst of my breakdown.

"He left you untied." She sounds amused, excited even. "He found me, and all he said was 'make sure she eats.'"

The outside world, even as drab as it is here in Sperantia, holds my gaze, and I can't be bothered to look away just yet. "Okay."

"It's a start," she tells me.

Now she's got my attention.

I spin around facing her. "A start to what?" I ask.

Hidi lowers her voice. "To start planning your escape, Princess."

I hold her gaze, trying to read the seriousness of her statement. Once again, hope flickers in my chest like a dying light orb, fighting for another minute of light.

Is she toying with me? Testing me?

When I don't respond, she smiles and continues. "Because we

both want the same thing. Nobody else knows what I can do."

"What do you want from me?" The question comes automatically. In my experience, people only do things for you when they want something in return. When your entire existence has been transactional, you get accustomed to the exchange. I want to trust her, but I'm not sure I can.

Hidi's face changes from amused to determined. "When we get you out of here, I want to go with you."

"Back to Tenuma?"

She nods.

"Why not just leave? You could go anywhere you want."

She shakes her head. "He has guards watching my family's home at all times. My mother and my brother are allowed to visit me here, but if I try to leave, they'll be killed. Even if we all made it out, where would we go? Any kingdom that we escaped to would surely turn us back into Lothar. But with you, we could enter Tenuma safely. We need you. I want my family to come with us. And Miri."

"Hidi, I don't know if you noticed, but I can't even help myself right now. What am I supposed to do?" Having been locked in a bedroom for weeks on end doesn't exactly scream heroine.

"Together we can. I'm a prisoner here too, Princess. My family will be killed should I ever flee. I've been the key to gaining the dragons' loyalty. Once the other dragons saw the way Miri trusted me and was affectionate with me, the others followed suit. Lothar and his army of monsters used that vulnerability to abuse them into submission and trained them to be weapons of war," she confesses.

Not only does this kingdom condone stealing animals and torturing them, but humans are used like pawns too. My heart aches for Hidi and Miri. For anyone who's been subjected to the king's wrath.

"The dragons are already here. Why not let you go home?"

She shrugs. "They're fearful that if Miri knows I'm gone, she'll rebel and take the others with her."

The stories I know of dragons always depicted them as intelligent, emotional creatures that had the ability to imprint on humans. It's not entirely unreasonable to think that Miri would follow Hidi, leaving the king without his weapons.

I nod in understanding. "Whatever you need me for, I'm in. But are you sure? Once you align yourself with me, people will be after you to kill you."

She hangs her head, then gazes out of the window we're standing in front of. "I've been held prisoner here for years. This isn't living anyways," she says. "If I can make it out long enough to get Miri free, that's all I want. I owe it to her. It's my fault she's here."

I can see the mist in her eyes, and it's clear to me just how much she cares for the dragon. Hidi would do anything for Miri. She's willing to risk her life to set her free. I'd be honored to take her back to my kingdom.

"Then let's get the fuck out of here," I say, feeling more confident than I've felt in a long time.

"I don't…" she starts, sounding unsure of herself. "I don't have a plan yet, but I know we can do it."

"So let's plan." She's in my room every day as it is, so her being here won't be alarming. The king doesn't seem to care whether I'm tied up anymore or not, and that alone gives me the strength to feel like we can escape.

"It won't be easy, and we may be killed before we can pull this off. He's cunning and crueler than he seems," she tells me.

"How so?"

"The reason you're here," she begins, "you're another weapon for him to use. You're the princess with the 'soul-snatching pussy'—forgive my language—that turns men into daemons. Men he could use for soldiers."

The words don't land the way she expects when a small humorless laugh escapes my lips. "What's so funny, Princess?"

"You would think that would be terrifying, and it still is, don't get me wrong. However, my own parents were using me as the same tool in their own political game." Saying it out loud makes me realize just how bad things have gotten.

Hidi quietly gasps, but her hand quickly covers her mouth to mask it.

My lips form a thin line, and the corners slightly lift upwards into an awkward sad smile that says, *"What can you do?"* Because as fucked up as it is, the simple fact is it's my life.

The people who were supposed to protect me are the very same ones who put me in harm's way. There are things I've been through that I *can* recover from, but I'm not sure this is one of them. Only the gift of time and acceptance can grant me that closure, and escaping Lothar's grip is the only way I get that chance. He made it clear that he intends to use my "gift" for his benefit, so I'm hoping we get the hell out of here before he does.

"Thank you." The sincerity drips off of her words like honey, so sweet and genuine I want to consume them whole.

"For what?"

"Trusting me, and helping me," she explains with a shrug.

"Thank you for doing the same for me," I say and squeeze her hand. I'm still not sure what made her decide to trust me. She's been like an angel sent to me, protecting and keeping me safe. Hidi has been my salvation. Like scar tissue, pulling me back together and filling the gaps of my wounds.

The week I arrived here, I recall guards attempting to come into the room while I was bathing and making excuses as to why they were inside. The men always tried to catch a glimpse of the "princess with the soul-snatching pussy." I wasn't a person; I was merely an object to be gawked at. A spectacle for men to be entertained by.

After that first week, I noticed Hidi was much more diligent about making sure my doors were always closed. She protected me from being violated by the guards, and went out of her way to keep me safe. Not only was she a human shield when I couldn't protect myself, she became a source of comfort. The small ways she made me feel like I was still a person who matters. The sweets she's been sneaking in for me, or a comforting touch. Her kindness saved me when I wanted to give up. A debt I hope I get the chance to repay.

In a matter of weeks, a perfect stranger has shown me more kindness and empathy than my family, or any of the men I've been with have ever shown me. Aside from Koen.

Except Koen might be a liar.

Well aware of the risk we're taking, Hidi doesn't seem fazed that she could be giving her own life. While there's a small voice warning me not to trust her, I feel the urge to fight it.

*Please don't let me down, Hidi.*

# 9

# KOEN

Please don't let me down.

Making my way up the street, I see Nik with Quirina by his side. The topic I was hoping to ignore for the time being is currently staring daggers at me.

Nik and Rina have been spending a lot of time together since Bellatrix was taken, and I may have reacted unfavorably when I noticed. I also may have accused them of sneaking around and hiding a relationship, even though it's no business of mine.

Like I said, I've been an asshole.

Nik and the men around town have come together to have his bar rebuilt as quickly as possible. There's still a lot of work to be done, but it's come a long way.

A sour, guilty feeling stirs in my stomach. I haven't been here to help at all. I've been lost in my grief and anger for so long that I've ignored the people I care about when they needed me the most. My chest tightens. I shouldn't be here asking him for a favor.

Nik regards me as I approach, and then whispers something to Quirina, who glares back in my direction. She gives him a nod, but disappears inside the new building to give us some space.

"The bar looks great, Nik," I tell him.

I'm hoping if I start light he might be more willing to hear me out. I've always considered Nik a friend who'd do anything for me, and I'm praying that's still true.

He's brushing sawdust off his hands with a rag, and glances up at me. "Yeah, thanks for all the help," he responds sarcastically.

Ouch. I deserved that one.

"I—" I start to apologize, but he holds up a hand, cutting me off.

"Don't. Why are you here?"

Okay, clearly pleasantries are not on the table today. Nik's not typically one to hold a grudge, but his response tells me how monumentally I've fucked up.

"The queen is finally putting together a mission. We're going to get Bellatrix back," I say, expecting to see him perk up.

He doesn't. I wish I could say it doesn't sting, but the pain in my chest would tell a different story.

"Great. Go get her back so you can stop being a dick to the rest of us," he shoots back.

I clench my jaw, knowing that this isn't the time to get into things with Nik. I'm also aware that I'm not entitled to hold the moral high ground after the way I've treated him, so I take a deep breath.

"I need my friend, man. Will you come with me?"

A cackle erupts from him like he can't believe what he's hearing, and it's a full minute before he catches his breath.

"You're kidding, right?" he finally responds after his laughter has died down. "For weeks, you have treated the rest of us like we're garbage. Unimportant and disposable. This isn't just about me, Koen. The way you've treated Quirina"—he gestures behind him to the bar—"to your mother, to poor little Mel. Do you have any idea what you've been putting us through?"

From Quirina's attempts to comfort me right after Bellatrix was taken, to the friendly way she always greets me when I run into her, I have rejected every kindness from her for no reason other than I'm angry. She didn't deserve any of it.

I'm aware I've screwed things up, and I don't know if I'm prepared to hear what it's been like on the receiving end of things.

He takes my silence as a no, so he continues. "I'll tell you. It's been *hell*. Aside from the complete asshole you've been acting like, you have everybody worried. You disappear for days at a time, show up at home in the middle of the night blackout drunk and even angrier. You haven't been here for me or for anybody, Koen. You didn't lose your home, your security, your family. They're all still there. Right in front of you. You've been selfish and punishing people around you who are already suffering, because you can't get over your own shit. I know you lost her, but we fucking matter too! Your pain is understandable, but your behavior is not excusable."

I know it's the wrong thing to say, but I can't stop it from coming out anyways. "How would you know any of that?"

Nik scoffs at me and tosses the rag on the ground like it personally offended him. "How the hell do you think, man? I go and check in on your mom and Mel, just as they've been doing for me. That's what you do for those you care about. You check in on them, lean on them, and they lean on you. Not whatever the fuck it is *you've* been doing."

"Who am I supposed to lean on, Nik? Everyone's been lying and hiding shit from me, for, I don't know, my entire life. So yeah, please, let me lean on them for support."

"I haven't been lying to you, Ko, so what's the excuse for treating *me* like shit?" he asks as Quirina walks back outside, no doubt hearing all our shouting and wanting to check on things.

I nudge my chin in her direction. "Oh yeah? You've been fucking Quirina and failed to mention it."

I'm a man possessed. I know I shouldn't be saying or doing these things, and yet I can't stop the words from leaving my mouth. It's like I'm watching myself from a distance.

Nik's eyes darken with fury, and his jaw clenches as his arms begin to rise at his sides. I mentally brace myself for the strike I'm sure is coming. Before Nik can lift his arm and swing, I feel a sharp sting of a slap rather than a fist, and my head snaps to see Quirina standing next to me with her finger pointed in my face.

"Fuck you, Koen. Trix would be disgusted if she could see what you've turned into."

I'm too stunned to react. There's not much I can say to get myself out of this mess, or justify why those words left my mouth.

Sometimes I think my heart needs someone to suffer with. Bellatrix is gone, and somehow the world keeps moving in spite of it. My family and my friends are moving on, and I hate them for it. The day she was taken, my world stopped. I'm not capable of comprehending that somehow, for others, it's continued to turn.

"Quirina—" I start, but she cuts me off, putting her hand back up to my face as if she can't stand to look at me. Behind her, Nik is silently fuming. I've never seen him this angry before.

"Don't. I don't care to hear it. Bellatrix cares about you, we all do. But this—" She waves a hand in front of me. "This isn't the Koen we know. Just go. You've caused enough damage, and a pathetic apology isn't going to cut it." Her face shifts from sadness and anger to pity.

This look is somehow worse.

Quirina, clearly finished with the conversation, turns to grab Nik's hand and pull him in the opposite direction. She doesn't seem fazed by the anger he's displaying right now, and as much as it's made me fearful of how far I've pushed him, I can't ignore the way they instinctively protect each other. Like they've known each other for years, old friends who know how to be rational when the other is driven by emotion.

I've been unable to be the friend they both deserve, and that makes me want to kick my own ass. The desire to be better is there, I can feel it. Unfortunately I feel the stinging pain of loss more.

It shouldn't surprise me that Nik has been so supportive and attentive with Quirina in her time of need. Nik is the one person you can always count on. Not once has he let one of his patrons leave overly intoxicated or alone. Nik makes sure every person makes it back to their families safely, never putting his business in front of anyone else. He cares more for others than he does himself.

I used to be that kind of man: selfless and driven by reason and rational thinking. I'd be lying if I said it's not hard to look at myself in the mirror each morning when my pores are seeping whiskey. It's a truth I try to keep buried along with everything else I've been feeling.

Turning away from the bar, I know that my walk home will need to have some serious soul-searching if I plan on mending any of the relationships I've been careless with.

Mellani draws quietly on the floor of the main room of our cottage in front of the couch, while my mother tends to a meal on the stove that smells divine.

Both of their heads snap up as I shut the front door behind

me. I give them an awkward half-attempt at a smile.

"Koen!" Mellani shrieks as she hops up and thrusts herself into my arms.

I wrap my arms around her and squeeze, and I must admit that the embrace feels nice. I hadn't realized how far I've really pushed everyone away. My eyes lightly mist. Human connection is something I never thought was a necessity, but in her embrace right now, I realize what a fool I've been and just how far I've fallen.

I pull back from the hug so I can see her beautiful face, and she rewards me with a bright smile. "Hi, sweet girl."

"You're never here when the sun is out," she says with delight.

She's right. I hate that she's right.

I brush a flyaway curl away from her cherub cheek. "I know, and I'm sorry. That's going to change," I tell her, needing it to be true for both of us.

"Come draw with me. I made a picture for the princess!"

As awful as I feel for my absence and overall attitude the last few months, I'm equally grateful for Mellani's resilience and positive attitude. She's been through as much as the rest of us, and the way she bounces back is impressive. The way she can still find joy.

I pick up her drawing, and sure enough, I see an image of a woman with black hair and red lips in a long dress.

*Princess Bellatrix.*

Even this drawing makes my heart ache with the way I miss her and fear for what she's going through. The picture depicts the princess in a large room, not unlike her own, looking out of a window where there's dragons flying around outside of it. A man stands by the door of the room, and I already know that it's Lothar. The accuracy with which she's drawn them both impresses me.

I'm always unsure what to make of Mel's drawings. On

occasion she creates something that comes to fruition, and other times it's just a regular picture. Is it random, or is she magically gifted? And if she's gifted, is she aware? I make a mental note to have a conversation with Mel at a later time. With everything she's been through, I don't want to confuse or upset her by bringing up the idea of being gifted to her. My gift was a shock, and I'm a grown-ass man. I don't want to worry her until we know for sure.

"What a great picture, Mel. Who are these two people? Is this one Princess Bellatrix?" I point to the woman staring out the window.

"Yes, that's the princess. She wants to go and be with the dragons."

"I see. Who's the other person in the drawing?"

"Two," she corrects.

My head tilts as I try to untangle her strange response. "Two what?"

"Two other people."

"Yes, the princess, but who's the other one, the man?"

She groans in frustration. "No. The princess is there." She points to the same woman. "And there's two more."

"I only see one, sweet girl," I say softly, curious where she's going with this.

Mel pulls me closer and whispers, "The other woman is hiding."

My head rears back like I've been struck.

"Who's hiding?"

She shrugs. "I don't know."

Without further explanation she grabs another piece of paper and begins on a new picture, the first one already forgotten. Leaving me bewildered, I ruffle her hair and tell her I need to go speak with our mother. She nods without looking up.

"It smells good in here." I inhale deeply as I walk into the kitchen.

"It's a roast with vegetables and gravy. I'm just finishing up the potatoes if you want to help mash them."

She holds out the utensil for me to grab like the olive branch it is. I take it and help my mother finish dinner. We stand side by side at the stove, and while neither of us speaks right away, it feels like there's an entire conversation swirling between us. So much left unsaid and stirring beneath the surface, screaming to be let out. After my conversation with Nik and Quirina, I can't trust my tongue right now. It's a tool of anger and vengeance. Upsetting those I care about isn't one of my typical personality traits, but lately it seems to be my favorite pastime.

After my mother's confession, I'd love to say that all the anger and frustration has dissolved. I know my mother isn't to blame, but I can't help the hurt I feel wishing she had been honest with me. I understand her motives, but I'm struggling with it all.

I begin to plate up the meal for us while my mother grabs three glasses.

"What would you like to drink?" she asks.

Usually this wouldn't be such a loaded question, but with the way I've been behaving lately, I know what she's really asking.

*Am I going to get drunk and be a jerk again tonight?*

"Water would be great, Mom."

Her bright smile makes me instinctively return one. I know it's a long road back, and we have a lot to sort out, but it's nice to know I still have one person in my corner.

We eat dinner, while Mellani carries out most of the conversation. Telling stories about her day, the pictures she drew, a bunny she saw hopping through the backyard in the snow, and her failed attempt to catch it. I almost forgot what it's like to feel carefree joy like her.

Grief swallows you whole and drags you down a dark pit of despair. It's a sick sort of comfort where you don't care what happens to you. It's easier. Loneliness becomes a desperate need to feel the pain. Eager to feel every sharp stab of it. Like pushing on a bruise, it hurts but you keep fingering the purple wound. Feeling joy is what's painful. Allowing yourself to feel a fleck of happiness feels wrong, and slices deeper than all the bad you're trying to suppress.

Now that I'm working with the queen to get the princess back, it feels like we're one step closer to righting the evil that Lothar inflicted on Tenuma. One step closer to having Bellatrix back in my arms.

One step closer to figuring out our next problem: breaking the curse.

# 10

# BELLATRIX

I can feel myself slowly breaking, coming undone at the seams.

Maybe this fate is payment for all of my sins. For all the men that have suffered by my body.

Sleepless nights spent tossing and turning, wishing I was anybody else. My days spent wasting away in a foreign land, wondering if I've been fooled by the one man who ever made me feel like I was more than an obstacle to the throne. Lothar isn't exactly a trustworthy source, but what does he gain from the lie? I want to believe in Koen, to be able to take what I've seen from him for face value. My own family had no issue sacrificing me, so why wouldn't he?

The only time my thoughts are drowned out and I'm pulled

from my self-pitying is when the dragons' cries ring through the kingdom. A reminder that those creatures are enduring far worse suffering than I am.

The moment I start to drift off to sleep, I hear the unmistakable squeak of the door handle turning. My heart begins to pound in my chest. Though I've been visited by Hidi during the night before, my stomach always lurches at the possibility that it's not her.

"Hidi? Is that you?" I whisper into the dark.

The dark shadow enters the room, and by the size alone, I know it's not her.

"Hello, Princess." Lothar's deep, gritty voice disturbs the quiet of the room.

I sit up at the sound of his voice, scooting as far back against the bed as I can with my knees pulled close to my body. The hammering in my chest intensifies, and my fingers grip the sheets tightly, my nails digging into the fabric. Any words I have get caught in my throat.

"Aren't you happy to see me?" he asks with a smug chuckle, making his way closer.

Another tall dark figure stands by the doorway, and I feel a chill run through my body.

It couldn't be him, could it?

"Koen?" I manage to squeak out.

"I'm sorry to disappoint you, Princess, but he no longer wishes to see you. But he did send his best wishes along with me."

A blow to my glass-like heart.

Lothar sits at the edge of the bed, and with the moonlight shining through the window I can finally see him. Those hateful gray eyes bore into me, and his sinister expression makes my skin itch. When he reaches a hand towards me, I all but shrivel up in an attempt to escape his touch.

The man at the door, who I now can see is one of his guards, lets out a low chuckle, which makes this all the more degrading. I may have had my fair share of men in my bedroom in Tenuma, but never with an audience.

Lothar's fingers trail up my arm, causing my skin to instantly prickle, like it's sizzling under his touch.

I search for any words to deter him, to make this all stop. "You know what will happen to you if you proceed."

My warning doesn't have the effect I hoped for.

"Drink this," he demands, retrieving a small vial of clear liquid from his pocket.

I shake my head, pulling my lips tightly together.

"Princess, I don't think you understand that you don't have a choice in the matter. I wasn't asking. Drink."

"Please."

A scornful laugh erupts from him, and he slaps a hand on his knee. "Please! The cursed princess has manners. That's wonderful! That will serve you well once you're my queen."

"Why do you want me as your queen?"

"So modest," he says. "You're the beautiful soul-snatching princess. You must know what a treasure you are. The power you hold. If not me, someone else would have taken you for themselves. Be lucky that at least I'm a king. A man *worthy* of you."

My lips curl back over my teeth, and I muster up all the saliva I've got and spit it directly into his face, sneering.

Lothar hardly flinches, as if he expected the recoil. He simply wipes the saliva from his face with his sleeve, and nudges the vial at me until I take it. "Drink it now."

When I make no move to ingest it, he pulls a dagger from his jacket and points it at me. I pull the stopper off the top and give the liquid a sniff. Odorless and colorless.

With no knowledge of what this could be, I send up a quick prayer to the Gods and tip the vial back, swallowing the contents. While it's tasteless, I can't ignore the burn as it spills down my throat. Letting the empty container fall to the bed, Lothar grabs my ankle and pulls my leg straight. He repeats this action with my other leg.

"You are beautiful. A beauty that has been wasted with those weak men. You need a powerful man like me."

"No," I attempt to speak, but my words feel slurred. My tongue suddenly feels too heavy and too big for my mouth.

"Shh, relax."

I try to stop my heavy lids from closing, but it's to no avail. The last thing I see is the guard standing in front of me smirking and Lothar's rough hand slithering up my leg before the drowsiness wins the battle.

When I awake, the sun is shining too brightly through the grimy window. My head is pounding, and my eyes feel heavy and dry. I'm not sure how long I've been asleep. I attempt to stretch my limbs, but they feel weak. Whatever liquid was in the vial is still wearing off.

"Good morning, Princess," Hidi greets me.

"Hidi. I didn't hear you come in."

Remembering that Lothar was in my room last night while I was unconscious has me feeling nauseous. I self-consciously run my hands down my body and thank the Gods I'm clothed. "I'd like to use the bathroom, excuse me."

I hop off the bed to make my way to the bathroom, only to realize how sore I am. I carefully make my way across the room and close the door behind me. I'm aching everywhere, so I know I need to examine my body. I strip my clothing off and stand naked before the mirror. My breasts have bruising on them, and are tender to the touch. Moving lower, my inner thighs have similar bruising. Too afraid to do any further investigation, too scared of what I might find, I decide to shower.

After scrubbing my flesh until it's red and raw, I emerge from the bathroom with the steam bellowing out after me.

"Are you okay?" Hidi can see something's wrong, but I'm not sure I can talk about what happened.

I shake my head.

Hidi has been my protector during my time here, but I now realize that not even she can protect me from the terrors of the night. Lothar will surely visit me again and do whatever he wants to me.

She slowly approaches me, taking my hand in hers. As she leads me back to the bed, tears begin falling down my face in shame. Shame for what happened to me, and shame that she can see what's happened without me having to utter a word.

Will everyone be able to look at me and tell?

Hidi gently guides me to the bed. "I am so sorry. Can I do anything? Bring you anything?"

I shake my head, unable to look at her directly.

"Princess, has this ever happened before?"

With my head still hanging, I shake it once more.

"Fucking monster," she curses under her breath. "Princess, we need to get you out of here now. This can't continue."

"I had an idea," I tell her hesitantly.

"About what?" she asks.

"Our way out. What if we escape during the night? Surely there will be less men around, right?"

She shakes her head. "There are more men on patrol at night. Sperantia is more vulnerable to attack at night."

I sigh, feeling defeated.

Her mouth pulls to the side as she contemplates what I've said. "I can handle the man who guards your door. However, there will be more throughout the castle and at the back exit, which is our best chance for escape."

Memories of Quirina helping me leave the castle alone to go into town flood my mind, and I try to recall if she ever told me how she cleared the pathway for me.

"My best friend used to help me sneak out of my castle sometimes," I tell Hidi, trying to remember how exactly Quirina was so damn good at always making sure the coast was clear.

"You had to sneak out of your own home?"

Another sad smile graces my lips. "I wasn't granted much freedom back on my own land. The one thing I enjoyed most was bringing money to children in town. My family..." I pause, thinking of how to describe them. "While they may not be as bad as your king, they're still selfish and greedy. Being a princess didn't come with much authority. While I couldn't change any of the terrible things my family enforced, I could make sure some of the families had money to eat and survive."

Her eyes bulge, and mouth falls open.

"You don't need to look so shocked. I'm not a completely horrible person." I know that my life has brought pain to many others, but it still hurts to be looked at this way.

Hidi shakes her head. "No, it's not that. I've never heard of anybody from a royal family doing such a thing. You're not horrible at all, you're a wonderful person," she says, her voice cracking from emotion.

I smile at her. "I don't know what you've been through, but I fully intend to make your life easier when we get back to Tenuma." She wipes away a few tears that manage to escape and slide down her cheek, despite the way she's obviously trying to prevent them from falling. We sit in silence for a few moments. Two women taken advantage of by the same man, fighting the emotion that we've been told makes us weak all our lives. Endure it, endure it all, they say, but never tell us how you feel.

"I want so badly for my family and Miri to have a better life. They don't deserve what's been done to them, or what they've been through," she confesses.

"It's just your mom and your brother?" I ask, trying to recall if she mentioned her father.

She nods.

"Can I ask about your father?" I ask gently, knowing it could be sensitive territory.

She sighs. "He became very ill when my little brother was just a baby. His sickness accelerated quickly. It was less than a year later that he passed. It's been my mom, brother and me since then."

Her story reminds me that I'm stuck here while my father is at home dying. As tense as things are between us, he's still my father, and to see him again and at least say goodbye is something I won't take for granted if I get out of here alive.

"I'm sorry you and your family have had such a hard life," I say, knowing it can't change anything and likely doesn't mean much. But it's a small token of understanding that I can offer.

"It hasn't been easy, no. But to know that there are still good people, people like you..." She pauses. "Hearing what you've done for the children and families on your own land makes me hopeful."

"Things will be different. You and your family won't suffer. I will be queen, and I plan to rule very differently than my parents did. Than your king does."

My statement kicks up the dust of another looming issue back home. If we do make it out of here alive, the urgency to find a king to rule with will continue. If Koen has in fact betrayed me, essentially taking with him my only prospect for a king, what's going to happen when I return home?

*One problem at a time, Trix.*

Hidi smiles at me, but our moment is interrupted when a loud screech echoes through the room, causing me to cover my ears.

The dragons.

The noise goes on for what seems like the longest minute of my life. When the commotion finally stops, I chance a glance in Hidi's direction. All I see is pain etched into her face.

"I should go. I need to be careful with how much time I'm spending with you. If anybody catches on…"

I nod in understanding. "I'll see you tomorrow then."

"Take care of yourself, Princess. I'll be back as soon as I can." She stands, taking the tray she brought in with her, leaving behind a piece of strawberry swirl cake. I catch a glimpse of the guard standing outside as she opens the door. He glares at me with something resembling disgust on his face, but when his eyes land back on Hidi, I see want and desire.

He might very well become our way out of here.

# 11

# KOEN

I need to get the hell out of here.

It's exactly what I'm about to tell the queen as I stand in the ground floor workroom with her.

We've been discussing her plan for the last few hours, and I don't know how much more of her nonsense I can take. She asked for my help, but instead of listening to me, she continues to offer up ridiculous notions and insults my intelligence. Knowing she had a plan in place was comforting, but now I realize just how out of her depth she is.

"Just tell everyone to help. It'll be easy," she suggests casually. As if I'd be asking my neighbors for firewood.

"Do you realize what you're asking?" I find my patience wearing thin with yet another frustrating conversation with the queen regarding the mission to get her daughter back.

Her cold eyes, that look far too much like Bellatrix's, stare blankly at me.

"I've tried. I cannot recruit a team to help rescue her because you've turned the entire town against your family. Nobody cares whether or not she comes back."

She rolls her eyes at me. "You could go alone."

Yep, it's a suicide mission.

She's asked for my help, but clearly despises me and doesn't want me to be with her daughter.

Gods only knows what she'd do if I revealed that Bellatrix and I were True Mates.

"Listen, Queen—" I start, but she cuts me off.

"Call me Charlotte."

My expression twists into one of disgust. Why the fuck would I want to be on a first name basis with her? "I'd rather not, if it's all the same to you," I tell her, hoping she drops the unnecessary argument.

"It's not fine. I cannot stand the mocking way you use the title. I get it. You loathe me, Koen. Message received."

My eyebrows pinch together, and I begin to see spots. I can feel my animal form begging to be set free. The audacity to be offended by anything, after what she's put me, Bellatrix, and the entire kingdom through.

"You're joking, right?" I ask in disbelief.

A quizzical expression is her only response.

"You force a despicable spell on your daughter. At my mother's hand, I might add. You then use her *gift*, as you like to call it, to turn the men she sleeps with into daemons. Which might be a step above death, but they're still mindless monsters. You use people. You're using me right now to get your daughter back. Why?" My words come out sharp, exactly as I intended. If I'm going to be in her presence for hours at a time for days on end, I'll be damned if I let her try to sit on the moral high ground and act as if she's owed a damn thing from me. I want Bellatrix back more than anyone, and she knows it, but I refuse to allow her to wield it over me like a weapon.

"Looks like you spoke with your mother, then," she responds coolly.

"Cut the shit. I know you only told me to take the blame off yourself, and attempt to destroy my family the way you have your own. But I've got news for you: not all families are quick to betray each other."

"Ah, yes. Well, you're doing that all on your own, aren't you?"

I can feel heat rising in my body along with the anger. My heart begins to race. I've been working on keeping my centaur form under control, but every time the queen opens her mouth, it takes all my willpower not to explode.

When I don't respond, she continues with a chuckle. "I hear things. The way you've been drinking and how you're hardly home anymore. You should be ashamed."

Why is this woman baiting me for a fight?

Why shouldn't I tear her apart right here?

Reminding myself that I'm nothing like her, I take a calming breath and try to let her words slide off my back.

"I thought you wanted my help getting Bellatrix back," I tell her, utterly confused at the way she's speaking to me right now. Every time I think she's starting to change her ways, she proves me wrong.

She is only friendly—and I use the term loosely—when I'm agreeing with everything she says. It's the same way she treats everyone, including her own daughter. Bellatrix is her perfect creation, as long as she's doing exactly what she wants her to. This woman is power-driven, and it must be killing her that it's all slipping away.

"Oh, relax. I just love the way you get fired up. You're going to be perfect for this mission."

"You know what? Fuck this. I don't need to be here." I begin exiting the large room, needing to put as much distance between us as possible.

"Wait," she pleads, her tone completely shifting and softening.

I spin on my heels, ready for a fight. "If you have something to say, you better say it quickly because I'm not listening to your shit anymore. I have a family who needs me."

She holds both of her hands up, surrendering. "Okay, but please call me Charlotte from now on."

I hear something new in her voice. I'm unable to place it, but it resembles something close to vulnerability.

"I'm here for one reason: to get Bellatrix home. Why does this matter to you?" I ask, confused.

Of all the things she should be worried about right now, a title shouldn't be one of them.

*Are there tears in her eyes?*

"I'm not the queen anymore. I ruled with my husband, but he's gone. My daughter is gone. Just, please, don't call me that anymore," she pleads.

This might be the first time she's shown any humanity. For a second, her icy exterior melts away, and I can see a mother. A widow. It's shocking and terrifying to see how quickly she can adapt. How she can shed her skin like a snake to reveal a new one beneath.

Her fragility allows me to see Bellatrix more clearly in her face than ever before. It's hard not to feel her pain through those intense green eyes.

My anger dissipates, and against my better judgment, I decide to stay. "Fine. I'm willing to put down my sword if you are. But if you continue this bullshit, I'm gone."

She nods slowly, and I mirror her movement, both of us coming to an agreement.

"She would want it to be you that saves her. It needs to be

you."

"Thank you, Charlotte," I say, temporarily waving a white flag.

I can offer peace to the queen until we get Bellatrix back alive. Afterwards, I intend to free Bellatrix for good. A price will need to be paid for what's been done to her. But I'll be keeping that to myself.

"I'll stay, but I need a favor," I say, attempting to make the most of this version of Charlotte.

She nods.

It's time to solve another problem while I'm here.

My muscles ache, and my limbs protest, begging for rest. I hunch over the ladder I'm working on, taking a momentary breather. I observe my work, feeling damn proud of the way Nik's bar is beginning to look.

I may not have been there for him when he started working to rebuild it from the ashes, but I'm going to help finish it.

The framework and walls were completed, but it still needed doors, windows, and the entire interior finished up. It's a lot of work, but I was happy to lend a hand. Actually, a dozen helping hands.

"Koen?" I hear Nik call from behind me as he approaches with Quirina by his side.

With a groan, I straighten out and climb down the ladder. Hesitantly I walk over to where Nik stands back, soaking in the progress we've made today. Quirina stands in silence by his side, a guarded look on her face. A look I can't blame her for.

"Hey, man," I say timidly.

"You did all this?" he asks in shock, pointing to the nearly finished bar.

I nod, pride and affection swelling in my chest. "Yeah. I, uh, thought you'd be here when we arrived. I hope this is okay."

"Yeah, this is…How?" he asks, running a hand through his thick hair in disbelief.

We have accomplished more than I expected to. It's amazing what you can get done when you've got the royal family's resources at your fingertips.

"Called in a favor for a friend that deserved it," I answer, hoping my attempt to make up for my shitty behavior will be enough to mend our friendship.

Nik bites his cheek, narrowing his eyes, no doubt attempting to decipher the sudden shift in my personality.

I rub the back of my neck, my head hanging slightly. "Look, I owe you—both of you—an apology. Hell, I owe everybody an apology. I've said some fucked up things I wish I could take back." I pause, making sure my words come across the way I want them to. "I should have been there for you, Nik, and I'm sorry for all of it."

Nik turns to face Quirina at his side. She throws her hands up in front of her, as if to say *I'm staying out of this*. When his gaze lands back on me, a small tug at the corners of his mouth indicates there might be hope for me after all.

He nods his head, giving me a friendly smile. It's enough to tell me that we can get past this.

"Do you want to go inside and look around?" I offer with a cheerful grin.

"Wow, my bar has a door again. Yeah, let's check it out," he says approaching the building.

Quirina doesn't move. Usually, she's easygoing and friendly, but she's currently shooting daggers in my direction. Regret sits heavy in my chest, knowing I could have been there for her. I had the opportunity to show up for her, and instead of being her friend, I became the salt in her wounds.

My mind is shouting at me to apologize, but it seems so insignificant for the pain I've caused her. I'm not sure I'd accept it if I were her.

I muster up a pathetic smile and open my mouth to speak, but she beats me to it.

"You look like shit," she says bluntly.

The comment takes me by surprise, and a laugh bursts out of my chest. "Yeah, I guess I had that coming. Turns out I haven't been handling losing the princess all that well," I confess, though it isn't news to her. Or anyone.

Nodding her head, she gives me a knowing look. "Join the club."

I take a deep breath, unable to shake the guilt. "I'm so sorry, Rina. I'm not proud of the man I've been, but I'm going to make things right. I'm going to get her back."

She sighs. "Koen, it's been what? A month? I hate the thought as much as anybody else, but it might be too late."

Thinking about the princess not being alive is an option I've refused to let my mind entertain. The morsel of sanity I have left can't handle those thoughts. I can't let them seep in now.

My heart squeezes, realizing that even though I've been dead set on getting Bellatrix back, Quirina has been mourning her. She lost her family and her best friend. Nik has been there for her, and instead of being supportive I lashed out at both of them. I get why she'd leaned on him. I misjudged their relationship. All she needed was a safe place, someone to comfort her in her time of need.

Rina gives me a sad smile when I don't respond and moves

past me to join Nik at the entrance of his bar. She stops and turns around.

"I'm glad you and Nik patched things up, for your sake." She and Nik exchange a knowing look and a chuckle, then disappear through the doorway.

*For my sake? What the hell does that mean?*

# 12

# BELLATRIX

"What do you mean?" I ask Hidi quietly.

It's the middle of the night and she shouldn't be here. Not only that, but with Lothar visiting in the late hours of the night, it's only a matter of time before we're caught together. The two have managed not to cross paths thus far. Thank Gods for Hidi's gift.

"Exactly what I said. I thought of a way to use him to get us out of here," she repeats confidently.

Hidi came into my room a few minutes ago, excited with an idea to get me—us—out of here for good. Turns out I wasn't misreading the look that the door guard gave Hidi a few days ago. Men are never as subtle about their desires as women are. He and Hidi have been secretly meeting for quite a while, which, according to her, we can use to our advantage.

I sigh, tracing my lips with a forefinger, and contemplate the cost. "Are you sure you want to do this?"

Hidi's firm voice pulls me back to the present. "Yes. Why wouldn't I?"

"We might not make it. This could get you and your family killed."

"This isn't living, Princess. My family and I have discussed the risk, and we're prepared to take that chance."

"Why now?" I ask her. Having the gift of invisibility, she could have left at any time. I can't help wondering why she's taking the risk now that I'm here.

Her face scrunches up, and I can see her mulling around the question. "I don't think I truly understood how bad it was getting until you got here."

"How can you say that with everything you've endured?"

Her eyes fall downward, avoiding my gaze. "It's harder to watch others suffer. Taking women from other kingdoms and doing what he's doing…I've never seen anything like it."

Me. The things he's doing to me.

It's a conversation I've been avoiding, but with new guards missing each day and the bruising she's observed on my body, she knows. Hidi knew the first day she saw me wincing in pain.

"If we make it out of here, I promise to protect all of you," I vow to her.

A heavy sigh slips through her lips as tears begin to fill her eyes.

I feel a wave of emotion wash over me, too. The woman before me has been a prisoner in her own life. I can potentially save her, her family and her beloved dragon. As angry as I want to be for being kidnapped, right now all I can feel is determination. Lothar captured me to gain more power, but what he didn't consider is that by bringing me here, he may have kicked off his own downfall.

"I should go for now, but I'll see you in the morning." Hidi leaves as quietly as she came, and for the first time, it feels like we're one step closer to getting the hell out of here.

The next morning Hidi brings me breakfast and coffee and water like she usually does. I don't tell her that Lothar showed up shortly after she left. Using my anger as fuel, I put all my energy into forging a plan with Hidi. After washing away the assault in the bathroom and assessing the fresh bruising, I join Hidi on the bed.

Without a word she hands me two painkillers. She doesn't ask what happened, or try to make me talk about it. With a large gulp of water, I swallow both pills. She holds up a tube of pain-relieving cream. Patting my leg, she asks for permission to slide the fabric of my dress up. After a few moments of covering some of the bruising with gentle massaging, she caps the tube and pockets it. Whatever was in the cream immediately soothes the wounds.

She hands me a ceramic plate with soft bread covered in a thin layer of butter and jam. I take a greedy bite, letting the flavor of the raspberry preserve momentarily become my only focus.

A bang on the door startles us seconds before it swings open, and I drop the ceramic plate I was holding on the tiles next to the bed. We both watch as the plate smashes into pieces.

*Shit.*

Turning our gazes towards the door, we see a man. Not the usual doorman, but a new guard with a stern look on his face. Dressed in the green Sperantia uniform, sword in hand, he addresses Hidi.

"You have been assigned to a different room. I've been told to escort you out immediately," he says.

*No. No, no, no.*

Slowly and calmly, Hidi rises from the bed and bends down to pick up the broken plate. "Sorry? Is there a reason why? I've been looking after the princess since she arrived."

His stern face never falters. "Not anymore."

Fighting my instincts to reach out and grab her, to pull her back and stand in front of her like a protective shield, I stay seated and keep my mouth shut. I have to bite my lip to keep it from trembling. As part of a royal family, I know how badly things can end if you say the wrong thing to any member of the kingdom.

Were we speaking too loudly and our plans overheard? Panic and anxiety surge through my body, anticipating what might happen next.

Hidi places the broken pieces of the plate onto the metal tray and shakily lifts it. She shoots me a look before turning around and exiting with the man.

What's going to happen to her?

My mind is wild with scenarios, and I fear that both myself and Hidi are now in grave danger. I've been under the impression that I'm more valuable living here than not, but there's no telling what Lothar might do to Hidi if he suspects she's turned on him.

I swallow hard, sorting through my thoughts when I realize the regular door guard is now standing at the open door, staring directly at me. The same man that Hidi has been seeing in secret. The same man that she was planning to use as a pawn in our escape plan.

My skin turns cold. I'm unsure how long he's been watching me, or why he continues to stare. A smug smile begin forming on his lips.

"Back to the drawing board then, huh, Princess?"

"W-what?" My voice cracks and betrays my calm exterior.

"Did you really think you could use her to escape? I don't know if you've been playing mind games or what, but I won't let you get her killed," he spews.

*Poor fool has no idea Hidi was willing to throw him to the wolves for her freedom.*

I don't respond. Anything I say could implicate one or both of us.

The man takes it upon himself to continue the one-sided conversation. "We may have to hide what we have together, but it's real. Not that you'd have a clue what that's like." His gaze is one of pure disgust. "You're not taking her from me."

Leave it up to a man to create his own scenario to deny the fact that someone's duped him. It'll be easier to fool him than it will be to convince him that he's been fooled.

The man shakes his head, and on his way out I hear him murmur, "I hope you know you're never leaving this place."

The door slams shut behind him, and though his words initially shook me, I can't help but smile at the closed door.

He might have gotten her assigned to another room, and he might know there's some sort of plan brewing, but he has no idea what's really going on.

And he doesn't know that before Hidi left, I slid a piece of the broken plate underneath the bed with my foot.

That is the last time a man tries to come between me and my freedom.

# 13

## KOEN

The open air feels like freedom.

My body is slick with sweat, and my muscles are straining and sore as I hack away at the wood on the stump in front of me. My gift of shifting into a centaur keeps my body temperature at a constant high, so even though I'm shirtless and there's fresh snow on the ground, my body still glistens with sweat.

Firewood isn't needed as much now that I fixed our windows up with the supplies the princess had sent over months ago, but making sure our cottage has a roaring fire is one of the many ways I like providing for my family. Ensuring they're safe and comfortable.

Though I've retired the title of raging asshole, I'm still plagued with shame for the way I behaved, how I almost turned into a person who resembles a man I've hated most of my life. I refuse to be my father. The asshole who left our family in ruins not once, but twice.

I raise my arms above my head, muscles taut, and let them

crash down in the center of the wood, splitting it in two. I may or may not be picturing his face on that piece of wood.

With a plan in the works, and me finally coming to my senses, I can feel life falling back into place. For so long I've been stuck in an angry haze, unable to see right from wrong. When we bring the princess home, she deserves a man worthy of her kind, selfless soul, and I fully intend to be that man for her.

Each swing and crack of the wood is another promise I make to myself to be better, not only for myself, but for the ones I love.

Another raise of my arms, and I swing back down on the last piece of wood, finishing for the day. I rest on the stump, wiping my brow with my forearm, admiring the large stack of wood I've completed. I've always been a man that finds happiness in the simplicity of providing for his family, so today's a good day. Optimism creeps in, taking an ax to the hard shell of misery I've let mold around me like a second skin, reminding me that there could be more days like this.

"Koen!" my baby sister shouts in the distance.

I call her that, but really she's almost seven. But to me she'll always be my baby sister. Taking care of her is one of my greatest pleasures in life. She's why I work as hard as I do; she's the reason I never considered meeting a woman and starting my own family. I never wanted anything to come between her and me.

The way she looks at me and the way she depends on me is an honor and a responsibility I don't take lightly. I've let her down the last few months, and I won't be making that mistake again.

With arms full of wood logs, I make my way back toward my cottage, where I find Mel standing out front waiting for me with eager, hopeful eyes. No matter what's going on in my mind, her sweet face never fails to calm the storm brewing inside me.

Once I reach her, I drop the wood next to our doorway and scoop her up in my arms. Although she's getting too big too fast, she still looks tiny in my embrace.

I kiss the top of her head, inhaling the inviting lavender scent her brown curls are emitting.

"You're all sweaty and stinky!" she shrieks, wriggling out of my arms.

"Sorry, Mel. Guess I'm due for a shower." I laugh and place her back on her feet. I'm smiling down at her, but she looks up at me with a strange expression.

I chuckle at her. "What's that face for?" I ask.

Her sweet smile fades slightly as she shrugs. "Umm, I don't know. Nothing."

Like me, she's never been a great liar.

Eyebrows cinching, I try again. "Come on, you can tell me."

Another shrug, and her eyes dart to the ground. "You haven't hugged me like that in a while."

The way her little voice quivers, as if she was scared to tell me, crushes me. I've been so oblivious, so out of touch and worried about what I've lost, that I couldn't see what I still had. I couldn't see the suffering right in front of my face. The suffering that I was causing.

Kneeling down so we're face to face, I use my fingers to lightly tilt her chin upwards. "Sweet girl," I say, calling her by the nickname I've used since she was an infant, "I love hugging you and being around you and drawing with you. Anything that involves you is my favorite."

Her eyes glisten, but she doesn't respond.

I try again, needing her to know how much she means to me. Internally I scold myself for allowing her to believe something so unthinkable. "Sometimes adults make really bad decisions. We act without thinking and accidentally hurt those around us. So, if you've been hurting because of anything I've done, I'm so sorry."

I see her bottom lip quiver. "But it's my fault," she says softly, her face twisted into guilt and shame.

My eyebrows pull together. "What are you talking about Mel? What's your fault?"

"The princess. It's my fault she's gone and you're so angry."

Her words burn like poison as I attempt to digest them. They leave me feeling blistered and raw. Shaking my head vigorously, I take both of her little hands in mine. "Hey, look at me," I say firmly. "None of that is your fault, why would you ever think that?"

My mind can't make sense of why this six-year-old feels like she's to blame for the evil deeds of adults.

"Because it was my dad that took her. It's my fault he left us, and my fault he took the princess."

Her dad.

Our dad.

"Mel, you're a child, and a really incredible one at that, so please know that whatever an adult does is *their* decision, and has nothing to do with you. None of this is your fault in any way. He is a bad man, and he didn't leave because of you, he left because of *him*," I tell her, hoping with every fiber of my being that she believes the truth, and not the lies swirling around in her own head.

The dam of tears has bubbled over, and she sniffles, wiping them away. I lift my hand and gently dry a few tears with the side of my index finger.

"He took Princess Bellatrix because he's a bad man. Not because he's your father."

"Okay," she responds, unconvinced.

"I mean it. None of this is your fault, and I'm so sorry you've been thinking that it is. Why didn't you say anything before?" I ask her, afraid I already know the answer.

"You've been so sad and angry. I thought you were mad at me."

This whole time I thought she was handling everything so

well, albeit a little more quietly than usual, when really she has been harboring as much—if not more—guilt than I am. If I had still been drinking, this would have been a very sobering moment. Hell, it still is.

I shake my head at her. "No, sweet girl. I'm never mad at you. I'm mad at him, and sad the princess is gone. But it's okay, because we are going to find her, and bring her home."

She nods and gives me a sad smile. Not wanting to make her continue to talk about this, I pull her in for another hug, giving her a squeeze. "I love you, Mel."

"I love you too," she says quietly into my chest.

When Tenuma was attacked, our town saw almost complete destruction, but unfortunately most of the damage *can't* be seen. The plight of the survivors, all attempting to find our way back, rebuilding the lives that have been shaken up and completely rearranged by an unhinged man who finds joy in others' misery. A monster who will never be satisfied with any amount of power he obtains.

"Come on, sweet girl, let's get inside. I'll make you a delicious meal, and we can color together," I say, hoping to find a smile buried beneath the sadness.

I do.

"When do you leave?" my mother asks as she slices up some bread that smells intoxicating after the strenuous activity I just finished.

"Next week."

"What exactly is this plan?" my mother asks hesitantly.

I can tell she both does and doesn't want to know. "I will be leading the mission with the Tenuman army as well as a few men I've managed to persuade to follow. They hope it'll leave them in the kingdom's good graces. We will ride as far into Sperantia as we can. There's a dense forest just before the castle that we can take cover in. From there we will break up into three groups, who will each approach a different attack point of the castle. The queen has ensured that there will only be one guard at each exit, because the rest should be attending war meetings at the time. We wait for the men to clear the front entrance and strike them first, while the other teams defend from the sides and back of the castle grounds."

"Do you trust what she's telling you?" my mother asks.

"About which part?"

"How would she know how many guards there's going to be?"

*Good point.*

"I'm not sure. I've been so anxious to get all of this together so we can go that I didn't even think to ask."

Taking an uncomfortable deep breath, my mom surges forward. "Then what?"

"My group will follow me inside the front, while the team in the rear will invade the back entrance. Together we should be able to take down the men on the front line and make it to the princess. The entire mission will have to be quick, considering that once the attack begins, backup will immediately be sent for. We also don't know how long those meetings will last."

The creases of worry around my mother's eyes deepened the more I speak. There's no certainty in this recovery mission, but we can't give any more time to Lothar. We don't know what the princess is enduring there, or if she's still alive. Reason tells me that she's more beneficial to him alive, otherwise why bother taking her at all? But until she's back in my arms, I can't assume anything.

I'm plating sliced meat and a small portion of steaming carrots and broccoli for Mellani when I hear my mother grunt to herself.

I place my hands flat on the countertop, giving her my full attention. "You can say it."

"Say what?"

"The warning you're about to give me, or order me not to go." My mother has always been protective over her kids, and I love her for it. Usually, I'd say she's being overprotective. But we both know death is a possibility on this mission.

My mother gives me a sad smile. "No. I know this is something you need to do. I'm so proud of you. Proud of the man you've become. But I can't lie and say I'm not worried."

"I know you are, Ma."

I fill my mother's plate next and place both hers and Mel's on the table before returning to my mother's side. I reach for the plate of warm bread across the table when she grabs my hand.

"Promise me you'll be safe. Use your head," she begs softly, trying to avoid upsetting Mellani who's sitting on the sofa a few feet away.

Mel seems to have recovered from our talk a little while ago, and now busies herself with the drawing she's working on.

"I promise. I will be smart. Nothing's going to keep me from coming back to you both."

"You and Mel are my greatest gifts. Sometimes it's impossible to think that you two are the product of that man. I feel guilty that I didn't give you both a better father. A better role model."

Her confession startles me. We don't often talk about him, or the things he's done to our family. Now that his evil has leaked out, blanketing the town like poisonous gas, I suppose it's an impossible topic to avoid.

"Mom," I say gently, "you've been the best role model. The

only one I've ever needed. His decisions have always been self-serving and reckless. You can't hold yourself responsible for that sort of behavior. The three of us have each other, and we're all we need." My attempt to comfort her has a dual effect, comforting me as well.

"And Bellatrix," she adds.

I grin, glad to know that my mother seems to be accepting that Bellatrix will be in our lives. "I know it's not your favorite subject to discuss, but I've always wondered what exactly happened between you and him. Why did he leave?"

She releases a heavy sigh. "He was never happy here with me. I was simply a placeholder in his life. Someone to pass the time with, while he continued the search for what he really wanted. Power."

"You two were never happy together, then?"

"There were happy times. But I think I spent more time trying to convince myself we were happy. Even before he left, he always had these crazy notions that he could work his way up in the kingdom and somehow take the throne. From the moment we met, it's all he ever talked about. At first, I didn't understand he was being literal, I thought he was simply a hard worker. But he had built up a real grudge at the fact that he never possessed any gifts."

"So he always planned to take over Tenuma?"

My mother looks lost in memory for a moment, but pulls herself back to the present. "Yes, sort of. He was drawn to my gifts, and wanted to use them to work his way into the castle. Something I never agreed to. But once my powers began to fizzle out after my deal with the queen, he lost all interest in me."

"That's when he stopped coming home as often."

"I'm sorry, honey. I know you've got some good memories of him, and even though he left us, I never wanted to taint those for you. Those were yours."

I chuckle. "I think it's safe to say that any good memories I had of him were wiped clean the moment he deserted us."

Tearing a corner of bread with my teeth, I swallow it down with all the fears that want to spill out. My mother's gaze lingers on mine, assessing the emotion left on my face.

"Are you nervous to see him again?" she asks tenderly.

I shrug as if not at all phased by the notion of coming face to face with the man that tore our family apart, waged war on our land after leaving, and kidnapped the woman that turned out to be my True Mate.

"It doesn't matter how I feel. What matters is saving Bellatrix," I say firmly. "But I suppose I can't hide that, yes, I'm dreading it."

A reassuring head nod is her only reply. She's giving me space to be vulnerable, and I suppose since I'm demanding transparency from everyone, I should reciprocate.

"I feel so much hate for him, but it doesn't change that he's my father. How the interaction will go once I see him again is something I can't foretell."

It's the best and most honest answer I can give right now.

The three of us sit down at the table for quite possibly one of our last meals together. I memorize every detail of their faces, focusing on what I'll be returning home to, rather than what I could lose.

Am I a fool to trust the queen in order to get Bellatrix back?

Attempting to create casual conversation over dinner, I ask Mellani about the drawing she was working on before she sat down to eat. Excitedly, she scurries over to grab it off of the couch, and runs it back over, placing it in front of me.

The drawing shows Bellatrix, with her rose tattoo, outside of a castle, not unlike the one in Tenuma, riding a dragon. She looks simultaneously confident and terrified on the back of a giant white dragon.

When I ask Mel about the drawing she shrugs and continues to eat, as if nothing is amiss. I can't help but wonder why she drew this.

*Where do these images come from, sweet girl?*

# 14

# BELLATRIX

*When* hen will he come for me?

My skin is hot, and my eyes refuse to close when I should be sleeping. My mind resists the sleep I so desperately need, fearing when Lothar will return. Fearing what will happen to Hidi. It's safe to say that the day's terrifying events have left me feeling anxious. Hidi became my daytime protector, a barrier between the men and me. But now that she's gone, what will that mean?

Outside the castle walls, the wind howls, blowing dust and pebbles into the glass. The moonlight shines through the window too brightly. A light that will force me to see Lothar should he come into my room tonight. I should be sleeping, but fear keeps me conscious, incessantly scanning the room. My eyes land on a strip of moonlight that hits the bedside table, and what sits atop of it.

*My bracelet.*

The gift from Fira, Koen's mother, sits drearily on the table, mocking me. After Lothar enlightened me about Koen, I tore it off my wrist and haven't touched it since. Learning that Koen's advances might be nothing but carefully calculated attempts to further his father's bid for power has messed with my head, the bracelet acting like a beacon, a tether in time connecting me to him. I needed to be free of it. Free of him and the memories. If only I could separate myself from those.

As hurt and confused as I've been, I can't bring myself to drop the bracelet into the sink drain and watch it disappear the way my anger wants me to. So here it sits, taunting me and questioning my beliefs.

While I haven't felt it tingle since I was in Tenuma, I needed the separation. Until I know what to believe. The truth lies somewhere between what I know and what I've been told, suspended between the two kingdoms. Do I believe Lothar, a man who isn't concerned with protecting others' feelings? Or do I believe the man that seems too good to be true?

Some nights I wonder if everything between me and Koen was a lie. A fabricated attraction that I was desperate to feel when I've kept every other man at arm's length. Other nights I can almost feel him in my soul. The warmth inside like his comforting embrace, cocooning me in his protective arms, telling me that he's going to find me. It begs me to hold on, to not let doubt corrode our connection.

I glare at the bracelet as if it will send my frustrations and anger to Koen, wherever he may be. Curled up in bed on my side, my hands lay in tight fists in front of me, and I have to remind myself to unclench them. Letting my thoughts consume me has always been a struggle. Being held captive in a room alone has exacerbated the issue, allowing me to over-indulge in the bad habit.

At the end of my exhale, I hear a scuffle of feet on the tile floors.

Please, not tonight.

I clench my legs together at the gruesome thought, and my mind screams "NO!"

Keeping perfectly still, I force myself to focus on the location of the noise.

They're inside the room.

Did the door open? The chaos of my thoughts must have drowned it out. I internally chastise myself for getting distracted. Remembering I have the broken piece of porcelain under the bed, I wonder if I can get to it in time. If Lothar has come back to drug me again, he'd better come prepared. I've endured enough, and I'm armed and ready for a fight.

"Princess. Are you awake?" a voice asks from the dark corners of the room.

*Hidi.*

I mutter a curse and thank the Gods it's her. I eagerly turn and sit up to see my friend, her form becoming clearer as she moves closer. I glance behind her, making sure we're alone.

"Hidi! Are you okay? Are you safe?"

She sits on the bed, and I quickly pull her into my arms. "I'm okay, Princess."

I'm unable to contain the relief that washes over me from seeing her in front of me. Hot tears sting my eyes and begin falling down my cheeks, the guilt overwhelming all else. If she wasn't trying to help me escape, she never would have been in my room plotting and arousing suspicion.

I pull back, but my hands grip her shoulders. "What happened? Where did they take you?"

Although calm, her words have an urgency to them. "I have been assigned to a different duty. The guard I told you about, the one I've been sleeping with, he knows what we're up to. He overheard us."

Hidi lays a tender hand on my knee. "It's okay. He didn't hear much. He only thinks I was trying to help *you* escape. Luckily, I was able to convince him that I felt bad for you but didn't realize what I was doing." She pauses, chuckling. "He told me I had a good heart, and that he got me assigned somewhere else so you could no longer brainwash me."

"So you're not going to be punished?" I ask anxiously.

She shakes her head. "No, he's grown too attached and is only trying to protect me. He won't tell anyone what he heard."

The guard told me he was suspicious, but I have to say I'm a little shocked that any of the men cared to pay attention to what we have been doing. In my experience, men only care what women are doing when they're either unclothed or disobeying them.

I lean back against the bed relieved that she's here, unharmed, and that for now we're both safe.

Hidi releases a deep breath. "Now that he's aware that you might try to escape, it's in our best interests to get out of here as soon as we can."

My palms start sweating, and I attempt to swallow. Talking about an escape and actually going through with it are two very different things. I can't help the doubt that begins to creep in, the fear that this could get us both killed.

I manage a tight nod. "I'm so sorry I got you mixed up in this."

"Princess, you didn't get me mixed up in anything. We're in this together. I trust you. Do you trust me?"

A smile stretches across my face as I realize that I do. I grab both of her hands in mine. "I trust you."

"I can't stay too long, I need to get back to his room before he wakes and realizes I've gone. But I wanted to go over a few things," she says.

"Once we make it outside the castle, we will be using the dragons as transportation. They're our only way out. They won't harm you, but you'll need to know some commands in order to communicate with and ride them safely."

She takes her time teaching me both hand and voice commands that will allow me to ascend and descend from the sky on dragonback. I try to commit them all to memory. One mistake could be the difference between life and death.

I demonstrate a few of the hand commands.

She smiles approvingly. "That's great. You're going to be fine. To get you out of this room, I will distract your door guard, luring him back to his room for a private moment. He won't fight me on this, since he's always trying to sneak away during the day. I will return once I've taken care of him."

I try not to think too deeply into her meaning of *take care of him*. "Then what?"

"The rest of the men will be in their scheduled war meeting at that time, so we will have a few moments to slip through the halls undetected. This weekly meeting lasts typically about an hour. The king will also be in this meeting, so we shouldn't have to worry about him, either."

"So we just sneak out the back door of the castle?" I ask skeptically.

Hidi nods. "Yes. There will be a few guards on the perimeter, but we will be flying out through the courtyard. My mother and brother will meet us there with the dragons. We should be in the clear, but we will have to move quickly."

She sounds so sure. Not a hint of doubt in her voice.

Could it really be this simple?

My body hums with excitement as we discuss our escape, freedom becoming more and more visible in my mind. Hope awakens like a sleeping limb, the static both painful and refreshing.

With an ally, a plan, and a weapon under my bed, I'm feeling surprisingly optimistic about how this is going to turn out. Maybe it's foolish, and maybe we wind up dead before we step foot outside of this castle, but I'd rather go down fighting. The days of letting life happen to me are gone.

Giving up would be too easy, and a few weeks ago if asked I would have admittedly wanted to.

But I'm not the girl I was a few weeks ago. Sitting here with Hidi, I know that I owe my life to her. Whether we make it out of here with our lives or not, she gave me another chance at mine. An opportunity to set things right. She gave me more time, and it's a gift I don't plan to fritter away.

After going over commands a few more times, I see Hidi wringing her hands and bouncing one knee up and down. She's anxious to sneak back to her room.

I set one hand gently on her bouncing leg to calm her. "I've got it. I'll keep practicing. Go back before he wakes up."

She pulls her lips inward, hesitating. She wants to say more, but part of her is holding back.

I cock my head at her, my eyebrows pulling down. "What is it?"

Her chest rises and falls dramatically as she takes a deep breath. "This needs to happen in the next few days."

The words land more like a command than a personal opinion.

*It's soon, but I'm ready.*

Letting my trust for Hidi guide me, I nod in agreement. In the next couple of days we begin the fight of our lives. For our lives. We sit in silence a moment more. Knowing we just sealed whatever fate life has in store for us, we hold onto each other like the lifeline that we are to each other. We are in this together.

"It's time we get our freedom back," I declare, knowing she's thought this through for longer than I've been here. If there's anyone determined enough to get us free from this hell, it's Hidi.

Eventually, the ones you try to suppress and make fall in line will rise up and do exactly what you feared they might do to begin with.

They fight back.

# 15

# KOEN

It's time to fight back.

If the decision and resources were within my control, we would have left weeks ago.

Unfortunately, the queen is insufferably stubborn, and for now she's still calling the shots.

Why she has delayed this search so long is anybody's guess. Perhaps the grief of losing her husband was too much to bear. Or maybe she's the same callous woman who forced her daughter to take suitors in order to become queen. Maybe she's altogether unaware of the ways she neglects Bellatrix.

The group of men spearheading this operation crowd together in the front sitting room of the castle, as we go over last-minute details. I had hoped Nik might come to show his support, but I'm not surprised he's not here. His decision to stay back is justified, and truthfully part of me is relieved that I won't have one more person I care about in harm's way.

Now that we're closing in on getting Bellatrix back, the nerves are starting to ignite. We don't know what she's been through, or if she's still alive.

The room immediately falls silent as the queen enters, sauntering over to the table in the center. Several pieces of paper litter the table, each containing different aspects of our attack. She picks one of the papers up, examining it as if she hasn't been a part of every detail of this plan.

She clears her throat. "Thank you all for being here. I want to make sure that everyone is on the same page. Koen Archer"—she points to me—"will be leading the rescue mission. All orders will go through him."

The queen's proud gaze holds steady as she lifts her head high. "I cannot express enough gratitude for those of you willing to go forth and risk death for my little girl."

I almost choke at the term of endearment the queen settles on. Even now she pretends to be the loving mother she's proven not to be.

"While this won't be an easy task, it's integral for the survival of Tenuma and its people. We will continue to rebuild, and with Princess Bellatrix home and ready to take over the throne, we will thrive once more," she assures them.

She gives the room a nod. "Thank you. I pray to the Gods of Tenuma that you all make it home safely."

With a flick of her wrist, she dismisses the room, and the group of men begin to filter out front to get the horses ready. I begin to follow but the queen stops me.

With her hand reaching outward she calls out for me. "Koen, a moment?"

My lips form a thin line, and I reluctantly step to the side, allowing the remainder of men to filter out before turning back towards the queen.

She stands before me in a dress that wouldn't shock me if

it had come from Bellatrix's closet. The figure-hugging material is a red velvet corset style with a deep neckline lower than she's typically seen in. The long train splays out behind her. Her long black hair hangs at her shoulders, and her gaze is intense. As much as I despise this woman, I can't deny the way she resembles Bellatrix. It's strange to hate a person who looks so similar to one you care so deeply for.

"I should really be out front helping the others get organized," I say, shooting a thumb over my shoulder.

"This will just take a moment."

I nod, allowing her to continue.

"I need you to do me a favor."

Confining my laugh to a snort, I swallow the irritation before responding. "Funny, I thought I was already doing you a favor."

She gives me a deadly smile. "Is this not for your own desires as well? Do you not also benefit from her return?"

I anxiously scratch the top of my scalp and release a huff. "What is it that you need, Charlotte?"

Her smile brightens, and her voice shifts from devious to cheery. "See! I knew we could be friends, Koen!"

I stare at her blankly, unresponsive to the fake niceties she's spewing my way.

She takes a few steps towards me, and I take one back.

She gives me a peculiar look and tries to hide a smirk. "After you get to Sperantia, once Bellatrix is safe, I need you to ensure Lothar dies."

My eyes narrow at her. "And I suppose you want me to be the one to do it?"

"I thought you'd be honored to be the one that gets to do it."

"Honored?" I can't contain my frustration and shock at her callous ideology any longer. "What is honorable about killing?"

Oblivious to the point I'm trying to make, she continues, "One would think all the hatred you have for him would be reason enough to want him dead."

I rake my hands through my hair and blow out another breath. "I'm going to rescue the princess. If she's still alive, that's my only mission. You got that?"

A bold statement like that might have gotten me killed at one time, but I know she won't do anything to me until Bellatrix is home safely. Afterwards, she can try it, but I'll be coming for her too.

There's no glory in death, but taking the queen's life will not hinder a single night's rest for me. I won't kill for honor, but I damn will kill to protect.

"She's alive," she says flippantly.

"How would you know that?"

Her eyes dart anxiously around the room as if she didn't mean to say that aloud.

"A feeling. A mother knows," she answers too quickly.

*Bullshit.*

A low growl forms at the base of my throat, and my hands form fists at my sides. I fight the urge to break into my animal form. It would be too satisfying to allow my centaur to erupt out of me and crush her, but she's hiding more. I need to know the information she's withholding. I've held my composure for months, I can hold it together a few more minutes.

Seeing my struggle, she rolls her eyes. "Keep it in your pants, boy."

"Fuck you. How do you know she's still alive? Tell me."

As if I'm a child she's exhausted with, she sighs heavily. "I have someone on the inside."

My fingers flex. "Elaborate."

"What does it matter?"

My eyes bulge, and I throw my hands up in the air. "It all matters. Your daughter's life is at stake!"

Charlotte's nonchalant demeanor is almost as rage-inducing as the information. For a moment, the anger ebbs and a thought flashes through my mind.

"How did you get an informant in there? Surely, they'd be killed," I speculate. "Are you—are you in contact with Lothar?"

Her lips form a thin line, and in the silence, I find my answer.

"I knew you were in on this shit with him," I seethe, hoping the sharpness of my words might cut her. Wound her, the way she wounds everyone around her, especially her daughter.

Admitting to working with the very man who took Bellatrix is a new low, even for her.

Throwing her hands up in defeat, she finally stops playing coy. "None of that matters now. Remember that today is about bringing Bellatrix home." She pauses, realizing her words are not easing the tension. "Lothar never planned to hurt her. He just wanted to build his undead army."

I'm horrified. "And you what? Handed her over to him? To allow your daughter to be…" I can't even say it. "How could you do that?"

She sighs. "I fell in love with him. I trusted him. Once my husband passed, the plan was to be together."

The bomb explodes in my lungs and sucks all the air out with it. I thought I knew anger before this moment, but that was child's play compared to what I feel now.

"How could you do that?"

"Lothar was going to build up the army, and together we would take over as king and queen of both kingdoms. We planned to merge the lands, creating a singular empire. Uniting the people. Once Bellatrix was ready, she would be able to take over Tenuma, but things changed," She pauses, and wipes at a tear that flows down her face. "Lothar never wanted me, only Bellatrix. I fell for him, and he betrayed me. I've been trying to get her back, but he's been refusing. I thought I could convince him otherwise, but I was wrong."

Suddenly it makes perfect sense why she's trying to convince me to kill him for honor. It's for *her*, because Lothar broke *her* heart.

Words are stuck in my throat, constricted by the fury that's demanding sovereignty of my body.

My head spins, and my vision temporarily blurs.

*She sent her daughter off to be used like a war machine.*

The explosion happens before I know it's happening.

Four long, muscular legs send me towering over Charlotte. My hands are in fists at my side, and every muscle aches with tension. I can't fight the thoughts telling me how easy it would be to snap her neck. I could lift my front two legs and trample her to death.

I grip her throat, restraining myself from breaking it with the little effort it would take. "You led your daughter like a pig to slaughter. Lothar doesn't love you, he used you for your daughter. And you *let* him. Because of you, he's been letting men take advantage of her this entire time. She's your daughter, and what you've allowed to happen to her can never be undone. I'm going to get her back, and once she's safe with me, I will deal with you."

I release my grip, and her hand immediately reaches up to soothe her throat, breathing heavily.

"Get out," I demand, needing to get my emotions under control.

I've spent the last few weeks agonizing over what might be happening to Bellatrix, and now that I know exactly what they're doing to her, I feel sick.

# 16

# BELLATRIX

"What are they doing to you?" I whisper to myself, as the agonizing cries ring through the kingdom.

Those dragons can't be free soon enough.

It's been three days since Hidi and I decided it was time to go. Three days of secret planning with her after the new courtier—her replacement—retired for the evening, and three nights of hell.

Night after night, Lothar came into my room with the clear elixir that left me unconscious. No matter how much I resisted, in the end I was forced to take it. He always showed up with two guards in tow. Three against one. I wanted to fight him off, but I need to choose my moment carefully. I wouldn't stand a chance against Lothar and his two giant guards. So each night I drank the liquid, and Lothar and his men did what they wanted to me.

New men arrived each night, the previous men never to be seen again.

Each morning I scrub my flesh raw, hoping it would make me feel in possession of my body again, but to no avail. I will never be whole here. Like the dragons, as long as I'm in Sperantia, my body will belong to Lothar and his men.

That all ends today.

I pull my long black hair back into a tight braid, then slip into a pair of black pants and a fitted top that Hidi dropped off last night. I don't intend on fighting my way out in the long dresses or nightgowns I've worn during my time here. The broken piece of plate sits on the bedside table, and I plan on slipping it into my waistband before we leave. With no other weaponry at my disposal, this will have to do. Hidi is working on detaining my door guard.

The thought of escaping on dragonback is terrifying, but I'd do just about anything if it means breaking us free from this kingdom.

Another cry ripples through the room. I curl up on the bed, squeezing my eyes shut, rocking back and forth as if I can stop it through sheer willpower.

A squeak of a door handle turning commandeers all of my thoughts. My eyes snap open and dart to the door. With one hand I lean over and snatch the broken piece of porcelain off of the table, gripping it tightly.

Like a terrified child, I'm hugging my knees to my chest. Heart racing, skin burning, just waiting.

Waiting for my fate, waiting for my doom.

A creak of the door echoes as it slowly pushes open.

My heartbeat pounds in my throat. All my senses are as sharp as the weapon in my grasp. Blood slowly drips from my palm from squeezing the shard too tightly. It stings, but I don't dare move to assess the wound.

"Princess Bellatrix, what an honor it is to join you in your quarters again."

*Lothar.*

Why is he here?

Hidi assured me he would be occupied in a meeting with the other men. But since he's standing before me, something has obviously changed.

Any words I attempt to voice die in my throat. My throat feels like it's closing in on me, similar to the current state of our escape plan.

Wounding and trapping Hidi's replacement was going to be my way out. By the time anyone realizes he's missing, we would have been long gone. The king being here changes everything.

"Come now, Princess, you must have something to say to your king after all the wonderful evenings we've spent together," he taunts.

Still frozen on the bed, I feel the anger start to thaw my bones and release me from my paralytic state.

"You are not *my* king, nor will you ever be."

A hearty chuckle erupts out of him, and he claps his hands one time in approval.

"That's my girl. I love a fighter."

My face twists into a grimace. *I'm not your girl.*

Lothar looks behind him, giving the two guards flanking the door a head nod, which they take as a dismissal. One of the men closes it, leaving me alone with the king.

As he turns back to face me, he slowly inches towards me, causing the hair on my neck to stand up, and my back snaps ramrod straight.

We are a mountain lion and a deer. Predator and prey. Hunter and hunted.

My clutch eases slightly on the shard of porcelain. I begin to feel a steady stream of blood drip from my hand down my forearm to my elbow, and I shift slightly to hide the blood cascading down my arm.

"What is it you want from me?" If it were the middle of the night, I'd know. But he doesn't visit during the daylight. This visit is different.

A disingenuous smile stretches across his face, as his eyes slither over my form. "You, Princess. I want you."

*No. I can't take it anymore.*

He clearly knows how this curse works, which is why I'm here to begin with. Why would he risk it? With all the money and power one person could ever need, why would he risk sleeping with me now? It's one thing to sacrifice his men, but I never thought he'd be foolish enough to participate himself.

"Why? You know what will happen."

His tongue sticks out and licks across both of his lips like he's about to devour his favorite meal.

*Keep dreaming, asshole. Not on this land or mine.*

If I can keep him talking, keep him distracted, it might give me enough time to figure out how to get out of here in one piece.

"What *might* happen," he says.

"You really think you can beat the curse?" I ask, mustering as much indifference as I can.

He nods his head, and continues to inch towards me. "Don't underestimate my powers, girl."

I don't know what comes over me, causing me to do what I do next. Lifting my arm to reveal my weapon, I hold it out and then place it at my own neck.

His eyes go wide, taking in the scene before him. The red

liquid running down my arm, the bloody weapon pressed to my own throat. "What are you doing, Princess?"

"Don't take another step closer or I'll do it. You need me. I'm of no use to you dead."

One of his eyebrows lift, and I see his jaw clench with frustration. The move he didn't expect.

*Your move, asshole.*

"Clever girl."

My hand trembles at my throat, and I hope he can't tell.

He takes another cautious step forward, and I press the shard harder into my flesh. I can feel small droplets of blood trailing down my neck.

Lothar lifts his hand. "Don't do anything rash. Let's talk about a new arrangement."

My teeth are clenched together so tightly it feels like they could shatter, crumble to dust, and blow away with the Sperantia gusts.

He takes another step and stands next to the bed. He hovers overhead, looking down on me with hateful eyes and a malicious grin. His expression reveals how little he thinks of me. He doesn't think I have it in me to go through with this, and while he might be right about that, he's underestimated what I'm capable of.

I see his mouth open to speak, but I've heard enough. All the anger I've been holding at bay has been simmering, waiting to be released. I sit up on my knees and turn my weapon on him, thrusting it into his stomach with all my might. I release it and plunge it back into his chest.

Shock paints his face a deadly shade of white. He stumbles backwards, and I have to jump forward and grab him to prevent him from crashing loudly to the floor. Stealth is the name of the game if I'm going to make it out of here.

As I lay him down, face up on the floor, I watch as blood

rapidly pours out of him. He's gurgling and grasping for words he can't articulate over his choking breaths.

I need to be quiet, but something inside me has been unleashed. Everything I've kept shoved down comes pouring out.

"You think you can bring your men in here to touch me as if I'm not human? Use me like I don't matter? Fuck you!" I shout and then spit in his face.

He gurgles, but his eyes are glued to me in disbelief. His mouth opens, but I pull my leg back and then strike him in the side with my foot. Again. And again. And again. I kick until I'm winded and my toes begin to hurt.

Leaning over him, I cover his mouth. With a smirk, I whisper into his ear, "You will never imprison another soul as long as I live."

Delivering another blow, I jam my weapon into his stomach one last time.

When he entered this room, he sealed his own fate. He convinced himself he had nothing to fear. He thought he had his prey cornered, but he had it all wrong.

I'm the fucking predator.

Bodies are significantly harder to carry than I expected. Carrying a dying body across a room is not something I ever thought I'd have to do.

My muscles ache and scream as I attempt to move quickly before the guards come back.

As quietly as I can, I lower Lothar to the washroom floor and throw a towel over his face. My frayed nerves can't tolerate looking at those cold eyes any longer. I'm not sure whether he's still breathing or not, and I can't bring myself close enough to check.

My bloodstained, sweaty palms grip the porcelain sink, my gaze driven downward out of fear. Looking in the mirror means facing what I've just done and who I've become. I don't know if I'm ready to meet her. Time is running out, but maybe if I stand here a little longer I can pretend I'm still somebody else.

I take a few calming breaths, slowly bracing myself for the monster I'm about to confront. But when I look up, I see my familiar reflection. I'm not sure what I expected, but this isn't it. A part of me thought I'd see the way I feel inside. Aside from the blood coating my face and upper body, I'm still me. The sadness still eclipses all other emotions in my eyes. Worry stretching from the corners of my eyes and mouth like tiny trenches that carry the sorrows of my existence. Nothing's changed.

A clatter on the other side of the bedroom door startles me, and my head jolts towards it.

Quickly washing my hands and arms, I vigorously scrub as much of the king's blood off my skin as possible. I watch the porcelain turn an offensive shade of red before it washes down the drain.

I slowly close the bathroom door with a soft click, keeping Lothar's body hidden away.

Swiping the only weapon I have off the floor where it lays from the assault, I use the bedsheet to wipe it clean. Ready to run for the door, I pause when the side table catches my eye.

My bracelet.

I tore it off and left it crumpled there, but now it beckons to me. My eyes zero in on it, and for reasons unknown, I can't find it in me to leave it behind.

Slipping it back on my wrist, I hurry to the door and swing it open.

Immediately my gaze is drawn to three men sprawled out in front of the door, lifeless.

*What the fuck?*

I quickly scan the corridor. But it's empty.

With shaky limbs I step over them, following the directions Hidi gave me to our rendezvous point at the back exit of the castle. But before I get very far, I feel a tug on my shoulder.

Panic seizes control of my body, and I freeze.

This is it. I've been caught. It's over. The panicky thoughts rush out like blood from a wound, leaving me terrified and cold.

Hidi materializes at my side.

"Hidi!" I whisper-shout.

Her eyes take in my body that's covered in blood. "Oh Gods, are you hurt?"

I shake my head. "Not my blood. Lothar came to my room. What the hell is going on?"

She grabs me by the elbow, pulling me forward while she speaks. "No time, we need to go now!"

I nod and follow her through the long empty halls of the castle. They're poorly lit and humid, the stench of dirt much more prominent through here. I have to hold my hand to my face to avoid breathing in the thick mildew-y air. The brick making up the walls appears as if it's sweating, and I do my best not to touch either side.

At the end of the hallway we turn right, then follow it down and take a left and race to the end where it opens up to a huge sitting room. One we need to pass through, in order to find the back door.

We are so close.

We're out of breath, terrified, and have been lucky not to run into another guard. Our freedom is within reach, but before we make it, we realize the room isn't empty. Out of my periphery I see a man rushing towards us from the side with a dagger stretched outward.

Like a puff of smoke, all my visions of freedom evaporate before my eyes.

# 17

## KOEN

The queen's words hang over me like toxic smoke, billowing overhead.

Jamming the sorrow and pain back down below, securing it tightly like a pin in a grenade, I am able to return to my human form. Once she leaves I quickly dress with the clothing strewn about the floor and join the men out front.

I will deal with her later.

Roughly fifty men stand huddled together, talking amongst themselves, awaiting orders. I fill my lungs with the fresh crisp air, making an effort to keep my emotions concealed. But when my gaze wanders upward, I can't help but notice that even the sky looks worried.

I repeatedly rejected Charlotte's suggestion to send in the daemons. Letting our friends and family involuntarily be led to their probable deaths wasn't a scenario I was willing to entertain. The men here volunteered for this fight. Their lives are in my hands, but I'm no soldier. All I want to do is save the woman I love.

Holding my head high, I start making my way over to the men when I'm stopped in my tracks by a familiar face in the group.

A smile slowly spreads across my face as I close the distance between us. "Nik."

His hands are in the pockets of his pants, his shoulders shrugging. "Yeah, well, I couldn't let you go and kill yourself alone."

His attempt at humor temporarily eases some of the tension. After how poorly I've treated him, he still has my back. He's not the friend I deserve, but the friend I'm lucky to have by my side.

I lean in for a hug and pat him twice on the back. "Thank you for coming. I wasn't sure I'd see you after our last conversation."

"You might be an asshole, but I'm always here for you, man." He blows out a breath. "Shit, let's not make a big emotional thing out of it. Let's go get your girl."

I nod, unable to hide the relief I feel now that my friend is here. "Let's go get her."

We've been traveling on horseback for hours through what seems like every possible terrain. Tenuma has seen its fair share of snow, so we've gone through some rough patches. The weather is brisk, and the clouds overhead threaten to wage war against us as well. The further we travel towards the foreign land, the further away those dark clouds become. The improvement in weather does little in the way of relief as we run headfirst into a much bigger problem.

Sperantia.

Opposite of ours, their climate is hot. A miserable desert-like kingdom covered in dirt known for its perpetual dust storms. We're coming from a much harsher environment, so our main concern isn't dealing with a little dirt. It's the front line.

I lie with the men crouched amongst the remaining trees that border Sperantia. It provides enough coverage to keep us hidden out of sight. Guards form a tight line on the other side, and from the looks of it, are heavily armed.

Swords. Bow and arrows. Daggers.

There's more men than Charlotte said there would be.

Shit. Weren't most of these assholes supposed to be in meetings?

"What's the order, boss?" Nik asks from my side.

My jaw clenches tightly. There's too many of them.

"We're outnumbered." I rake my hands through my thick hair, lost in thought. "I have an idea, but it's kind of crazy."

This wasn't the plan, but with what I know now, it just might work.

"Nik. Stay here with the men. I'm going in by myself and—" I'm cut off before I can finish the thought.

"Like hell you are!" Nik whisper-shouts. "I promised your mother I'd keep you from being an idiot."

I scrub a hand down my face and release a tense huff. "I know how it sounds. But you need to trust me."

Nik's lips form a grim line, and he reluctantly motions for me to continue.

I direct the men to split up into the assigned groups, and make their way to their designated posts, but to hold back.

Once we are left with our smaller group, I turn to the men. "The queen was having an affair with Lothar. They were planning on being together once her husband died."

Nik's eyes go wide in disbelief.

For the next several minutes I explain what the queen revealed to me, and the direction of the new plan with me going in solo to extract the princess from the room they've got her in. We weren't supposed to split up like this, but it could work. There's a lot of understanding nods and raised eyebrows, but nobody protests. Not even when I waltz right up to the armed guards by myself, and multiple weapons begin pointing in my direction.

Staring down more weapons than I ever hoped to, I stand before the men of Sperantia, ready to fight, ready to kill.

Nobody says a word.

They don't need to. I'm outnumbered, so one wrong move on my part would lead to a pretty swift kill.

Clearing my throat and raising my hands in a display of innocence, I greet the men. "I, uh, I'm the new informant sent from Tenuma. The queen has sent a message for the king."

With no clue how the other informant usually comes and goes, I take my best shot and hope it doesn't result in the firing of weapons.

A man to the right of me is the first to speak up. He has a slightly different uniform than the rest of the guards. They're all wearing the green uniform with the unmistakable Sperantia serpent, but this man has a crown over the serpent symbol and a multicolored ribbon on his shoulder. I take him to be the one in charge.

"Who are you? I've never seen you." His suspicious eyes roam my face.

I swallow, trying to take with it the nerves and hesitation that I fear might come out with my words. "The previous informant was compromised. He was taken by our army after admitting to having plans to kill Lothar."

The man's eyes narrow to slits as he considers my claim. "And I'm to believe you don't have the same plan?"

Sweat begins to form around my hairline, as the lies pour out of me. "I'd have to be pretty stupid to show up here alone and attempt to take down an entire kingdom. My message is urgent, so I'd like to deliver it to the king as soon as possible."

Just because I *am* dumb enough to try taking down Sperantia doesn't mean he needs to know.

Or that I have my own army of men ready to strike once I've found the princess.

My story must have been believable enough, because he waves a hand in front of a few men, and they part, exposing the gate entrance to the castle.

He takes a key from inside the breast of his jacket, sticking it in the heavy-duty lock that secures the castle. With a turn and a click, the gate slides open.

"You two." The man in charge points to two other guards standing next to him. "Escort him inside, make sure he only does as he says."

I'm given a wave to proceed and a glare from the man as I step forward with the two guards following closely behind. Just as I pass through the gate, he calls my attention. Blood begins to pump violently in my veins.

Turning quickly on my heel I see the man pointing a dagger in my direction. "You have ten minutes, then I send in the rest of my men to kill you."

For fear of saying the wrong thing, I nod tightly at the man and take slow steps towards the entrance of the castle. Careful not to make the wrong move, I slowly raise my arm to wipe the sweat collecting at my brow and surge forward.

The castle is as large as Tenuma's, though not as impressive. The size itself is grand, but it lacks the personality and life that the castle back home holds. It appears cold and covered in the same dirt that's swirling around us.

There's no rose gardens or hedge mazes, but it holds my sweet princess inside of its walls.

*Hold on, Princess, I'm coming.*

It takes all of my effort to stay calm with two armed enemies at my back. I expect to find more guards through the front door, but the area is vacant.

*Odd.*

My gaze bounces from one side of the entrance to the other, assessing any immediate threats.

Empty.

Something doesn't feel right.

I peer into the room on the left, anticipating my first target.

Empty.

There's nothing I want more than to run directly to the princess's room and bring her home, but something is nagging at me to stay put.

"We'll need to search you for weapons before we go any further," one of the men tells me.

Turning to face the two men, I feel my insides twist. The dagger in my jacket feels like a beacon, like they both know it's there. I resist raising my hand to it.

"I told you, I'm just an informant. I have no need for weapons."

"Well, as you've stated, our last *informant* planned to kill the king. This isn't a request."

For a long moment, I lock eyes with the man, unsure what to do. They will find the dagger, and they will kill me before I get to her.

Suddenly, it's not what I hear or see, it's what I feel.

Confused at the sensation, I glance down at the location of it, and tears sting my eyes.

My wrist is tingling.

The bracelet connecting me to Bellatrix vibrates with life. She's alive, and she must be close.

I glance back up at the men with renewed confidence. I didn't come this far to lose her now.

"I have nothing to hide," I say steadily.

One begins to approach me, and before he can find my secret, I pull the dagger, slashing it across his neck. He immediately falls, and when the other man is distracted, watching in horror as his comrade goes down, I slice his neck the same way.

Like I've taken a dose of adrenaline, I feel suddenly emboldened to surge through the fear regardless of what lay ahead. I'm about to take off in a sprint when I see two women racing toward a door at the back of the room.

My body tenses, fear tearing through me. Without hesitation, I raise my dagger. But as my eyes adjust to the newcomers I realize that it's not just anybody. It's my girl.

*Princess.*

My feet take off before I tell them to, closing the distance between us. Like a mirage, I worry it'll disappear if I dare look away. Seeing her is a dream. Though the closer I get, the more worried I become. There are splotches of blood all over her arms and clothing, and some splattered on her face. I can see the fear and panic sitting deeply between her eyebrows. Her mouth is tense as she shouts something at the woman beside her. I don't make out the words with the buzzing in my ears.

I stop short of where she's shooing away the other woman, lowering my weapon and attempting to hold back the urge to wrap my arms around her. Though she doesn't look nearly as happy to see me.

The tone of her voice when she says my name aloud all but confirms that something is very wrong.

# 18

# BELLATRIX

$S$omething is very wrong.

What is Koen doing here?

Has he been here all along?

We stand facing each other, neither of us moving. Neither of us speaking. But he's not trying to hurt me, either.

"Princess," he whispers. "Are you okay?" he asks, surveying my body.

Time slows, and for a moment, everything around us blurs. I smile at him, a knee-jerk reaction from seeing his familiar, handsome face. A rush of emotions I couldn't hold back almost have me falling right into his arms.

I try to hold them back, but memories slip through my fingers.

Meeting Koen for the first time, and the first time we kissed. The protective way he's always stood up for me. Hearing that he collaborated with his father to betray me. My head is swimming with emotion, and like an overfilled balloon, I burst open, letting everything out.

"Am I okay? No, I'm not okay! What are you doing here?" I scream at him with bleary eyes. My weapon shakes in my grip, and I try to display any semblance of confidence and strength, failing brilliantly.

He sheathes his weapon inside his thick jacket. As a show of submission, he lifts both hands to me, displaying empty palms. "Princess, I came to bring you home. Why else would I be here?"

His response is slow and controlled as if I'm a grenade, fragile and quick to detonate. The look in his eyes is so hauntingly sincere, that I almost give into a moment of weakness and believe him.

But *he's* never given me reason to doubt him, has he?

My emotions are currently playing their best game of tug-of-war, each side desperate for the win. I can't bring myself to hate him, but I don't think I have it in me to trust him either.

"I'm leaving. Don't try to stop me."

Koen winces at my words when they land exactly as I intended them to. He takes a few deliberate steps backwards, extending his arm outward to the door, signaling that I'm free to go. "I don't know what's going on, but I want your freedom as much as you do. I would never take that from you. Be careful, there's a line of guards out front."

He's warning me?

The bracelet I forgot was on my wrist tingles, urging me to move closer. A current running beneath my skin almost thrusting me right into his arms, as if controlled by another entity all together.

I shake my wrist, doing my best to ignore it.

I move backwards toward the back door, and the obvious mistrust earns me an anguished frown. I don't let it deter me. I need to get back to Hidi. I all but shoved her through the door while I dealt with Koen. Not knowing how things would play out with him, at the very least I wanted her to escape.

The door swings open before I reach it, and Hidi bursts through the doorway with a concerned expression as her gaze swings between me and Koen. "We have to go. NOW."

We exit out into a large courtyard in the center of the castle grounds. There are high brick walls and multiple doors leading to other parts of the castle.

I pause when I feel the wind blowing through my hair, causing the strays to dance around my face in celebration. After weeks of being held captive in a muggy room, fresh air, even a Sperantian dust storm, feels like paradise.

"We must hurry," Hidi urges me forward, and as much as I want to lose myself in the moment, I continue on.

"Agh!" I yelp as I trip over a large chain in the middle of the ground.

Hidi prevents my fall by grabbing hold of my arm before I go down. I stare back at the chain, wondering why it's there, when I hear a noise that clears up any question.

I glance up to see rough white flesh. Long talons. One golden eye, one green.

*Miri.*

Hidi's dragon.

The dragon tilts her head downwards and releases a noise that's equivalent to a cat purring, making my heart ache. Listening to Miri and the other dragons crying out in pain the last few weeks has been heartbreaking, and I can't imagine the damage it's done to Hidi's heart, knowing this has gone on much longer than I've been here.

"Miri will be the most cooperative with a new rider. I'll help you up and show you how to stay on her back, but we need to get the others out. I'll be on another dragon. They're accustomed to soldiers riding them, and they know me, so it should be fine," Hidi says, gesturing for me to walk with her.

We cross the common area, through an archway that leads to another, much bigger space. My eyes go wide, and an involuntary gasp escapes my lips.

"There are so many of them," I whimper as my eyes take rows of dragons chained to the castle walls.

Hidi huffs. "This is only where they keep the ones they plan to work with next. We won't be able to save them all. These are the ones we can free, but we need to hurry."

I nod, and she hands me a key. "This will unlock all the chains. I have another key if *he* plans to help." She gestures to where I left Koen inside.

My eyes furrow. "He isn't here to help. That's Lothar's son, the one that helped him put me here."

Her head jerks back with shock. "I don't think so, Princess. I've never seen him here before. Surely I would have seen him with Lothar at some point in all my years here."

A spark of hope flickers in my chest.

"You've never seen him before?"

"Princess, I've never seen that man before in my life."

The conviction in her voice rocks my already unsteady compass.

My bracelet begins to tingle, and as I glance behind us, I see Koen cautiously making his way over. Though it's hard to decipher whether the fear is coming from his proximity to me, or the dragons.

This new information further confuses me. I don't know what to believe. But if there's anyone I'd put all my faith in, it's Hidi, so

I don't stop Koen when he approaches us.

"How can I help?" he asks timidly.

Hidi holds out a key and drops it into his outstretched hand. "Unlock all these chains, and I will show you how to mount a dragon and keep yourself on."

"Why chains? Can't they use their fire breathing to break free?" Koen asks.

Hidi shakes her head. "One of the trainers has a fire protection gift, and he's enchanted all of the chains so they're impenetrable."

"Will they try to kill me?" Koen asks, and I'm glad I didn't have to.

"No, they've been around humans and have had enough training that they wouldn't harm us unless given an order to."

Memories of the dragons ripping through Tenuma, leaving everything in rubble makes my stomach feel queasy. The day of the attack changed everything for Tenuma, and I can't help but wonder how many innocent men and dragons were killed at Lothar's command.

"I'll help, but I can't ride a dragon out. I have my men waiting for me out front. I came with them, and I plan on leaving with them. Bellatrix, you can come with us." His eyes plead, filled with dread as they bounce between me and the dragons.

He came here with an army?

Fuck. So he has been forthright all along.

I shake my head, not trusting myself to speak to him. But the plan was to leave with Hidi, and that's what I intend to do.

At the other end of the large open area, a man and a woman are working together on the other chains.

"Hidi, is that your family?" I ask as we quickly move towards the first set of dragons.

She gives them a quick wave. "Yes, that's my brother and my

mother. They will be riding a dragon out as well. We'll follow you and Miri to Tenuma."

Koen approaches the dragons, quickly releasing their chains, while the rest of us work our way down the other rows. I'm shocked to find that the dragons don't immediately take off when the chains fall from their limbs. Their strict obedience is firmly intact from the horrid "training" they've endured. For several minutes, the only sound is the clanging of heavy chains falling to the ground. The sound of freedom.

"Will they follow us?" I ask, trying to recall every signal she taught me.

"Yes, Miri's their leader. They'll fly together in a pack, so once they see Miri take off, the rest will be close behind."

Sirens begin to blare all around us, and either we've just been caught, or the king has been found in my bed chambers.

The dragons are all released, yet stay surprisingly docile. They rise on their legs slightly, snouts in the air, sniffing around, waiting for their commands. Even with the ear-splitting noise, they're seemingly unaffected.

"We're out of time, Princess!" Hidi shouts at me over the blaring.

We rush back over where Miri has been sitting, waiting for our return. Quickly, Hidi helps me up onto the dragon's back. "Do you remember the commands I taught you?"

I quickly nod, coughing through the dust. "Yes, I think so." While I don't feel confident, it's going to have to be enough.

"Shouldn't you be riding Miri? You two have a connection. I can—"

"No," she insists. "She's the only one who's been exposed to *good* humans. It's best if you ride her. She'll make sure you get home safe. I will be okay with one of the others."

Miri lowers her giant head, and Hidi nuzzles herself into

the side of her dragon's face. Holding on tightly as she says her goodbyes. I can see tears streaming down Hidi's face when she pulls back. Miri is nudging her nose into Hidi, encouraging more rubs and affection. The moment is tender, and I feel like I'm intruding as I watch from Miri's back.

"Take care of the princess, girl. I'll be with you soon. I'm sorry I let you down, but you're free now. My sweet Miri. You *are* a miracle. I love you." Hidi presses her face back into the dragon, kissing her affectionately.

I receive an encouraging head nod as Hidi races back toward her family and the other dragons. Droplets of water splash on my hands, and I curse the weather for turning on us right now. Flying through a storm isn't exactly a challenge I needed. It's not until I see Koen lingering nearby with a somber expression that I realize the wetness comes from my own tears.

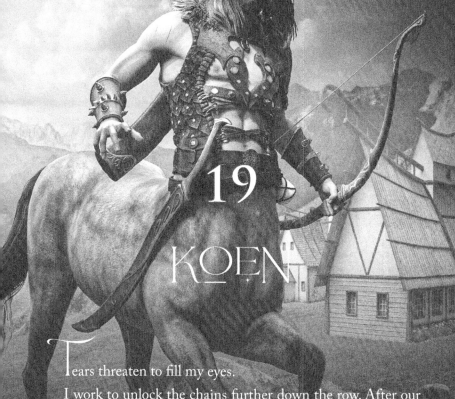

# 19

## KOEN

Tears threaten to fill my eyes.

I work to unlock the chains further down the row. After our tense and confusing reunion it's clear that Bellatrix doesn't want me near her. I was elated to see her, but her gaze was that of murder. It's taking all of my restraint not to pull her aside and clear things up right now, but unfortunately that conversation will have to wait.

When I set out on our mission today, I didn't expect to be rescuing dragons in lieu of the princess. I knew there was risk in facing Sperantia's armed men, but coming face to face with dragons unveils a new layer of fear. Glancing around, I see the women fearlessly facing the dragons, so I muster all the courage I can and soldier on.

One by one, the locks come off, and to my surprise, none of the dragons break for the sky. They remain on the ground, glancing around anxiously, but I'm not sure for what. I expect the chaos of fluttering wings, and a show of flames shooting from their mouths, instead they do nothing.

The tanned woman with intense brown eyes with Bellatrix seems confident that we can trust these creatures, but my last encounter with one was having to slay it, a memory I don't care to revive.

Before I can ponder the strangeness of it all too long, sirens sound in every direction, piercing the air. I frantically glance around at what the others are doing and if Lothar and his men are storming us. The woman's family members climb up two separate dragons, and I see Bellatrix and her friend take off towards a white dragon. After releasing the last animal, I jog back over to where the women are locked in discussion.

Bellatrix climbs up onto its back, and to my surprise she doesn't look afraid. She declined my offer to travel back to Tenuma with me, and I try to tell myself it's not personal, though clearly it is. I only wish I knew why.

Not wanting to further upset her, I hang back and wait for her to ascend. Assuming she's going to take off after mounting, I brace myself to watch her slip away. Instead, I notice her friend has what looks to be a somber goodbye with the white-fleshed dragon.

She's hugging the animal's leg, saying something I can't decipher over the siren. It looks sweet and sad, and unlike any interaction I'd expect with a dragon.

Suddenly, it starts to come together. These aren't just an exit strategy, transportation. She's *saving* the dragons.

I hang back, staying alert to our surroundings, and watching for the inevitable rush of guards.

Their absence thus far has been odd, but I know our luck won't hold out.

Bellatrix sits solo on the white dragon. I don't rush to her side like I want, but I can't resist studying her face. Where I thought I'd see fear, I see an overwhelming sense of sadness. Though she's emanating strength, I can see what lies beneath. What she's been through during her time here, I can only imagine. There are so many factors about this situation that I don't understand, and I want more than anything to know how to reach her

In the weeks that she's been gone, the experience here has changed her. I can see it. She's full of sharp edges, and I was immediately cut with her accusation. As much as I wanted to be her savior, it seems like all I've brought is more distress.

*She doesn't need you.*

*You took too long.*

*She rescued herself.*

Bellatrix makes a command to the dragon with her voice and hand, but I can't hear it over the sirens from where I'm at. The dragon rises and extends its large wings. I have to step back even further to avoid contact with them.

The dragon she's on is quite spectacular. Not gruesome like the one who chased us in the forest, but then this one isn't currently trying to kill us. This animal has magnificent white flesh that almost glows, and dual-colored eyes, one a brilliant golden brown, and the other a bright emerald green. I've never seen anything like it, and I find myself captivated by its beauty. Bellatrix looks powerful on its back, despite the fears I'm sure are flowing through her.

My eyes stay glued on the princess, pleading for any sign that she won't cast me away forever.

Any indication that there's still a chance for us, an opportunity to be heard. I think she'll leave without a single word when the bracelet tingles on my wrist. The princess turns her head to meet my eyes, and holds one arm up revealing her matching one.

It's a small gesture, but it's all I need. Hope blooms through me like a rose, surpassing all other emotions. But hope is dangerous when I don't know where we stand.

As the dragon prepares for liftoff, the entire courtyard

explodes into chaos. Armed men flood the open space. The siren continues to wail, drowning out almost all other sounds.

We've taken too long. I came prepared to fight, but never expected the princess to have to join.

I need her to get the hell out of here.

I try repeatedly to call out to Bellatrix, telling her to leave, but she doesn't hear me. Waving my arms in the air, I signal for her to get her dragon in the air. My efforts are futile. There's too many guards, men pouring out from every corner, and everyone is scrambling. The tanned woman is struggling to get her family airborne on their own dragons, and she has yet to mount one of her own. Meanwhile, all of the animals are frozen in place, awaiting the appropriate command.

Bellatrix looks frozen with fear, and her dragon isn't moving. No matter what she thinks of me, or how she feels about me, I won't let her be captured again. She can hate me, but I'll continue to fight for her with my last breath.

For a moment, everything goes black. My muscles scream, and my head spins as I take my animal form. My clothing drops to the floor beneath my hooved feet. Towering over everyone else, my centaur body stands strong and agile. Though we're outnumbered, I now have the upper hand and a better chance at picking more of these men off.

Time to fight my way out.

In the few seconds it took for me to transform into a centaur, the atmosphere changes, and it's clear something terrible has happened. The siren finally begins to wane, and through the ringing in my ears, I hear the princess's distressing screams.

# 20

# BELLATRIX

My mind is screaming. With fear, with confusion, with yearning.

As I raise my arm, I reveal to Koen the bracelet secured on my wrist. Our connection and beacon to each other. I may not have all the answers yet, but looking into Koen's eyes, I remember the man he is. My mind flashes back to the man who was determined to protect and set me free from the bonds of my own life.

I thought it would be easy to hate him. To turn him away and never look back. As it turns out, enduring pain and betrayal from the ones we love is easier than letting them go.

Love might be the real curse.

None of the confusion matters right now. There's a good

chance one or both of us won't make it out of here alive. If this is the last time we get to see each other, I don't want it to end with hate.

I give a quick hand and voice command, and Miri rises up on her long legs and leans back to prepare for flight. I brace myself to be airborne, but everything changes before she manages to flap a giant wing.

New noises come from behind us. Loud noises.

Something isn't right.

Miri crouches back down and freezes, both fearful and curious.

Whipping my head around, I see guards begin to fill the area. Hidi is securing her mother and brother safely on the back of the dragon, so she has yet to climb onto the back of her own. The guards split off in all directions, going after her family on the dragons, and straight towards me.

The dragon Hidi's mother is on takes flight first, and seconds later her brother's dragon follows suit. The guards begin firing off arrows, but miss their target in the chaos of large flapping wings. The strong force of the wind it creates knocks some of the men backwards, but a few arrows must have struck the dragons, as evidenced by the cries they emit.

Hidi rushes to her dragon. Before climbing on, her gaze is cast upwards as her family escapes the castle and Sperantia. Relief splashes across her face, quickly fading as she lowers her eyes to see four armed guards closing in on her. Her gaze flicks to mine where more guards are closing in on me, aimed and ready to fire.

I'm certain time has stopped. A moment pulled and stretched over an eternity. I'm frozen along with it, unable to do anything but watch as an arrow releases and flies in my direction. I can't force myself to flee. Numbness seizes my body, and instead of recognizing that I'm about to die, I'm wondering if Hidi has time to get herself and Miri out.

*Take me, but let them live.*

My chest rises and falls slow but heavy. I can feel myself breathing in sync with Miri as we both watch warily. Neither of us move to avoid the incoming threat. The arrow inches closer and closer, and I can't hear anything around us. I turn to find Koen, desperate for the comfort of his kind and reassuring eyes. In my last moments, my heart still craves him. One last look into his eyes, where I know I can find compassion to give me peace.

A tear runs down my cheek as I realize he's not looking at me. He's nearby changing into his animal form while the situation intensifies. He's getting ready for battle.

I don't get to say goodbye.

Closer.

I prepare myself for the affliction of imminent pain.

Closer.

My body is thrust backwards into the dragon as something hits me hard from the front.

I scream, and my hands reach for the arrow I'm sure is sticking out of my chest.

No arrow. No wound.

Hidi is on top of me, her body pinning me down for a moment before she flies off the other side of the dragon. Reaching for her hand, I try to save her from falling, but it's too late. My fingers barely graze hers. I'm not fast enough, and all I can do is watch. She descends with an arrow meant for me, plunged through her.

There isn't a drop of fear in her eyes, but it fills my heart with dread.

She slams into the ground and the guards immediately surround her, weapons drawn and aimed directly at her.

"Hidi, run!" I shout, tears swelling in my eyes.

But there's too much going on and she can't hear me.

Why isn't she using her gift?

Two slow blinks. That's all it takes for everything to change.

The arrow protrudes from Hidi's chest, and blood drips down from the wound. My eyes focus on her face, her lips. She mouths her last words to me, and then with a peaceful smile her eyes shut. I gasp when one of the men approaches and thrusts his sword through her abdomen. He throws his head back and releases a maniacal burst of laughter. Surrounding men cheer along with him. The sheer joy it brings him to cause pain to another human being sends a wave of nausea through me.

I try to scream, but no sound escapes. My skin feels hot and itchy, uncomfortable like a barrier that's holding my anger hostage. Desperate for relief, I want to tear through my seams. The ringing in my ears and hot tears in my eyes are in a race for who will outlast who, but it doesn't matter. We lost.

My moment of grief is cut short when the weapons are turned back in my direction. As quickly as they're drawn, they all drop, as the men clamber to cover their ears against the piercing cry. A noise so shrill and ear-splittingly painful. A sound I didn't know I could make.

Only it's not coming from me.

*Miri.*

For weeks I've heard the dragons cry out in pain, but I've never heard this level of anguish and utter despair coming from any of the animals. This is very different.

This is heartbreak.

Daring a look at Miri I see her long neck craned backwards, and realize she just watched the same thing I did. Those who say animals can't feel pain have never witnessed an animal lose their human, their soulmate. The level of anguish she's exhibiting could never be confused with anything else. The desperate wail that begs the Gods to let you keep them. The plea for five more minutes. A language only grief knows.

My eyes are raw from crying and from the dirt blowing around us. The screeching goes on for what feels like minutes, but really it's mere seconds. Seconds too long. Seconds that will get us killed.

"Bellatrix! Princess!" I hear faint shouting over Miri's wails.

My blurry eyes wander, searching for the source.

*Koen.*

"Get out of here. Go!" he shouts again, but it's hard to hear. I only understand by reading his lips.

Turning back to Miri, I attempt a few hand commands and shout the verbal ones. She doesn't budge, and the wailing continues.

"Miri, please!" I manage over choked sobs. The sorrow in her cries magnifies mine, making it difficult to breathe. "Miri, please, we have to go!"

*Come on, miracle girl. We need to save you. For Hidi.*

Fighting the urge to give up, I resolve to try one last time. Her large eyes finally meet mine, and the screeching fades to a controlled whimpering.

"Miri, we can't let her die only to be caught again. Help me! Please," I beg through my own tears. I don't know how much she can understand from what I've said. I'm not sure if she cares.

Losing someone you love makes the importance of everything else fade away when they're all you want. The one thing you can't have. My head falls at the realization that I can't get her to fly.

Sorrow and defeat begin taking up residence in my chest when I feel a jolt. My head snaps up when I feel Miri shift into her takeoff position. I grab hold of her, and feel the rush of thick air as we make our way above the castle.

Braving a look below, I see Koen and the guards watch our escape slack-jawed and wide-eyed.

Arrows begin flying into the sky towards us, but quickly the men grow smaller the further away we get. Before they disappear beneath the dirt swirling in the air, I see the guards turn on the centaur in front of them.

How many will I lose today?

They were all here for me, to set me free, and now they're all going to die.

Guilt and dirt suffocate me as we climb higher. The desire to give up is all consuming, but I owe it to Hidi to get her dragon to safety. Up ahead, I see the other dragons flying slowly with Hidi's mother and brother on their backs, allowing us to catch up to them.

Pulling my shoulders back, I sit up higher and somehow will the tears to stop. I can be strong for them.

Their eager eyes search the sky behind me, and I pull my lips inward and shake my head. Once we get home, I will have to explain to them why Hidi isn't with us, but for now I bury it as deep as I can. I make another command, and Miri pulls ahead of the other dragons. Glancing back, I see that the rest of the riderless dragons have also joined us. I lost the only human any of these dragons trusted, yet here they are following me to a new life. As a pack, we fly toward Tenuma.

I won't let them down.

# 21

# KOEN

I'm going to let them all down.

The thought hides in the corners of my mind, like the stag avoiding the mountain lion. It tries to evade capture, but only delays the inevitable. I know it's there.

I'm not a praying man. If I was, I'd be on my knees right now, begging to rewind the last few minutes. If I knew it would help a damn thing, I'd kneel down in the dirt for as long as it took. But she's already gone. The woman who helped Bellatrix escape lays lifeless on the ground. The men look to me next. We've invaded their kingdom, taken their greatest assets, and now they're looking for retribution.

The princess burst into the sky with the magnificent white dragon, and whether or not I make it home alive, that knowledge fills me with comfort. Part one of the mission is complete. Now I need to get myself and my men the hell out of here.

While I tower over enemy soldiers who are currently contemplating their best course of action, I know that I'm greatly outnumbered. The shock of seeing my animal form will wear off and they will resume their attack.

Two of the men step forward with their swords extended. Their first mistake. Not rushing me all at once allows me to quickly disarm them. I yank the swords from their hands, tossing them behind me with ease, and use my front two legs to kick the soldiers backwards. I watch one man fly through the air and crash into a nearby wall. The other man is sent in another direction, crashing into the ground with a thud.

The remaining men surge forward together. Their weapons are drawn, some with swords, others with a bow and arrow. An arrow whizzes past my head, splintering into pieces when it slams into the concrete wall behind us. I grind my teeth, turn toward the man that shot it, and rip the weapon and arrows from his hands. I turn it around on him and shoot the arrow back at him. I hit my target, piercing through his chest. I nock another arrow and release it, sending it puncturing through the next man's leg.

Every movement, every decision is sped up, as if time itself is eager to find out what happens. Split-second decisions become the factor on which my survival hinges. Just as I eliminate one threat, a new one generates from the side. Even with my increased strength, I can feel my muscles beginning to exhaust. Blocking and issuing the continual blows is rapidly wearing me out, and my limbs begin to resemble jelly.

A leg injury isn't enough to immobilize one man, and he jumps on me from behind. Standing on my hind legs, I spin my body to fling him within arm's reach. I pull him off and toss him across the enclosure. The loud crack he makes against the concrete lets me know he will no longer be an issue.

Just as I think my body is about to give out, I launch the last man into the air by his throat and slam him into the ground. A quick 360 turn shows me that all the men are dead, and with gasping breaths I try to revive my burning lungs before finding my way out of here. But once my eyes land back to the doorway, a fresh obstacle presents itself.

New armed soldiers stand in the doorway.

Like ants pouring out of an ant hill, they file out of the door. There are too many of them for me to take on myself.

I retreat backwards into the courtyard, quickly retrieving extra arrows from the fallen soldiers. I hold my bow high and tight, ready to fire. But it won't matter. I can only take down one man at a time with an arrow. Judging by the smirk on a few of the men's faces, I'd say they know that too.

I'm not sure if it's exhaustion or the realization that this is over that leads me to start mentally preparing for death.

*Mother, I'm so sorry. Keep yourself and Mel safe.*

I feel my throat begin to ache, and there's a stinging at my eyes. When I was angry, I never wanted to speak to anybody again, but right now all I can think about is everything I want to say to my family, my friends, my girl. I spent so much time being angry, taking advantage of their presence, and now I'll never get to make any of it right.

*Princess, keep fighting for the life you deserve. I'm sorry I won't be there to fight with you. We never got our chance to be together, but I wouldn't change a thing. You're worth every drop of blood.*

The men move forward, closing in on me.

After I mentally let go, a strange sense of calm washes over me. This is the reality of war. Some survive, and some don't. I'm okay being one that doesn't survive if I know my loved ones are safe. I will endure the pain so they won't have to.

Like arriving home right before a storm hits, or finally getting that kill at the end of a long day of unsuccessful hunting, the eleventh-hour save emerges behind the new army of men.

My men.

Nik.

A new surge of energy ignites beneath my skin, giving me the momentum I need to keep going. Nik, followed by the rest of our men advance on Sperantia's soldiers from behind. Tenuma's army is here, and we are going to make it out of here alive.

With restored hope, I tighten my grip on the bow and arrow, firing at the smirking Sperantian man. It lands in his chest, and he goes down, the smirk dying on his face.

Nik and his men charge from the back, picking the men off one by one. I'm no longer outnumbered, and Lothar's army is rapidly vanishing.

I reload my weapon and release it over and over until I'm out of arrows. Tossing the weapon aside, I rush Sperantia's remaining men, and feel them crush beneath my hooves.

"Koen!" Nik calls.

My eyes scan the area for him. Our eyes meet, and he tosses me a sword.

"Thank Gods you're here!" I shout at him.

"Bellatrix spotted us from a fucking dragon, and signaled for us to get back here. We would have been here sooner, but we had to fight off the line of guards at the front. On your left!" Nik alerts me, but I'm not fast enough.

A man rushes me from the side, and before I can defend myself, his weapon sinks into my side.

I scramble backwards as blood begins to pour out of the wound.

Fuck, that hurt.

I groan when my back meets one of the walls. Nik stabs him, and with a lethal slice across the throat the man goes down. The two opposing kingdoms continue their fight. I sink to the floor, unable to make myself keep going. Weakness is setting in, and I can't hold my animal form any longer. I shift back, but feel no relief. It feels like somebody shook the earth beneath me, and my vision is getting blurry.

Is this what it feels like to die?

I feel a grip on my shoulders as a figure appears in front of me. Shaking the dark from the corners of my vision, Nik comes into focus. "Shit, are you okay, man?"

Nik must have retrieved my clothing from where I shifted, as I see him drop it next to us and begins dressing me while the rest of the men hold the Sperantian soldiers at bay. My bottoms are pulled on, but Nik rolls my shirt into a ball and hands it to me. Guiding my hand, he presses it to my side, instructing me to firmly hold it in place. With my free hand, I press down firmly on the other. A jolt of pain sparks through my body as I anger the wound. I suck in a sharp breath.

"Hey, Castor!" he shouts for another one of our men. "He's losing a lot of blood, I need to get him out of here."

Castor assesses my injuries with a grim face. "Yeah, we've got this. The rest of the army is still out front, don't go back that way."

"Wasn't planning on it," Nik states matter-of-factly.

I watch as they both gaze upwards. The same path the dragons took.

All the dragons followed Bellatrix out. We can't fly out.

I intend to tell Nik as much, but Castor nods and rushes back to the fight taking place on the other side of the enclosure.

"So, don't freak out, man…" Nik begins, taking a few large steps backwards.

He raises his arms in the same strange fashion he did in front of his bar, only this time I see what would have happened if Quirina hadn't stopped him.

An explosion of heat and feathers fills the air, floating around us like falling ash. His clothes are strewn at his now-clawed feet. My eyes travel the width of his wingspan, the length of his newly formed tail. The sheer size of him is astonishing.

Holy shit. He's a *phoenix*.

My mind spins, and whether it's due to blood loss or the revelation, I'm having a hard time adjusting to everything in front of me. Nik has been in my life for as long as I can remember, and he's never alluded to having any sort of gift or changeability. Then again, I just recently found out about mine.

Maybe he did too.

Another burst of chaos ensues as more men rush in from inside the castle. This fight won't be ending any time soon.

"Nik, get him out of here! Go!" Castor shouts.

Sliding my body down, I kick my leg out and slide back Nik's clothing with my foot. As a fellow shifter, I know what it's like to forget about clothing once you've shifted back. He'll be glad to have these if we make it out of here.

With a large taloned foot, he reaches over and clutches me gently but firmly and shoots into the sky. Large wings flap against the wind, taking us higher, until the castle is lost beneath the swirling dirt.

We made it out.

There's an uncomfortable feeling sitting in my chest when I realize that I never saw Lothar. I can't help but wonder where he was hiding, and why he let everyone else do his dirty work. While I wasn't looking forward to seeing him, I wanted to look him in the eye after all he's done. To hear what he had to say to the son he abandoned. With too many thoughts racing through my mind, I tuck that one away to deal with another time. A time where perhaps I'm not bleeding out in the grip of a phoenix.

I'm grateful that Nik can't see my face right now. As the adrenaline is wearing off, pain and fear settle in, making themselves comfortable. Tears prick my eyes, and Gods, I finally let them fall. I give into the wave of emotion because what's one more thing out of my control?

# 22

# BELLATRIX

*This fucking thing is out of control.*

Humans shouldn't be able to experience this degree of speed. Miri is tearing through the sky, eating up the distance while I do my best to avoid losing my grip, thus dropping to my death. I manage a glance behind to reassure myself that Hidi's family is still with us.

*Hidi.*

She showed me the broken pieces of her life, and it was my job to put them back together, put her family back together. Her face flashes through my mind, all the kindness she offered me. When she'd bring me food no matter how often I refused. The strawberry swirl cake she brought because it reminded me of home. Countless times she kept the guards from entering my room. Learning about her family and her past. Talking with her in hushed tones in the early hours of morning when nobody was the wiser. Remembering stings, leaving behind a residual ache. Memories trapped in time.

Miri takes a drastic descent, as if she can sense where my thoughts have wandered to. I nearly slide off, and am forced to shove all thoughts of Hidi away for now if I want to survive this trip. Closing up the door in my mind, I seal it until I'm prepared to unlock it and deal with those demons.

Another dip.

*Fuck, Miri.* What is she doing?

We pass over a mountain range and, though it's nearly dark, I can see life begin to take shape. Buildings shoot up towards the sky, our lush snowy forest stretches ahead like a welcoming embrace, and…

Tenuma.

The castle I used to look at as a prison. Now that I've experienced what that truly means, I couldn't be happier to see my home.

Miri takes another sharp descent, and I give her a command letting her know to slow down and prepare for landing. When her feet finally touch down, I feel immediate relief, finally able to loosen my tight grip on her back. I wrap my arms around her giant body and squeeze, an acknowledgement of what she's done for me, and an apology that I couldn't save her rider. Her person. Hidi's last words still spin around in my head.

Like a house pet showing submissiveness, Miri lays down with her chin touching the cold ground, allowing me to safely slide off.

Thank Gods for land.

My feet hit the snow-covered ground, and I throw myself at the dragon. Devoid of any fear I once had for these creatures, I embrace Miri with the same gentleness and affection Hidi had, scratching her chin and nuzzling myself into the crook between her neck and arm. She turns her head towards me, enclosing us in a tender moment of mourning for our friend. It's enough to almost break me, but I force myself to hold it together.

The rest of the dragons land next to us a few moments later in the open expanse behind the castle, where we can all breathe again.

Quickly, we begin to draw attention, and a handful of people begin filing out of the back entrance of the castle.

Armed guards.

My mother.

Quirina.

Giving Miri one more arm rub, I wave and break into a sprint towards Quirina. My best friend. The one person who won't mind that I'm still covered in dirt and blood. The person who forgave me when I betrayed her in the worst way. Not just any person, *my* person.

She runs towards me, and we collide in an emotional embrace. She smells like home, and I break. I let everything free fall. I sob until I can't breathe, and she caresses my back and reminds me to.

I don't want to breathe. I don't want to breathe if Hidi can't.

Quirina doesn't ask questions. She holds me, letting me unravel in the freezing cold. We stand there for I don't know how long. Forever maybe. She only lets go when my mother approaches us.

"Bella," she coos softly. A tone I haven't heard from her since I was a young girl. I'm scared to speak and shatter through to the coldness I'm accustomed to. I'm not sure my fragility can shoulder her routine cruelty right now.

Reluctantly, I lift my head finding her gaze as she examines my appearance. Torn clothing, covered in blood, bruised, and I'm sure there's dirt streaking down my face. The braid I had in my hair has been blown apart by travel, and sits in a ratty mess at the nape of my neck.

I don't care, but I'm sure she will. Appearances always matter for a royal family.

"Bella, are you okay? Whose blood is that? Is it Lothar's?" she asks.

"It's not the time, Your Majesty. I'm taking her to her quarters, for a shower and rest." Quirina is apparently no longer afraid of my mother.

"I'm okay," I lie, but it's the best I can offer.

Quirina has her arm around me as we walk towards the castle, leaving my mother gawking at the pasture of dragons we just acquired.

With the emotional reunion, I briefly forget about our new guests. I turn to Hidi's family who have dismounted their dragons and stand awkwardly next to them, unsure what to do next. "Please, follow me. I will show you to your quarters."

Hidi's mother and brother begin walking towards me wearily.

Before my mother can attempt any protest, I introduce them. "These are very important people." I get choked up. "They saved my life. They are to be treated as family."

I expect my mother to protest, but she surprises me by nodding in acquiescence. Hidi's mother and brother bow to my mother, showing their respect and appreciation, and I notice they're shivering. This must be a drastic change from what they're used to. They left everything behind at the prospect of a better life, and only escaped with the unsuitable clothing on their backs.

I make a mental note to find them warmer clothing.

Unable to discuss Hidi's death with her family yet, I instead ensure that they're settled with warm clothing, bedding, towels, and a hot meal, and retreat to my own quarters. It's a miracle I'm still standing, and as much as I want to go back outside and make sure the dragons are going to be kept somewhere safe, staying upright is no longer an option.

My fingers throb from the tight grip I held, and every muscle in my back and shoulders are aching.

I told Quirina to inform everyone that there are to be no restraints used on the dragons, and they are not to be harmed in any way. Hidi's family showed her a few commands they could use to make the dragons follow them somewhere discreet and safe for the night until we figure out what's next.

Rina is kind enough to bring me a whiskey and a plate of my favorite foods once I've showered. Gratefully I accept, but my appetite is nonexistent, so I opt for the whiskey. I drain the glass and drop my head to the pillow. It doesn't take long for it to be soaked with tears, needing to be flipped over. I'm overrun with emotion and guilt. I'm home, and while it should feel amazing, it feels wrong.

Not knowing what happened to Koen or his army. Leaving Hidi behind. None of it settles in my gut, instead stays swirling like a virus, needing to be ejected from my body. While I've only had one drink, it doesn't stay down very long. The emotion pouring out of me makes it hard to breathe, and I find myself running to the bathroom to empty my stomach. As it turns out, whiskey has the same sensation coming up as it does going down.

Quirina rubs my back while I'm hunched over the toilet, holding my hair back with the other hand. Her care is simultaneously comforting and agonizing when I feel so undeserving. My existence is cause for so much suffering, and yet I'm the one who lives. It's not right.

Once I'm back in bed and I've finally caught my breath, I see Quirina's curious gaze on me. I can't blame her. I'd have a million questions too.

"Do you want to talk about it?" She asks so gently, I'm not even sure she meant to say it out loud.

I shake my head, the tears immediately welling back up, blurring my vision. The skin under my eyes is sore and raw as I continuously wipe the tears away.

She doesn't push. "That's okay, Trix. You don't have to talk. Whenever you're ready, I'm here. I'm so sorry for everything you've been through."

Her voice cracks, and when I glance up at her, I realize she too looks like she's emotionally wrecked. The purple and red under her own eyes tell a similar story of heartache and worry. While I've been gone, life has continued, but so has the loss and devastation.

I open my mouth to speak but with all the crying and emotion, my voice is strained. Clearing my throat, I try again. "How are you doing?"

Her head bobs up and down, but I can see it's a mask.

"I don't know. Everyone is gone," she starts shakily. "My parents, my friends, my home, Nik, Koen."

The man that can't keep his eyes off of her.

I can see another emotion in her eyes.

Yearning.

She's missing Nik.

"I'm sorry I wasn't here," I say. All I do is hurt those around me. As if it's my destiny to forever be a thorn embedded into the sides of all my loved ones.

Wiping her runny nose with the side of her sleeve, she lets out a confused chuckle. "Trix, why would you apologize for that? Please don't do that. It's not your fault."

"Isn't it, though?"

Rina furrows her brows at me, and her lips turn downward. "No. It's not."

I let out a heavy sigh, and shrug into the mattress.

"I'm going to let you sleep. Do you need anything before I go?"

"No, I just want to sleep," I say, even though the night will likely be filled with self-blame and crying.

Quirina gives me a hand squeeze and a sad smile. She stands to leave, but there's a knock at the door. We exchange a look of confusion. It's late, and most everyone has gone to bed.

Walking over to the door, Rina swings it open to reveal a courtier.

"Yes?" Rina asks warily.

"The queen wanted me to inform the princess when Mr. Archer returned."

At the sound of Koen's name, I shoot up in bed, my eyes wide with disbelief. Quirina quickly looks back at me, and the relief on her face makes my heart swell. She hasn't only been worried for me.

He's back.

And since when is my mother team Koen?

The confusion rocks back and forth like a pendulum in my chest, making me queasy once again, but I think I can hold it down this time. That is, until the man continues to speak.

"And he's been injured."

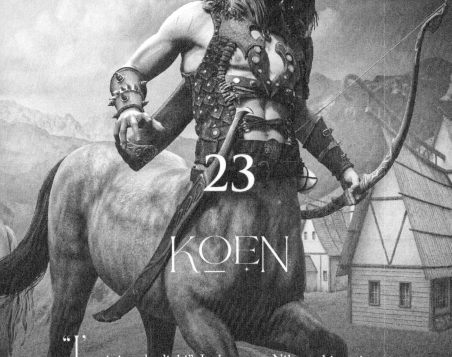

# 23

## KOEN

"I'm injured, dick!" I shout at Nik as his grip on my midsection tightens.

I can see Tenuma up ahead, and thank Gods this trip is almost over. As grateful as I am that Nik was able to get us out of Lothar's castle, it hasn't been a pleasant journey. The wound in my side is throbbing, and the grip it's been caught in likely hasn't helped.

"Take me to her!" I shout over the wind rushing past us and the flapping of the giant phoenix wings.

Uncertainty lies between me and the princess. She somehow has the notion that I have betrayed her, and now feels unsafe around me. It couldn't be further from the truth, so I need to see her. Now. The desperate need to prove her wrong is all-consuming. If it's my destiny to bleed out and die today, I need to see her one last time.

Nik dives down and then carefully lands on one clawed foot as he slowly lowers me to the ground with the one I'm clutched in. As the grip releases me, a fresh rush of pain shoots through my body, and I groan in agony.

I'm lying on the ground, clutching my side, bracing myself to walk again when it happens. I feel a blast of heat followed by a flash of light, like fire exploding to life. My neck strains to look at my friend, but now he's back to being Nik.

Taking the clothing I was carrying for him, he quickly dresses before coming to my aid.

He rushes to help me up, throwing an arm around my back and slowly lifting me up. "You doin' alright, man?"

I chuckle, and try to lighten the shit situation we're in. "Yeah, but would it have killed you not to squeeze so tight?"

His low laugh barely escapes, as if it feels wrong to laugh at a time like this. "I was trying not to drop you! Forgive a man for still getting used to his gift."

We make our way slowly across the front lawn, each step sending a surge of pain through my body. "Yeah, since when can you shift?"

He shrugs. "It just happened one day."

I think back on a conversation I had with my mother when discussing my own gift. Realizing the likely cause makes the corners of my mouth tug upwards.

"Fuck," Nik groans. "It was a lot easier to carry you in my talons."

A deep chuckle erupts from my chest, followed immediately by a shooting pain. "Aaaagh, fuck."

"Sorry, man. Let's get you inside."

The courtier's set me up in a bedroom upstairs not far from Bellatrix's bedroom. A healer was brought to my room once we were admitted inside, and I've been thoroughly cleaned and stitched up.

I had attempted to get up to find Bellatrix, desperate to talk to her and make sure she's okay, but Nik and the healer informed me that I needed to stay in bed and that Bellatrix was resting. Nik disappeared while the healer worked, and I realize he must have sent for my mother and Mel. When he returns hours later, they trail right behind.

My mom slowly approaches with a hand over her mouth, likely debating if she can stomach seeing me in this condition. Mel, however, bursts across the room and to my side. She throws herself over me, squeezing a little too tight, but it's worth all the pain.

I nuzzle into her small frame over the side of the bed, and inhale her lavender scent. "Sweet girl. I missed you so much."

Her big brown eyes are glued to an injury that's now wrapped up in gauze and tape. "What happened? Are you hurt? Are you going to die?" The questions shoot out of her, getting more panicked as they go.

I tilt her chin upwards to meet my gaze. "Hey, look at me. I'm not going to die. Okay?"

Mel nods reluctantly, like she's not sure if she believes me.

My mother approaches the other side of the bed, and lowers her hand to the injury. Immediately there's a warming sensation. My eyes travel from where we touch, to the concentration on her face. I'm not sure whether the heat is coming from her gaze or her hand.

I open my mouth to ask her what the hell she's doing, but she holds up her forefinger on the other hand, silencing me.

A few more minutes go by, and the sensation continues to intensify. I'd press her for information, but the warmth is nice. All the stories my mother told me as a child from her years as a healer and enchantress come flooding back.

Having never seen my mother use any form of magic, I don't know what to make of this. I'm certain she's trying to heal me, but is it going to work?

I don't dare make another noise until my mother is finished with what she's doing, but I do look at Mel. She stares at our mother in awe. Her beautiful brown eyes dance with excitement. She knows something amazing is taking place and soaks in the moment of silence with us.

The heat dissipates when my mother pulls her hand away, and she slips it into mine, giving it a squeeze.

"My boy," she says, caressing my face with her free hand.

"Hi, Ma."

Her sweet smile immediately relieves the tightness I've held in my muscles, and the stress I've felt for weeks is numbed. Though that could also be due to the magic she just performed on me.

"How are you feeling?" she asks.

With my opposite arm, I reach over and slightly press on the wound, assessing the pain level. "Surprisingly not bad."

While I don't feel completely better, the pain is nearly gone. I mostly feel sore and tired.

"Good."

"Did you save the princess?" Mel asks excitedly.

A shallow laugh bursts from my lips. "Sort of."

A tight smile from my mother tells me she's itching for answers but willing to wait until Mel is out of earshot. Not that I'd admit it aloud, but a small part of my pride takes a hit knowing that Bellatrix didn't need me.

"She's home safe. We made it back, and that's what's important," I say instead.

The sound of a throat clearing draws our attention to the door where Nik still stands. "I'm going to head out and give you all some privacy," he tells us with a thumb pointed over his shoulder.

"Thanks for saving my ass, man," I say, earning a dramatic gasp from Mel.

"You said *ass*," she whispers.

"Mellani," my mother warns.

Her little hands shoot in the air in defense. "I was just repeating it. How can I say what he said without saying the word?"

Sometimes I think this kid is too clever for her own good, though I can't deny it feels good to hear her being silly again. Life has been so challenging and intense lately that I'd hate for it to squander what's left of her innocence and childhood. I believe the short-lived fragility of it should be protected at all costs.

Our mother simply rolls her eyes at her. Nik chuckles, giving us a wave before exiting the room.

I realize that I came very close to never seeing my family again. Being able to sit in silence with them is a luxury I never want to take advantage of, though I am shocked to see them both here.

"I'm surprised that you felt comfortable being here with the queen," I tell my mother.

"Nothing could keep me from my son. You're hurt. A mother would never let anything stop her from showing up to protect her child."

A knock at the door has my eyes glued to the entrance with anticipation that I might see Bellatrix.

The queen appears in the doorway. I haven't seen her since I've been back, and I can only imagine what it's been like to see her daughter come home the way I saw her last.

"I don't want to interrupt. I wanted to thank you for your help, and inform you that the rest of the men have returned home," she says stiffly, her hands clasped together in front of her.

The army must have left shortly after Nik and I departed. Evidently the mission was a success all around. It's the early hours of morning, though the sun has yet to rise, and I'm feeling myself fading. My poor mother and sister should be at home resting.

I nod to the queen, unsure what to say to the woman that's repeatedly put us all in danger. Now that Bellatrix is home safe, it's time she pays the price for what she's done to her daughter.

"Do you have any news on the other part of the mission I requested?" she asks.

My jaw tightens, and I shake my head. Even if I had news of Lothar, this wouldn't be the time to discuss it with my family present.

Feeling the unwelcome atmosphere, she gives a tight smile and then shocks us all by addressing my mother. "Fira, could I speak to you for a moment?"

My gut instinct tells me this is a bad idea and I attempt to sit up.

My mother lays her arm across my chest, refusing to let me rise. "I'll be right outside."

"Mother, are you sure?"

She nods and steps outside with the queen, leaving the door cracked. Unsure whether or not they realize we can still hear them, their entire conversation leaks into the room as Mel and I listen in in silence.

"Thank you for allowing your son to help rescue Bella," Charlotte tells my mother.

Silence.

Charlotte tries again. "I wanted to apol—"

"Enough. I don't need to hear it. What is it that you really want?" my mother asks.

"How do I undo it?"

"The curse?"

Silence, and I presume an affirming nod.

"You know how. There's only one way," my mother responds.

"There has to be another way. What if—"

"Your Majesty, you were well informed what the rules of the curse were before it was cast. You made that decision, and now it's your burden to bear. I begged you to reconsider, but you refused. But it's never too late to make things right, and after everything that poor girl has been through, don't you think you owe it to her?" My mother's words make my heart ache.

There's silence for a few beats before the queen replies. "I heard what you said in there, about a mother not letting anything stop her from protecting her child."

"Just because you bear a child doesn't make you a mother. There's more to it than simply having one. Love and protection make you a mother. You haven't earned that title."

"Things weren't always like this."

"They are now. If you want to be a mother to her, fix this. Do what needs to be done."

"I'm sorry I got your family mixed up in this," the queen says quietly, and it almost sounds sincere.

"My son's intentions were always to go and find her."

"No, I mean before she was taken. I never should have requested your son personally. I wanted to be sure that you hadn't revealed our arrangement to him," the queen confesses.

There's a few more moments of silence before I hear my mother's voice again. The tone has shifted from scolding to downright terrifying. The words resemble a growl. "You hand-picked my son for that job to check if I had exposed your dirty little secret, thus exposing your cursed daughter to him?"

Every word is slow and intentional. I can't see their faces, but I know one thing for certain, my mother is livid. While we knew this was a possibility, it's just as shocking to have it confirmed.

More silence.

If she was looking for absolution, she came to the wrong place. Knowing my mother, the look on her face is as dangerous as the curses she casts. The fire in the corner of the room mimics the tension crackling around us. I hold Mel close and pray that the queen doesn't make things worse by telling my mother what she asked me to do. Coming home should be a relief, but there are enemies in our own kingdom that need to be dealt with.

# 24

# BELLATRIX

I don't want to deal with anything.

Sun shines through my bedchamber windows, and I reluctantly lift my heavy lids. I'm not sure how long I've been asleep, but it doesn't feel like it was long enough. Quirina left to check on Nik after we were informed they had returned, and I haven't seen her since. Truthfully, I haven't wanted to face anyone yet.

I turn on my back to stretch out my aching muscles. They scream back at me to stop. Aside from that, my head pounds from the crying I haven't been able to stop. There are many things I should be doing, conversations that need to be had, but I can't make myself care about any of it.

Somebody knocks on my door, and I sit up and shout for

them to enter. I hope it's Quirina with more whiskey—anything to numb the pain.

Hidi's mother and brother appear as the door swings open.

My heart rate speeds up, and my blood runs cold.

Oh Gods, I have to tell them.

"Hello," I say as they hesitate entering. "Please come in."

"I'm sorry if we woke you, I know we didn't have the opportunity for proper introductions yesterday. I'm Valeria, and this is my son Theo."

They both look so much like Hidi. Valeria has the same dark features and facial structure, while her son is taller and has a wider build. His hair has a lighter hue to it, but the nose is identical, and eye color is an exact match to Hidi's golden brown.

I clear my throat, not trusting that it won't crack when I speak. "Lovely to meet you both. I'm Bellatrix."

They both give me a knowing head nod. I swing my legs over the bed, wanting to stand face to face with them while I deliver the worst news of their lives.

As I open my mouth to speak, Valeria approaches and holds out her open hand to me. I place mine in hers.

A sad smile quivers on her lips as she speaks. "It's okay, dear, we know."

The calmness of her voice, gentle in the way a mother comforts a child, feels foreign to me. I find myself forgetting who's breaking bad news to whom. I try to keep myself from coming completely undone the way I want to.

She rubs my hand. "A mother knows."

At that, I lose all control and my head falls to her hands.

"I'm so sorry, I'm so sorry," I sob.

Wave after wave of grief rolls through my body, each one threatening to drown me for good. I don't have the strength to stop it.

"Shh," she whispers. "It's not your fault."

I expected her to cry, yell, maybe lash out at me. But not this.

"We've been planning our escape from Sperantia for a long time," she says quietly. "While we had many chances to escape before, we never had anywhere to go. Until you came along. Yes, she was trying to save you, but she was trying to save herself as well. All of us. You made escaping possible."

"I should have protected her. She should have used her invisibility, why didn't—" As I'm speaking the words aloud, I realize exactly why she didn't use her gift to disappear.

She sacrificed herself for her family.

Staying visible meant that the attention stayed on her, and not on me or her escaping family members.

The realization only forces my sobs to come out faster and even less controlled. It does nothing to lessen the blame I feel in my soul. The cause of her death falls on me, the feeling like a tattoo etched into my flesh. A permanence I can't wash away.

It's Theo who speaks next. "Please do not blame yourself, Princess. She knew what she signed up for. We all did. Death was a possibility for each of us. She sacrificed herself for years to stay close to Miri and work up a plan to save us all. I know she's at peace, seeing us all free."

How can they be so strong in the face of loss?

I can feel their sadness, but unlike me, they're not letting it crush them. They stand atop of it, like a rock jutting out from the sea, refusing to be taken under by the wave.

My sobs begin to ebb, and I wipe my face dry with my fingertips. "Is there anything I can do for either of you?"

They both shake their heads.

"You've done more than enough. We're not sure where to go from here, but we won't stay long," Valeria tells me.

I shake my head at them. "No, please stay. I want you to. We have more than enough room. I owe you that much."

Reluctantly, they look at each other, but then give me a gracious nod and leave me to my thoughts again.

I pad over to the windows. The light dusting of snow Tenuma received last night creates a view that never fails to leave me in awe. Being alone and secluded to one room in a castle should be the last thing I want, but right now it feels like the one thing I need. Everything outside seems so unsure, so foreign. My bedchambers are the only comfort I have left.

I lift a hand and rest it on the window when I notice a small fleck of red on my wrist. A speckle of blood that refused to be washed off in even the hottest of water last night. A not-so-subtle reminder that yesterday can never be erased and will always be a part of me.

I'm a killer.

I yank my hand back down and cover it with my other. As if concealing the spot changes anything. For now, I'll hide in my bubble and pretend that this has all been a nightmare.

"Bella," a quiet voice pulls me from my mental turmoil.

Speaking of nightmares.

I spin around to find my mother slowly entering the room. Her black suede corset dress hugs her body, and the small beads on the end of the long train trails behind, the small beads on the end making an agitating scrape against the floor with each step she takes. Her hair hangs in one long braid swung to the side over her shoulder, and I notice the absence of her crown. The look on her face is hard to decipher, but it's something akin to shame.

"Mother," I reply emotionlessly.

"How are you doing?"

I shrug and cross my arms over my chest.

"I wanted to check on you before, but I wanted you to get

some rest."

Pulling my lips inward, I contemplate how to respond.

"I'm fine," I lie.

She takes a step towards me, and her arm reaches out as if to touch me, but she pulls back. "I've been so worried about you."

*Then why did it take so long to send help?*

"Well, I'm back now. And I'm fine," I lie again.

Her eyebrows pull together. She looks sad, hurt, confused. "I wanted to wait, but there's something you should know."

"What is it?"

I watch her take a deep breath, preparing for what's about to leave her mouth, and my stomach somersaults anticipating bad news.

"Maybe you should sit," she offers, extending a hand towards my bed.

The tangle of sheets and blankets tell a tale of a restless night filled with bad dreams that mimicked a worse reality.

Taking a seat on the edge of the messy bed, my mother joins and takes my hand in hers. I reluctantly let her. "While you were gone, we lost your father."

I let the words sink in, letting them feel their way around, searching for an emotion to latch onto. It's before I know what I'm feeling that the tears begin to fall. My lips quiver, and I pull my hands to my face. The tears keep coming from somewhere deep inside. From a time when I felt like my father's daughter, and not a pawn in a political game.

"I'm so sorry, sweetie." My mother's tenderness surprises me, and only stirs more emotion. For the first time in a long time, when I need her to show up for me, she actually does.

"That doesn't feel the way I thought it would," I reply honestly.

Knowing he was sick made death feel inevitable. But with the decay of my relationship with my father, I never expected to feel the devastation that's currently coursing through me.

My mother pulls her hand back, and when I glance up at her, she appears upset, and not for her own loss. She looks upset *for* me.

"I can't talk about this right now. Please just leave me alone. This is all just— it's too much." My emotions start to bubble and boil over the edges. "You couldn't have waited to drop this on me?"

She has the nerve to look wounded. "Now that you've returned, there's a lot to sort out. Finding you a king, your crowning ceremony, and what to do about Sperantia and those dragons."

"What does that matter right now?" I ask, irritated.

"With your father gone, and the dragons in our possession, Lothar will be looking to attack."

"Lothar is dead."

"W-what? He's dead? How?" she asks, her face turning a ghostly shade of white.

"What does any of this matter right now?" I shout at her. "I've been back less than a day, and already you're hounding me to find a king. I won't sacrifice my body for one more night for the sake of this kingdom. Those days are gone."

"What about our family's lineage? We must ensure we remain in power."

"You're joking, right? I don't care about lineage, because it sure as hell doesn't care about me. So, get the fuck out and stop pretending you ever gave a damn about me!"

Screaming at her won't change anything, but for now it serves as a balm over my emotional wounds. It helps to relieve some of the pressure that needs to be expelled. The anger feels good. Instead of reeling it back in like I normally would, I lean into it.

Grabbing the empty whiskey glass off my bedside table, I fling it at my oval vanity mirror, smashing it to a million pieces while my mother watches on in silent horror. The glass cascades to the floor like confetti decorating the room, signifying the celebration of a new me. Someone who is unwilling to please her or anybody else. That bridge was burned when she lied to me about what my curse actually was. I thought if I kept doing what I was told that eventually I'd earn the respect and love of my parents, but that was an illusion I created in my mind.

My mother looks at me like I'm a stranger standing in her home, and she's right. To her, I am a stranger. Someone she never knew or cared to know. The daughter she sent to the wolves to protect herself.

I stare back at my mother in defiance, with the only thought I've had since she told me about my father dancing on my tongue.

"It should have been you."

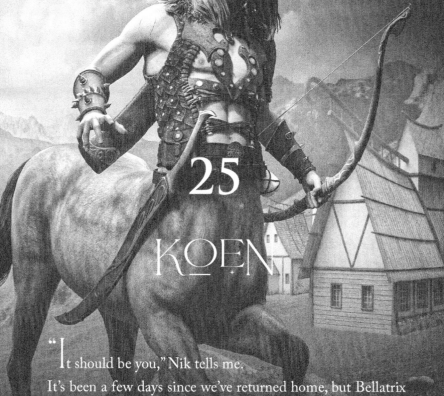

# 25

## KOEN

"It should be you," Nik tells me.

It's been a few days since we've returned home, but Bellatrix has refused to leave her room or see anybody. Being with her is all I can think about, and I can't stop wondering how she's doing. How she's *really* doing. Is it me she's avoiding, or people in general?

"Koen, hello?" Nik snaps his fingers in front of my face, pulling me out of the thoughts swirling in my mind.

I'm still recovering, but needing to escape the growing tension in the castle, Nik and I are walking through the rose garden out front.

The thin layer of snow squeals under our boots as we make our way through the untouched ground. The very same place I first saw the princess express the way she felt about me.

I shake my head in frustration. "She won't see me. What am I supposed to do?"

"You've been hovering outside her door for days. She needed

time to decompress, but I think it's time go to her."

Quirina made it clear that Bellatrix wanted to be alone. She's within reach, but hurting and refusing talking to anybody.

My family went back to the cottage a few days ago. I know my mother was uncomfortable being here. Poor Mellani was so eager to see Bellatrix, it was difficult to disappoint her when I told her no. Right now, she's not the *tattoo lady* she knew from before the attack. We've all changed, the princess most of all.

"Her mother is already asking Bellatrix about who she wants as king," Nik asks.

Of course she is. I scoff. "All that woman cares about is getting Bellatrix to the throne and making sure her family stays in power."

Nik's mouth forms a thin line. "Do you think that you'll be the one to rule with her?"

Becoming the king of Tenuma has never been on my radar. It was never something I aspired to be. Though, now that I know Bellatrix is my True Mate, I might not have a choice in the matter.

Could a working man from the village really be worthy of becoming king?

I shrug. "I'm not sure. There's a lot on her plate. So I'm sure this isn't her priority right now. Sperantia is probably planning a counterattack as we speak."

"Unlikely," Nik says under his breath.

I turn to face Nik. "Why do you say that?"

He rubs the back of his neck anxiously like he didn't mean to say that out loud.

"I mean they're probably just in recovery mode. We have their dragons." He attempts to give a half-assed answer, but I'm not buying it.

"Don't pull that shit. Tell me."

He glances around. "I shouldn't say anything. Go talk to

Bellatrix—you should hear it from her."

"Hear *what*?"

Nik sighs heavily. "The princess killed Lothar. That's why she was covered in blood. It was his." "He's dead?"

He nods.

"How do you know?" I ask.

"Quirina told me. Bellatrix told her."

"Oh," I say quietly, wrapping my head around the new information.

"Are you alright? I wasn't hiding it, but I didn't think it was my place to tell you."

"Yeah, I'm… it's fine." I say, but I don't know if that's true or not.

Though there's enough reason to hate my father, it doesn't replace the parts that tied us together. The flicker of affection for the father he was, for the father he could be, in the off chance that the man I once knew returns, is now forever extinguished. "Fuck, I need to see her. This must be killing her."

No wonder she's been reluctant to see me.

This must be weighing heavily on her. Likely she assumes I'll be angry with her for killing my father. The truth is, I don't care what she's done. She did what she had to do to survive. I would never condemn her for that.

"What are you going to say to her?" Nik asks.

"I'm not sure, but I need to see her. She needs to know that nothing she did was wrong."

Racing out of the flower garden and through the entrance to the castle, I climb the large staircase two at a time, and pray to the Gods that she lets me in. But one question suddenly nags at me.

If the king is dead, does that make me next in line for the throne of Sperantia?

The noise of three strong raps on the princess's door settles into the hallway. I press my ear to the door for any sounds of life. No footsteps, no shouts to enter.

She could be sleeping.

I debate knocking again, the urge to comfort her becoming too much to bear. I can't pretend to know what she's gone through, but I can be here for her. Letting her suffer on her own isn't something I can stomach any longer.

"Princess," I call.

After what feels like an eternity, footsteps sound on the other side of the door. Hesitation, and then the door slowly swings open.

My reflexes have me smiling at her like a moron at the sight of her, but I'm met with a blank stare. Her eyes are swollen, her face is puffy, and her cheeks are red. The silky black hair that usually cascades freely down her back is tied up in a messy knot on top of her head. She's dressed in a simple black silk knee-length nightie, with a black floral robe that's untied and hangs open.

My smile fades. Like a rose, she's still beautiful, but she looks withered and neglected. I ache to reach out and touch her, hold her, but something tells me I shouldn't.

"Is it okay that I'm here?" I ask softly.

I wait, thinking she'll reply, invite me in, or kick me out. Instead, she just leaves the door cracked open and walks to the other side of the room. Following behind, I close the door with a careful click.

The room is littered with empty drinkware on her bedside table. Her bed is a mess of tangled sheets, and glittering shards of broken glass are strewn about the floor.

What the hell happened here?

"I wanted to come see you sooner, but Quirina said it might not be the best idea."

A humorless laugh sounds while she gazes out the window.

"Can I get you anything?" I ask.

I watch the back of her head as she shakes it.

Taking a chance I stride over and stand next to her at the window. "Princess. Will you tell me what happened? Did I do something wrong?"

Her head slowly turns to me, like she's scared to look at me. Her eyes meet mine, glossy and overfilled with an emotion I can't quite read. "Your father told me that you helped him. That you were using me all along."

"Oh Gods, Princess, no. I would never do that." I lift my arm, my fingers itching to touch her, but lower it when she steps out of reach.

The water in her eyes spill over her lash line and she quickly wipes them away. "I was isolated for weeks in that room. I never thought I'd leave. When I saw you at the castle that day... I didn't know what to believe."

No wonder she wasn't happy to see me.

"I don't know why he would say that. You know me, my family. I would never, ever do that. That's not the kind of man I am."

She crosses her arms, and the sleeves of her robe cinching up with it. On her wrists I see dark red and purple bruising around her wrists, along with multiple cuts along her arms. Her eyes travel to where my eyes are glued in horror. She quickly unfolds her arms and pulls the fabric back down.

"Koen, why are you here?" Her words are harsh, but at least

she's talking. I'd rather be cut by her words, than die by her silence.

"I wanted to see if you were okay."

She releases an irritated sigh. "Go ahead, ask. Everyone wants to know what happened to me. Do you want to know if anyone touched me in Sperantia, Koen?"

After learning about Charlotte's arrangement with Lothar, I'm fairly certain that multiple people had their grimy hands on her.

Before I can respond, the princess starts pacing around the room, like she's being led by her rage. "Go ahead, ask me!" Her words turn into shouts as she continues her pacing, her bare feet crossing over a path of broken glass. She doesn't flinch. If she feels any pain, I can't tell.

"Princess," I say gently, not wanting to fan the flames.

"Are you jealous, Koen? Are you here to tell me what I should do with my body?" She begins to strip her clothes off.

She's falling to pieces in front of me, and all I can do is watch. Her feet are bleeding and she's completely naked. My princess, stripped down to nothing but her anger. There's more bruising on her thighs and breasts. Each one tells a story of the hell she endured. Stories she might never be able to talk about.

"Go ahead, take a look!" she shouts, her arms held wide open.

I've never felt so helpless.

I avert my eyes. It doesn't feel right to look at her, not like this. "Princess, your feet. Let's sit down so we can get the glass out of your feet."

"I don't need your help, Koen. Not back in Sperantia, not now!"

Her words hit me right in the chest. I'd take the injury I got from Sperantia's army repeatedly if I never had to hear those words out of her mouth.

I meet her wild gaze. "Princess, I was there. I came to save you."

"I didn't need you to save me!" she shrieks, and then lowers her voice. "I always wanted a man who was willing to risk everything to save me, but what I wanted more was to be a woman who didn't need saving."

She didn't need me.

"I'm sorry I wasn't there sooner," I tell her. "I wanted to be."

"Do you have any idea what it was like to know that others were risking their lives for me? *Me*. I have caused so much agony already in one lifetime. Tenuma was attacked because of me, and then Lothar took me, and I knew you would be looking for me. I knew you would risk your life for me. Do you know what that felt like? The guilt that ate away at me every single day? Until I had a conversation with your father, of course, and he told me you were working with him."

Fuck, she blames herself for all of it.

"Bellatrix, first of all, that man is not my father. He didn't even have that name when I knew him. I'm sorry that he planted doubt in your mind about us. I'm not upset that you killed him, and I would have never collaborated with him and used you in that way. I'm sorry for everything you went through. Not just in Sperantia, but here at home too."

She sucks in a breath that lets me know that her adrenaline is wearing off and she's starting to feel the glass stuck in her feet. Shifting her weight from one foot to the other, she still won't meet my gaze, either out of anger, frustration, or embarrassment, I'm not sure. I'd venture to say all of the above, since she's still fully naked.

Angry, and splitting at the seams, she's still the only woman I could ever want.

She turns away from me, and I take it as my cue to leave. While a part of me knows she wants to be alone to recover from her outburst, I never want her to hide from herself or me. I want every version of her. I'll be the light to outlast all her darkness.

I walk away from her, but instead of leaving, I make my way to her bathroom and turn on the warm water. She expects me to leave her, betray her like everyone else has, but I'm here to show her that I never will.

# 26

# BELLATRIX

I expected to hear a door slamming shut, but instead hear the sound of water running. I twist around to see hot steam wafting out of the washroom, and Koen emerging through the cloud.

He's drawing a bath for me?

He extends his hand out for me to take. All I can do is stare.

Pleading eyes ask me for a chance. "You're bleeding. Let me help you."

My feet are beginning to throb and I can feel blood pooling under my feet, but I can't bring myself to assess the damage. I want to let him in, but I'm not ready to. Do I really think he is to blame for what I went through? No. But I'm still trying to make sense of everything, and until I do, I'm not sure it's smart to have him around clouding my judgment.

"I'd like you to leave," I say, folding my arm under my bare chest.

His shoulders slump, and his lips pull downward. It's not the response he was expecting, but I can't give him what he wants right now.

"Trix, is everything okay?" Quirina peeks around my door, attempting to assess the situation. Her eyes go wide when they land on my naked body and bloody feet. She rushes to my side and tosses a blanket over my shoulders.

"What the hell, Koen?" Her accusatory voice unfreezes the tension keeping us still.

Standing in the bathroom doorway he gives her an incredulous look, throwing both hands up.

"Whoa, I just came here hoping to talk."

Quirina has her arm around my shoulders, rubbing softly. "I know you mean well, but I think it's time to go."

"But—" he starts, but I cut him off.

"Get out! You're not who I want to talk to. She's gone! She's gone!" I'm shouting, as Quirina rubs my back and shoulders trying to calm me, but it's no use. Emotion spills over like angry lava. I can't keep being held hostage to men who refuse to hear what I need.

I feel like I've been broken open, all my ugly parts seeping out, bleeding on everyone around me. Hidi's death is the one thought I can't shake.

"Koen, you need to leave. Now," Quirina tells him firmly, and without waiting for his exit, she leads me to the bathroom, carefully avoiding the broken glass.

"I'm going, but I'll be right here if you need me. I don't scare that easily, Princess. I'm not going anywhere," Koen calls over the running water.

All he's trying to do is help, to comfort me. But how can I let him near me when anybody that does is destined to get hurt? It's better for us both if he forgets all about me.

I fall to the washroom floor, my inconsolable wails no doubt terrifying Rina, when I can't stop myself from repeating the same mantra. "She's gone. She's gone. She's gone."

Desperate wails combine with pained sobs that I can't hold back. My personal grief chant.

"Shhhh, it's okay," Rina whispers, holding me close.

Shaking my head, the pain floods me. Grief, the relentless bitch, suffocates me as I try to take breaths between sobs.

"Trix, who are you talking about?" she asks gently.

"I couldn't save her. It should have been me!"

As I glance up at Quirina, the look on her face is nothing short of horror. I know I'm scaring her, yet I can't stop. I don't care that I'm scaring everybody. I'm scared every day.

Who will be hurt next because of me?

How can I let anybody close to me when I'm destined to harm them?

"Talk to me, Trix."

I wish I could.

Quirina holds me until my sobs slow enough that she can get me cleaned up and into the bath. I don't know what I did in this lifetime to find a friend like her. I don't deserve her. She's been through enough on her own, and yet here she is, holding me together. Just like Hidi did. The tears start flowing again.

The setting sun turns the sky a bright orange, signaling another snowstorm on its way into Tenuma. The frigid air bites my skin, but I don't mind. It makes me feel alive.

It's been about a week since I returned to Tenuma, and a few days since I've seen Koen. He went home the day after our conversation, which was probably for the best. I've been closed up inside the castle long enough, and I've been anxious to see the dragons, Miri especially. Quirina has been taking the lead on their safety, making sure they've been fed and treated well.

Today, I finally pulled myself together and assured Quirina it was safe to leave me alone. She told me she'd be back later with dinner, so I figured it was a good time to check on Miri.

Exiting through the back of the castle, I'm stunned to find most of the dragons are still present.

They are free to go where they choose, and yet they seem to be meandering around like dogs in a yard.

It should be terrifying to see these giant animals moving about, but I know I don't have to fear them.

Animals are far less harmful than humans are.

Miri sits at the far end of the open space, just before the strip of trees that lead into the forest. I don't know how I'd categorize her current state, but she seems to be curled into herself. She looks peaceful, yet sad. The brilliance of her color is still just as shocking to me, as is the coloring of her eyes.

Slowly as not to startle any of the dragons, I pass through the herd making my way over to where Miri sits. Her eyes track my movement, though she doesn't shift her position as I get closer. If she's bothered by my presence, she doesn't show it.

Once I'm standing in front of her, I raise a hand to caress the rough flesh of her leg. "Hi, girl. How are you doing?"

My question is met with a huff.

I sigh softly. "Yeah, me too. I wanted to thank you for getting me home. You saved me, Miri."

She tilts her head down so we're looking right at each other. The way her eyes glisten and shift, it feels like she really sees me. I can see her pain, and I know she can see mine. Kindred souls navigating through their grief.

Miri's head dips down, nudging me with her nose. The affection makes me smile, and I lean into her, gently wrapping my arms around her face. For the next few minutes, we simply sit together. Miri lets me hold onto her, pulling her close. The desperation to feel close to Hidi has us both leaning on our last connection to her. I only let go when I hear someone approaching us.

Theo walks towards us, offering a warm, sad smile when our eyes meet.

"Princess," he greets as he approaches.

"Please, call me Bellatrix."

The title feels even more insignificant than it usually does. Maybe once I'm able to protect my friends and family, I'll feel worthy of it.

He nods. "Bellatrix."

"She's beautiful," I say, gazing up at Miri. "Hidi said you found her together when you were both kids?"

He winces at his sister's name, and I instantly regret saying it.

"We did. I couldn't believe what we were seeing. She was just this little thing—well, little compared to what she is now," he says. "She was all alone, and made us feel like we were dreaming. Hidi said it was a miracle. She's the one that named her."

His eyes glaze over as he retells the memories of his sister and Miri, a smile dancing on his lips.

"Life was so harsh for a very long time. Greedy rulers left very little for the rest of us. We were frequently told stories of the dragons and what their return could mean."

"What does it mean?"

"It's been said that the dragons would return during a time of great change. When they came back, there was to be a power shift, an end to the suffering. Hidi was so optimistic. She looked at Miri as a new beginning. But for years, nothing happened. And then things got worse when Lothar took over the throne a few years ago."

A full body shudder runs the length of my body at the mention of the man that violated and kept me captive, but I stay silent, eager to hear the rest of Theo's story.

"The king was ruthless, cruel. We tried to keep Miri a secret the best we could. We knew she would be in danger if the king found her." He pauses, reigning in the building emotion. "We were right. She was found and taken. They wanted to make her submissive, and then break her. Hidi was their way to do that."

The story is hard to listen to a second time. "That's awful."

Theo gives me a sad smile. "It was. But then you came along, and Hidi's faith in the stories about the dragons' return was renewed. She said you were the key. It's why she was so eager to save you. She believed change was in your hands."

Why me?

What did she see in me?

"I'm not sure what I could have done or said to make her think I could change anything. There's nothing special about me. I don't save people. I end up hurting them."

His brows furrow together, then soften. "You saved us. Took us in."

I shrug.

"No ruler in my homeland would have done so. Don't discredit what you've already done for us."

I'm not ready to feel good about anything I've done. It hurts too much to feel good when I'm in pain and when so many others are struggling. I want to believe what he's saying, but I don't allow the words to penetrate. Don't allow them to fester inside my mind, for fear of them turning into anything other than the dark sludge of misery I've been accustomed to.

Miri nudges her nose in the direction of her old friend, so I stand back watching the sweetness of their interaction. A bittersweet reunion. An entire conversation passes between them without a single word.

Theo scratches the top of Miri's nose, and she closes her eyes, letting herself enjoy the feeling. A soft noise sounds deep in her throat, akin to the approving purr of a cat. She looks serene. Safe. When I glance down to Theo, I realize he's crying.

The tears fall silently down his cheeks, as he comforts Miri. Seeing him this way makes my own eyes water. My voice breaks the silence. "I don't know what I'm supposed to do. I don't want to let your sister down."

He wipes away the wetness on his cheeks and lays his head on Miri. When he pulls back to face me, he looks so much like Hidi I can't help but pull him in for a hug. At first, he doesn't return the embrace, but after a moment I feel his arms wrap around me. The awkwardness of being strangers melts away.

It's a desperate kind of embrace, and I wonder if he will let himself go and allow himself to really feel her loss. I've checked in on him and his mother a few times, and they always seem so upbeat. He portrays such impressive strength, but a person can only outrun grief for so long.

I've been hiding out thinking I can ignore mine, but am quickly reminded of the issues still plaguing my reality when Koen shows up and rips us apart.

# 27

# KOEN

I rip him off of Bellatrix, shoving him away from her.

"Get the fuck off her!" My angered voice slices through the quiet area, ricocheting off Bellatrix and the man touching her.

I've gotten a glimpse of the wounds inflicted upon her when she was away, and the last thing she needs is another man putting his hands all over her.

The man immediately stumbles backwards, confused by the encounter.

My face feels hot, like flames licking up my face. But Bellatrix steps in front of him, a barrier between me and the man.

"What the hell are you doing?" she yells.

"He had his hands on you!" I shout back.

"We were hugging. This is Hidi's brother, Theo. I do not need you to save me, Koen." Each word is enunciated to be sure I receive the message clearly.

I can't help the wounded look I give her. The need to protect her and pull her close is overwhelming. I lost her once before; I can't lose her again. But the harder I try to hold on, the quicker she's slipping away.

Theo stands awkwardly behind her and throws his hands up peacefully, stepping around her.

"Sorry for the misunderstanding. I'm going to head inside and check on my mom."

We watch as Theo quickly removes himself from the situation unfolding. Once he's far enough away, Bellatrix turns her attention back to me. "What the hell is your problem?"

"I'm sorry. I misread the situation and panicked."

"Why are you so insistent on 'saving' me?"

"Because it's all I can offer you! I can never offer you power, money, security. But at the very least I should be able to keep you safe."

Bellatrix's face softens. She closes the distance between us and takes my hands in hers. "Koen, I don't need any of that from you. I never did."

The sudden affection tugs me closer to her. It's the most I've gotten from her since our return, and I want to cherish every second of this. With my thumb, I trace circles on the side of her hand.

"If I could have gotten to you sooner, I would have, Princess."

"I know."

"And I was never working with Lothar or Sperantia, I promise," I say desperately.

Her eyes study my face, like she's looking for the man she knew before the attack. Before she was taken. "I know that too. I just… I just need some time, Koen."

I finally have her in front of me talking, and I find myself wanting to scream, "But you're my True Mate!" But at the risk of scaring her back into hiding, I decide to keep it to myself for now.

Forcing a smile, I nod while we stand together, hands still intertwined. There's so much to say, but for now, just being with her is enough.

A snort bursts out of the large white dragon we're standing in front of. Bellatrix smiles, dropping my hands to caress the dragon like it's her pet. She's comfortable around these animals. I can't say the same for myself, and I don't think they'd appreciate knowing I killed their brothers and sisters. But I can't deny the beauty of this one, with the striking color of its eyes, and the way its white flesh blends in with the snow covering Tenuma.

"It's a beautiful dragon," I say, glancing up at the animal.

"She. Her name is Miri."

"Miri," I echo.

"She belonged to my friend Hidi before..." She trails off when her voice cracks. "Well, she's here now, and I want to give her a good life."

My sweet princess is always trying to take care of others.

"I know you will," I tell her.

She looks up and smiles at me. Unfortunately it doesn't reach her eyes. It's a polite smile, but not a real one.

"Look, I'm sorry about what happened before, with your friend. I shouldn't have—"

"I think I just need some time to process everything. My father's gone, and I killed yours, so that means both kingdoms are without a king. I don't know how I'm supposed to take the throne and lead Tenuma."

"I'm here for whatever you need. If I can do anything to make things easier for you, please let me know."

"Thank you, Koen. I have a lot of big decisions to make." Her voice is laced with uncertainty, and I fear that it's only applicable to me.

"I'm sure your mother will be more than happy to handle

things until you're ready to," I tell her, knowing how much Charlotte loves being in control.

One side of her mouth lifts into a sarcastic grin. "Yeah, I'm sure she would."

"I'll let you and Miri have some time together."

Miri coos in approval, and I try not to take it personally.

"Thanks, Koen."

I turn to leave, but Bellatrix calls after me. "Don't be a stranger," she tells me with a warm smile, and it feels like hope.

As I make my way back to the castle, weaving through the hoard of dragons that rest calmly together on the castle ground, I glance back at the princess. The smile she's giving Miri can be seen from afar, and it suddenly occurs to me how much has changed. She might feel lost and broken, but when I look at her all I see is how strong she is. The fact that she can still smile after what she's had to endure shows me that. Everything has changed since the attack on our kingdom, and while there's plenty left to repair and figure out, I feel confident that Bellatrix is well on her way to becoming the strong queen she aspires to be, whether or not she sees it yet.

"Is she talking to you again?" Quirina asks, catching me off guard as I exit the front entrance of the castle.

I glance to my right where she's sitting on a bench, head tilted upwards with her eyes shut. She's soaking up the sun while it's out. With Tenuma's unpredictable weather, one has to take advantage while they can. Since she no longer works here, she's able to enjoy the property without waiting on everybody inside. Being the princess's best friend definitely has its perks.

"Not really," I say, coming to stand beside her, resting a hand on the top of the bench.

"She'll come around. You mean a lot to her."

An huff forces its way out of me before I can stop it. "I'm not so sure anymore. I can't seem to say the right thing to her."

Quirina opens her eyes to really look at me. "You're caught up in all of the words you can offer her. But you can't fix this. Stop trying. Just be there for her. What she needs is to know she's not alone."

"I'm pretty sure being alone is exactly what she wants," I tell her, running my hands through my hair.

She rolls her eyes, giving me an exasperated look. "Look, we've all been through a lot, her more so than anyone. On top of it, she blames herself for what's happened to us all. She's coping the best way she can, but she doesn't want to be alone."

How can I be there for her when she's pushing me away?

As if reading my mind, Quirina continues, "You show up every day. Show up. Be there for her, but for the love of Gods, keep your damn mouth shut."

We both chuckle, knowing she's absolutely right. "When did you become so wise, Quirina? Wasn't it just yesterday that I was walking your drunk ass home when you were upset about some other guy?"

"Gee, thanks for bringing that up," she says with another smiling eye roll.

"You might be right about me keeping my mouth shut," I joke back.

Her tone turns serious. "What do you think is going to happen with them? The daemons?"

I realize I have absolutely no idea. "I wish I knew. But I'm sure we'll find out soon enough."

As the words leave my mouth, I don't know if they're comforting or distressing. Sometimes we're better off not knowing, so we can still believe any outcome we want. Knowing eliminates them all, forcing us to face reality.

Will the daemons return to their human forms? Or will they be forced to continue fighting a war they didn't agree to for eternity?

"What if they come back?" she asks, and I know she's wondering about her ex.

I won't look forward to walking among all the men the princess has had sex with.

It will be hard to see them and not want to beat their faces in, knowing they had their grimy hands all over her for their own selfish desires.

"We'll have to wait and find out. Something tells me you wouldn't even notice if Edwin came back around."

Her eyebrows cinch, and the corners of her mouth twitch as she tries to hide a growing smile.

"What do you mean? Of course I would notice. But he's an asshole so I wouldn't care, if that's what you mean."

Pursing my lips, I give her a knowing look. "Come on. Nik's gift is a dead giveaway."

Genuine surprise slips over the playful demeanor she just had. "What do you mean? What about his gift?"

I hesitate telling her, until she flicks her wrist impatiently urging me to speak, and I realize she isn't going to let me leave until I tell her. "My mother told me that gifts only present themselves once the person has met their True Mate."

Quirina sits back against the bench in shock.

"Are you okay?" I ask her when she doesn't reply.

The look on her face tells me she's somewhere far away, lost in thought. I wave a hand in front of her face.

She jerks back to the present. "Sorry. I, uh, I've heard the tales, but the thought of that never crossed my mind."

Laughing, I try to ease the shock. "For what it's worth, I had a similar reaction when my mother told me Bellatrix and I were mates."

"Do you think it's true?"

"I think it's hard to deny the way we're drawn to each other. The fact that my gift showed up when I was in her presence. Hell, I didn't even know I had a gift up until that point. So yes, I do think we're mates. I think aside from all of that, It's clear how different I feel with her."

"You never really were much of a dater, Mr. Archer," she says playfully.

"No, I guess not. There was never a woman who took my breath away like Bellatrix does. I tried to keep my distance from her, but somehow, we always ended up back together. It feels like I've been waiting for her all this time." Like two magnets trying to go in different directions, only to be pulled back into each other's orbit.

"Koen the heartbreaker. I would watch women throw themselves at you at Nik's bar night after night. You never did look at a single one of them the way you look at Bellatrix," she says, making my chest squeeze.

It's easy to forget that when you have an attraction as strong as the one between me and Bellatrix that others pick up on those things too. We were fools to think our families would never find out.

"It's hard to look at her the same way I look at others, when they can't compare to her," I reply honestly. Whatever happens between us, I know I'll always feel this way.

Quirina gives me a knowing look that tells me she's becoming very familiar with the feeling.

"Hey, you want to get a drink at Nik's with me?"

I like the sound of being able to go to my friend's bar again. Life may not be back to what we considered normal before the attack, but slowly we're rebuilding and repairing our lives. Piece by piece we will get it all back.

# 28

# BELLATRIX

I want it back.

My sense of security, and most of all privacy. Closed behind my bathroom door shouldn't feel as nerve-racking as it is. I can't help but fear there's a slimy guard outside waiting to get in. When I close my eyes, I often forget that I'm home in Tenuma where those men can no longer touch me. The nightmares that wake me in the middle of the night refuse to let me forget what happened, widening the tears in my soul that nobody but me can see. All my life I've been expected to give others pieces of me. The only thing I really want is my body to myself.

So, after spending days in my bedroom wallowing, I made the decision to begin combat training to overcome the helplessness I've felt. The man I've hired is a tank. He's exactly what I need to gain back my confidence, and learn the skills I'll need when we come face to face with Sperantia again.

Today was my first session with him, and after an hour and a half of grueling training, I stink and desperately need to wash up. The bathtub is calling me, and I cannot wait to sink beneath the water with my wine. I start the water in my oversized tub, letting it heat up before I plug in the stopper. Stripping my dirty clothes off of me, I kick them to the side and then stand in front of the mirror to assess the bruising. The bruises are beginning to finally fade, but serve as a reminder that my time in Sperantia was real.

I climb in the warm, inviting water when I realize that I left my glass of wine on the bedside table. I throw on my silk robe and pad over to grab it when I hear knocking at my door.

The tub is only about half full so I let the water keep running and make my way towards the door. Swinging it open, I see a tall handsome man. One that still gives me butterflies despite all of my reservations. The rift between us has been slowly mending, and though I have my guard up, he still continues to show up.

Koen stands in front of me with an abashed expression. "Hi, Princess."

"Hi."

"This is for you," he says, offering me a single red rose.

"Thank you."

He smiles as I take the rose from his hand. " Can I come in and talk?"

I glance back at my bathtub that's still filling. "Umm, I was about to wash up."

"Oh, okay." His face falls. I can't help but feel for him. My outbursts towards him weren't his fault, but they weren't mine either. It's a tough position for us both to be in, when we had such an intense chemistry before his father got in the way.

"It's okay, come in. Let me turn the water off." I wave my

hand, inviting him inside. I turn around, place the rose on my vanity, and walk over to turn off the faucet.

When I join him back in the bedroom, he's standing awkwardly in the center of the room. He's wearing dark pants, his work boots, and a black long-sleeve shirt that hugs his rippling muscles. I can't deny that he's a gorgeous man.

I take a few steps towards him, leaving just a few feet between us. "What did you want to talk about?"

"I wanted to see if you needed anything. If you wanted to talk, or anything. I'm not very good at this, but…it feels like you're slipping away again."

His confession makes my heart ache. Koen has a heart of gold. I feel stupid to have ever believed Lothar, to even imagine that Koen would have ever hurt me. "I'm right here."

"Are you though?" he asks slowly.

"I'm trying my best, Koen."

"I know you are. I don't pretend to know what you've been through, Princess. Whatever happened, I know it was awful. Please don't think that I'm expecting anything from you, or expecting you to be anything. All I want is to be there for you, and you won't let me in."

I *want* to let him in. If only it were that easy. He's a good man, and I don't want to hurt him. But us being together might not be an option anymore. I don't know what was done to me when his father drugged me, and my vague memories have me absentmindedly rubbing at the abrasions on my wrists from the restraints I wore for so long. Unfortunately it draws Koen's eyes downward too.

With a tense jaw and misty eyes, he takes a step forward.

I squeeze my lips together, unsure what to say. Unsure what I want. He takes another step forward, closing the distance between us and gently taking my wrist in his hands. His thumb rubs softly over the bruised flesh. "Is this okay?"

I nod with bleary eyes.

My skin tingles under his touch. Everything I remember feeling in his presence returns. The lust, the longing, how he feels absolutely right. But my mind betrays me, showing me flashes of Sperantia men coming towards me. I can almost feel their hands on me, as if my subconscious remembers things I don't.

My bedroom door squeaks, and my mother pokes her head inside. "Bella, I wanted to ask you a question. Oh," she says, her face turning into a scowl once she sees Koen next to me.

"I'm busy right now, but I'll be out shortly," I tell my mother, averting my gaze so she can't see my watery eyes. My mother has been making an effort to show up and be attentive. She doesn't always say the right thing, but I can see that she's trying. It doesn't make up for the way she's treated me, but I can't discount her efforts. I will always be her daughter, and like it or not, I can't shut off my love for her.

My mother gives me a tense nod and leaves, shutting the door. Koen is glaring at the door even after she's left.

I shake my head, taking a step backwards, our hands falling between us. "I can't. I need time."

"I know, Princess. I'm so fucking sorry for everything." His voice is thick, strained with grief.

Tears cascade down my cheeks. He hasn't done anything except try to be here for me. I know he means well. "I'm sorry I doubted you."

His shoulders instantly relax the moment the words leave my mouth, and I can see the relief it's given him. "It's okay. None of that matters."

"It should have been said sooner."

"It's okay."

I shake my head. "It's not. None of this is okay."

"You're right."

The tears continue to stream down my face, so Koen lifts a hand and gently wipes them away with his thumb. Each touch sends a tingle through my body.

"What do you need, Princess? Is there anything I can do?"

I chew on my lip, unsure of what to say. There's so much I wish he could do. Save me before his father had the chance to put his disgusting hands on me. Erase every memory I have of waking up the mornings after Lothar came to my bedchambers. Make it so I never have to remember anything about Lothar. I can't seem to scrub him off of me, no matter how hard I try. Lothar's scent seems to be a permanent resident in my nostrils. Most of all, I wish Koen could turn back time and bring Hidi back. Everything I want and need are things that he could never give me. As I stare into his desperate gaze, I can see that he'd give anything to take any of my pain away.

I shake my head.

"I will always be here for you. Things are hard right now, but I'm not running away. There's nothing you could ever show me that will make me walk away, Princess. You're it for me. When you're ready, I'll be waiting for you." He leans forward, planting a soft kiss on my cheek.

His words are perfect. They're everything I ever wanted to hear. The nights I spent alone in my bedroom after entertaining a new suitor had me dreaming of a man who'd want me for me. Someone who would say things exactly like this to me. A man who'd see me hiding in the dark shadows of my pain and pull me to the light. But as we stare into each other's eyes, I think we both realize the woman I was before is no longer here.

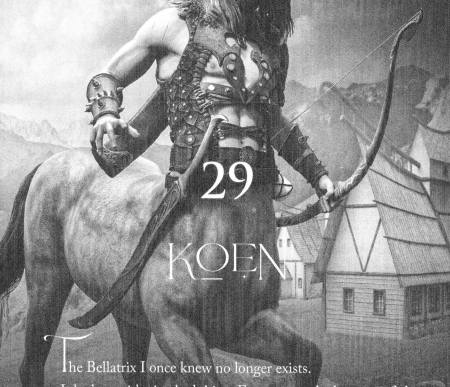

# 29

## KOEN

The Bellatrix I once knew no longer exists.

I don't consider it a bad thing. For starters, she has more fight in her. Seeing her stand up for herself, even against me, makes me proud. I don't want her taking shit from anybody.

I have a lot to think about on my way back to the cottage today. Usually I break into my animal form and let my centaur body lead me home. It cuts the time in half, and truthfully it's more enjoyable. More freeing. Today, though, I feel the need for the extra time to think.

Bellatrix still cares for me. But how do I give her time *and* let her know I'm not going anywhere?

I'm not sure I can handle the truth of what happened to her while she was gone. Her body is covered in bruises and strange wounds that make my blood boil. Lothar did things to her, or made her do things that have forever changed her. If he were alive, my only purpose would be to make him suffer, make him regret it all. I know Bellatrix needs to get through this on her own, but she's hurting and all I can do is watch.

Inside the cottage, my mother and sister are sitting on the couch reading a book together. My mother has her arm draped around Mel, who holds the book with both hands reading aloud. They both look up with delight when they see me.

"Koen!" Mel tosses the book on the couch and launches herself out from under my mother and into my arms.

I wrap my arms around her tightly. "Hey, sweet girl. Are you having a good day?" Mel nods against my chest.

"Until I made her eat the carrots on her plate at lunchtime," my mother chimes in.

I pull us apart, glancing at her chagrined expression. "You used to like carrots. What happened?"

She shrugs. "I don't anymore. I changed."

A half-hearted chuckle escapes my lips. "Yeah, you're not the only one, sweet girl."

Mel doesn't acknowledge my comment as she bounces back to the couch. But my mother's keen awareness doesn't miss it. "Did everything go well with the princess today?"

I sigh heavily, running my hands through my hair. "I guess so."

My mother eyes me warily. "That's not very reassuring."

Taking a seat in the chair next to the sofa, I cross an ankle over my knee and lean back. "I don't know. It didn't go badly. She's just *different*."

"Of course she is. She's been through hell. A person doesn't survive what she has without being forced to change."

"You're right. I just don't know what to do."

"About what?" She leans forward, ready to give me advice.

"She said she needs time, but I want her to know I'm there for her. I don't want her to think that her anger, her grief, any of it is going to scare me off."

One side of my mother's lips lifts into a half smile. "You're a good man. Have I told you that lately?"

I scoff. I haven't felt like a good man in a long time.

"You are, my son. An amazing man. I'm so proud of who you've turned into. She says she needs time, okay. Give her space, but show up. Keep showing up, but do not smother her. Don't force her to talk; she'll come to you when she's ready. One thing you need to know about women is that we pay attention to the little things. So, if you can make small gestures that don't disrupt her healing, she'll notice them. And she will remember them. Women always remember who was there for them in their darkest hours."

"Like what?"

My mother throws her hands in the air dramatically. "What, I have to think of that for you, too?"

I raise one eyebrow.

She laughs. "You'll come up with something."

"I can't believe she thought I'd actually betray her that way with *him*."

I explain to my mother the lie Lothar told Bellatrix, but she isn't all that shocked. "You have to remember that he can be very convincing. He's fooled a lot of people, women especially. He's a skilled manipulator."

Somehow, my father managed to deceive my mother, Bellatrix, and the queen in his pursuit of power. I've seen the way he can lie and manipulate. One day he was the father teaching me to hunt and be a man, and the next he was drinking and screaming at my mother. He was nothing but a monster in disguise.

"Why did he change his name from Adrian to Lothar?" The question has been plaguing me for some time now. Had we known that Lothar was really my father all along, would things have been different?

"I wish I had the answer for that. With a fresh start and a thirst for power, I suppose a new name was his way of shedding the life he once had. Maybe it was his way of convincing himself it never existed at all."

"Who's Adrian?" Mel chimes in, sitting on the floor in front of my mother, doodling a new drawing on the coffee table.

My mother pats her head, smoothing her brown curls. "Nobody, sweetheart."

"Hey Mel, why don't you go help yourself to a piece of that strawberry swirl cake you love while Mother and I talk for a bit?" I suggest.

Her eyes go wide with excitement, and although I can tell my mother isn't thrilled at the idea, she nods in approval.

Mel shoots up from the floor with an excited squeal as she scampers off to the kitchen for her treat.

"I don't like discussing these things with her listening ears so close."

My mother nods in agreement. "You'll be an amazing father one day."

A loud laugh bursts out of me. "I don't know if that's in the cards for me, Ma'."

There's only one woman for me, and that woman just so happens to have a deadly curse that prevents us from being physical, even if she wanted me around at the moment. So it's safe to say that kids are an unlikely prospect.

"Do you want kids someday?"

I'm surprised by her question. We've never discussed my future with any woman, or having children. "Sure, if it were up to me, I'd like to have a few. But if I can't have that with Bellatrix, then I'm okay with that."

"I'd love to see you as a father."

"Does her curse even allow for children?"

Since finding out that my mother is the one who put the curse on Bellatrix, we haven't gotten to discuss the details of it. All I've done for months is badmouth the "monster" who put the curse on Bellatrix, so I don't think my mother has been eager to strike up the conversation either.

"Yes. If you were to survive…" She trails off, not wanting to discuss Bellatrix and I having sex. Feeling equally unsettled, I wave a hand for her to move forward. "Well, you know, then yes, you two would be able to bear children."

"Wait, you said she's my mate. Does that mean I'd survive the curse?" Not that having sex with her is on the table for us, or a priority for me. But it is an intriguing question.

Her lips form a thin line. "Not necessarily."

"But I thought—"

"There's still a risk. It's magic, it's not foolproof. If you're even thinking of—"

"No, Ma, relax. It was just a question. I'm just trying to make sense of it all."

"The only way is to break the curse."

I nod. Now that Bellatrix is home, I still intend on making her mother pay her debt for that curse.

"One last thing," my mother starts, as she leans forward placing a hand on my knee. "In the spirit of knowing what a woman needs…"

"Yeah?"

"Don't ever tell a woman to *relax* unless you want her to show you just how un-relaxed she can be." My mother slaps my knee twice, and gets up to join Mellani in the kitchen.

# 30

# BELLATRIX

Miri looks relaxed for once.

Though she's been tortured and bullied for her entire existence, you'd never know. The affection and kindness she shows me magnifies the grief I have for what's been stolen from her. The pain she's had to endure. Her resilience keeps me going, and I've made it my mission to visit with her regularly and get better at flying with her. It's clear she doesn't feel comfortable wandering off on her own, so I want to ensure she's still getting some exercise and stretching her wings as frequently as possible.

Miri lowers her head, and I offer her scratches. Her eyes blink slowly while she makes the purring sound in her throat. The comforting vibration of noise that tells me she's fond of me too. "I missed you, girl. Are you ready to fly?"

Her nose thrusts upwards, bumping into me. I can't help but laugh at her playfulness. "I'll take that as a yes."

My hair is gathered in a tight bun on the top of my head, a few of the shorter strands hanging loose in my face. Dressed in boots, thermal pants, and layered long-sleeve tops under my jacket, I'm ready to fly. Tenuma at ground level is freezing, so on top of a dragon at high speeds with the icy wind slapping you in the face, the cold air nips like needles penetrating your skin.

Over the last few weeks, I've grown quite close to Miri, and it's hard to imagine Tenuma without her. I've seen so much patience, kindness, and forgiveness from her in such a short time. The same can't be said for my family throughout the duration of my entire life. If she's able to keep a soft heart after all she's endured, then maybe there's hope for me.

"Princess!" I hear shouting in the distance, just as I'm about to climb up the back of Miri.

I turn to see Koen jogging towards us. Our relationship is still mending. I wasn't sure what to expect from him after my meltdown and telling him I needed time. But he keeps showing up, so he hasn't given up on me yet.

"Hi," I greet once he's approached us.

"This is for you." He extends a hand holding a single red rose. This has been his daily routine, to bring me a rose and check in on me.

"Thank you. I was about to go flying with Miri." I accept the flower and give Miri a loving pat.

"Oh!" he responds, eyes going wide.

"I wanted to get better at it, and it makes me feel close to her."

"To Miri?"

"Yeah. Her too," I say with a sad smile.

I miss Hidi. I've been giving her family space to grieve in their own way, so I can't talk to them about Hidi. But Miri seems to enjoy my company, and I really enjoy hers. I never thought I'd be bonding with a dragon, let alone flying one. But here we are.

"Can I come?" Koen asks, surprising me.

"Flying?"

He nods. "I want to fly with you."

Am I ready to share Miri with him?

Koen was forced to battle many of the dragons during the attack, so I can't imagine how terrifying and strange it must be for him to suddenly see them on our land as allies. Yet here he is willing to climb on the back of one, for me. I've made very clear how important Miri is, and without question he's accepted her as an extension of me.

"Yeah, I'd like that." While his request caught me off guard, I think I like the idea of having this experience with him.

It's been difficult letting my guard back down around him, but I've been working on it. My mind and heart are in a constant state of tug of war when it comes to him. Koen doesn't force me to be anything I'm not, though. My whole life I've felt trapped, always wanting to escape. But he cares for me in a way that staying put makes me feel free.

Koen steps forward, reaching his hand out towards Miri's nose. He allows her to sniff him a few times like he always does, and then once they've both said hello, she dips her head and allows him to scratch her. He rubs her nose up and down a few times while I stand back watching. It would be so easy for him to hate these creatures, but he's kept an open mind and allowed his view on them to shift.

"Okay, girl, ready?" I ask Miri, and using her front leg, hoist myself up on her back. I direct my next question to Koen. "Are *you* ready?"

It may be my imagination, but it looks like his face has turned a mild shade of green.

But he nods. "Yeah. It can't be any worse than the last time I was flown somewhere."

My eyes automatically travel to his abdomen and the injury he received in Sperantia. Having been flown home by his phoenix best friend while bleeding out must have been a traumatizing experience. While I wasn't there to witness it myself, Rina has retold the detailed version she received from Nik. The way Koen has healed is nothing short of a miracle. From the sounds of it, a wound like that never should have left a viable body behind.

I offer my hand as he begins to climb to help him up. Once he's seated behind me, I turn to see his worried gaze lowered to the ground.

"Are you okay?" I ask, stifling a giggle. I kind of like seeing this rugged man be vulnerable with me.

He chuckles, eyes cast down. "Not really. That's a far distance to fall."

"Well," I say, taking his hands and folding them across my waist, "you'd better hold on then."

At my voice command, Miri leans back on her hind legs and her large wings expand with ease and grace. Koen's hands latch tighter around me, forcing me to smile.

"Do you trust me?" I ask him.

Lowering so his lips are pressed to my ear, he lowers his voice. "With my life, Princess."

His words send chills through me, and I know he isn't only talking about being on the back of a dragon.

With one swift slap of her wings, Miri sends us soaring into the air. We rise higher and higher until the castle becomes a miniature model of my home. Tenuma has gifted us with a beautiful sunny day. A rare occurrence, given all the snow we've gotten lately.

Miri whips through the sky with perfect grace. She's truly

in her element, and getting her back into the sky makes me emotional. Seeing her depressed each day, huddled on the ground was crushing me. She exudes such strength that sometimes it's shocking to think of the way she was imprisoned. Miri is proof that we are capable of coming back from anything.

Koen's face remains close to mine as he shouts over the wind hissing around us. "She's incredible!"

I nod, turning my head slightly to smile at him. His gaze bores into mine. I have to look away from the intensity of it. As I'm turning to face forward, he shifts. Koen's hand leaves my waist and catches my chin before I've fully turned, keeping my eyes on him.

I know that look.

Am I ready to start things back up with him?

It's not that I don't trust him. Trusting Koen is the one thing I can do. Ever doubting him to begin with was a mistake that I'm painfully aware of. I've been avoiding him, and avoiding his gaze. I think I was scared to see his father in his face. To be reminded of the awful things that man did to me. That's not at all Koen's fault, but unfortunately he's been a casualty in my path of healing.

"Bellatrix, can I?"

When I look into his eyes, filled with hope, filled with love, I only see my handyman, my Koen. My eyes zero in on his lips, and when I nod, he leans in fusing our mouths together.

Every concern I have evaporates. The way his lips and tongue move in sync with mine feel intentional and thorough. It's not hurried or rough, but slow and intense. He's taking his time, getting lost in me, and exploring every inch of my mouth. Like the first pull of water after a grueling workout, it's satisfying and quenching. His lips against mine feel right, reigniting every feeling I had for him.

My grip tightens on Miri, and I allow myself to get lost in Koen. Lost in how easy it is to be with him, fall for him. I'm suddenly wishing for this flight to be over, as my desire to fully turn around and straddle him begins to overpower everything else.

Moments ago, the cool breeze blowing past us was chilling me down to my bones despite my layers, but the heat from this kiss is enough to incinerate my flesh. Enough to tear down the walls I've built up in the last few weeks. Like the relentless waves that overtime begin to corrode boulders, Koen keeps finding his way through. The resistance I've put up hasn't deterred him for a second.

We pull apart, and as we're locked into each other's eyes, I see Koen's attention shift past me, and a grin spreads across his face. "Look," he says, nudging his chin ahead of us.

I turn my head around to face forward and don't have to search long for what Koen was referring to. Just ahead of us, a massive rainbow arches over the sky. The colors are so vibrant they're almost blinding.

Koen gives my waist a squeeze as his arms find their way back around me, and I find myself sinking comfortably into him. With Koen wrapped around me, everything else fades away. All the pain. All the suffering. The heartache, and the fear, all blowing right past us. With unwavering trust in Miri, I release my hands and embrace the moment.

I raise both arms in the air, feeling the wind whip through my fingers. Koen holds me tight, either out of fear or affection, and briefly I find myself completely at peace. A feeling that's been lost since my abduction. As if surrendering to her own euphoria, Miri glides us directly through the rainbow, and though I can't feel it, my fingertips pass through the colors. A once-in-a-lifetime experience, and I had both Miri and Koen with me. My heart swells, and fills with something new.

Possibility.

A glimpse of the peaceful life I've always wanted flashes

before my eyes, and for once it feels like it could become reality. Like a child chasing a bubble, always reaching for it, I usually see my dreams pop before they can ever become real. Only this time, it feels like I finally caught one.

Miri tips her head back and lets out a deep roar, startling us both. Having heard the agonizing and angry cries from these creatures for weeks in Sperantia, I can confidently say this noise is vastly different. It's a burst of joy that couldn't be contained any longer. That tickle of laughter that you can't seem to hold back or stop, until tears are running down your face.

She's happy.

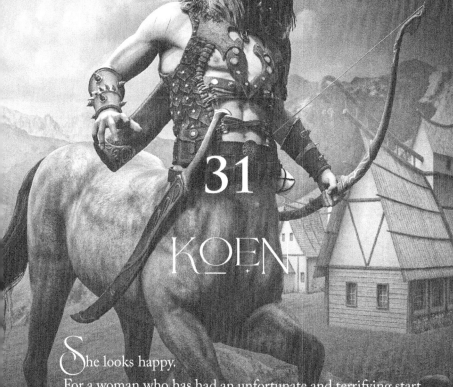

# 31

## KOEN

She looks happy.

For a woman who has had an unfortunate and terrifying start to her life, Bellatrix doesn't show it. She actively seeks out love and joy, regardless of the way she's been used and abused. Despite the many people who've taken advantage of all her goodness, she's decided to let me back in, and for that I'll forever be grateful.

Miri begins her descent as the castle comes into view, and she brings us safely back to the grounds. I slide off first, using Miri's slanted front leg as a sort of slide, and help Bellatrix down as she follows.

I just rode a fucking dragon.

"That was amazing. Thank you, Princess."

She shoots me a shy smile. "What for?"

"For giving me that experience. For letting me share that with *you*," I say, grabbing both of her hands in mine.

I don't want to let her go. But I don't want to smother her.

"You're welcome," she says but doesn't make a move to leave.

It would be so easy to pick her up and carry her inside to do all the things I've been daydreaming of doing with her. *To her.* Just be close to her. The look in her eyes tells me she wants it too, but her trembling hands tells me she's not ready for it. It's not lost on me how she looks at me. I know she's seeing my father. I can see the way she avoids my gaze, looking anywhere else. I wish she would feel comfortable opening up about her experience, but she's like a tightly pinned grenade, holding all those dangerous parts inside of her.

As much as I don't want to leave, I know I need to. Our kiss was perfect, and I don't want to push it. She will let me know when she's ready. "Well, I should probably get back to Mel and my mother."

She nods in understanding. "I miss them. I'd love to see them soon."

"You should come to the cottage. They'd love to have you over. My mother has been asking when she can make you dinner." It's been difficult for my mother to spend time at the castle with Charlotte there. Her connection with Lothar has been upsetting for us all.

"I'd like that."

I can tell she means it.

Turning towards Miri, I say my goodbyes. "Thanks for the ride, girl. I appreciate you not doing any rolls or flips."

Miri snorts at my joke, and the princess giggles softly.

My heart pangs hearing the sweet sound of Bellatrix laughing. It's something I've seldom heard, and never thought I would again. Slowly, she's coming back to us.

Miri takes off suddenly.

"Where's she going?"

"Probably to find something to eat. She likes a snack after

flying."

I slowly nod. "Ah. Well. Until next time, Princess."

Leaning in, I place a kiss on her cheek. I'm not even ashamed that I linger there a moment longer than necessary. The way I feel her cheek rise into a smile under my lips tells me she doesn't entirely mind it either.

"Bye, Koen."

As I watch her walk away from me towards the castle, I'm filled with hope. Hope that we can overcome the things that have tried to tear us apart. As much as I want her to be mine, I want her to be fine more. Today I caught a glimpse of the girl she wants to be: carefree and happy. There are more obstacles I need to get out of her way, but once I do, I know she stands a shot at a new life. A fulfilling one that she can be proud of. It feels good to know that maybe, just maybe I'll get to be a part of it.

"Koen, to what do we owe the pleasure?" Charlotte asks.

I was almost out of the castle before she found me. We both know why I'm here. My eyes turn to slits at her question. "What do you want?"

"Oh, come now, don't be that way. Why don't you come and chat with me for a few moments?" she asks, gesturing towards the entrance of the castle.

I sigh heavily and reluctantly follow her inside. Walking under the enormous staircase to a hallway behind it, we take a left down a long dark corridor. Its walls are adorned with lit torches giving the space an eerie red haze.

Where the fuck is she taking me?

Charlotte stops before a large metal door. It consists of three large locks, which can only open from the outside. A chill shoots down my spine. I know I'm not going to like whatever's behind this door.

Charlotte pulls a large key out from between the fabric of her dress and her bosom. Sticking it into one lock at a time, she fully unlocks each one with a loud thunk. Her hand moves to the large brass handle, but I stop her.

"Where are we going? I thought you wanted to talk."

The cunning grin crosses her face once more. "I do. Let's talk inside."

With the force of her shoulder against the entrance, she shoves the heavy door open. The tangy smell of rusted iron immediately fills my nostrils. It's overwhelming, and I fight the urge to cover my face with my shirt.

We travel down a cold narrow hallway, and on the right I see an opening. The further we get, the more audible a metal clanging noise gets. Once we reach the end of the hall, it opens up into a large room full of...

What the fuck?

I fight the competing urges to run or to end Charlotte's life right here. "Why are we here?" I ask angrily.

"I thought it was time to remind you what you're getting yourself into," she responds smugly.

I can't help the scoff that bursts from me. "You mean what you've gotten Bellatrix into?"

She's brought me to the daemons. Rows of metal bars form prison cells that fill the room. Each cell is packed with so many men, they're barely able to move about the space. Not that they're trying to. A few men clang metal mugs against the bars. Their eyes are dead, soulless. They look like the men they used to be, but they hold no expression, no human-like movement. Flesh and bones.

"This is your future with her. You two can never have a real life together. You seem to have forgotten that."

Is this the same woman that momentarily showed remorse and handpicked me to rescue her daughter? Why the fuck is she trying to tear us apart again?

"Why did you bring me here?"

"To remind you that you're not good enough for her. You never will be." She arrogantly tilts her head up, her nose in the air. "You have served your purpose, but now that she's home, she will begin looking for a suitable king to rule with her."

If it wasn't for Bellatrix, I would end Charlotte here without a second thought. But I know, whether Bellatrix will outright admit it or not, she still loves her mother. She may have done awful things to her, treated her unimaginably, but it's not up to me to decide what her mother deserves as punishment for that. Only Bellatrix can make that call.

"Look, I don't know what you're trying to do, but you need to stay the fuck out of our relationship."

She has the audacity to laugh. "Is that what you think you have? A relationship? Oh, Koen, no. You're a hobby for her. She will remember who she is, find the man worthy of being king, and become queen of Tenuma."

Ignoring her taunting, I focus the conversation on the horror in front of us. "What are you planning on doing with these men? They're trapped this way because of you."

She shrugs.

I feel my blood boiling at her cavalier attitude. "How can you not care? You're destroying innocent people's lives!"

"I did what I had to do to survive. This is the real world, boy.

Some of us had to make hard choices. I had that spell cast on my daughter for her protection, so she could have a fighting chance at having a worthy partner."

"At the expense of her body, and her choice."

"I'm not hurting her, I'm helping her. I was once a foolish young woman like her, wishing and waiting for love. But then I grew up, and those silly notions quickly fell away."

I refuse to give her the satisfaction of getting a rise out of me again. "Hurting people is all you do, Charlotte."

She doesn't respond, and the only sound is the banging of the tin mugs on the metal bars. The daemons don't seem bothered by our presence, or even aware of it. It's unsettling. Like men caught in a living nightmare, they have no control over their bodies.

My eyes travel across the groups of men, and I see the face of someone I never thought I'd see again.

Landric.

Before deciding to go to the castle as a last resort, he was a good friend of mine and Nik's, and a good man who always took care of his family. With money and work being hard to come by, he thought he stood a chance at beating the curse.

He was wrong. They were all wrong.

Seeing him here causes the bile in my stomach to rise.

"You need to let them go. Please, give them their lives back. This is evil."

We both know there's only one way the daemons have a shot at getting their souls back.

"There's no guarantee that will even work. What if they die when I do?"

"By doing this in the first place, you've already decided that your life is worth more than all of theirs combined."

"I didn't know the men would turn into *this*!"

"Maybe not at first, but you did eventually find out, and you let it continue. Why?"

She looks away. "Because of your father."

Lothar lied and abandoned her the same way he did to me and my family. Charlotte's face is filled with longing. Her eyes, red and swollen, tell me that her affection for him was genuine.

My eyes narrow at her. "Is that supposed to make me feel sorry for you? The man deserted his own family. Were you under the impression that he was a good person?"

Charlotte manages to look ashamed. "I'm not proud to say he fooled me. I thought my actions were preserving my family. But—"

I can't hear this anymore. "But all you did was ruin a hundred other families." I turn to walk away from Charlotte.

"All I wanted to do was protect her," she whimpers.

Before I've turned down the hallway, I turn back around. "All that your choices have ever done is put her in harm's way. Do us all a favor and leave Bellatrix the hell alone."

With tight fists at my side, I storm out of the horrific room as quickly as I can. Every encounter with that woman solidifies my desire to wipe her from the earth for good. But before I do, I need to be sure where Bellatrix stands with her. There's not a chance I'll risk losing Bellatrix again.

But oh, when she tells me she's done, revenge is going to feel so damn good.

# 32

# BELLATRIX

They say time heals all wounds, but that's a lie. Revenge does.

"Faster! Again!" Harding shouts at me while I gasp for air.

Harding is my trainer, but I refer to him as Hard-ass since he seems to enjoy inflicting pain onto my body. He has dark skin and a shaved, shiny head that mirrors back my pathetic reflection, reminding me how much work I still need to put in.

When I groan out in agony and frustration, he yells back, "Hey, this is what you wanted. Get up! Do you want to keep fighting, or do you want to be weak?"

His specific brand of training is cutthroat, but his lessons teach me exactly what I'm trying to avoid: getting killed. Not everyone would find his style motivating, but it's what I need.

He doesn't let me forget what happened to me. Doesn't let me forget how it felt to be weak and trapped, imprisoned by a power-hungry monster.

Digging deeper, I search for more strength, any remaining energy.

*Fight through the pain, Bellatrix.*

*You will never be weak again.*

*You will be ready when they come back for you.*

The weeks since my return have been quiet. There has been no word from Sperantia, especially after my mother exiled the informant that helped her keep tabs on me. Nevertheless, I know this isn't over. I've killed their king, and Sperantia has been left without a ruler. Knowing that the next in line to take over for the fallen king would be his heir, I can't help but wonder what that will mean for both Koen and Sperantia.

Along with training with Harding, I have been attending mandatory daily meetings with my mother and the lieutenant general of the royal army. Slowly, I'm being groomed to take over the throne. Only a few know that my father is gone, and now that it's only my mother and me, getting me trained and ready to take over as queen is top priority. I've hardly been in the right mindset to be concerned with the politics of either land, but my mother has been surprisingly helpful, stepping up to continue her duty when it should be me.

There's been talk of sending men to Sperantia to ensure the kingdom isn't in ruin without their ruler; it's just a matter of when and how. We have to play our cards carefully, since our own kingdom is also in a fragile state.

A sweep of Harding's leg behind mine knocks me off balance, slamming me backwards to the ground and back to reality. He's over my body right as I've hit, pinning me to the earth.

"Fuck," I shout as he restrains my hands above my head, and his powerful legs trap mine beneath his own.

Images of strange men hovering over my unconscious body flood my mind. My breathing becomes erratic, and I can't hold back the screech that rips from my throat.

Harding immediately releases me, and his eyes widen with concern.

This isn't the first panic attack I've had while training.

I rise and work on steadying my breath. Reclaiming control over my mind is exactly why I'm here.

"Keep your focus," he commands.

"I *am* focused," I snarl back, brushing snow off my limbs.

Standing back with his hands propped on his hips, he watches as I struggle to get up. He reaches out a hand to help me off the ground. "If you were, it shouldn't have been that easy to knock you down. You won't always be the stronger opponent."

"So you keep reminding me."

"Why do you keep trying to overpower me then?"

"Just because I'm not as strong as you right now doesn't mean I won't be," I snap. I'm not sure I believe my angry words. But I can't stop the stubbornness pouring out of me.

"I'm already stronger than you, which means even though you keep training and gaining strength, so will I. This will be true of your enemies as well. I'm not saying you're not strong. I'm telling you this to make you better. Assuming you're the weaker person in the room can work to your advantage. Be smarter, be faster. There is more than one way to win."

He's a six-two, two-hundred-and-twenty-pound tower of steel. Knowing he's stronger than I am is not news.

Defeat must be written on my face, because I see a smug smile as he gives his next order. "Again. This time, focus on moving your body around mine. Stop trying to take me down. Wear me out. Outlast me."

We train for another thirty minutes until I'm covered in

sweat, despite the snow on the ground.

I have yet to be able to take Harding down, and there's only so much failure I can take for one session. My limbs are aching and in desperate need of a hot bath, so I call it a day and head back to my chambers.

I climb the stairs that taunt me after my grueling workout, but when I turn the corner I find a visitor waiting outside my door.

"Princess," Koen greets, smiling at me.

"Koen," I reply warmly.

Why does he always have to look so good?

Leaning up against my doorway with one leg crossed over the other, he's wearing black boots, dark pants, and a tight black shirt with a heavy jacket over it. In one hand he holds a single rose. The urge to press my hands against his chest to feel the ripples of muscles overwhelms me, and I fight to keep my face neutral.

"Good workout?" he asks, grinning at me.

I chuckle. "I suppose that depends on your definition of good."

"Fair enough," he laughs back.

We stand silently in front of my door for a moment, as I try to keep my eyes from roaming his body, undressing him in my mind. "Would you like to come in?"

"Do you want me to?" he asks cautiously.

I push past him to open the door. "I wouldn't have asked if I didn't want you to."

While the attraction and draw still exists between us, we're slowly getting close again. The effort on his part has been the reassurance I needed. Not to mention it's attractive as hell. Every day he shows up to check on me. Snipping a rose from the garden and leaving it on my bedside table. Instead of crowding me or completely avoiding me, he asks what I want. I think that's what I'm loving the most.

What I needed the most was simply for someone to ask what I wanted. He's been patient, considerate, and genuinely kind to me while I worked through my trauma. Between training and meeting with the royal counsellor once a week, I've slowly been able to let go of the past, and I've been reminded of the man I was falling for. The man that stuck by me and stuck up for me when nobody else would.

Koen explained some of the things that his mother has revealed, as well as what my mother has done behind my back. Finding out my own mother had teamed up with Lothar at my expense has been another crushing blow. I'm grateful that Koen told me; I'd rather know the truth than be comforted by lies. He's been my rock, the one I can always count on to show up no matter what kind of day I'm having. He shows up on the good days, but more importantly he shows up on the bad ones.

I thought being intimate would forever be ruined for me, but I the urges are still there. I would be lying if I said there weren't times that I wanted to ravish him. Have my way with his hard body. That feeling awakens nearly every time I'm with him. The impulse lingers close by, reminding me of what I want. Reminding me that I'm still me. A person who's survived unforgivable acts, and can still be a woman who wants to be loved and feel sexy and strong. I'm not one thing, I'm all things. All at once.

Koen follows me inside the room, and I close the door behind us. Turning around, I take the red rose he's holding outstretched for me.

"Thank you," I say, placing it in a small vase of water next to the flower from yesterday.

"Are you sore?" he asks as he watches me limp over to the bed.

I chuckle. "What gave it away?"

"Would you like a massage?"

Though his offer was devoid of any seduction, instantly my belly swirls with warm desire.

Imagining his hands on me sends a thrill through me.

"I was actually going to take a hot bath. That's all I've thought about for the last hour."

His face falls, but he forces a smile. "Oh, I'll go then. You've earned it. Enjoy."

"You can stay, if you want," I say, surprising us both.

He nods, and sits on the bed to wait for me while I make my way over to the bathroom. I start the bath water, turning it to a hot, but comfortable temperature. As the tub fills, I start to close the door, but when my eyes find Koen's intense gaze, I stop and swing the door in the other direction.

Too much was taken from me while I was in Sperantia, and I refuse to live in fear in my own home any longer. I can't erase what happened, can't take away the anxious feelings, but I can create new experiences. Ones I want to remember.

He leans back on the bed, and his eyes fill with desire. I turn and face the bathroom mirror and begin to strip my tight clothes off my body. They fall to the floor, and I fight every urge I have to let my gaze wander back to where he sits. Where he watches. If I look at him, I won't be able to overpower the way he stares into my soul.

Now completely naked, I lift my arms to tie my hair in a knot at the top of my head. All the while, I'm completely aware that Koen is only a few feet away. I can feel the heat of his gaze on me. I let the moment linger, soaking up the way he desires me. The same desire that stirs within me, so intense it's almost painful.

The tub is about half filled with water, and I dip a toe in, slowly letting my body adjust to the heat before sinking all the way in and letting the warm water cover my aching muscles. The immediate relief has me sinking down and leaning back into the water with a quiet moan of pleasure.

"You can't be making noises like that, Princess," Koen's deep voice sounds from the doorway.

Startling me from the relaxing state I was sinking into, I jerk my head around to see his dark gaze glued to me. His hands tightly gripping the doorframe.

"Why not?" I ask innocently.

"Because it's hard enough keeping my hands off you. I want to be the only reason I hear those perfect lips moaning."

Oh.

Being wet in a tub just took on a whole new meaning.

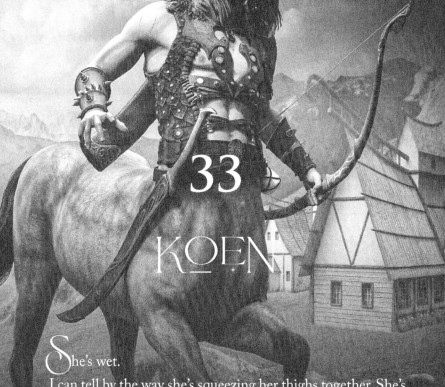

# 33

## KOEN

She's wet.

I can tell by the way she's squeezing her thighs together. She's having an equally difficult time keeping her hands off me. We've made great strides the last couple of months, but when we start back up, I want to know for certain it's because *she* wants it.

The way her gaze lands on me warms and excites me better than any whiskey ever could. It's intoxicating me before I've laid a hand on her.

"What are you saying, Mr. Archer?"

She's taunting me, trying to seduce me, and it's working. "You know exactly what I'm saying." "Say it."

My lips curve into a devious smile. "I want to touch you, Princess."

Her lips pull inward. She doesn't speak, but her worried eyes say enough.

She's not ready.

"Forget I said that. I don't want to pressure you," I say, hoping it will relax her nerves.

She shakes her head. "No, it's okay. I want to."

Without breaking eye contact she slowly spreads her legs, inviting me, giving me access to her pussy. Access I would have gladly begged for. Access I would have waited forever for.

"Can I?" I ask.

She nods.

Stepping forward, I kneel down next to the tub and dip my hand into the warm water. My fingers dance on her thigh, squeezing and caressing her flesh. I move slowly, grateful just to be near her. I want to make this moment last. Bellatrix begins breathing deeper and faster, her chest rising and falling as her perky breasts pop in and out of the water. They look delicious, and I would love to make a meal out of them.

Her body begins to tremble slightly.

"Are you okay?" I ask.

She nods.

Pulling my hand from the water, I turn the nozzle until the water stops running. The only sound is a small drip from the faucet, and her heavy breathing.

She surprises me by grabbing my hand and pushing it between her legs. A grin spreads across my face.

That's my girl.

Slowly, I take my thumb and rub small circles on her clit. I let her sounds guide me as I increase pressure and tempo.

"Mmm," she moans, laying her head back against the ledge of the tub.

"Does that feel good, Princess?"

"Yes, keep going. More."

"Are you begging me to fuck you with my fingers?" I ask,

needing to hear the words. I've been careful not to cross any boundaries with her, so I won't do anything without her approval.

"Yes, Koen. Please. Fuck me."

As those sweet words leave her lips, I spread her open and slip a finger inside.

*Fuck,* she feels good.

I push one more finger inside her, and begin pumping my fingers in and out of her warm cunt. I recall why getting so close to her was dangerous in the first place. Like a sugary cocktail, she's sweet and addictive. How the hell am I going to restrain myself after touching her? I need more.

"You feel so fucking good," I praise.

She mumbles her approval and grinds against my hand, trying to get deeper, closer. Whatever hesitation she had is long gone. My eyes can't decide where to look. The look of pleasure on her face is beautiful, but I'm equally drawn to where my fingers caress the most tender parts of her.

My dick is throbbing against my pants, not only because of the view in front of me, but from her willingness to be open and vulnerable with me. I pick my pace up, curling my fingers to hit her sweet spot and rubbing a thumb over her clit, pumping them faster and faster.

"Fuck! Right there, keep going."

Bellatrix telling me how to please her while my fingers work inside of her has me rock hard and ready to explode sitting next to her. Her breathing picks up rapidly and I know she's close. My fingers are soaked with her arousal and my other hand kneads her perky breast, rolling her nipple between my fingers.

"That's a good girl. Let go, Trix, let me hear it. Come all over my hand."

And she does, with a scream of ecstasy I've never heard from her before. This will be the sound playing on repeat in my mind for the rest of my life.

"Koen!"

My name sounds perfect on her tongue while she comes. She rides the wave of pleasure as her body tenses, and her pussy clenches around my fingers as if she intends to keep me there forever.

I'm already undeniably hers.

Once the pleasure fizzles out, she lifts her head and looks up at me. "Well, fuck me."

"We already did that," I reply playfully. I grin as if I'm the one who got to release.

"Right, well, I suppose it's your turn then."

As if I couldn't get any harder, somehow my cock stiffens further at the thought of Princess Bellatrix getting me off.

"There's nothing I'd love more than whatever you have planned in that beautiful head of yours, but right now all I want is to make you feel good."

As much as she wanted this, I know that this was also challenging for her. Getting to this point was no easy feat, and I want her to know I appreciate every step of the way with her. That I'm okay going slow, and that I never need anything in exchange. This was for her.

A look of confusion crosses her face, and she waits for me to elaborate. I pick up the clean white washcloth at the end of the tub and lather it with some of the soap next to it.

"Sit up," I request, rubbing the washcloth together between my hands until it's nice and sudsy.

She leans forward, and I run the cloth down her back, over her shoulders, and across her neck. Once I've finished with her back, I gently press her against the tub so I can reach her front. "I've never had anybody wash me."

I can't help but smile knowing I have one of her firsts. "And what do you think?"

She takes her time with a response, while I take my time washing—who am I kidding, caressing—her chest.

"Hmm," she replies playfully. "It's not terrible."

I motion for her to stand so I can move down her stomach and over her backside, until I'm between her legs again. My touch is soft, but she winces.

My eyes shoot up to hers, worried I've hurt her.

She gives me an apologetic look and a giggle. "Sorry, still sensitive."

"I love seeing you like this," I tell her, glancing up to see her eyes heavy with relaxation.

She takes the cloth from my hand, and drapes it over the tub. I rinse her off and grab a white towel from the stack on the counter, wrapping it around her shoulders.

Bellatrix steps out, drying any excess water off of her body, and then wraps the towel around her chest, securing it with a tuck. "Come lay with me." She grabs my hand and leads me over to her bed, where I find myself suddenly full of nerves.

She pushes me down so I'm sitting on the bed, and kneels in front of me and begins undressing me, first unlacing and removing one boot and sock, and then repeating with the other side. Her hands move to my belt, unbuckling it and then snapping open the button on my pants. She reaches for my zipper, but I place my hand over hers, holding her in place.

"You don't have to do this," I remind her.

She nods and pushes my hand away. I lay back on my elbows so she can continue unzipping my pants, and she yanks them down in one quick move.

As she comes face to face with my already rock-hard cock, her eyes widen, and I swear I see her lick her lips.

I finish undressing, pulling my jacket and shirt off, sliding back on the bed so she can position herself better. She straddles my legs and lines up her mouth with the head of my cock, then takes it in her mouth, giving it a hard suck and pulling back to swipe her tongue around the tip. The attention she shows my dick, like she doesn't want to leave a single area untouched, is going to make me quickly fall apart for her.

I groan as my pleasure builds. We may not be able to have everything we want, but what we do have is pretty damn good. Truthfully, if all sexual activity was off the table, it wouldn't change a thing for me.

She pulls back, letting her saliva coat my cock, and begins stroking up and down my shaft.

"How's this?"

"So fucking good, baby," I tell her.

I am so gone for her.

Her tight grip on my cock is firm and possessive. Her touch has me feeling inebriated, making it challenging to lift my head, but I'm dying to watch her in action. When my gaze meets her, she wraps her mouth around my cock and takes it as far into her mouth as she can.

"Fuck!" I involuntarily groan as I feel my dick hit the back of her throat.

She pulls back and repeats it over and over while she moans and simultaneously strokes my cock with her hand. The combination threatens to make me burst. I could watch her do this all day, but I know I won't hold on much longer with how good this feels.

She's the soul snatcher, *my* soul snatcher.

She's stolen mine, and I wouldn't have it any other way. While the title is one she's been ashamed of, I want to make her see that to me, it's recognition of how in love with her I am. We've been through hell and back, and though we have a rough road ahead, I would do it a hundred times over just to be with her.

"Fuckkkk." I try to pull her off as my orgasm starts to shoot through my body, but she stops me. Bellatrix holds onto my thighs and tightens her mouth around my cock, sucking hard as I explode down her throat.

Gods damn, I would let this woman ruin me.

She may be royalty, but she makes me feel like a king.

I finish, and she pulls off my dick with a pop, licking her lips. A devious grin spreads across her face, like a cat who devoured the mouse she's been chasing all day. She looks proud and satisfied.

"Fuck, that felt amazing," I tell her when the stars start to fade from my vision.

Bellatrix crawls up to lay by my side. Her towel has long since fallen off of her and lays in a heap on the floor. We lay side by side, completely naked, staring into each other's eyes. It's blissful, yet I know we both want more.

The princess is the first to break the silence. "So, what now?"

# 34

# BELLATRIX

"What now?" I ask the general in today's war meeting.

"We have been sending groups of men to the border of Sperantia for any intel as to whether they're preparing a counterattack. So far, we have seen zero movement. Nothing suspicious," the lieutenant general of our army informs me.

"What about our border?" I ask.

"We have doubled our security around the perimeter and throughout the forest. We are patrolling through the night as well," he reports.

"And what about the daemons?" I ask, glancing at my mother, who quickly looks away. Koen revealed my mother's impromptu field trip with him to where she's keeping the daemons, and I haven't been able to stop thinking about it since.

"What do you mean, Princess?" the general asks.

My eyebrows pull together. "I mean, what are we doing about those men? Surely the plan isn't to keep them in their current state forever?"

The general glances over to my mother. "The queen has requested that we keep them on standby for any future attacks."

My head rears back. "What? Absolutely not. Mother, you cannot do that. They are still *people*. They have families. They're someone's father, brother, son."

My mother coolly sits a few chairs away at the big oval table with her hands placed on top of one another when she responds. "What do you care, Bella? These men are the same ones that used you."

The room is completely silent, the rest of the men not daring to speak. Tension fills the room.

My eyes narrow at her. "*You* used them. Letting them suffer indefinitely is not an option." I turn back to the general. "How's the search going for an enchantress who could reverse the spell?" I ask.

"We stopped the search at your mother's request, but the few we found before refused to risk their magic with that curse," the general informs me.

I scrub a hand down my face. "Continue the search, please. Surely there's someone out there willing to help."

The conversation moves forward to discuss other pressing matters. Once the meeting ends, I quickly exit the room, hoping to avoid any further interaction with my mother, but she catches up with me.

"Bella, will I see you at dinner?" she asks.

"No."

I can hear a heavy sigh, evidence of her pouting.

Why is she still surprised?

In the weeks since Koen and I started our sexual relationship back up, I've spent a lot of time with him and his family. I'd choose dinner at their cottage any day. Being reunited with Mellani has been the refreshing boost I needed to pull me from the darkness.

"Bella, please. You never spend time with me."

"And I don't intend to."

My mother loses her mind when she no longer has control over the people she's used to manipulating. She may still have nominal control of the kingdom, but she no longer has power over me. Her reign is coming to its end.

As much as she loves ruling over Tenuma, I know that it lost its luster without my father. All of her energy has gone into planning my crowning ceremony that will officially announce me as queen. Though the matter of who will be king still hangs in the air.

"Have you put any more thought into the men I've told you about? Any one of them would be a perfect ruling king."

If it were up to me, Koen would rule with me. It will be a lot to ask of him, to give up the only life he's known, and put himself and his family under a constant microscope.

"Mother," I say, stopping to turn and face her. "You know damn well that Koen and I are together.

What are you trying to do?"

"I just thought…"

I cut her off. "You chose wrong for yourself *twice*. You don't get to choose for me."

Her shoulders slump. "Will you ever give me the chance to explain myself? To make things right?"

I sigh. "For what? For you to lie to me again? To force me into some new arrangement?"

The sharpness of my words seem to stun her for a moment, and she doesn't respond right away.

I know she's trying, but she can't seem to put her need for power aside to see that she's hurting me.

"Mother, I'm busy. I'm grateful for the ways you've held Tenuma together, but unless you have a way to reverse this curse once and for all, I'm not interested in anything you have to say."

Making my way towards the front door, I try to move past her but she catches my arm before I can leave. Her fragile voice is foreign to me. "Bellatrix, please. Give me a chance."

It's hard to ignore the tears in her eyes, the desperation in her voice. I'm all she has left, but she turned her back on me long ago. What words could ever undo all the hurt she's caused?

Against my will, tears well up in my own eyes. "I'm your daughter, and you just handed me over.

How could you do that?"

I jerk my arm out of her grip.

"But I'm your mother."

"Are you? Because instead of being able to come to you for comfort, I find myself running from you because you're the one who keeps hurting me." As the words leave my lips, I know they'll sting. I don't say them to be hurtful. I say them because they're true.

Theo and Valeria, Quirina, Nik, Koen and his family. They're who I consider family now. I will protect them as they've protected me.

I push past my mother and walk away from her, leaving her stunned and silent. After this ceremony, I will be queen, and I don't know what will become of my mother. Frankly, I'm not sure what to do about her. I suppose that's a problem for another day. This feeling, somewhere between love and hate has fractured our relationship in an irreversible way. While I would love nothing more than to have a close relationship with my mother, I can't move past what she's done.

"That's beautiful, Mel." I compliment Mellani on her recent drawing while Koen's mother busies herself over the stove preparing a delicious meal for us this evening.

Koen sits next to me on their couch, with his hand laid tenderly on my knee. His warmth is soothing, and I love being close to him. Simply being in his presence calms me.

"Thank you, Princess!" Mel chirps.

An easy stillness falls over me whenever I'm around the Archer family. I find myself comfortable and wholly myself. While it's not typical for anyone from the royal family to spend time in a "commoner" home, I find them anything but common. They're the most caring, selfless people I know, and I'm grateful to be welcomed here.

"Bellatrix, honey, would you like some wine with dinner?" Fira, Koen's mother, offers.

While it was strange at first to be in the home of the woman who put the curse on me, I remind myself that if not threatened into it, she never would have agreed. My mother is solely to blame. Fira has been nothing but warm and inviting. I can sense the guilt and shame she's carrying over the curse, but none of the blame falls on her. Likewise, it's been nice not to have been blamed for her son's near-death experiences. I've put her son in danger more than once, and she's never held it against me. It's a behavior I'm not accustomed to, but quickly learning comes natural for this family.

"I'd love some, thank you. Are you sure you don't need some help?"

"No thank you, dear. Would your"—she gestures to the front door where two armed men stand guard—"friends like something to eat or drink?"

The man on the left speaks up before I get the chance to. "No, ma'am. We are here to protect our queen."

*Our queen.* I don't know if I'll ever get used to it.

Though I don't yet wear the crown, only a queen in practice, the entire kingdom seems to be honoring it. Evidently we're all ready to move on from the reign of my parents.

I have yet to feel comfortable wearing the crown, and the title feels foreign. So when Mel calls me "Princess," I don't correct it. I've been a princess for so long that being called queen is like trying on someone else's clothing.

Fira laughs, clearly feeling strange that her dinner will be watched over again by two royal guards. But she takes it all in stride. She always offers, and they always decline. That's what I love about her. Though I'm sure there's plenty about my lifestyle that makes hers more difficult, she's never made me feel like a burden. Fira isn't one to complain. It's a stark contrast from my own mother, who complains about every little inconvenience.

I hand Mellani's drawing back to her, one that depicts a replica of the tattoo on my arm. For whatever reason, it seems to have stuck with her. She always asks to see it and still refers to me as the tattoo lady from time to time. That little girl could call me any name and I think I'd love it.

She takes my hand, jerking me off the couch. "Come on, let's go eat. You can sit by me!"

"Mel, relax, you're going to yank her arm out of the socket," Koen warns as he follows us over to their dining table.

I take a seat next to Mellani, with Koen on my other side, and Fira across from me. The table is filled with an array of options. A bowl of white sauce chicken pasta sits in the center, next to a bowl of mixed greens with chopped vegetables. It looks like a vegetable rainbow. On the other side is a wood slab of sliced bread and a small dish of whipped butter. The aroma of the garlic in the pasta and the steaming bread swarms my senses, and I find myself salivating, eager to taste the feast she's provided. Though the castle has a full kitchen staff, there's something so special about a home-cooked meal like this.

Koen lifts his wine glass. "I'd like to toast to our guest of honor." He winks at me. "*Queen* Bellatrix."

Laughing, we all raise our glasses and clink. He gets a kick out of using the word *queen* to mess with me. Truthfully, I think he just enjoys seeing me smile.

He gives my leg a squeeze under the table, causing my skin to flush. Any time his hands are on me, there's an instant reaction. I take a sip of my wine, and the red liquid slides easily down my throat.

"Thank you for having me. I love being here. It feels like home."

"Thanks to you," Fira comments, pointing her own glass towards the windows.

I shrug, not wanting admiration for helping a family when I had the means to. The only thing I wanted was for the Archers to have a safe, comfortable place to live. The castle had more than enough material to cover what we used it for. It feels silly to be thanked for kindness. Though there is one thing I wouldn't mind accepting in lieu of all the praise.

"I have been thinking about what you told me the day of the attack. If I brought Koen back safely."

*"My son was right about you, My Lady. Bring him back to me, and I will make a way for you two to end up together, if that's what*

*you wish."*

Fira nods with recollection, and sets her glass down.

"Have you found a way to break the curse?" I ask, hopeful.

She shakes her head. "Not yet. But I am still in search of one. There's only one foolproof way I know of."

I exchange a look with Koen, whose hands form tight fists on top of the table.

My mother's life will have to be taken.

As much harm as she's done, taking my mother's life isn't something I'm willing to entertain. I've already killed once before, and I refuse to do it again for my own selfishness. I know it's not the decision Koen wants to hear, but I know he'll respect it.

I shake my head.

Fira gives me a sweet smile. "I won't give up, sweetheart. I'll find a way."

Nodding, I try to change the subject. "While I love being here, I did have another reason for my visit this evening."

Koen squeezes my leg again reassuringly, and Mel and Fira look at me with wide excited eyes. "Go ahead dear," Fira tells me.

"My mother is hosting an official crowning ceremony in a few weeks to announce my title as Queen. I'd love for you all to be there."

I won't tell them that I have plans to ask them all to move in with me after I have a much-needed talk with Koen separately.

"Yes! Oh, Mommy, I want to go to a party at the castle!" Mel shrieks excitedly, almost jumping out of her seat.

Fira hesitates, not answering right away. I understand, and it's probably the same reason she's not been a frequent visitor since I've been back, despite how much time Koen spends there.

"I don't know, honey. Let's think about it, and we can discuss it later," she tells Mellani, patting her hand.

While it earns a pouty groan from Mel, I nod. "There's no pressure. I would love to see you all there, but I understand."

Koen gives me another squeeze, and I turn my head to see him smiling sweetly at me. "I'll definitely be there. I wouldn't miss it."

Though we haven't discussed what this ceremony will mean for us, I already know. Surely his mind must be going in a thousand different directions, wondering what fate has in store for us, but my confidence in our relationship grows stronger every day.

We've been challenged with plenty of circumstances that should have broken us. Koen and I will figure this out together— but will he be willing to uproot his entire life to be with me?

# 35

# KOEN

"Are you with me or not?" Quirina asks, holding a shot of whiskey in front of my face.

She invited me out for a drink at Nik's bar, and it seemed like a good idea until she started ordering shots. The bubbly side of Quirina has finally begun to resurface. She spends most of her time with Nik, and while I haven't asked, I'm pretty sure she's been living in the loft upstairs with him.

"I don't know if that's wise, Rina," I tell her, holding onto my beer.

"Come on, man, it's just one. Humor our girl," Nik chimes in, and I can't help but notice his choice of words.

*Our* girl.

Taking the whiskey from her hand, she squeals and picks up another.

"Okay, cheers to…" she trails off, waiting for me to finish.

"Being back at Nik's."

Nik's bar officially reopened a few weeks ago, with a huge turnout from the rest of the town.

He's well-loved in the community, and everyone has been incredibly supportive.

The new wood bar top is dark and smooth, running three quarters of the length of the entire room. There are booths with a deep red velvet cushion and gold trim along the left wall and the backside. Each booth is softly lit by a low-hanging chandelier. The wall next to each booth is decorated with framed paintings of buildings around town, and even a few drawings from Mellani.

There are low tables down the center of the giant room, with matching red velvet chairs, and low-lit light globes in the center of the tables. Red high-back leather stools that far exceed the comfort of the simple wood ones that he used to have line the bar top. Above the bar are black oval fixtures with light spheres inside, complimenting the red used throughout the room. The entire building gives off a warm upscale vibe. Bellatrix offered her men to come and turn the bar into whatever Nik wanted. It's romantic and intimate, while still being the fun, relaxing spot to go after a hard day's work.

Quirina squeals in agreement, shooting Nik a beaming, slightly off-kilter grin. The alcohol has clearly already begun working its way through her bloodstream. We both shoot the whiskey, its smoky caramel flavors going down smoothly and settling warmly in my stomach.

"Maybe that should be your last one, my friend." I laugh as I take the empty glass from her, and scoot her water glass closer.

She sighs dramatically, with a lazy grin. "Yeah, maybe you're right."

I laugh watching the instinctual way her gaze lingers back to Nik. The way she watches him behind the bar, and how he watches her back. Their eyes always seem to find each other. If either of them are aware, I'm not sure, but from where I'm sitting it's pretty clear what's going on.

"So, Rina, do you think you'll ever go back to working at the castle?" I ask, drawing her eyes away from Nik.

Immediately she shakes her head. "No. Being there with her mother, it's too much."

I know what she means.

Trying to be there for Bellatrix, while knowing I have to see Charlotte has not been easy. But for Bellatrix, I'll endure it. Any form of suffering is worth existing next to her.

I nod my head. "I'm sure Bellatrix is grateful you show up for her. She loves you so much."

A knowing grin spreads across her face. With her elbows propped on the table she rests her chin on her hands. "She's my best friend. I'll always show up for her. That girl loves you too, you know."

One side of my mouth lifts into a shy smile. It's strange to hear others talk about us loving each other when we haven't said it ourselves yet. Telling Bellatrix I love her is always on my mind, but I don't want to spook her. It's the same reason I have yet to tell her that we're True Mates. Things between us were intense when she came home, and it finally feels like she's starting to be comfortable with herself again.

"Maybe."

Quirina dramatically shakes her head again, those brown curls bouncing as she does so. "No, she really does. Trust me."

"I guess I'll find out."

Bellatrix could have her pick of any man on this land or the next, and I'm nobody special. As much as I feel the love from her, it's still possible that I could be a placeholder until she finds someone more suitable to rule with.

Nik comes back to the conversation after helping some patrons at the other side of the bar. "Find out what?"

"If Bellatrix looooves him," Quirina answers, her intoxication becoming more evident.

Shaking my head at her shenanigans, I take a long pull from my beer.

"Is that even up for debate?" Nik asks.

Quirina holds her hand out to me dramatically as if to say, "See, I told you."

I shrug. "I'm just glad things are starting to get back to normal again around here."

Nik looks proudly out over his bar, full of customers laughing and enjoying themselves. "It's nice."

The tenderness in his voice is a reminder of how fragile things are. The life we have is always one moment away from being torn out from under us. We've all begun to heal, and I pray to Gods that we don't see another attack.

I finish the rest of my beer and watch as Nik silently takes the glass and refills it for me. He hands it back to me, and I can't help but realize how far we've come too.

"Thanks, man," I tell him.

"No problem, but if you start acting like her"—he gestures playfully towards Quirina—"you're cut off."

"I wasn't talking about the drink."

His eyebrows pull together.

"Thanks for having my back. Coming with me to Sperantia. Risking your life to save mine, even after I was a raging asshole to you and Rina."

Rina lets out a drunken giggle. "You really were! Koen the asshole."

I watch as Quirina drunkenly mocks me, amusing herself. Though it's mostly the alcohol talking, she's right.

"Maybe it's time we get you up to bed, Rina," Nik suggests

tenderly.

I offer to take her since Nik is working.

He shakes his head. "It won't take long to take her upstairs."

Quirina hugs me goodbye and slips her hand comfortably into Nik's, as if it's something they've done a hundred times. He helps her through the back hall towards the stairs in the back.

Nik returns a few minutes later when I've just about finished my new beer. "Did you want another one?"

Tipping the glass towards me to gaze inside, I contemplate whether I should.

"No, I think I'm okay. I should probably get going. I don't want Mel and my mom to worry whether I'm coming home or not."

Nik gives me a nod like he's proud. "Alright, man, thanks for coming in. And I know I've said it before, but thanks for helping out with the bar."

I drop some money onto the bar top for my drinks. "Hey, it was the least I could do."

"Yes, it was," he deadpans, collecting the money and putting it into his register.

I laugh as I stand to shake his hand. "See ya later, man."

"I'll definitely see you at the ceremony."

"You'll be at Bellatrix's ceremony?"

He nods. "Apparently so. Quirina was invited, and she asked me to accompany her. Apparently there will be dancing and food."

I want to ask more, but the smile on my face says enough.

Without me responding, he continues, "As *friends*."

"Sure, sure."

"We are. I've told you this."

I throw my hands up in surrender. "Hey, I'm not judging

anything. It's none of my business."

A pained look crosses his face, and it's one I can't decipher. I decide to leave things be. "I'm happy for you."

If there's anyone in this entire kingdom who deserves good things, it's Nik.

I exit through the large black front doors into the cold, and reflect on the ceremony we'll all be attending. Soon Bellatrix will officially be crowned Queen of Tenuma. I know the night holds more than the crowning. It will unveil what's to come for me and Bellatrix. I'm ready to move things forward with her, no matter what that looks like, but does she feel strongly enough to include me in her plans? Either way, it will be an important and life-changing night.

For us all.

The focus that evening will be on our new queen, but I have plans of my own for that day.

Plans that could change everything.

# 36

# BELLATRIX

Sometimes change is scary, but I love the woman I'm becoming.

"Great job! That was much better," Harding appraises me from the ground.

I reach my hand out to help him up, and we both stand to catch our breath for a moment.

"Thanks. I told you I'd get it."

"I've never said you wouldn't."

"Well, it felt like I never would." I chuckle, reaching for the water canteen on the ground nearby.

"You will always triumph in battle when you put your ego aside and open yourself to new ways to overcome obstacles. At first you fought it, but I can see you've taken my advice seriously and altered your tactics. It's showing."

I thank him, my chest swelling with pride and confidence. Two things I never thought I'd feel again.

"Your mother doesn't want me to train you, you know," he confesses.

Tossing the canteen to the ground, my eyes snap back up to him. His dark eyes reveal his hesitancy. I shouldn't be surprised, and yet I am. "Seriously? What did she say to you?"

He shrugs. "It doesn't matter, I shut it down. You're the queen my loyalties lie with. But from day one, she asked me to decline."

"The nerve of that woman," I say through gritted teeth, my jaw tense.

Every time I think I'm being too hard on her, I turn around only to find out more lies and betrayal.

"She's not in control anymore, Bellatrix." He jabs his forefinger in my chest for dramatic effect. "You are."

I give him a grateful smile. Not only for his kind words, but for having my back. It couldn't have been an easy decision to ignore my mother. She can be very persuasive. I would know.

"Okay," he starts, getting back to business. "Let's see if you can do that again."

Getting back into position, we face off and I wait for him to make his first move. One of the first things he taught me.

*Wait for your opponent to make their first move. Figure out how to block and counterattack.*

Harding takes a swing at me, throwing a right jab, and I successfully duck out of its path. I return a jab to the side of his abdomen, aiming for large organs.

A loud groan leaves his mouth as he hunches over to nurse his wound, for just a second. A second too long, and it allows me to shift into my next move.

I sweep my left leg behind his, knocking him off balance, and he goes down hard. Surging forward, I launch my body on top of his, pulling out my dagger and pressing it to his throat.

He raises both hands in defeat. "Okay, okay!"

A devious smile spreads across my face, as I climb off of him. Knowing I'm getting faster and cleverer is the confidence boost I've needed. Exhausted, I throw myself on the ground to rest, and the unexpected happens.

Despite the cold weather, my face turns hot as emotion rushes over me like a tide. My shoulders begin to shake. Tears are falling down my cheeks before I've realized they've filled my eyes. Harding stands over me silently watching. My body is racked with sobs, and I let them freely descend.

I've forcefully taken my power back, and I now know what I'm capable of. It's been a long road, but I'm here. And now I know that I have it in me to protect myself, to never be the girl who needs to be rescued again. This moment is mine.

When you're violated, much more is taken from you than the stolen moments. You lose your confidence, self-worth, safety, security. In an instant, everything washes out from underneath you, leaving you on unstable terrain.

I'm taking it all back.

"Are you alright, Bellatrix?"

I sniffle, nodding my head as the sobs begin to fade. "I am. I'm good."

My voice comes out more confident than I've felt in a long time. When I began training with Harding, my goal was to protect myself. Somewhere along the way though, it turned into so much more than that.

"I'm proud of you," he says, offering me a hand to get up.

I wipe my eyes with the sleeves of my long thermal top. Nobody tells you that healing comes with a lot of crying.

"I am too."

"Don't get me wrong, this doesn't mean we're done training. I still expect to see your grumpy ass down here every day."

I mock gasp. "After I kicked your ass? I think my training is done."

Harding's deep chuckle at my joke makes me smile. It's not often that Mr. Hardass laughs.

"You've won this round, I'll give you that. But there's still much to learn. We can't slow down now," he says, crossing his arms.

"You're right," I reply, deflating a little.

"Now isn't the time to let your guard down. The enemy gets you just when you think you're safe."

His words send a shudder down my spine. Considering there's been no word from Sperantia since my return, Harding's words are exactly what I've been thinking, fearing this entire time. I don't want to be fearful anymore; I want to be prepared. "I'll be here tomorrow."

There's nothing like a hot shower after pushing and stretching your muscles to their limits. Slowly, my aching muscles begin to loosen. I've been standing under the warm spray for ten minutes now, and haven't found the energy to start actually bathing yet, when I hear my door creak open.

"Princess," Koen calls over the water.

I turn around to see his silhouette through the frosted glass doors of the shower. Swinging one of the doors open, I poke my head out.

"Hi," I greet warmly, water dripping off of me onto the tiled floor.

He looks good. He looks happy.

"Would you like some company?" he asks, smiling sweetly.

Instead of answering, I grin and push the shower door open wider. Koen quickly undresses, leaving his clothes in a heap next to mine, and joins me under the warm water.

"Gods!" he shouts, turning the nozzle to change the temperature.

"Too hot?"

"Not if your goal is to burn off a few layers of skin, Princess."

"Mr. Archer, do you plan on calling me 'Princess' when I'm officially the ruling queen?" I ask, laughing as he wraps his arms around me.

Okay, the cooler water feels good too. Maybe his embrace is warming me up enough by itself.

"Hmm," he ponders. "Maybe I will. You are very worthy of the title, but I don't know if it suits you."

I squeeze my arms around him, holding him close, and we stand swaying slightly side to side.

Though I'm sore and exhausted, he manages to awaken all of my senses, making my heart flutter.

"Well, tell me then, what name suits me?" I ask playfully.

"Mine."

One second we're smiling at each other; the next, our lips crash together. The kisses are needy and passionate. There's a sense of desperation to them, as if neither one of us can get close enough to the other.

Koen is the only man I've ever kissed, the only man I've ever wanted to kiss. Despite my curse and the acts my parents had me performing to become queen, kissing is the one thing I reserved for myself. With the way our lips mold together, I'd say I made the right choice.

*Mine.*

The only thing I want for myself is to be his, and him to be mine.

For the next few minutes we're all hands and tongues and lips. Neither one of us wanting to come up for air, or disturb this bubble we've cocooned ourselves in. Right now, nothing and no one else exists.

"Koen, touch me."

Koen takes a fistful of my long black hair, and spins me around until I'm facing the shower wall. I place both hands on the wall to brace myself, and automatically find myself arching back into his body. He's pressed against me as the water continues to spray over our left sides, but the only heat I feel is from him and the hard length against my backside.

Leaning closer, he whispers in my ear, his deep voice creating goosebumps over my entire body.

"Is that what you want, Princess?"

With his hands still gripping my hair, I can barely move my head but do my best attempt at a nod.

"What was that?"

"Yes," I say breathlessly.

"Tell me what you want."

"I want to be yours." My voice is weak and needy.

My body craves him in all the ways I can't have him. Not without consequence. I want him in every way I could possibly think of. But the question is, does he need me the same way?

# 37

## KOEN

"Do you want me to be yours?" Bellatrix asks me.

A devious grin spreads across my face, and though she's facing the shower wall with her perfect ass arched against my hard dick, I'll make sure she understands clearly.

I press my erection further against her, earning a delicious moan from Bellatrix's perfectly plump red-stained lips.

Do I want to be hers?

Can't she see that she's the only one I could ever want?

With my lips against her ear, I respond in a low voice. "You've always been mine."

As the words leave my mouth, I feel her legs turn to jelly and threaten to give out. I wrap my arm around her torso, holding her up.

"Stay with me, baby," I tell her, which only causes her to go limp in my hands. I can't say the same for my rock-hard cock.

"I want to feel you," she whimpers.

"Where?"

"Everywhere." The neediness in her voice is insanely sexy.

Fuck, I wish we could.

Bellatrix twists around in my arms, so she's facing me. She grips my hard cock in her hand without hesitation. Like it belongs to her.

It absolutely belongs to her.

"Look at you, being such a good girl for me."

She bites her bottom lip. With one hand she begins stroking my cock firmly, and I lower my hand and rub circles on her clit. Our faces are so close together we're moaning into each other's mouths. Bringing my other hand to the back of her head, I draw her to me, fusing our lips together. Bellatrix wastes no time plunging her tongue into my mouth. When she catches my tongue slipping into hers, she latches on and sucks it hard.

As if reading my mind, she backs away and gets on her knees. She takes hold of my cock, licks the precum off the tip, and then wraps her juicy lips around me. She's sucking and stroking me at the same time, and Gods I don't ever want to leave this shower.

The water continues to pour on her head and body, so I slightly shift us out of the path so she can breathe, even though she's doing a decent job making sure she can't. The way she's shoving my cock down her throat and the heaving gags that follow tells me she's taking it as far as she can.

"Good girl, you can take it," I praise.

My approval earns a loud moan from her, and the vibrations on my dick feel incredible. Every interaction with my girl feels so fucking amazing. I can only imagine what it'll be like when we can finally be together.

Even without the curse, her pussy might kill me.

She continues to suck, her tongue working magic swirls around my dick, and I feel my pleasure climbing higher. "Princess,

I'm close. Where do you want it?"

Releasing me for just a moment, she says, "Come down my throat. I want to swallow all of you." Then goes right back to sucking and stroking.

A goddess on her knees for *me*.

My orgasm climbs, and with a groan I explode in her mouth. She continues to work, sucking every last drop and swallowing everything I give her.

"Fuuuuck!" I groan. Stars are in my eyes, and the corners of my vision go dark as pleasure surges through my body.

As she pulls back, her hair is a sopping wet mess, her lips are swollen, and she's never looked more perfect, more mine.

"Fuck, I love you." I can't stop the words from coming out. I'm enchanted by her. Amazed that someone like me ever got a shot with her.

Her head snaps up to me. Her wide eyes and slack jaw tell me that neither one of us expected me to say that.

"I—I mean…" I start trying to ramble off an excuse, but it's pointless. We both know I meant it. I take her hand and help her up so we're standing face to face. "I love you, Bellatrix. My queen."

Her eyes well up with tears. I keep my eyes on her, trying to hold her gaze, but she quickly looks away.

She bites her lip. "Are you sure?"

I can't help but chuckle. "Yes, I'm sure."

A smile spreads across her face when she looks up at me.

I caress her cheek with my thumb. "You don't have to say it back. If you're not ready, I don't want you to feel pressured."

"It's not that I don't, because… I feel it. There are some things I want to make sure are sorted out before I say that to you."

Is she having second thoughts about being with me?

Could there be someone else I don't know about?

"What sort of things?"

She hesitates. "I was planning on talking to you at the ceremony."

The day she chooses her suitor.

"Can you talk to me now?" I ask, knowing I'll go crazy with ideas if I have to wait until then.

"I've been worried you might not want the same things I do. I know being in my life hasn't been easy, and I'm scared."

"You're scared? I just told you I loved you. What could you be scared of?" I ask, perplexed.

She shrugs. "Love doesn't mean the same thing in my world as it does yours. My mother claims to love me, but look what she's done to me."

My jaw tenses at the mention of her mother. "Princess. You're right, we've experienced love differently. But let me be clear. The weeks that you were gone were some of the lowest of my life. I felt lost without you. I love you, which means I will always put you first. I will cherish and protect you at all costs. I loved you then, and I love you now."

Her eyes gloss over and she wraps her hands around my waist, bringing us back together and plants a few tender kisses on my chest.

My girl has been used for so long that she can't recognize, can't trust when someone genuinely cares about her.

"Turn around. Let me wash your hair," I say, grabbing the shampoo. Normally I'd offer to finish her off, but it's safe to say the mood has shifted.

She smiles and turns around as I begin to lather her hair. A fresh floral scent fills the shower as I scrub her scalp. Her head tilts back lazily, and I can tell she's enjoying it.

"I like making you feel good."

"I like you making me feel good," she replies playfully.

"Nobody has ever washed my hair for me before."

"Really? Not even your mom?" I ask, thinking of the countless times I've washed Mel's hair in the bath, but as soon as I ask the question I regret it. I know enough about that woman to know she doesn't have a motherly bone in her body.

"Uh, maybe when I was really little. We used to be close. But it's been a long time since she's shown me that kind of affection. Or maybe all of the terrible things she's done have overshadowed the memories." The last part feels like a thought that slipped out rather than something she meant to say aloud.

"I'm glad we have some firsts together. I'd do this for you every day."

Once I finish her hair, I grab the loofah that's hanging on the wall above the nozzles and lather it up with soap. "Can I wash you?"

She nods in approval, so I begin washing her shoulders. Once I reach her chest I slow down, savoring the way the bubbles look on each of her breasts, glistening like an orb of light, showcasing their perfection.

I work down her stomach, caressing her in slow circles. I'm hesitant to move lower, not wanting to cross any boundaries. I don't want her to think I'm only after her body. Before I can act, Bellatrix's hand covers mine and shoves it downward, between her legs.

I shoot her a smirk, loving when my girl gets feisty. Bellatrix has many sides to her, and I love each and every one. She's strong, yet soft. She's shy, yet she knows what she wants. It's insanely sexy.

My hand moves between her legs, washing her gently but thoroughly. Kneeling, I trail my hand down each of her legs. Once I've finished and the water is rinsing her off, I prop one leg up and place one of her feet on my knee.

I glance upward, and once I get the nod of approval I spread her legs open wider, giving me a better view of her. All of her.

"Gods, Princess, you're perfect."

"What are you waiting for? Eat."

# 38

# BELLATRIX

"Don't stop!"

His face is pressed against my pussy, while his tongue works magic on my sensitive flesh. I've been aroused and eager to feel him since he walked into the washroom. It might not be his dick, but Gods, his tongue is incredible.

He pulls back, then uses two fingers to open me up. A wide grin plasters across his face before his tongue dives back into place, fucking my pussy. He uses a thumb to put delicious pressure on my clit, massaging slow circles.

"More," I beg, and he obeys by slipping a finger inside me. Then another finger, pumping them in and out with perfect rhythm as he sucks on my clit. My arousal covers his face and beard, and the gentle scratching on my thighs feels euphoric.

This man loves me. Really loves me.

The pressure is building, and it feels so fucking good. Being spread open and exposed while his face is buried between my legs makes me feel powerful. There are many ways to embrace strength, and I'm taking back control of them all, my sex life included. Koen's face belongs between my legs, licking, sucking, biting, fucking.

He moans, and the vibration against my pussy feels as good as the scruff of his facial hair.

"Moan again, please. Let me hear it."

Without missing a beat, he drags out a few more moans against my pussy, turning me into putty.

My legs want to give out, and I have to hold onto the wall for support.

"Almost, don't stop. Oh Gods, please. Don't. Stop."

He continues the movements without changing speeds, or rhythms, and I love him more for it. My orgasm builds and it erupts with his face still buried between my legs. I grab the back of his head, holding him in place.

A scream escapes my lips, while Koen keeps licking, lapping up every last drop of my wetness. His eagerness tells me it would never be enough. He's a parched man, lost in the desert, and I'm his oasis.

Once I've come back down, Koen kisses the inside of each thigh, and gently sets my foot back on the floor of the shower. He stands back up right as shouting starts outside the washroom.

"Your Majesty! Everything okay there?" A man's voice shouts from the other side of the washroom door.

He's too close, and I can't help but feel suddenly exposed in an unpleasant way. Memories of being watched in Lothar's kingdom come flooding back, and my heart begins to race. That familiar panic of needing to cover my body creeps in, bursting my lust bubble with Koen.

He must sense my alarm, because he shoves me behind his body, using himself as a shield.

I quickly shout back, almost choking on my words. "Yes! I'm fine. Please do not come in! I will be out shortly!"

"We will be right outside your chamber doors. Please report to one of the men once you're decent," the man shouts back, retreating back outside as evident by the door snapping shut.

"Can you make sure they're gone?" I ask, trying to stop my hands from shaking.

Koen turns to me, glances at my clasped shaking hands, and nods before exiting the shower and peeking around the door. "They're gone, Princess."

Koen dries me with a towel once we've finished showering. I grab my red knee-length silk robe from behind the door, securing it around my waist. I open my chamber door to let the guards know that I'm decent and unharmed. They peek around me to look at Koen, and once they're satisfied there's no danger, I close the door.

"You should keep some of your clothes here, so you don't have to keep throwing on the same ones after a shower," I say, feeling bad that I don't have anything to offer him.

"It's fine, Princess. I'm used to making do with very little."

It's a harmless comment, yet I can't help feeling responsible for it. For my family's policies and the burden they've put on our people. The hardships they've endured for years.

I release a deep breath. "I plan on making sure that changes."

"You already have, Princess," he tells me, lifting my chin and planting a soft kiss on my lips.

My shoulders lift in a shrug.

"It's true. You made it possible for people to rebuild their homes. Made sure they had supplies. Helped families get back on their feet. Provided food to those who needed it."

His words warm my chest, but it's not enough. None of that would have been necessary if it weren't for me. I'm the reason Tenuma was attacked, and why our beautiful land was burned down.

Koen sees the defeat in my face, the guilt I can't seem to shake. "You have to stop blaming yourself. You never asked for this. I know who you are, and you are not the cause for anything that's happened. You can't control who your parents are and what they've done."

I want to believe his words. If there's anyone who understands this feeling, it's Koen.

"I'm trying."

The large fireplace crackles, startling us both. Exhaustion begins to set in as I pad over to my bed. Koen follows behind, sitting next to me on the bed as I get comfortable beneath my silk sheets. I find myself without the strength to stand any longer.

My eyelids feel heavy, and I'm vaguely aware of the way Koen sits next to me holding my hand as I begin to drift off to sleep. Knowing he's next to me is comforting, relaxing me even further, and I find it difficult to open my eyes. Like knowing, with him watching over me, I can finally let my guard down.

He whispers in my ear, "Sleep well, Princess. I'll be back tomorrow."

My attempt at responding is more of a lazy grunt, and I'm not sure if he's heard it. I feel him lightly kiss my forehead, and I fall into a deep slumber.

"We need to talk," Quirina shouts from inside my large closet.

My hands rest underneath my head as I lay on my side in bed. The training session earlier left my body completely worn out, and I don't have the energy to move.

"What about?" I ask with a yawn.

"Well, your mother's forcing you to go through with this ceremony, so what do you plan to wear?" she asks, peeking her head out of the closet.

"I don't know, Rina, a dress isn't exactly at the top of my priorities list."

Holding one of my favorite emerald green corset dresses, she saunters over to the bed, sitting beside me. "I know you have a lot on your plate, but you're allowed to focus on good things too. This ceremony is a good thing."

"Oh yeah, why's that?" I ask her.

"Because you'll be able to officially declare Koen as your king."

I chew on my lip.

"That is what you plan on doing, isn't it?" she asks, her eyes going wide at the possibility that there could be anyone else.

"It is. I just feel stupid thinking about such trivial things when there are much bigger ones," I reply.

Being queen isn't something I want for myself, I just don't trust anyone else to do it. The way our people have suffered at the hands of my family is enough. It's my job to mend the wounds. To heal the kingdom.

"I get that. All I'm saying is, you're allowed to focus on good things, too."

"Like Nik?" I ask, playfully nudging her with my foot.

Rina's cheeks instantly heat, and a smile spreads across her face before she has time to stop it. Or maybe she's not trying to hide it anymore. At this point we've all seen the way they gravitate towards each other, and the way she lights up around him. They can say whatever they want, but the body doesn't lie.

The smile spreads wider as she speaks. "Yes. Like Nik."

I can't help but mirror her smile. Seeing her happy after all she's been through sends a wave of warmth through me. "I can't find you without him nearby. You became a package deal."

She shrugs and nods her head in agreement. "Yeah, I guess we are."

We both giggle. "How did this even happen?"

She bites her bottom lip, concentrating on her reply. "He was just… there."

Giving her an understanding nod, I let her continue.

"After my parents were killed, he was there. When you were taken and I had nowhere to go, he was there. When I was grieving the three of you, he was there, always making sure my head was above water even when I didn't want to. When everything was falling apart, he was my stability."

My eyes instantly water. "I'm so sorry I wasn't there for you, Rina."

She reaches over to give my leg a squeeze. "All things considered, I think I can forgive you for that."

"I'm still sorry I wasn't there. You've been by my side since I've returned home, and I can't imagine having to get through all of this without you. I'm really happy you have him."

"He's pretty great. And you're my best friend, so stop apologizing. It's my job to be there for you. Now, back to the dress…"

I groan dramatically.

"Come on, you used to love this sort of thing. Plus, I know

that you want to look and feel your best when your king walks in."

"If he shows up."

"What do you mean? Why wouldn't he?"

I'm not used to people showing up when I need them the most.

"I invited his family, and Fira was very hesitant about it. Which I understand, but I just wonder if they don't show up, will he?"

She clicks her tongue. "Girl, you know damn well there's nowhere else he's going to be."

"I guess. Things are going to change. Not only for me, but for him. If he chooses to stay with me."

I can't stop the worried thoughts that flood my mind. Asking him means giving us a real chance and changing not only his life, but his family's life. Koen tells me he's all in, but does he really know what that entails? He could decide that all the danger and chaos is too much for him and his family. Maybe he'll decide to walk away.

"He's already changed his life for you without you asking." She pauses, opening and closing her mouth twice like she wants to say more but is hesitating.

"What? Tell me."

"When you were gone, he was unrecognizable. He was a mess. There's not a thing that man does that isn't for you, or about you. He loves you, and I think you should focus on enjoying your special day. Because that's exactly what it is. It's your day. *Queen.*"

My heart knows she's right. Time and time again, he shows up. Koen's been there when no other person has. When fear kept everyone else from standing up for me, myself included, he had my back.

"You're right. Let's find a dress," I tell her.

"Oooh, I think I know the perfect one!"

# 39

## KOEN

There's no perfect way to start this conversation, but it needs to be had.

Mel sits next to me at our kitchen table, and my mother sits across from us. A pile of Mel's drawings lay sprawled across the table between us like a timeline of current events.

The most recent one is tucked into my pocket, away from my mother's curious eyes. The one that shows what I have planned for the night of the ceremony, the decision I've made. It cannot be seen by another soul.

"Mel, can you tell me why you drew these?" I ask gently, pushing them towards her.

She shrugs. "They felt important."

My mother and I shoot each other a look.

"Where did the images come from?" my mother asks her in the same cautious manner.

"Sometimes I dream about them, but they're not regular dreams. They're more real."

"Real how?" I ask.

Mel chews on her lip for a moment before answering. "Like they're really happening. Sometimes they scare me."

I reach over and grab her tiny hand in mine. "Hey, you're safe. I won't let anything hurt you."

"That's not all," she admits.

"What do you mean?" my mother and I ask in unison.

"Sometimes I see things when I'm awake, too. If the picture won't go away, I'll draw them."

*Sweet girl.*

My heart aches for her. It must be terrifying not to understand your own mind.

"I see. Mel, have you told anybody other than Ma and me about these images you get?"

She shakes her head.

"Good. I don't want you to be afraid, but I want you to know how important it is that you don't tell anybody about…this." I choose my words cautiously, not wanting to heighten her fears.

She seems to understand and nods.

"Mel, sweetheart, are there any other drawings you've made that we should see?" our mother asks.

She grabs a stack of papers from a shelf next to the couch depicting images of our family, flowers, and other seemingly innocent drawings.

Our mother scans the pictures then hands them back. "Will you be sure to let us know if any new ones come to you?"

"Sure, Mama."

We both smile sweetly at her, trying to keep her from picking up on the tension. Mel, thank Gods for her innocence, doesn't seem to be affected.

"Can I go outside and play?" she asks.

"Of course. Stay in the yard, and I'll call you in when it's time to wash up for dinner," she tells her.

Mel hops out of the chair, slips into some snow boots and her coat, and disappears into the backyard. I remain seated at the table with my mother.

"Do you think we should have told her more? Maybe tell her that it's a gift?" I ask.

My mother considers the question, and then shakes her head. "In time we will. Let her enjoy being a kid. She has a very powerful gift. I think for now, the less she understands about it, the better."

"I thought you said our powers reveal themselves only after we've met our true mates. Mel is just a kid."

She shakes her head. "Not for women. Our gifts can show up at any time. I had my gift long before I met your father, not that he was my true mate."

"Mel could know when the next attack is coming. She could save lives," I say with bewilderment.

"Maybe, but we must be very careful with this information. The more people that know of her gift, the more danger she could be in. Soothsayers are rare and powerful. Her safety must always take priority over any information she might possess," she tells me with a stern expression.

I nod. She's right. Now that we're aware of her gift, we will have to pay better attention to it, and whatever drawings she creates.

I let out a deep breath. "If you two are okay here, I think I'm going to go for a run. Maybe I'll stop by Nik's."

My mother reaches across and squeezes my hand. "Okay, be safe. I'm happy you and Nik patched things up. He's a good man. You both are."

The corners of my mouth lift into a bashful smile. "Thanks,

Ma. I know I wasn't myself for a while. I'm not proud of the things I did, the things I said. I'm really lucky that you were all willing to give me another chance."

She gives me a warm smile. "Pain and suffering are inevitable. But you can't let it turn you into someone else. You may have gotten derailed for a bit, but you found your way back to us. I'm proud of you, my son. I think it's time you let go of the guilt you've been carrying around. Let yourself breathe."

Maybe she's right. I can't change what's happened, but I can choose what happens here on out.

"Thanks, Ma. I love you."

"I love you, my boy."

While my mother and I haven't always seen eye to eye or been fully transparent with each other, we always show up for each other. Our protection and love for each other knows no bounds, and it's exactly what I plan to bring to my relationship with Bellatrix.

Walking through the large doors to Nik's bar, I can see that he's got quite the crowd to attend to, so he doesn't see me. The sweet and spicy scent of tequila and beer hops invade my senses as I work my way through the sea of people. I spot a single seat at the other end of the bar and quickly make my way over before it too is occupied. Nik and Quirina tend to the bar, working quickly in order to keep up with the demand. Multiple workers are carrying out trays of food from the swinging doors next to the bar.

After a few minutes I manage to catch Nik's eye, and without having to ask, he pours me a pint of my favorite beer. I thank him as he places the mug in front of me.

"Wow, is the whole village here?" I ask jokingly.

He laughs. "Seems like it. Are you hungry?"

"No. I just needed to get out and see my friends."

He smiles and raps his knuckles on the bar twice. "Well, let me get through this rush and I'll be back to catch up."

Sipping on my beer, I release a breath and allow myself to relax into the plush high-back barstools. The beer enters my bloodstream, and it's exactly what I needed after my talk with Mel. While the conversation was what I suspected, it caused new fears to surface.

Does Mel know what's coming?

What if somebody finds out about her gift?

I'm taking another long pull of my beer when the collective chatter of the entire bar comes to a halt. I turn my head to see the front door swung open, but I can't see who's entered. I immediately reach for the dagger sheathed above my ankle.

At the other end of the bar there's movement, and I see Bellatrix and her new companions come into view. Like a tornado clearing a path, the crowd divides down the middle so they can move easily through the bar.

"Bellatrix?" My voice isn't louder than normal, but in the silence of the bar, it captures everyone's attention.

Surprise etches her face as her eyes meet mine, and she quickens her pace over to me.

"Koen. Thank Gods," she says quietly, looking around. "Should I be worried? Am I in danger here?"

I chuckle, and wrap my arm around her waist, pulling her into me. "No. Not when you're with me, Princess."

I'm about to greet Theo and Valeria, only to realize we're still being heavily scrutinized by every patron in the bar, in complete silence.

Standing and addressing the whole bar, I offer a gentle warning. "Go back to your meals. Bellatrix is one of us. She's not to be bothered."

As quickly as it stopped, the conversation resumes.

"Thank you," she tells me, wrapping her arms around me.

I give her a squeeze. "Of course. And here I thought it was strange to see you in my *cottage*. This is definitely a sight I'll never forget."

"Oh, please." She laughs and playfully smacks my chest. I fake a groan and grip my chest as if in pain.

"Hey, man," Theo says, sticking his hand in mine.

I've apologized to him, and we've run into each other a few times since my outburst. Luckily we've gotten past it and can be cordial. Admittedly he's a pretty easygoing guy.

Bellatrix has been spending a lot of time with Hidi's family, and I know that, for her, it's a way of coping with Hidi's death.

"Hello," his mother says with a nod.

"What are you all doing here?" I ask.

"My mother was her usual charming self and ruined dinner by repeatedly referring to them as 'the help.' So, I thought I'd save us the agony of sitting through an awkward meal and come to support Nik. Quirina swears by the food here."

"I'm glad you all came."

"You guys hungry?" Nik shouts over to the four of us.

I nod my head. "Yes, they haven't eaten."

Nik hands me a couple of menus, and I go in search of a free table. A couple rises from a large booth just as I'm walking by, so I set the menus down and wave over at Bellatrix. We slide in, and a staff member immediately arrives to take our order. The woman looks nervous but smiles at Bellatrix the entire time.

Since her return, Bellatrix's reputation has greatly improved. Gone is the woman that everyone feared. People are now seeing all the good she's done. Families discovered that she was responsible for all the money their children were bringing home. That she helped Nik's bar get up and running. That she provided the supplies for families to rebuild their homes. She's no longer the Soul Snatcher—though the curse remains—she's just Bellatrix.

A whiskey on ice sits in front of Bellatrix, a glass of wine in front of Theo's mother, and a beer in front of Theo and me.

I hold my beer up. "Cheers to the princess slummin' it."

She feigns shock, flipping her hair back over her shoulder. "I am not a priss. You might remember I shared a weekend getaway with you on a cold cave floor."

The memory of us trapped in a snow-covered cave together flashes before my eyes. It was the first time I had spent a significant amount of time with her, and I immediately knew she was different. Knew she was something to be cherished. It was also the same night we almost crossed a very dangerous line.

I chuckle at her words. "You're right. It's what I love about you."

The word hangs suspended between us. Apparently I'm unable to prevent that word from leaving my lips around her. When she's near I feel like a child, speaking uninhibited and unfiltered, letting my heart do the talking. Bellatrix has yet to say it back, and I'm trying not to let it bother me. I know she's been through a lot, so I'm willing to be patient. She doesn't draw attention to it, and luckily the server shows up with bread and whipped butter, so we let the moment pass.

Bellatrix clears her throat. "How was your evening at home?"

I rub the back of my neck. "It was okay."

"Did you talk to Mel?" she asks.

I nod.

We've have had multiple conversations about Mel's drawings and what they could mean, but I'm not about to divulge my family's secrets in front of people I've known for such a short time. Though Bellatrix seems close with them, I'm not sure how much I trust them. I guess that comes with the territory of being betrayed by your own father.

Bellatrix places a hand on my knee underneath the table. She knows there's more, but she doesn't push me. My mother made it very clear not to let anyone in on Mel's gift, so I'll have to discuss this with the princess at another time.

Taking a large gulp of my beer, I'm reluctant to say more with others listening in. I change the subject and ask Theo and Valeria how they've been settling in and if they'd like to see more of Tenuma.

Once we finish our drinks, Valeria and Theo head to the bar to get us another round, and Bellatrix takes the opportunity to dig deeper.

"What is it?" she asks.

I lower my voice and lean in closer. "Mel is a soothsayer. She said all of her drawings come to her. Some in dreams, some while she's awake."

Bellatrix gasps. "What does this mean?"

I sigh. "Well, it means that she could very well know if we're in any immediate danger. She could see what the future of Tenuma holds."

"But?"

"But my mother and I discussed it, and we don't want to exploit her. Or make her feel like she's a tool to be used for other people's purposes."

Bellatrix looks away from me, but not before I see the shame in her eyes. We haven't talked much about her curse since her return. There are no more suitors, but the past remains. Like an inkblot on the story of her life, it will never go away. She's still the princess who slept with enough men to create an undead army against her will. The way Bellatrix carries the responsibility for it kills me. She should never wear the shame her mother should be covered in. It's not something I'd ever wish upon Mel.

"Hey," I say, tilting her chin towards me with my thumb and forefinger. "None of that. You did nothing wrong. It never should have happened, but you are not to blame."

The sad smile she reveals tells me she's not convinced, but nods regardless. "I don't want her to feel that way, either. This is a very different circumstance. You and Fira would never treat Mel that way. But if there's any chance it could prevent another attack, don't you think it's worth knowing?" she asks.

I nod. She's right, but I know my mother won't agree, even though knowing could prevent great loss for Tenuma.

I sigh heavily. Getting Mel involved in this war is the last thing I want for her. I wouldn't be able to live with myself if she got mixed up in anything dangerous.

Theo and Valeria return with the drinks, and we cheers. I lift my mug, draining the entire beer. I watch Bellatrix do the same with her whiskey. Her tense shoulders drop, and she says the last thing I expect her to.

# 40

# BELLATRIX

"Fuck it. Shots for everyone."

The bar erupts in hoots and hollers at my announcement.

Throwing back shots might not be my brightest solution, but I think we're all due for a little release. Tonight, I want to loosen up and focus on the good things.

Koen is a very good thing.

My friends. Miri. The town standing on its feet again. These are the only things I want to think about.

Rina bounces through the room a few minutes later with a tray full of shots, handing them off along the way. She approaches our table and sets the tray down. Koen slips out of the oversized booth, and I scoot out to greet my friend.

"Trix! I can't believe you're here!" she squeals, squeezing me in a warm embrace.

I pull back and see the warm smile gracing her lips. "I had to see where my best friend was spending all her time."

Crimson colors her cheeks, and her eyes light up. "So, shots, huh? Can I assume something happened with your mother?"

Giving her a knowing smile, I nod. "Always. But we aren't talking about that tonight. Tonight we are drinking."

Quirina distributes the shots to everyone at the table, greeting each person with a smile and a warm hello.

Taking the lime off the edge of the glass, I hold it up. "Rina, are you taking one with us?"

"Can you drink while you're working?" Koen asks, grinning at her.

She makes a pfft noise. "I actually don't work here. I only help out when he needs it. Besides, I would be honored to take a shot with our next queen!"

The title causes me to shrink a little. Self-doubt and insecurities creeping in, telling me I'm not worthy. But Koen wraps his arm around my back and pulls me into him, smiling encouragingly.

He sees me when nobody else does.

Holding up his own shot glass, Koen makes a toast. "Here's to our girl coming home, and to a better life ahead."

With so much uncertainty, his hopefulness and positivity manage to seep out, reminding me that things aren't all bad. Like the sunflower that intentionally faces the sun for warmth, I lean into him and try to soak it all up.

The five of us raise our small glasses, clink them, and throw them back. Theo's mom surprises me by taking one with us and is the first to ask for another one.

"Valeria! I knew I liked you!" Quirina tells her playfully, before scurrying off to the bar for another round.

The strained atmosphere we initially walked into made me think coming here was a mistake, but I've quickly gone from lost doe to one of the pack. Blending into the crowd as if I belong. As if I've always belonged.

We spend the night drinking, laughing, and enjoying each other's company. Something so simple, yet it feels monumental to me. A luxury I've never been able to participate in. My entire life I've felt like an outcast, the topic of whispers in every room, but not tonight. Tonight, all of that feels kingdoms away. I pretend for a moment that I'm a regular woman out with her friends.

After we consume our food—much needed after the two tequila shots—Theo and Valeria decide to call it a night and head back to the castle.

"I'll head back with you," I offer, but Valeria waves me off.

"No, no, you stay here and enjoy yourself. We can manage to find our way back," she tells me, but it's more of a demand. A mother's way of not wanting to burden the ones around her.

"I don't mind. You're still new to Tenuma, and I would hate it if—" I start, but she cuts me off.

"We can manage, Princess. Please don't let us ruin your evening."

Koen gives my leg a squeeze under the table. "They'll be fine. We will head back soon."

"Thank you for everything tonight, Bellatrix. This was— we really needed this," Theo tells me.

I nod. "I'll see you back at the castle then."

They slip out the front door, and my attention cuts back to Koen. "We?"

"Hmm?" he asks.

"You said we would head back. Are you staying with me tonight?"

A grin spreads across his face. "If you'll have me, Princess."

I lean in closer, pressing my lips to his ear. "I would have you every day if it were up to me."

His body gives a slight shudder, and as I pull away to sip the drink in front of me, I see his eyes have gone dark. Where I once saw light and playfulness, I now see hunger.

"Be careful what you wish for, Princess." His voice is so low that if I wasn't watching his lips like they were the quenching beverage to my dehydrated soul, I would have missed it.

"Or what?"

His grip on my leg loosens, as his hand trails up my leg higher, higher. "Maybe we should head back too."

"What did you have in mind?" I ask, letting his fingers trail dangerously close to the aching between my legs.

"Because I'm suddenly starving." His words send full body chills, and I instinctively squeeze my legs together to dull the growing ache, trapping his hand between my legs.

Picturing his face between my legs, the lush beard rubbing against my thighs, nearly leaves me in a puddle in this bar.

It's definitely time to go.

"I better feed my man, then."

"That's my good girl." His praise nearly makes me moan aloud.

"What is it that you're craving?"

He gives me a devious smile. "Your mouth-watering pussy."

I bite my bottom lip, and his thumb comes up to stroke it.

"These lips are mine too."

"Let's go put your actions where your mouth is, then."

"I plan on putting *you* where my mouth is."

Tipping my glass back, I empty the contents and nudge my chin for him to get up.

Quirina slipped back behind the bar to help Nik, so I wave her down to the end of the counter to pay and say our goodbyes.

"Hey, are you leaving too?" she asks, scooping ice into a clean glass.

"Yeah, it's getting late."

She raises an eyebrow. "Girl, look at those eyes sparkle. You are wide awake. There's no need to lie to me."

I lift an eyebrow at her. "I could say the same to you."

I nudge my chin in Nik's direction, and she knows what I'm referring to without even looking. She playfully rolls her eyes and then pulls me in for a hug across the bar. "Get out of here, and please be safe out there."

"Always," I tell her, handing her money to cover our bill and then some.

"You better be."

The flicker of worry I see behind her eyes tells me that just because I'm home, the fear hasn't left. If anything, we're all more on edge, constantly worried when the next disaster will strike. With more secrets being exposed and gifts revealing themselves, everyone's a little uneasy.

If only my curse would turn into a gift.

Koen says his goodbyes to Nik, and then joins me at the front door. As we walk out together, he takes his hand in mine, and I finally feel like I'm home.

# 41

# KOEN

**B**ellatrix has always felt like home to me.

I loved seeing her let go tonight. Watching her laugh and talk with our friends as if it were a typical outing for us. Like a real couple. Without all the doom and gloom.

Once we return to the castle, she changes into a silk, strappy black nightgown, and climbs into her oversized bed. I strip down to my undergarments joining her.

The slightly inebriated smile she's wearing turns me to jelly. She still has her reservations when it comes to us, but this version of her can't contain her true feelings for me. They're written all over her face.

*She loves me.*

I've let the L word slip a few times, but she's hardly acknowledged it. There are moments when I know her feelings mirror mine, but she's protecting her heart. Refusing to let herself fall.

"Thank you for coming home with me tonight," she says

lazily, like the words are rolling around in her mouth.

"Happy to. I'm glad you want me here."

"I always want you here. And soon, you'll never have to leave," she says cryptically.

"Oh really? Are you asking me to move in?" I joke, squeezing her hip, laying facing each other a few inches apart.

Her big green eyes find mine, and in her drunken haze I can see her wheels turning. "Don't you want to?"

Is she really asking?

"I want to be wherever you are."

The sluggish smile appears again, and her eyes drift close. "Good, because I'm going to ask you. Ver-very soon."

I watch as her breathing deepens, and her eyes flutter when she starts to dream. I lightly caress her arm for a few minutes, and then pull the covers up to her chin. A relaxing moan escapes in her unconscious state, and I can't help but smile. The way she eases into sleep tells me she feels safe, and that's all I ever want for her.

"Good night, Princess," I whisper before dozing off next to her.

"Aaahhh, no! Hidi! Run!" Bellatrix screams.

My heavy eyes snap open to see the moon still shining brightly outside her windows. I roll over to see her thrashing next to me in her bed. Her arms and legs are flailing, eyes closed, face pinched.

"Stay away from me. No, I don't want to drink it," she pleads, eyes still shut.

I reach over and softly stroke her arm. "Princess, wake up, you're having a bad dream."

She continues to swing her arms, like she's trying to escape something, or someone.

My grip on her arm is firmer now, and I try to gently shake her awake. "Bellatrix, wake up, you're safe."

Her arm comes swinging at me, but my half-asleep reflexes are too slow to dodge the blow before she makes contact with my cheek. I take a fist to the face, and groan in agony.

Her eyes snap open and dart back and forth in confusion. "Koen, what's going on?"

With one hand I rub my cheek. Her gaze meets mine, and I see the moment it all comes together for her. "Oh my gods, did I do that?"

Her hand reaches for me, and I grab it between both of mine. "I'm fine."

Her eyes fill with water, and her bottom lip trembles. "I'm so sorry. I can't believe I did that."

Placing one hand on her cheek, I hold her face close. "Hey, I'm fine. Are *you* okay?"

She nods. "I keep having these dreams. They're awful, and I can't make them stop. I should have told you."

I shake my head. "My jaw can take a hit or two. I want to make sure you're okay. What can I do?"

"Hold me."

A smile stretches across my face. "I can do that."

I hold her tightly against my body, my arm draped over her. If another nightmare comes, I'll be right here to see her through it.

Tenuma after a fresh snowfall. Mellani's smile. My mother's proud face after finishing a new project. And Bellatrix's serene face in the morning are a few of the most perfect and beautiful things I've witnessed.

Her eyes flutter open, and she stretches her limbs. I caress her cheek with my thumb, earning a jolt from her.

"I'm sorry, I didn't mean to scare you," I say with a rueful expression.

Her initial shock is replaced with a bashful grin. "Oh my gosh, I forgot you stayed here."

"Wow, I must have made quite the impression on you last night," I reply playfully.

"I'm sorry. I'm not used to having you here, I guess."

I debate whether I should bring up her nightmare or not, but decide to let her bring it up if she decides. Grinning at her, my hand slides down to her back, giving her a gentle rub. "I had fun last night.

You did reveal some interesting information, though."

Panic flashes in her eyes. "What do you mean?"

I can see her mind racing, and now I feel bad for taunting her. "You may or may not have asked me to move in with you."

Turning to lay on her side, she buries her face in her hands, causing her words to come out muffled. "Please tell me I did not."

"Afraid so."

She looks up at me from under her long dark lashes, giving

me the sweetest expression.

"Let's blame the alcohol. Those shots were not my brightest idea."

"Maybe not, but I like the way it lowered your guard."

"What do you mean?"

I take a moment before I speak, carefully choosing my words. Unsure if it's the right time. It could scare her off, and I sure as hell don't want to ruin all the progress we've made. Trust doesn't come easy for her. All I can do is hope that my actions thus far have proven that she can trust me.

I cup her cheek with my hand, softly pressing my lips to hers. Pulling back, I let my confession pour out. "Princess, I love you. I'm so in love with you. I know I've said it before, and I can see the way you're hesitant to move forward. And that's okay. I want you to know I'm not going anywhere. No matter how long it takes you to feel the same. Last night you showed me how much you care about me. I know that those feelings are there. And even though you haven't said it back I know you want more for us, too. Just know that, whenever you're ready, I'll be here."

Silence takes over the room, but I swear I can hear her frenzied thoughts. She rolls her lips in and out, mulling over what I've said. Her eyes glisten, and her gaze is glued to mine. My finger gently strokes her cheek as I patiently wait for her to sort her thoughts out. "You don't have to say anything," I say, smiling.

She gives me a wide grin back. "I love you too, Koen."

*She loves me.*

"Princess, I need to kiss you."

"Kiss me."

My heart explodes, and I can't keep my lips off of her another second. Our lips crash together. It's fast and fervid. Our tongues dance together as if the other contains the remedy for a lifelong affliction, both of us desperate for relief. Her hands weave into my hair, pulling us closer together, and my hands instinctively wrap around her midsection, my fingers digging into her back. We can't get close enough. Can't feel enough. Can't taste enough.

I want to consume every inch of her.

I manage to pull us apart, and I lay her onto her back. My fingers search for the bottom of her satin nightgown, moving deftly as I inch it higher until it's gathered at her stomach.

My gaze wanders back up to hers, making sure she's okay with me touching her. She nods, pushing her hips upward. With her panties exposed, I slip my thumbs into the sides of the waistband, awaiting an approving nod to proceed, and then slip them down to her feet. I drop them at the bottom of the bed, turning my attention back to the goddess on the bed. "Be a good girl and open up for me."

She spreads her legs open, and it's like gazing into the heavens. My cock hardens when she obeys. She's perfect, and she's all mine.

I take my time moving higher. Working my way upward, I plant kisses on her legs, giving her a gentle nibble when I feel her flesh turn prickly under my lips. Giving her goosebumps just became one of my new favorite pastimes. I kiss the inside of her thigh, issuing another gentle bite. A quiet moan slips from her lips, and my cock twitches in response.

"I never got my meal last night, Princess," I say with a sinister smile. "What do you want? Tell me," I demand.

She's already panting, and her words come out choppy. "I want your mouth on me."

With one hand on each of her knees, I push her open wider, giving myself full access to her pussy. I lower my head as my tongue darts out to make a few circles on her clit. Before I dive in, I look up and notice she's dropped her head back and her eyes are closed.

"Hey," I say firmly.

She startles, quickly lifting her head to meet my gaze. The confused look she gives me makes my cock twitch again, and I cannot wait to eat this woman alive.

"Eyes on me, Princess," I tell her and then, flattening my tongue, give her a long lick from bottom to top like she's the last meal I'll ever enjoy.

I glance up again. "You're going to watch me devour you. Keep your eyes on me while I lick, suck, and fuck this pretty pussy. I want you to watch me worship your body the way it deserves to be treated."

A devious grin spreads across her face. "It's all yours."

Bellatrix giving herself to me fully, telling me her pussy is mine, drives the animalistic side of me wild. It takes all of my restraint and brain power to remember that I can't fuck her the way I want to. Not yet anyways. But I can taste her. And I plan to, until she begs me to stop.

# 42

# BELLATRIX

"Don't stop!" I cry out.

Koen licks my pussy like it's his job.

Maybe I'll make it his first official duty once he's king.

His tongue darts in and out of me, as his thumb rubs aching circles on my clit. As my hips thrust against his face his tongue replaces his thumb, and he slips two fingers inside of me, curling them to hit the spot that makes me explode.

He pumps his fingers in and out of me, while his tongue works my clit, making my body climb closer and closer to orgasm. The current starts at the top of my head and my toes, building and traveling further to my core.

"Gods, please don't stop."

I might be known as the Soul Snatcher, but with the way he makes my body feel, I'm certain he's stolen mine.

Thick fingers fuck me steadily, and a deft tongue works my throbbing clit, creating the most agonizing pleasure. I grind my hips against his face, still needing to be closer. I need more. As I buck into him, he growls against my pussy, causing a delicious vibration.

If this feels this good, I'm not sure I can handle his dick inside me.

My orgasm hits its peak, causing my body to tense as I cry out in pleasure. But he refuses to stop and keeps licking. Lapping up all of my juices, making sure he works until my orgasm has run its course, giving me every ounce of pleasure. Koen gives me one last long lick, then lifts his head and runs his tongue over his lips for any remaining wetness. "Delicious."

All of my limbs feel like jelly, and though we just woke up, my energy is zapped.

"Fuck," I murmur. "What did you just do to me?"

He climbs the bed, and lays next to me with a chuckle, but his voice holds a serious tone. "The same thing you did to me. Snatched my soul."

Did he read my mind?

Though the nickname has always left a sour feeling in my gut, when he says it, a new emotion rises.

Love.

Devotion.

That's what it means to him. We've been forever changed since entering each other's lives. And, while I can't speak for him, I've never felt anything close to this in my life.

I turn on my side, laying my arm on his bare stomach. "My turn."

My hand begins sliding downward to release his giant dick

from the tent he's created in his trousers, but a hand on top of mine stops me.

"You know I would love nothing more, but I need to get home. Mellani gets upset when I don't come home at night."

Now I feel worse. "That's so sad. Why did you stay?" I can't hide the guilt in my voice.

"Because my other girl needed me."

"I would love it if all of you stayed here with me."

I love both his mother and sister. Nothing would make me happier than having them all here, like a real family. I want to make Koen my king. But I don't know how this will work when his mom refuses to step foot on the castle grounds. I know he would never leave them behind, so where does that leave us?

"You know how my mother feels. It has nothing to do with you. She loves you. They both do."

I'm not used to having people that care about me, and it's still foreign to hear someone use that word so easily and know they mean it.

Giving him a disappointed smile, I nod. "I understand."

"Soon," he tells me, planting a kiss on my lips, then stands to dress.

Soon?

Soon what?

I dress in my favorite silk robe, and pad to where Koen sits on the bed, tying his boots. Once finished, he pulls me into him, planting a kiss on my belly. A moment I'd love to freeze in time, so I could keep it forever. But like trying to catch a snowflake, it melts away too soon.

Koen stands and kisses the top of my head. "I love you, Bellatrix."

My face is pressed into his muscular chest, greedily inhaling his manly scent. "I love you too," I respond with the biggest smile. "Promise you'll come back?"

He kisses my forehead. "Always."

I look up at him with pouty eyes. I have a training session with Harding and a ride planned with Miri today, but I can't help the way I miss him already. My eyes must show it, because he smiles down at me, tucking my hair behind my ear.

"Hey, it's temporary. Soon we won't have any reason to be apart. Okay?"

My eyes narrow slightly. The cryptic things I keep hearing from him have me wondering if there's more to his words. Is he being hopeful and positive, or is he planning something? I need to get to the bottom of this. Koen is definitely hiding something.

# 43

## KOEN

"Where've you been hiding?" my mother asks as I walk through the front door of our cottage.

The space smells like fresh-brewed coffee. It's warm and inviting, and I'm practically salivating as I pour myself a mug of it.

I give her an apologetic smile. "Sorry, I didn't plan on staying at the castle."

I take the first satisfying sip of coffee, letting it rouse my senses. It's no longer my favorite way to awaken my senses in the morning, but it is a close second to being between Bellatrix's legs.

"Where's Mel?" I ask, but before it's answered, I see brown curls bouncing towards me at high-speed.

"Koen!"

"Sweet girl," I say, giving her a loving squeeze.

"I missed you," she tells me, and I'm pleased that the sadness that usually accompanies her words is absent. "Were you with the princess?" she asks as her big brown eyes look up at me with excitement.

I tousle her curls. "I was."

"I miss her too. When can I go back to the castle with you?"

I nervously glance towards my mother who's shaking her head. "Uh, that's not really up to me, Mel. You might need to ask Mother about that."

My mother gives me a "what the hell" look. I shrug apologetically.

Mel spins her body around and gives my mother a pouty face. "Can I go back with him today?"

"Sweetie, I don't know if he's going back today," she tells Mellani.

"Mel, I just got home. Maybe another day?"

She surprises me by turning around and rolling her eyes at me. "Oh please, you're there every day. I'm sure you'll go back later."

I chuckle, and give my mother an incredulous look while pointing at Mellani. When did she get so sassy?

My mother throws both hands up. "Hey, she gets that from *you*." Mellani giggles and prances out the backdoor to play outside.

"That girl is becoming quite the little character."

"She sure is. Quite talented too," she says bluntly, picking up a paper from the kitchen counter and handing it to me.

As I unfold it, my breathing halts and body turns cold.

*Fuck.*

"Care to explain this?" she asks coolly.

I try to keep my face as neutral as possible, hiding the sheer panic I'm feeling inside. "One of Mel's drawings?" I feign ignorance. "What about it?"

"I found it in one of your coat pockets."

*Busted.*

"Really? That's weird."

Cocking an eyebrow, she props a hand on one of her hips in a no-nonsense stance. "Don't play stupid with me, boy."

With a shaky hand, I fold the paper up and put it in my jacket pocket. "It's nothing, Mother."

A humorless laugh explodes out of her. "Do you know what you're doing?"

Since the conversation we had with Mel, it's very clear that the majority of her drawings come to fruition at some point. This particular one is the very picture I've been trying to keep from both my mother and Bellatrix.

"I have it handled."

"Handled? How exactly do you have *that* handled?" she asks, pointing to the pocket with the drawing.

My words are bullshit, and we both know it. Nobody can read me better than my mother. I don't know why I thought I could ever hide this from her.

"What did you think was going to happen? That everything was just going to go back to normal? You know that can't happen."

She sighs. "You're too involved, son. I don't think you really know what this will mean. The way it will change things. The way it will change *you.*"

Of course I'm too involved. It concerns my True Mate.

I don't respond. My mind is made up. Nothing she tells me will change what I've been planning.

When she realizes I'm not going to respond, she tries again. "Please, really think about this before you decide anything."

I've already decided.

But I nod to appease her, placing a kiss on the top of her head. I don't enjoy keeping secrets, but I hate seeing her upset. I should have been more careful.

"It's something I have to do, Mother."

Her brows pinch together. "*You* don't have to."

But if I don't, who will?

"Everything will be okay. I love you," I tell her.

"Don't shut me out. If you intend to go through with this, let me help you."

"You'd help me?"

A low laugh escapes her. "I used to be a very powerful enchantress, my boy. People from all over the kingdom used to seek me out."

"What would people seek you out for?" I ask, curious. We've never had an in-depth conversation about her gifts.

"Healing, mostly. That is the one power left that's most potent. Protection. I also used to share Mellani's gift. Oh, the things I could tell you I've seen."

"Like what?"

For a moment her eyes glaze over, lost in memory, but then she pats my arm. "Oh, maybe another day I'll regale you with my old tales. Now, you're behind on chores. The firewood is all gone."

Leave it up to my mother to jump from talking about magic and gifts to laying down the law of chores to her adult son. Whatever voice in her head that's telling her she doesn't still have any power is lying to her.

I chuckle. "Sure, Ma. I can do that."

I know my mother only wants to keep me safe, but dealing with Charlotte is not something I can put off any longer. I owe it to Bellatrix.

The day I found her in the woods now feels like a miracle. A chance encounter, as if time was tired of waiting on us. Too impatient to keep waiting for us to figure out how much we needed each other. There's only one more thing standing in our way. One loose end that needs to be dealt with. I will give her the life she's always wanted, no matter what it costs me.

# 44

# BELLATRIX

The road to becoming queen has cost me far too much. My freedom, my sanity, and my guilt that an entire kingdom is suffering right along with me. But once I'm queen I'll be able to enact real change. Positive change.

"You're going to be beautiful," Koen tells me, catching me by surprise.

Holding a long gown in each hand, I quickly place them back on the rod in my closet. "Don't look. I wanted to surprise you."

He approaches from behind, wrapping his arms around me and snuggling his face into the crook of my neck. For just a moment we melt into each other. Our breathing syncs up, and everything else fades away.

"Princess, you could wear my smelly hunting gear and you'd still be the most beautiful woman in any room."

The smile that stretches across my face is so wide, it's almost painful. "I'm not sure I'd be taken seriously as the queen if I did that."

He chuckles into my hair. "You'd be beautiful in anything. Or nothing."

I tilt my head to the side against his chest, giving him better access to my neck. "Oh, now that's an idea. Maybe I'll go naked."

He bites my neck, and gives me a gentle squeeze with his arms, his voice deep and gravelly.

"Don't. You. Dare."

I squeal at the pinching sensation of the bite, unable to suppress the giggle that escapes me from my playful taunting. "Why's that, Mr. Archer?"

He spins me around so we're facing each other, and gazes down at me, his eyes are dark and fierce. "Because you're mine. Nobody gets to see you that way but me."

I bite my lip. The only thing exceeding the allure of his protective side is this possessiveness.

"Is that any way to speak to your next queen?"

"You're right. You are *my* queen," he says, tipping my chin up with his forefinger. "And I take care of what's mine."

My eyes automatically lower to his lips, and a zap of excitement courses through my body. The anticipation of our bodies connecting.

"Forever?" I ask.

Koen has made his feelings for me very clear, telling me he loves me any chance he gets, but it doesn't quiet the voice in my head that tells me he still might walk away. If his family can't support him ruling with me, the ceremony might very well mark the end of our relationship. As much as I want him to say yes, to declare his loyalties to me forever, the pit in my stomach warns me not to get my hopes up. A wicked grin spreads across his face. "Is that what you want?"

Though my limbs feel like noodles, I manage a weak nod.

Koen dips his head, fusing our lips together in a deep kiss, as his hand slides around the back of my head to press us even more firmly together. My tongue desperately searches for his, needing his taste inside my mouth. Needing any part of him inside of me. As our physical relationship has expanded, the ache and the longing have only intensified. A moan slips from my mouth to his, and as if given a hit of caffeine, his hands and kisses begin moving more frantically.

"Gods, get a room!" Quirina shouts from a few feet away.

We jump apart in embarrassment, and I quickly wipe my mouth.

"We do have a room. In fact, this *is* her room," Koen snarks back.

"Relax, handyman. I'm here on official business. Sort of," she says with the flick of a wrist.

I notice she's holding a folder under one arm. "What's that?"

She pulls out the folder I'm pointing at, waving it at me. "Said official business. Details for your crowning ceremony. It's in two days, so we need to get everything finalized."

Quirina has taken over what my mother would have usually been overseeing, per my request, and my mother has reluctantly, but peacefully, stepped aside.

"Ah," Koen remarks. "We can pick this back up later, Princess."

Biting my bottom lip, I try to disguise my lovesick grin for him. Koen plants a quick kiss on my lips, and says goodbye to Rina.

Quirina sticks her forefinger in her mouth, pretending to vomit.

I roll my eyes. "Oh please, like you and Nik aren't just as bad."

She laughs. "At least we hide our shenanigans. You two don't censor yourselves around anybody these days."

I shrug. "Life is too short to pretend I'm not stupid in love with Koen Archer."

She gives me a knowing smile. "It's sweet. I like it."

"You do realize that's the first time you've really admitted there's something more going on with you and Nik?"

"Like you said, life is too short," she says with a wink, handing me the file.

I groan. "Can't we just send out a memo to the entire kingdom declaring me queen?" Quirina gives me a "don't be ridiculous" face. "This is a big deal. You should celebrate it." How can I celebrate when we could be attacked any moment?

Knowing that I could be turned down publicly by the man I love, thus effectively ending our relationship?

I shrug.

"We're not doing this again. This ceremony is two damn days away. I know you're nervous, but Koen is not going to hurt you. You are going to wear a gorgeous gown and blow his damn mind. You are going to drink, eat, and mingle. And you are going to be crowned in front of half the damn kingdom, because this is *your* time to shine. It's your chance to show everybody who you are. You're not the Soul Snatcher anymore. Show the town who you are. What you plan to do as queen."

She's right. No matter what happens with Koen and me, there's much more at stake.

"Thank you," I tell her.

"For what?"

"For being my person."

For the next hour we go over details for the ceremony. What

kind of food will be served, the kind of drinks that will be tray passed, my outfit details, my grand entrance, my speech. Most of the details are merely window dressing; what I'm more focused on is the speech. This is my chance to inform the kingdom of the changes I plan to implement.

A new Tenuma.

A new queen for a new era of ruling. One that doesn't bleed its people dry. I plan to show our people that my family lineage doesn't define who I am, or who I will be as Tenuma's queen. If it takes the rest of my life, I will do whatever's necessary to undo all the hurt the rulers who preceded me have caused.

After helping me with my speech, choosing from an endless parade of flowers, and sampling food, both Quirina and I are ready for a drink. Now I want to enjoy my last few days before I officially hold all the power and responsibility of Tenuma.

"Are you ready to head over to Nik's with me?" she asks.

"Let's do it. But no shots this time."

"Hey, that was all you, Trix."

"I know, I was reminding myself," I joke, heading to my closet for a jacket.

"Hey, I wanted to talk to you about something," she says, and by her tone I can tell it's serious.

"Of course."

"The daemons. Is there any update?"

I have a feeling she's asking for one particular reason. One particular person.

I sigh. "Well, the general told me they've found an enchantress in another kingdom that's willing to help reverse it. They've sent for her, but it will be a few days until they return."

"What if she can't do it?"

I shrug. "I'm not sure. There's only one known way to end the curse. But even then I don't know what it means for the men."

"So, if your mother dies, then they could potentially turn back to the person they were before?"

"That's been our understanding."

Her teeth worry her bottom lip, deep in thought.

"Are you okay?"

Shaking her head out of whatever thought bubble she was caught in, she nods. "Me? Oh yeah. I was thinking about, you know, him."

Edwin. Quirina's ex-boyfriend that led her on, and then, to his own demise, wound up in my bed.

"Nik told me he loves me," Quirina confesses.

"He did? Did you say it back?"

"Did *you* say it to Koen?" she counters.

"Not at first, but yes, I did. And don't change the subject. Would your feelings for Nik change if Edwin were to return to himself? Could you forgive him?"

"It's hard to say. As fucked up as what he did was, and it was…" She pauses, looking for the right words. "Those feelings are still there. We never had any closure. There was no explanation. He was here one day and gone the next. As hurt as I was by his actions, I can't help but remember the good moments we had together. The love I had for him. *Have.*" The last word is harshly spoken, as if she's annoyed with herself for it.

"There's nothing wrong with loving him still. You have the biggest heart, Rina. You wouldn't be you if you didn't care. I hope you get the chance to get your closure."

"It's strange to think that he could come back and I could bump into him in town again one day."

"I never thought of it that way." I haven't given much thought to me having to see all the men I've had sex with, either.

Guilt creeps up the back of my neck, as the memory of unknowingly sleeping with the man she loved comes flooding back. Nothing can ever take away the pain I caused her, nor can I escape the guilt that plagues me for it.

Grabbing both her hands in mine, I face her when I speak. "I am truly sorry for everything, Rina."

"You've apologized so many times, please stop."

"Just making sure you hadn't forgotten," I say, giving her hand a squeeze.

Despite the tears I can see glistening in her eyes, she doesn't let them fall. She pulls me in for a hug. "I don't want to hurt Nik."

"Rina, he's a good man, and no matter what you do, he'll still love you," I reassure her. "I think it's time for a drink."

When we part I see her red, swollen eyes and know that we're both carrying too much.

*Maybe shots aren't such a bad idea after all.*

# 45

# KOEN

Maybe this is a bad idea after all.

Tonight is Bellatrix's crowning ceremony. After today, she will officially be the Queen of Tenuma. My girl is going to be queen. I originally had a solid plan going into the evening, but after seeing Mellani's latest picture, I'm having to rethink my approach. I stuff the drawing in my back pocket.

"What do you have there?" my mother asks from behind.

The way she always manages to sneak up on me, I swear she must have worked for the army in a past life. Meanwhile, I can't slide anything past her.

"A reminder for myself," I lie—poorly, as evident by my cracking voice.

"My son, you have always been a terrible liar. I love that about you. Now, hand it over," she says, holding out her hand for the picture.

I pull it out and pass it to her. There's no use fighting her. She already knows what I intend to do, but this new drawing is a clear warning.

Her face turns white as the snow blanketing Tenuma. "Did she just draw this?"

I nod, confirming her fear. She fingers the paper, tracing lines as if making sure she's really seeing it correctly. When Mel showed it to me earlier, she was clearly shaken. The images are becoming too much for her to handle. With her visions coming more frequently, we are going to have to find a way to help her process this gift.

"You can't go tonight."

"I have to. Bellatrix is expecting me there."

"Tell me you're not still considering this," she replies, exasperated.

Silence falls between us as my reluctance to argue with her weighs in. My mother can't stop me; this drawing can't stop me. I'm going this evening no matter what.

Despite my original notion that the decision should be left up to Bellatrix, this is the only way we can be together and end her suffering. Bellatrix might be upset, but I'm hoping she'll see it's for the best.

"Koen, baby. All of her drawings have come true at some point. If this one does too, it will kill me. Please."

Her eyes fill with tears, and I can't stop the aching in my chest. The pain gnawing at me, a punishment for hurting her.

After tonight, the suffering ends.

For all of us.

I take the drawing from her and place it in my back pocket, then take her hands in mine. "I know what's going to happen, which means I can change it. Everything will be okay. I promise. Don't worry."

Her tears push over the ledge and cascade down her cheeks. "I'm your mother, it's my job to worry."

"I know," I say, leaning in and kissing her cheek.

We both know I'm going, no matter what's said today. And we both know why.

"Mel and I won't be going. If this is what you've chosen, I can't support it," she tells me firmly once we separate.

I had asked her last week if she'd reconsider attending, and she seemed to contemplate it. But this new information has changed things for us both.

"Does this mean you won't support me being with Bellatrix?"

She worries her bottom lip. "I'm not sure how I can."

My mother removes something from the top of a shelf and walks it over to me. She opens my hand, dropping it into my palm. It's my black bracelet.

"Please wear this at least."

After experiencing her healing power handiwork when I returned with a near-fatal stabbing, I'd be foolish not to wear it.

I nod and place it on my wrist.

Without a word, she pulls her jacket on and heads for the backyard where Mel is playing in the snow.

"I love you, Mom," I say softly, as she closes the door behind her.

I'm doing this for her too, after all.

Y ou take as long as Quirina to get ready, man," Nik shouts from the other side of his bathroom door as I finish dressing.

At the risk of further upsetting my mother, I decided to pack a bag and get ready at Nik's. I've filled him in on my plan, but unlike my mother he didn't have such an emotional reaction to it.

"Why don't you do us both a favor and go find her so you can give your mouth something else to do?" I quip.

My snarky comment earns a full-belly laugh that travels through the door, causing me to return the sound.

"Not a bad idea," he shouts back.

The ceremony is quickly approaching, and I'm filled with nerves. Bellatrix could decide that I'm not worthy enough to rule beside her and pick one of her mother's suitors. Hell, I don't *feel* worthy enough to rule with her, but she's what I want. No matter what she decides, I'll be by her side until she says otherwise. Tonight will be a turning point for us all.

Swinging the door open, I see Nik at a nearby table pouring us two fingers of whiskey into crystal glasses. Handing one to me, he holds the other in his hand in a cheers position.

Nik's place is a one-room dwelling above his bar. The door at the top of the stairs opens up to a large space. His large bed is pushed against the far left wall, and a simple kitchen is nestled to the right. The washroom is just beyond the kitchen. There's no decoration, no frill. The place is plain and tidy. Just like Nik. What you see is what you get.

"You ready for this, Ko?" he asks, offering me a glass.

One side of my mouth lifts into a grin. "Ready as I'll ever be."

"I've got your back," he says, and taps his glass into mine with a clink.

We tip our glasses back, draining the liquid. My stomach immediately feels warm, settling the nerves I initially had coming over here. I'd be lying if I said Mel's drawing hadn't left me feeling uneasy.

But it's more information. Information that I now have, and

can use to be smarter and stay one step ahead.

"Another?" Nik offers.

I hand back the glass. "No. Not tonight." One drink takes the edge off. Two drinks leaves room for error. In this case, error equals death. "Where's Rina?" I ask.

I was surprised to see she wasn't here when I arrived. It seems like she and Nik have been inseparable the last few months, and when I gaze around his place I notice pieces of her laying around. Hair ties on his small round dining table in the corner. A pair of women's shoes next to the bed. Hair styling tools in the washroom. Taking a few deliberate breaths through my nose, it smells undeniably like women's perfume.

She definitely lives here.

"She's at the castle, getting ready with Bellatrix."

"Aw, how 'bout that, our girls getting ready together before the ceremony," I say playfully.

Nik gives me an eyeroll. "Hasn't that joke gotten old yet?"

"What's the deal, man? She's a great girl. There's no need to be weird about it. It's clear you're into each other."

"Me."

"You what?"

"I'm into *her*. I don't really know what she wants."

*Oh.*

"Sorry, man. We all just assumed you two were together."

He pours himself another drink, swirling it around in the glass. "She's been through a lot. At first, I was just being helpful. Offering her a place to stay, letting her help out around the bar to keep busy. Somewhere along the way I fell for her. But I don't think she feels the same."

"She's told you that?"

He nods. "Sort of. I can't blame her, though. Losing her

family, her home. Almost losing Bellatrix. That shit with her ex. It's a lot for one person."

"That makes sense. The way she looks at you, though, it's not in your head. She can say what she wants, but I know what I see. What we all see."

"It's hard, though, when there's no closure with her ex. Her feelings are unresolved with him still a daemon, and nobody knowing what's going to happen with them."

"Would she give him a second chance if he came back?"

He chews on the inside of his cheek, and I can tell it's a question he's asked himself many times. "She said she's not sure. You know Rina. Even though what he did was awful, she can't snap her fingers and stop loving someone. As much as I hate it, it's what I love about her."

Quirina is like Bellatrix in that way. Strong women with bleeding hearts.

"You're a good man, Nik. She'd be lucky to have you," I tell him, not meaning for it to come out as mushy as it did. But maybe that's just who I am now, a corny man that roots for love.

He shrugs, rubbing at the back of his neck. "Yeah. Anyway, should we get going to this ceremony?"

I've hit a nerve. One I didn't mean to touch. We've been best friends for as long as I can remember, but rarely have we discussed women. We've both been focused on work, not looking for someone to spend our time with. Our lives didn't revolve around women, and we were content with that. These conversations are new and uncomfortable, but I'd know that lovesick expression anywhere.

He loves her.

# 46

# BELLATRIX

I am not loving this.

I'm beginning to feel sick sitting at my vanity mirror where I'm currently getting ready. Tonight is my crowning ceremony, and the nerves have worked their way into my bloodstream.

It was finally time to replace the mirror I smashed. For so long I wasn't ready to fix it. I wasn't ready to face the person I'd become, the person I let fear and pain turn me into. I had reached a breaking point, where I stopped trusting, stopped caring, stopped feeling. I'll never forget the look on Koen's face as I stood naked before him, covered in blood. The memory is seared into my brain. With the crowning ceremony tonight, I feel ready to take on my new title and make a positive change for Tenuma. I only hope that when I ask Koen to stand by my side, he will.

I'm applying makeup while Quirina is fussing over her curls in the washroom. The air is filled with tension as we both get ready in silence, weighing everything on our minds.

Quirina's worries about Nik and whether she can let go of what happened with Edwin to move on. I worry whether Koen will accept my offer to become my king.

I add the final touches and twist around in my chair as Rina comes out of the bathroom. I take in her perfectly styled curls and the subtlety of her makeup. "You look beautiful, Rina."

She gives me an unsure smile. "Thank you. You're stunning, Bellatrix. What do you say, Your Majesty? Are you ready to become queen?"

A nervous laugh bubbles out of me. "No, not really."

"What are you so worried about?"

I sigh heavily. "Everything. My mother. Koen. Facing the kingdom. What if I say the wrong things? I want to show them that I'm not like my family, but I worry that they won't see it."

Rina gives me a warm smile. "Trix, everyone already sees it. The way you've generously given, the reparations you've made. You're not like your family, and everyone knows that. I'm so proud of you, and I cannot wait to see that well-deserved crown on your damn head."

I laugh, absentmindedly touching the top of my head at the mention of the crown.

"What are you worried about your mother for?" she asks.

I chew on my lip. "Well. I haven't told her yet that I've chosen Koen. She has two royal suitors from another kingdom attending tonight, waiting for an answer. I've been avoiding her."

Quirina squints her eyes at me, a dumbfounded expression painted across her face. "I'm sorry, is she blind? Or stupid?"

A laugh bubbles out of me. "Usually."

She lifts her hand in front of her dramatically. "The fact that

that woman refuses to acknowledge your and Koen's relationship is beyond me. She's insane."

"She has a hard time accepting that I'd choose a man with no social standing."

"What the fuck?" she blurts out. "Wasn't she the one sending man after man to your bed every night? All those men were from the village, so what is her issue with Koen?"

"Well, I guess that was my father's doing. *She* only wanted men of royal heritage."

Her eyebrows raise to her hairline in disbelief. "She's something else. I'm surprised that you haven't kicked her ass to the curb already."

I stand and walk over to join Rina on the bed. "I know nobody understands. But she's my mother. In a lot of ways, she's all I have left."

Rina puts her hand over mine. "You have me. And Koen, Nik, Theo and Valeria. We're all here for you."

I give her a sad smile. "I know, Rina. That's not what I mean. You're all my family too. It's hard to explain. I guess it's like you and Edwin. He betrayed you, and even though it hurts, it doesn't magically erase what you feel for him."

She mulls over what I've said before giving me an understanding nod. Aside from Koen, Rina is always the first one to have my back.

Everyone wants me to turn on my mother and cast her away like garbage. But if I do, what does that say about me? It's not as simple as shutting her out. Forsaking her means leaving another hole in my chest. I've already lost my father, and even though my parents put power over my feelings, I know they care for me in some way. Sure, things progressively worsened the older I got, but does that mean I have to let go of the good times with them? Who says I can't hold onto those too? People aren't only made up of the bad or good things they do; they're a blend of it all.

I do think my mother put this curse on me for protection. Over time her motives may have changed, but I know it began with good intentions. And how do I turn my back on her, the only family I have left?

"You're right. It's not easy to change what you feel for someone. What do you think she'll say when you announce Koen as your king?"

"She's going to be angry, but she'll have to accept it."

Quirina cocks an eyebrow at me, as if to say, *When does that woman take anything lying down?*

I shrug. "We're about to find out. I'm more concerned with what Koen's going to say. I worry that he might not be ready to jump into that role."

"Why the hell not?" she asks, surprised.

"Because of his family," I say, picking at my nails.

"Girl. That man loves you. How many times do we have to go over this?"

"I know he loves me. I don't question that."

"Well, then?"

I inhale deeply. "It might not be enough."

"What are you even talking about?"

"His family hasn't been at the castle since we returned. I've been over to their cottage countless times, but I can still sense his mother's hesitation. He will never choose me over his family. Nor would I want him to. This might be as far as we can go. If his mother hasn't gotten on board with him becoming king of Tenuma, then that's it for us. He's going to walk away, Rina," I confess, my eyes cast down.

She scoots closer. "Hey, look at me," she says, tilting my chin upwards. "That's not going to happen. That man damn near gave his life to bring you home. He's not going to throw in the towel now."

I suppose she's right. But why then am I filled with such doubt? Why can't I share her unwavering faith that it's going to be me and him in the end.

I sniffle, holding her gaze with watery eyes. "But what if it does?"

She pulls her lips inward, a strained expression hanging on her face. "I shouldn't tell you this…"

Using my hand, I fan my eyes to stop the tears threatening to fall. "Tell me what?"

She hesitates, her mouth pulling from side to side.

"Rina. What is it?"

"You and Koen are True Mates."

"What? How do you know that?" I ask, eyes going wide.

"Koen told me a while back. He said that Nik and I are also likely True Mates."

My head spins, wondering why all this time Koen has neglected to tell me when he knew. My jaw tenses, and Quirina must sense my irritation.

"He wasn't hiding it, Trix. He just didn't want to scare you away. You've been through so much, and he wasn't sure how you'd react. He wanted you to make your decision about your relationship on your own, without any persuasion," she reveals.

Koen should have told me, but I suppose I can understand why he didn't.

"True Mates," I say aloud, wanting to hear the way it sounds on my lips.

I reflect on our time together. The way he's recklessly protected me and loved me. The way he's never hesitated putting his own life on the line to protect mine.

Rescuing me from the dragon in the forest.

Standing up to my mother.

Coming to Sperantia to rescue me.

Braving the back of a dragon for me.

How have I not seen it before? Of course he's my mate. The way the bracelets drew us together, the desperate way we thirst for one another. The evidence was always there.

"Are you okay?" she asks.

It's not what I expected to hear before this momentous night, but it makes me more confident going into it. Not only does Koen love me, but he's my mate. Surely he wouldn't turn his back on his mate. Would he?

I nod with a shy smile. "Better than ever. I think we're going to be okay, Rina."

She smiles back. "Yes, you are. We all are. Are you ready?"

I nod.

"Good. It's time."

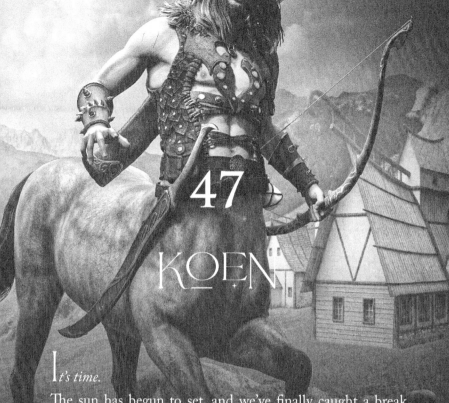

# 47

# KOEN

*It's time.*

The sun has begun to set, and we've finally caught a break from all of the snowfall over the last few days. As Nik and I approach the castle, we can already see how much work has been put into tonight. The walkway is lit up with dimmed light orbs on both sides trailing up to the doorway. The hedge maze on the left looks immaculately manicured, and I can't resist the urge to sneak into the rose garden and grab a flower for my girl.

The entrance is heavily patrolled, and every guest is being questioned and patted down, except for Nik and me. The guards at the front no longer give me a hard time when I visit, and haven't since the rescue mission. Where I once saw hostility from them, I now see respect.

When we enter the main room, we're met with a mixture of welcoming aromas, trays of champagne on both sides of the door, and endless flowers. Nik and I both grab a glass of champagne, clink our glasses together, and sip. The bubbles tickle my lips, and sizzle on my tongue as I swallow it down. Feeling the slight buzz from the whiskey, I decide I've had enough and quickly hand the server back my glass. We make our way inside making room for others to file in behind us.

Once inside, the aromas intensify as they swirl around us. The fresh floral fragrance of roses, the warm, tantalizing scent of freshly baked breads and meats, and vanilla candles lit around the room somehow blend together perfectly.

The staircase is adorned with densely packed white roses trailing up both sides. There's added greenery to fill in the banister, and oversized candles sit at the bottom of the stairs in tall glass vases. The whole room is elegant and sophisticated. They've gone all out for Bellatrix tonight.

I glance down at the one red rose I plucked for Bellatrix, feeling inadequate.

How could I ever be enough for her when this is all I can ever offer her?

"She's going to love it," Nik tells me as if reading my thoughts.

I chuckle nervously. "Should we go sit?"

"You don't want to go find your girl?"

"I'm sure she's still getting ready. Besides, I want to keep an eye on things."

He nods, knowing exactly what I'm referring to.

We make our way into the sitting room to the right, and sit on one of the velvet couches. This room is also decorated with vases of flowers. A server approaches us with a tray of assorted cheese and meats.

I decline, and the waiter continues circulating.

There's only two things I'm focused on tonight, and neither of those are food.

"Koen!"

The hairs on the back of my neck stand on end recognizing

the voice.

"Charlotte," I reply meekly as she approaches us.

Her eyes widen at my attire. Having mostly seen me in either my hunting gear or my work wear, the dark suit and tie I'm wearing must be jarring to her. A stark contrast to the dirty man she's convinced isn't good enough for her daughter.

Bellatrix refused to show me her dress, so I wasn't sure what to wear. I decided on a black suit, black vest over a black button-up shirt, and red tie. I also included a red pocket square that I don't care for, but Nik insisted that it pulled the look together. For a man who doesn't put much stock in his appearance, I worry it's a little over the top. But I wanted to look good for Bellatrix. This is her big day, and there's nothing I wouldn't do for her.

"Don't you look like a whole new man?" She tries to make it sound like a compliment, but her tone betrays her.

My lips press into a thin line, and I hear Nik snicker.

Charlotte's gaze flits from me to Nik and then back. "Can't I give a compliment? I'm just being nice."

"You're never nice," I retort.

Her head rears back, as if in shock, and she smooths her hands down her gown. The indigo dress she's wearing is silk and floor-length, a train with gold detailing around the edges flowing behind her.

It's form-fitting and strapless, accentuating her petite curves. The bust contains the same gold detailing of the train. Her black hair is pulled back into a tight bun, so her shoulders and back are bare.

"I'm glad you're here for her," she says softly, then exits the room.

Nik and I stare at each other for a moment trying to figure out what the hell that encounter was about. Having a non-combative conversation with that woman has never been possible.

"That was interesting," Nik says.

"Definitely strange."

"She seemed sincere."

"Don't be fooled. It's all for show. There's always a motive with that woman," I tell Nik, but it's also for me. I have to keep believing this if I'm going to go through with this tonight.

"I know, man, I know."

Rising from the couch, I stick my hands in my pocket and lean against the entryway of the room, tracking her movement. My future hinges on how this evening plays out. There are myriad things that can go wrong very quickly if I'm not smart.

Luckily, I'm a skilled hunter, and I'm used to getting my kill.

I trace the outline of the dagger in my jacket pocket to comfort myself. More people flood the castle while we wait for the night to begin. I knew this would be an enormous event, but with the way the room is quickly filling up, it's going to exceed what I envisioned.

The room explodes into a cacophony of laughter, conversation, clinking glassware, and tapping of heels and dress shoes on the tile floors. In a short time, Bellatrix has managed to win over the entire kingdom of Tenuma as evident by the large attendance tonight. Everyone is here to show their support of her officially taking over the land.

My girl is incredible.

"Hey!" Quirina shouts, waving her arm in the air as she weaves through the thickening crowd. Nik greets her with a warm embrace and a quick kiss on her cheek that turns it a slight shade of pink.

Her outfit is nothing like I've ever seen her in. It's a long way from the uniform the royals had her wearing. Quirina wears a floor-length teal silk dress that hugs her curves and accentuates her tan skin. The slit up one side of her dress has Nik's eyes ready to bulge from their sockets. Her brown curls hang loose, with a few pieces on each side of her pinned away from her face. Her makeup is flawless.

"How is she?" I ask.

"Bellatrix? She's stunning," she replies with a mischievous grin.

"She's always stunning," I state.

"You should go up and see her before everything begins. It would mean a lot to her."

I nod, and retrieve the rose I set down on the couch. "I'll see you guys in a bit."

"Stupid shoe," Bellatrix mumbles to herself.

I quietly enter her room, silently chuckling at the frustration she's showing her heels. With a lowered head, she sits on the bed fussing with her shoe. I watch as she struggles with one of the straps, getting angrier by the second.

I approach, kneel in front of her, and take her ankle in my hand. "May I?"

She startles, and then smiles brightly at me. "Koen. Hi."

"Hi," I reply softly, taken aback by her beauty.

She's breathtaking. I don't want our voices to shatter the moment. There's a haze around us, and Bellatrix is all I see. Each of my senses are heightened, and they all have her name on them. Her skin feels soft and smooth under my fingers. Her perfume fills my nose; like a drug entering my blood stream, it's intoxicating. It's citrusy and floral. Her red lips are like a beacon calling me home, begging to be tasted. We've come so far from the woman I saw tempting me in the garden, and now I know exactly how sweet she is.

The straps of her shoe wind across her ankle in a crisscross pattern. Still knelt before her, I set her foot on my leg, and loop the strap through the back of her shoe, securing it to her. Pressing a soft kiss to her ankle, I lower her foot to the ground and glance up at her, taking in every detail.

Gods damn.

That's my queen.

My eyes slowly travel upwards, absorbing every inch of her perfection. Her strapless gown is black with gold embellishments down the center of the gown and a gold brooch just underneath her breasts. It hugs her chest and waist tightly, while the skirt flares out wide at the hips with a high slit on one side, giving me a glimpse of her creamy thigh.

"Bellatrix, you're perfect," I tell her, wishing I had better words to describe the way she looks right now, because they don't do her beauty justice. She's not just a queen worthy of worshiping, but a *woman* worthy of it.

She extends her hand, and I grab it to help her to stand. "Aren't you going to call me princess?"

"Not today. You're my queen. No doubt about it," I say looking up at her from my knees. Memorizing every detail, every curve.

"You plan on staying down there all night, Mr. Archer?" she asks seductively.

"That's not a bad idea. I could think of a few ways to keep busy down here," I say, running my tongue over my lips.

Moving her body closer to me, she places a hand on my cheek, her thumb caressing me softly.

"After today, that's exactly what I hope every day looks like for us."

Is she saying what I think she's saying?

Holding her hand in place on my cheek, I stand to face her eye level. "Is that what you want?"

The corners of her mouth lift into a shy smile. "Koen, I want you to be here. Permanently. I want you to be my king. I want you to rule with me. I choose you. There was never any question. I hope you know that."

Like a shock to the system, hearing those words sends me reeling. My heart races, and my ears are buzzing. I want to ask if I heard her right. This is everything I've wanted for us. Though we've both revealed how we feel about each other, the hesitation she showed for so long made me wonder if we'd ever get here. But she loves me, and she wants me to rule with her.

"Is that what *you* want?" she asks, and I see it in her eyes. The fear. The concern that I might not choose her back.

Cupping her face in both my hands, I pull her close. "Nothing would make me happier, my queen."

"Really?" Her voice cracks and tears fill her eyes.

"It's everything I could hope for."

"Not just you. I want Fira and Mellani here too. All of us, as a family."

The grin I thought couldn't be any bigger manages to stretch even wider across my face. "As a family."

Our lips fuse together, sealing the deal. Not only has this incredible woman accepted me and chosen me to rule in her kingdom, but she's asking to be a part of my family.

She pulls back, with a serious expression. "What about your family? Do they want this too?"

"Don't worry about them. They want me to be happy. And you make me very happy."

"Choosing this life is dangerous," she warns.

"My queen, there's nothing you could say or show me that would change my mind. There's no pain I wouldn't endure to be with you. Show me the darkest parts of your soul so I can love you despite them."

She tips her head back in an attempt to keep the tears from falling. "Ah, this makeup took me so long."

We both chuckle, and I grab two handkerchiefs off her vanity and hand her one. I use the other to wipe the lipstick off my face. As she dabs her eyes, neither of us can stop smiling like idiots. Love is definitely a drug. Bellatrix is my drug of choice, and I intend to take heavy doses of her each day from here on out.

A knock at the door pulls us out of our love bubble, and an armed man appears in the doorway.

"Your Majesty, we're ready for you."

Bellatrix nods, and the man leaves.

She exhales heavily. "It's time."

Bending down, I present her with the rose I set on the floor while I helped with her shoe. I gently kiss each of her hands. "Let's go, my queen. Your people are waiting to celebrate you."

# 48

# BELLATRIX

*My people are waiting to celebrate me.*

A phrase I never thought I'd hear. For as long as I can remember I've been the Soul Snatcher, the hated whore of Tenuma. All I've ever wanted was to do something good for the kingdom. My family never shared my desire to better the kingdom. In their eyes, ruling was always about gaining more power, more money, more more more. Well, I want more too.

"Bellatrix Madison Bardot, daughter of Charlotte and the late William Bardot of Tenuma, your kingdom calls on you tonight to step forth and take this crown with the intent of overseeing the people of this kingdom," the lieutenant general intones. "Will you create a better, more harmonious land for all its inhabitants? Do you agree to rule with integrity, abandoning all selfishness and greed? Will you rule with your king, never to turn your back on each other or this land?"

I'm standing a few stairs from the bottom, facing the crowd, as he recites the oath. Peering into the sea of faces, I spot Harding, Quirina, Nik, Valeria, and Theo who all smile brightly at me. Even my mother watches nearby with a smile on her face, though I know she's holding out hope that I will choose one of the two royal men she invited.

Koen stands next to the stairway, right at my side, exactly where he belongs. His black suit and red tie make it hard to focus on anything but him.

It's me and him forever.

It took going through hell to get here, to find each other, but somehow we did. To feel the way I do right now, watching the way he can't keep his eyes off of me—it's indescribable. Whatever happens tomorrow or the next day, we have this moment, and we fucking earned it.

When I don't answer, the man in front of me clears his throat to get my attention. My eyes snap back to his. "Yes, I will."

"And whom have you chosen to rule as king by your side?" he asks, which immediately sends my attention right back to the crowd. To my mother.

Her eyes are tight. What I say next is sure to disappoint her, but I've given enough of myself to others, made myself small to appease those around me. Now it's my turn to be bold and take what I want.

"Koen Archer," I say clearly.

The fire in her eyes threatens to set ablaze the entire castle. I knew my defiance wouldn't sit well with her, but my life is no longer in her hands.

"Mr. Archer," the man announces, waving for him to join me on the stairs.

Koen walks around the man, climbing the few stairs, to claim the spot next to me. With his nerves near the surface, he misses the last step and almost falls. I catch him, along with the paper that floats out of his jacket. I giggle and grab the folded paper. I stuff it into the side of my corset to give back later as he scrambles to collect himself. Once he has his bearings, I give him a reassuring smile.

"I love you," I mouth.

Together we face forward, and the lieutenant resumes the oath. "Mr. Archer, do you accept the crown, and the responsibility of ruling with integrity with your queen by your side? Do you vow to never leave her side or betray your kingdom? Will you abandon all selfishness and greed and always honor the crown as well as your queen?"

Koen nods. "Yes, I will."

Zero hesitation.

The crowd becomes a buzzing of gasps and murmurs. No commoner has ever been chosen to rule the kingdom this way before. Though many knew of our relationship, the assumption was that I would choose a more *fitting* suitor.

The lieutenant general turns to the crowd briefly to quiet them down, then turns back towards me and Koen. We finish the formalities of swearing us both in, and the moment I've been waiting for has come.

Koen and I are both about to be crowned, in front of more than half of the kingdom.

The queen's crown is lifted off of its dais and held over me for a moment before it's slowly lowered onto my head. I can feel the change as soon as the crown rests comfortably on my head. Everything has changed. A slight buzzing starts at the top of my head and moves down to my feet.

The gold and black of the crown compliment my dress perfectly. The silence in the room turns to a quiet gasp as the large central jewel catches light. The jewels are lovely, but not what I love most. Underneath, two swords cross and appear to hold the large jewel in place. The representation of strength upholding the beauty calls to me. I hope that from here on out, people see me for my strength rather than just as a pretty face.

Koen is next to be crowned, and he looks even more in shock than I do. It's a similar black and gold jeweled crown, but without the swords. Once the crown is set on his head, his beaming face meets mine.

We are officially king and queen. Together.

"People of Tenuma, I am happy to officially introduce our new king and queen, Koen Archer and Bellatrix Bardot!"

Mimicking the pounding of my heart in my chest, the room erupts into a roar of cheers and applause. Looking out at the genuinely happy faces of my friends, I feel overwhelmed with love and acceptance for the first time in my life. As of tonight, I'm no longer the Soul Snatcher. I'm the Queen of Tenuma.

While being crowned is the main event, I'm more looking forward to what comes after. The flow of food and drinks, the music, the dancing, the laughter. I plan to make my speech later this evening to express my plans for a better Tenuma, but for now we celebrate.

After receiving individual congratulations from each person I walked by, I'm happy to have champagne in one hand and Koen's hand in the other. He's stuck close by me all evening, though he seems slightly on edge.

I give his hand a squeeze, leaning into his ear. "Are you okay?"

"It's a lot to take in," he replies, but it feels like there's something more.

In my bed chambers he was steadfast and sure. There was zero hesitation in accepting the title. There's something else he's not telling me. Quirina comes barreling up to me with Nik hot on her heels. "Bellatrix, my queen! It's official!"

"It's weird, isn't it?" I say.

She makes a pfft noise at me. "Not at all. You've always been queen in my eyes." Quirina gives me a wink, and we grin at each other.

"Congratulations, Your Majesty," Nik offers, lifting his own champagne glass in a cheers.

"Oh Gods, please promise the three of you will not start calling me that."

"Yeah, I would also like to make that same request for myself," Koen says.

"Too late, it's already been decided. I can no longer refer to you as Bellatrix," Rina taunts, her hand clutching her chest.

"Okay, well, then if you want to be formal, I guess it's improper to buy everyone shots at Nik's tavern anymore."

Rina exchanges a mock worried look with Nik. "Bellatrix, I would like to apologize. I think it's the champagne."

"Oh, really?" I ask playfully.

We both laugh, and I pull her in for a hug. This night is more than I hoped it would be. Being surrounded by the man I love and incredible friends who have my back no matter what. A dream that once felt so far away is now my reality.

My mother disappeared once the crowd dispersed and hasn't spoken to me, but I expected as much. I only hope that with time she can learn to accept that I chose a different path for myself than she did. My father may not have been her mate, but Koen is mine. Tonight, I want to drink with my king and sway with him on the dance floor.

I realize I'm on my second champagne while Koen hasn't had a drop. "Want me to get you a drink?"

His eyes dart around the room, as if he's looking for someone. "Not right now. Maybe later."

What is going on with him? Is he having doubts or second-guessing his decision?

"Who are you looking for?" I ask bluntly, impatient with his standoffish behavior.

His gaze snaps to me. "What?"

"You heard me. Are you looking for someone?"

His expression softens. "I'm sorry. I was just hoping my mother and Mel might show up."

Oh.

Now I feel like a bitch.

"I didn't mean to snap. It seemed like…"

"Like I was having second thoughts?" he finishes for me. I nod, and he shakes his head laughing.

"Never, my queen."

Relief washes over me. He leans in and kisses my cheek.

"Would you like to dance?" he asks, gesturing to the dance floor on the other side of the ballroom.

Unable to hide my smile, I loop my arm through his and let him guide me through the crowd. The dance floor is filled with couples slowly swaying side to side.

Koen places a hand on the small of my back, taking my hand in his other. My free hand moves to curve over his shoulder, and I pull his body into mine, not wanting any space between us right now. I can't get close enough to him.

For the next three songs, our bodies sway together, and we gaze into each other's eyes with goofy grins. Neither of us able to contain the bliss of being together. Though I no longer wear the bracelet that tingles in his presence, I still feel that connection between us. My entire body is ignited at the mere presence of him. If Koen is nearby, my body feels it.

As we continue to sway, tucked tightly between his arms, I realize that for the first time, I feel safe.

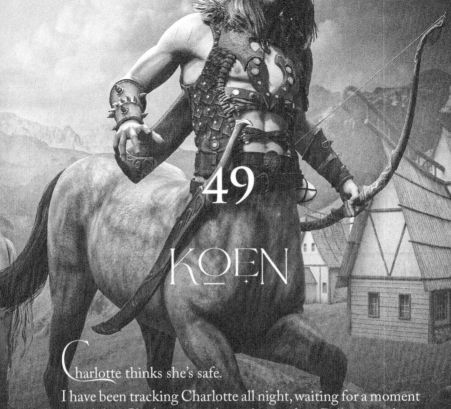

## KOEN

Charlotte thinks she's safe.

I have been tracking Charlotte all night, waiting for a moment alone with her. She has spent the night avoiding Bellatrix and me. It's no secret that she's not thrilled with the decision her daughter made tonight. When Bellatrix and I were dancing, I saw her make a hasty exit from the ballroom and knew this was my chance.

Hiding this from Bellatrix doesn't sit well with me, but truthfully we're all better off without Charlotte. Tonight, I'm choosing to ask for forgiveness rather than permission. Tonight I'm setting up our future.

I tell Bellatrix I'm going out for some air and excuse myself. I climb the stairs and turn towards the queen's quarters. I slowly push the door open, only to find an empty room.

I know I saw her come up here. Where did she go?

Bellatrix's room is open, and I glance inside to find that it, too, is empty. There's only one other place she could be.

The study at the other end of the hall. It's complete with a mini library, reading chair, and a desk where a majority of the royal paperwork is held. Bellatrix once told me this is where her father spent most of his time.

Maybe she's feeling contemplative tonight?

I pat my jacket pocket once more, fingering the outline of the dagger, before letting myself inside. The door swings open, revealing a large space with magnificent floor-to-ceiling shelves that take up the far wall. A large wooden desk sits in front of it, and that's where I find Charlotte.

She's hunched over the desk, and her shoulders are shaking.

Is she crying?

I tiptoe into the room, but my dress shoe squeaks against the tile, startling Charlotte from her private moment.

She whips around in terror, relaxing when she recognizes me. "Oh, Koen, it's you. What are you doing here?"

The relief I hear in her voice sends a trickle of humor through my body. She has no idea what I'm here for, and it almost makes me feel bad for what I have to do.

*Almost.*

I take slow, deliberate steps towards her. "Paying off a debt."

I watch as my words sink in, and the realization of what's about to occur flashes across her face. Her eyes water, but she doesn't move.

"Aren't you going to run?" I ask, pulling the dagger from my jacket, holding it down at my side. I try to conceal my trembling.

She shakes her head. "She deserves this. It's time."

Her words startle me. I'm not sure what I expected. A fight, maybe? Pleading, or trying to explain why she deserves to live? But not this. I'm not a man who kills for pleasure, nor do I enjoy the act. A few moments of uncertainty pass as I try to muster up the strength to do this.

"Fuck!" I shout, throwing my hands in the air. Can I really do this?

"It's okay, Koen. We both knew it would come to this." Her voice is eerily calm. Accepting.

"Please stop talking."

As the seconds tick by, I feel myself becoming less inclined to follow through. That's the tragedy with good versus evil. Those who cause pain always get away with it. Even when they're confronted, the good guys seldom find the strength to inflict what they deserve. Their hearts aren't wired that way.

My heart isn't built for revenge. "I'm sorry, Koen."

I snicker. "For what, Charlotte?"

Quickly, she wipes away a tear from her cheek. A movement she didn't want me to see. A moment of weakness.

She takes a deep breath before speaking. "For all of it. For trusting a man like your father, thinking we could be together. Thinking he wouldn't betray me the way he did you and your mother. For the way I hurt Bellatrix. For not protecting her the way I should have. Inflicting the curse upon her was a mistake. I never should have prioritized power. I..."

"You betrayed everyone around you," I finish for her.

She nods. Doesn't fight it, doesn't make excuses. Finally forcing myself to really look at her, I see it. Remorse.

Gods help me.

I can't go back now. I have to do this.

"There's no other way. You did this," I tell her through gritted teeth.

"I know."

"You stole the first part of her life. It's up to you to give her back the rest of it."

I see her swallow hard. "You're right."

"Why aren't you fighting this?"

"Koen, she's all I have left. This *is* me fighting. I'm fighting for her by giving up," she confesses, and I don't miss the way she sounds so small, so defeated.

I groan. I'm not the man for this. Frustration builds, while my courage wanes and withers like a dying rose. Everything I had planned for this evening just blew up in my face.

Suddenly Mel's face pops into my head, and I wonder what she'd think of me if she knew. Will she grow up and be proud of the man I am? Can I look her in the eyes if I kill an unarmed woman? Will I be able to face myself? Does the reason justify the act?

I want to be a man that the women in my life can be proud of.

I can't do this.

I thought this would be doing Bellatrix a favor. That even if she resented me for it, in time she would come to understand it was beneficial for us all. But this isn't the man I am. I'm not one to kill without provocation, nor am I one to lie and hide things from the woman I love.

It's unclear to me whether strength or weakness wins out.

Placing the dagger back into my jacket, I stand tall, facing Charlotte. "You will help us find another way. Your daughter deserves a mother that fights for her. She deserves a real life. A happy life.

You took that from her, so you will find a way to give it back."

She's silent, and I see the tears uncontrollably flowing down both cheeks as she nods. I don't know if she was bluffing, or if she had made her peace with death, but either way, it feels like she won.

"I mean it, Charlotte. You will make this right."

"I will. Bella deserves everything," she says in between sobs.

I give her a skeptical look. "And stop calling her Bella, she hates that. She's our queen now, and you will give her the respect she's due."

She nods.

I turn to walk away, unease settling in my chest when I realize I don't have a way to get my queen her life, her body, her freedom back. This is not how tonight was supposed to go.

"Koen, wait," Charlotte calls before I reach the door.

Turning on my heel, I take a few steps back towards her, and then everything slows.

My head lifts to meet her terrified, angry gaze.

Charlotte reaches across the desk to grab a dagger I hadn't seen sitting there.

My eyes shift from the dagger, back to her face.

She extends it towards me, lunging forward.

This is how it ends.

I gave her a second chance, only to have her turn on me.

Her movements are swift, leaving me without enough time to reach for my own dagger. I brace myself for impact, for the pain of the blade ripping through my flesh. Charlotte places her bladeless hand on my shoulder, shoving me to the ground. Not down, but out of the way.

She's aiming for someone behind me.

My chest and palms slam to the floor. I ignore the pain and whip my head around to see Charlotte launching towards a large man. But not just any man.

My father.

How the fuck is he alive?

I roll onto my back and, with shaky hands, pull the dagger from my jacket. Unable to move, I'm glued to the floor. All I can do is watch as everything unfolds in front of me.

Charlotte stabs and misses.

Lothar extends a sword into her abdomen. When the blade is removed, it's crimson, dripping with life. Charlotte falls to the ground with a loud thud. I feel frozen in place, watching his hateful expression morph into sinister humor. Like he's enjoying this.

His gaze lingers on her for a moment before shifting to me. "Good to see you, my boy."

His eyes scan me in a predatory way, and I know he's not here for a reunion. I'm in danger, but there's too many thoughts fighting for answers. I should be getting up to fight back, but all I can do is cycle through everything I never got the chance to say to him.

There's a thousand things I *could* say to him. That he's a disgusting monster that betrayed our family. I could tell him he's a shit father, a sorry excuse for a man. That all the power in the world won't make up for the fact that he'll never have a gift. But none of this would be news to him. He doesn't care how he's viewed. All he cares about is power. So, instead I ask him the one thing I might get a reply to.

"What did you do to Bellatrix in Sperantia?"

He laughs. "She sure is a beautiful whore. Hard to resist, isn't she?"

"Fuck you!" I shout, spitting at him.

"You ignorant boy. She could have given you all the power in the kingdom and you let your foolish heart get involved. Love isn't real. It's what gets you killed," he taunts as his gaze lingers back to Charlotte. "Right, Queen?"

"That's where you're wrong. She did, and as the new king of Tenuma, I plan to kill you." My lip curls, and I bare my teeth at him. The animal instincts are preparing to take down the threat. Before I can get to my feet, Lothar darts from the room, disappearing down the hall. I could chase him down, but I find myself instead running to Charlotte's side.

I place pressure on the wound, but it's too large, too deep. The gash hit the upper left side of her chest, and as the puddle underneath her expands, I know she won't survive this night after all.

Desperate eyes stare back at me, and in my distressed state, all I can do is scream for help.

# 50

# BELLATRIX

If I keep drinking this champagne this way, I'm never going to survive the night.

After Koen left to get some air, Quirina joined me on the dance floor, and we danced until our feet throbbed.

"We need to eat something," I tell her, feeling the buzz of my drinks flowing through my blood.

She nods. "That's probably a good idea."

We grab a dish and pile it high with hors d'oeuvres. As we eat, I can't help but wonder why Koen was acting so bizarre before. The hard part is over. Surely he can't still be feeling this anxious about things, right?

"Rina, have you noticed Koen behaving strangely tonight?"

She finishes the bite in her mouth, eyebrows moving as she considers my question. "I don't think so. Why?"

"He seems really on edge. All night it's like he's been searching for someone. He said he was hoping his family would show up, but I don't know."

"I'm sure it's all overwhelming for him," she assures me.

"But then he said he wasn't feeling well and wanted to go get some 'fresh air.' Which was weird too."

Her head jerks back.

"What?" I ask.

"I last saw him heading upstairs."

"What would he be going upstairs for?" I ask, immediately darting towards the staircase, my mind buzzing with worry. Quirina follows behind.

Glancing up to the second floor, it appears empty, but he could be up there. Remembering the paper that fell from Koen's jacket during crowning, I pull it from my dress and unfold it.

Nik walks over, putting an arm around Quirina's waist. "What's going on?"

"Gods," I say, my hand covering my mouth.

"What is it, Bellatrix?" Quirina asks.

It's the way Koen's going to die.

A drawing from Mellani depicts my father's study, as evident by the floor-to-ceiling shelves. In the room Koen stands facing my mother, as she lunges towards him with a large dagger. Mel's gift shows us what's going to happen.

Koen is in danger.

"Help! Somebody!"

The three of us glance up the stairs towards the sound of shouting.

"Who is that?" Quirina asks, her voice filled with concern.

Koen.

Gods, please save him. I need him.

Bolting to the stairs, we take them two at a time and head in the direction of his voice. Just below, the gathering is still roaring with life, but all I can focus on is the door at the end of the hall. Nothing could prepare me for what I find inside.

Koen is crouched on the floor, his jacket balled up and pressed into the chest of a woman. My mother. There's a pool of blood around her, and she's staring up at him with red-rimmed eyes. Koen's head snaps around as we enter, his gaze wild and frantic.

"Fuck," Nik mutters.

I have to quickly adjust myself from expecting to see my mother killing Koen, to seeing Koen comforting my wounded mother on the ground.

What the fuck happened?

As if reading my mind, he replies, "Lothar. He's here."

Panic seizes in my chest, and I spin around like he's right behind me. Cold zaps my entire body from the inside out. With chattering teeth and shaky limbs, I force myself to stay upright.

Lothar is alive.

But I killed him.

"I'll alert the general," Nik offers, already taking charge. He bolts from the room.

"Bellatrix," my mother's frail voice calls me from where she lies.

I'm confronted with the clash of emotion currently pulling me in every direction. My mother lies before me bleeding. She cursed me and fed me to the hungry wolves. But she's also the person who read me stories at bedtime, taught me to braid my hair, and comforted me during storms. Simultaneously she's the woman I hate, and the mother I can't stop loving.

I kneel down beside her and Koen, taking her limp hand in mine. "W-what happened?"

Weakly, she shakes her head. "None of that. I wanted to tell you how sorry I am. I let you down. I should have protected you. I've made so many mistakes, but hurting you is what I regret most."

"Shh, we can talk about it later," I tell her, but as we look into each other's eyes, we both know there won't be a later.

My mother now lays dying before me, and it doesn't feel the way I thought it would. I expected to feel nothing, or maybe relief if anything, but in this moment, I feel my heart cracking open. I can feel her slipping away as her grip weakens by the second. What will I do without both of my parents?

Though I've been misguided most of my life, I've had them to rely on in this world, and now I'll be alone.

"My beautiful girl, you will be an incredible queen. And now you'll get to live your life any way you like."

"Mother, no. Hold on, help is coming." I turn to Koen. "Koen, can you get your mother here?"

He stares back at me, eyes blinking rapidly.

"Koen!" I shout when he doesn't answer.

"There isn't enough time," he answers gently.

Panic doesn't leave room for common sense or reason. I know there's not enough time, I can tell by the rapid blood loss. But getting his mother here gives us a chance. That's all I need.

My eyes beg him, overflowing with tears, and I force out a cracked plea. "Please."

"Bellatrix, it's okay. You…" She stops to cough and winces at the pain it induces. "I'm happy to give my life for you. I love you."

Her fingers go limp in my hand, and the rapid way her chest

was rising and falling finally stills. As I watch her take her last breath, the room begins to go black, and a piercing pain rips through my abdomen.

I clutch my stomach with both hands, groaning out in pain.

What the fuck is happening?

"Bellatrix, are you okay?" Koen asks with bulging eyes.

"I- I don't…Agghhh!" I shriek again, as another surge of pain lances through my abdomen.

Koen wraps his arms around me, pulling me close to his chest. "What's happening?"

"I'm not sure. I think it might be…" I start, and Koen finishes with me. "The curse."

The magic rips from my flesh, threatening to tear me apart from the inside as it claws its way out. My forehead is covered in a sheen of sweat, and my jaw is clenched so tightly, I'm afraid I'll crack a tooth.

Koen scoops me up and lays me on top of the desk gently as I ride through more waves of pain. Quirina runs back to my room for a blanket and places it underneath my head. More pain surges through me, and Koen holds my hand the entire time. Each burst of pain gets more and more intense. My grip on Koen's hand tightens, and I wonder how I'll survive the next wave of pain.

"How long will this go on?" Quirina shouts at Koen, as if he has the answer.

He ignores her, keeping his gaze glued to me. "You're okay. You'll make it through this. Don't leave me again, Bellatrix."

This entire time we've known what breaks the curse, but we never thought to ask if the curse would break me along with it.

His hand trembles in mine. My eyes squeeze shut with every new current of pain, silently begging the Gods to make it stop.

A few minutes pass by, and the sharp pains finally begin to diminish. I feel my breathing return to normal again.

Koen rubs a thumb across my sweaty forehead, caressing me softly. "Did it stop? Are you okay?"

I nod, and slowly begin to sit up. "I am."

After the worst pain I've ever experienced, I now feel revived. My head is clear, my body feels rejuvenated. The pain has completely ceased. Glancing down to where my mother lays lifeless, it all hits me at once.

"Koen, it's gone." Emotion overwhelms me, and I break down. "She's gone."

He wraps his arms around me, letting me weep into his chest. Holding me through my storm, protecting me, refusing to let me endure it alone.

"Lothar is here somewhere, we need to find him," Rina says urgently.

Koen nods in agreement, pulling out of our embrace. "Can you move?" he asks me.

"Yes, I'm okay," I reply, standing with Koen.

We don't make it to the door before we hear a commotion and see Nik racing back through.

His breathing is heavy as he tries to speak in between breaths. "We have to go!"

"What's going on?"

"The castle is on fire! Everyone is evacuating." "Oh Gods!" Rina shrieks.

"Let's go! We stick together!" Koen orders.

Everyone is on edge as we exit the room, smoke visible throughout the castle. Our eyes scan every doorway, every hallway, looking for Lothar.

Where did he go?

"My mother," I tell Koen once we reach the top of the stairs.

"Bellatrix, we have to leave her. I'm sorry."

My lips tremble, but he's right, so we keep moving forward.

The majority of the crowd races through the front entrance. The doorway is backed up and moving slowly.

"Let's go through the back," I suggest.

We make it down the stairs and turn down the hallway to the back door. We pass the hallway under the stairs when we hear a strange noise that has all four of us stopped dead in our tracks. "Is that what I think it is?" I ask nervously.

We freeze, all eyes glued to the door at the end of the hallway to the left. The room that contains all of the daemons. Only now we hear men shouting from the room.

"Help! Help us! Let us out! Please help!"

"We're locked in!"

Male voices call out from behind the door, and it can only mean one thing.

"The curse is broken. The daemons are human again," Koen says, stunned.

Everyone turns towards Quirina, who looks like she might be sick. Nik slips his hand into hers, and we all stare back towards the locked door.

I grip Koen's hand, holding onto him like an anchor. As the new king and queen, all of this lands on us. He squeezes mine back. Whatever happens next, we are in this together.

*To be continued…*

# ACKNOWLEDGMENTS

They say it takes a village to raise kids, and the same is true for publishing books. There are so many people that have played pivotal roles in bringing Curse Breaker to life.

First off, to my fiancé Leo, your unwavering belief and encouragement along the way made becoming an author possible. I love you for that.

To my best friend and alpha reader Hannah Sulewski, you saw this book in its most imperfect form, yet your positive words and love for CB kept me going when I wanted to give up. The excitement you had each time a new chapter hit your inbox was like caffeine for my soul. You believed in this book even when I didn't.

To Hannah Bird and Ali Salvino, thank you for the time and dedication you took reading through with a keen eye and giving me such valuable feedback. I am so grateful for everything you ladies have done for me. Thank you for the round the clock conversations that helped me sculpt CB into the best version possible.

Hannah Bird, my angel on earth, thank you for seeing things that my eyes never could, and making me laugh with your commentary. Thank you for reminding me to clothe my characters. Without you, this entire story would be told in the nude. My battle scene is officially dedicated to you, my angel, and you know why. I love you!

Ali, thank you for being my first alpha reader and giving CB your full attention when you already had a full plate. I am so grateful for your friendship. I could not have done this without you.

Rachel, thank you for being the most incredible beta I could have asked for! You have an incredible eye for key elements that CB was desperately needing. Thank you for the time you put into reading, and the invaluable feedback you gave me. You are my beta for life! You're stuck with me, like it or not!

To everyone in the indie author and bookstagram community who has been sharing and commenting on my posts, and recommending my book to all their friends, thank you from the bottom of my heart. (Sam, Jennalee, Simone, Jen Davis, Amanda, Helen, Sarah McGuire, Blake, and so many others that I can't possibly add you all) The excitement you all have had for this series is what keeps me going when I have wanted to throw my manuscript in the pool, and believe me, there were lots of those times.

This book truly would not be possible without all of you. To my tribe, I am honored and forever grateful. Because of you guys wanting to read what I write, I get to call myself an author. Thank you for taking a chance on such a wild idea.

# ALSO BY JACKIE EGAN

Standalone:
One Last Message

Weapon of Mass Seduction Series
Soul Snatcher
Curse Breaker

# ABOUT THE AUTHOR

Jackie lives in SoCal with her two beagles. She enjoys spending time with her fiancé and two daughters, staying active, and visiting the local wineries. She has turned her lifelong love of reading into creating stories for others to enjoy. When she's not in mom mode, you can catch her writing, or enjoying a new book.

**Instagram:**

https://www.instagram.com/author.jackie_e/

**Amazon:**

https://www.amazon.com/stores/author/B0BYTHNBLP/

Printed in Great Britain
by Amazon

49688383R00209